Wells 10/07

PRAISE FOR
DOROTHY GARLOCK'S MOVING NOVELS IN
THE ROUTE 66 TRILOGY

MOTHER ROAD

"Bestselling Garlock's endearing characters and vividly depicted milieu will enchant her legions of readers. Garlock's claim, 'I write to entertain my readers,' is fully validated with this suspenseful romance." —*Booklist*

"A(n) engaging tale, spiced with Depression-era detail." —*Publishers Weekly*

"*Mother Road* is a colorful personalization of a highway and the people who work and play along its byways. Garlock captures the work ethic and spirit of Americans during the Depression years with understanding. *Mother Road* is a novel of tribute to the common men and women of that era." —*Bookreporter.com*

HOPE'S HIGHWAY

"Delightful. . . . This is a story that reminds us that dreams do come true." —*Rendezvous*

"An entertaining cavalcade of characters. . . . Garlock, known for her heartwarming Americana, does not disappoint here . . . a heart-throbbing romance." —*Publishers Weekly*

"No one evokes the Depression like Garlock. . . . A great, hopeful read." —*Romantic Times*

DOROTHY GARLOCK

Song of the Road

DOUBLEDAY LARGE PRINT HOME LIBRARY EDITION

WARNER BOOKS

NEW YORK   BOSTON

Copyright © 2004 by Dorothy Garlock
All rights reserved.

Warner Books

Time Warner Book Group
1271 Avenue of the Americas, New York, NY 10020

Printed in the United States of America

ISBN 0-7394-4487-5

Cover illustration by Wendell Minor

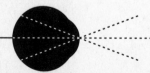

This Large Print Book carries the
Seal of Approval of N.A.V.H.

For my children: Lindy and Herb Jr.
When you were teenagers
and going over Fool's Hill,
I feared that you would never
amount to a hill of beans.
Surprise! Surprise! Surprise!
You turned out just . . . WONDERFUL.

Song of
the Road

COMING HOME

Mary Lee:
The bus bumps along on Route 66,
Its wheels warning, "Girlie, you're in a fix."
No husband to help me—he never did.
Would he be happy I'm carrying his kid?

Jake:
I can sleep on this bus, sick of staying alert,
Watching my back so's I don't get hurt.
Someone in Cross Roads means trouble for me;
He set me up once, but who can he be?

Both:
We're two weary travelers on the way home.
Home, "where the heart is"—after you roam.
Home, where the pain was that sent us away.
Home, where we never wanted to stay.

—F.S.I.

Chapter 1

1935
New Mexico

When the bus slowed to turn off the high-way at Cross Roads, Mary Lee was the only passenger awake. Or so she believed. It was hard to tell about the man across from her. He had climbed on at Amarillo. In the brief time it took him to find a seat, she had seen that he was tall, lean and unsmiling, with a level, direct gaze.

Now he sat sprawled in the double seat, his head back, his hat covering his face, awkwardly trying to sleep on a seat de-signed only for sitting. He seemed vaguely familiar, and she wanted to keep looking at him.

Mary Lee's worry for the last hour had been that she might throw up. The lurching, swaying vehicle and the fumes from the motor were a combination she'd had to endure since she got on the bus in Tulsa. Now she had a throbbing headache, her back hurt and her stomach was queasy as well.

Thank God, the journey was almost over.

Before the bus came to a complete stop at the station located in the lobby of Roads Hotel, the cowboy was up and standing at the door. She didn't know why she knew he was a cowboy. Boots and Stetsons were worn by most of the men in New Mexico whether they were bankers, bootleggers or ranchers. The distinction lay in the quality of the Stetsons and the boots.

The lights came on in the bus, and the door folded back. The cowboy bounded down the steps while Mary Lee was gathering up her purse, hat and a small sack that contained the last of the crackers and cheese she had brought along to munch. She stepped off the bus onto the dark street illuminated only by the street lamp on the corner and the light coming from the hotel lobby. When she looked up and down the street and saw no one, her shoulders slumped. She moved wearily to the side of the bus and waited for the driver to remove her suitcase from the luggage compartment.

"Here ya are, ma'am. It's pretty heavy for ya to be carryin'. Got someone meetin' ya?" The driver had obviously observed her condition.

"No, sir. I was intending to leave it here at the station. I'm going out to the Cross Roads Motor Court. I know I can't carry it that far."

"I'll be goin' right by there. Get back on, ma'am, and I'll stop and let ya off. I ain't supposed to, but ya ain't ort to be walkin' out there this time a night."

"Thank you. I was dreading the walk. It's been a long ride from Tulsa."

The driver set the suitcase inside the bus and went into the hotel. Mary Lee got back on and sat down on the front seat. She was so tired that her legs were trembling, her nerves were raw, and she feared that given the slightest provocation she would burst into tears. Her mother had surely received the letter saying she would be arriving on the eleven-thirty bus. She had mailed it over a week ago.

It would be strange going home to the motor court when her father was not there. She blinked away the tears that came to her eyes. Six months had passed since she received word that he had died suddenly while shoveling snow, and at times she couldn't believe that he was really gone.

She had not been able to come to the funeral. The little money she made at the five-and-dime had covered the rent with not much left over for food. She couldn't have arrived there on time anyway. He had died on a Thursday, and her mother had had him buried the following Saturday.

Now her husband, Bobby, was gone as well. Poor, weak Bobby, killed in an alley behind a beer joint. What a waste of a young life. Gambling was his passion. If he thought he had a good hand and had nothing else to bet, he would wager his life. He seldom drank, but the police said that he was drunk when they found him. The police didn't hold out much hope of finding his killer, and it wouldn't do her or Bobby any good if they did.

The driver returned, and the bus moved up the main street, turned and headed back out toward the highway. It wasn't much more than half a mile as the crow flies from the center of town to the motor court, so only a few minutes later the bus stopped again. The lights came on, and the door opened.

As Mary Lee was getting off, a voice came from the back of the bus. "Jesus Christ, why are we stoppin' here?"

"Just hold your horses. This'll take only a minute." The driver set the suitcase beside the drive leading to the house.

"Thank you. I appreciate the ride."

"You're welcome. Will someone be down to help you?" He glanced at the lighted house.

"Yes. I'll be fine."

With a nod and a tip of his cap, the driver got back into the bus. Mary Lee waited until it went some distance down the highway before she picked up the case. With slow steps and several stops to rest along the way, she finally reached the house. Exhausted, she leaned on a porch post to catch her breath.

The front door was open. Light shone from the kitchen. Voices, both male and female, carried to where she stood. Her heart sank to her toes when she recognized the slurred, giggly laughter coming from inside the house. It was a dreaded sound from her childhood. She felt the old hurt creep around her heart.

Her mother was drunk.

All the way from Tulsa she had hoped against hope that the shock of her daddy's sudden death had caused her mother to stop drinking. She should have known what would happen without her father here.

Mary Lee sighed. She ached in a hundred different places. Pushing herself away from the porch post, she opened the screen door and went through the front room to stand in the doorway leading to the kitchen. Her mother, another woman and two men were playing cards at the kitchen table.

Her mother's back was to her. The man opposite her was grinning and pouring whiskey into her glass from a tall bottle. Mary Lee recognized him at once. He looked up, saw Mary Lee, and the grin left his face. The bottle tipped in his unsteady hand.

Her mother licked the whiskey from her hand, then turned toward the doorway to see what the man was looking at. She gave

Mary Lee a blank stare, then stood and held on to the back of the chair.

"Hi, hon. When did . . . ya get here?"

"Just now." Mary Lee hated the silly grin on her mother's face.

"That's nice. Didn't know ya was . . . comin'."

"I sent you a letter telling you what time I would be here."

"Ya did? I don't remember it. We was just playin' a little cards. Bobby with ya?"

"Bobby died two months ago, Mama." Mary Lee couldn't keep the irritation out of her voice. "I wrote and told you about it."

"Oh, yeah. I did hear somethin' about that. This is my girl," she said to the others, still looking at Mary Lee. "She's come on a visit."

Mary Lee looked directly at Frank Pierce. His thick black hair was streaked with gray. He might have been a handsome man long ago, but now dissipation had reddened his eyes and slackened his jaw. His whiskered cheeks were sunken. He had only four lower teeth, and a few upper ones were missing.

She had known who he was for most of her life. He was what her father had called a ne'er-do-well, a man who never held a job for very long and always seemed to get by without working. She hadn't liked him when he was the school janitor, and she didn't like him now.

"I'm Pearl." The woman who spoke had black penciled eyebrows and thin blond hair looped behind her ears. Her dress was so low in front that you could see the tops of her breasts, and probably more when she bent over. The word "trash" came to Mary Lee's mind.

Mary Lee glanced at her and nodded.

"Mama, I'm tired." She was also hungry, but she didn't mention that. "I'll get my suitcase and go to my room."

"Pearl and . . . ah . . . Jim—Pearl's been stayin' with me. You know, I don't like bein' out here on the highway by myself."

"You won't be by yourself now." Mary Lee's eyes scanned the messy kitchen, then back to the four people at the table. "I'm here now."

"You stayin'?" Frank Pierce asked.

Mary Lee ignored him. "Mama, I noticed that there isn't a car parked at number one. I'll use it tonight. We can make different arrangements in the morning."

"Number one's mine." Frank Pierce spoke again. His voice held a belligerent tone.

"You've rented it for the night?" Mary Lee looked steadily at him.

"For the month," he retorted crisply.

"Are all six cabins full, Mama?"

Dolly's eyes were on the floor. "Number four is empty, but it's not been cleaned. We . . . ah, had a little fire in number three."

Mary Lee stepped around the corner to reach the board where the cabin keys were hung. All the hooks were empty.

"Where's the key?"

"It's in the door so it'd not get lost."

Mary Lee turned frosty eyes on Frank Pierce. "I asked Mama."

"And I'm tellin' ya."

She bit back a reply. Something was going on here that she didn't like at all, but there was nothing she could do about it tonight.

"I'll take clean sheets and go to number four, Mama."

"I don't have any, hon. I've not washed this week."

"See you in the morning." Mary Lee

abruptly turned on her heel and went back through the living room to the porch.

Tired and disappointed, she couldn't hold back the tears that blurred her eyes. She sat down on the steps and wiped her eyes on the hem of her dress. *Her mother had not even noticed that she was pregnant, but Frank Pierce had.* Once when she was looking at him, he had deliberately lowered his eyes to the bulge below her waist.

Knowing that she shouldn't carry the heavy suitcase all the way down to number four, she fumbled in her purse for the key, unlocked it and took out a nightgown, two sheets, a towel and soap. After locking the case she scooted it into the living room.

Scott Finley had built the motor court back in 1929 just before the stock market crashed. At that time Route 66 was just a gravel road and already the main highway through New Mexico to California. With the promise of pavement, Scott was sure that the traffic would increase, and it had. The drought and the dust storms had driven thousands to leave the farms and head for a better life in the fertile fields of California, and the highway had gained another name: Route 66, America's Mother Road.

The Cross Roads Motor Court was made up of six identical cabins, strung out in a row, with spaces between them for motor cars. The entrance to the road fronting the cabins led to the main house.

On her way down the lane to number four cabin, Mary Lee could see weeds in what used to be carefully tended flower beds. Partly hidden in the high grass were sundry items of trash. A mattress with a large burned spot in the middle lay outside the door of number three. Seeing the run-down condition of the motor court stirred her to anger.

A car was parked next to number five, and a truck next to the last cabin, where lights shone from the windows.

The key was in the door of number four, but the door wasn't locked. Mary Lee went in, turned on the light, shut and locked the door. Why in heaven's name would her mother leave the key in the door? Was a friend of Frank Pierce coming in late?

The odor from cigarette butts and from a coffee can that had been used as a spittoon sent Mary Lee hurrying to open the window in the back and reopen the front door. Anger held her tears at bay as she took the ashtray and coffee can outside. She yanked the soiled sheets from the bed and piled them beside the door. After remaking the bed with her own linen, she washed her face, then turned off the lights before undressing and putting on her nightgown.

Mary Lee would have preferred to leave the door open, but fearing tentative arrangements might have been made for the use of the cabin, she closed and locked it. She wedged the one straight-backed chair beneath the doorknob and sank down on the bed.

Lying on her side with her knees drawn up, she rubbed her rounded stomach and let the tears flow. She cried because her back hurt so badly that she felt as if it were being stabbed with a thousand pitchforks. She cried because of the sorry mess she had come home to.

Her mother obviously hadn't been glad to see her. She hadn't even noticed that she was going to have a grandchild. And how had she become tangled up with that sorry, good-for-nothing Frank Pierce? Mary Lee's mind went in a dozen different directions.

"It's going to be hard, baby." Mary Lee had assumed the habit of talking to her unborn child. "Daddy worked hard to build this place. I'm not going to let her run it into the ground. He loved Mama and tried to help her. Even when she came to my high school play so drunk that she staggered, he'd said she couldn't help her craving for alcohol. He had taken her home. I'd had to stay and endure the whispers of my class-mates and the pitying glances from their parents.

"I'm not going to let Daddy's motor court go to wrack and ruin. The first thing I've got to do is to go see Mr. Morales and find out what authority I have here. You're all I have, baby, now that Daddy's gone. I've got to take care of you, and the only way to do it is to make this place pay."

Mary Lee drifted off to sleep thinking that she and her daddy were a lot alike. He had married her mother hoping to cure her drinking habit. She had married Bobby thinking that he needed her, that she could make him face up to his responsibilities. Both of them had failed.

Mary Lee awakened to the sound of a car. Someone was revving the engine. By the time she swung her feet off the bed, a flatbed truck was passing the window.

The person in number six was leaving early.

In the light of day, the cabin was even more filthy than she had noticed last night. Thankful that her father had bullied the Cross Roads city council members into bring sewer and gas out to the motor court, Mary Lee used the bathroom, squatting over the toilet because she couldn't bring herself to sit on it.

Feeling better, although she was so hungry she was weak, she washed and dressed, putting her bare feet in her shoes and carefully rolling her hose into a ball to take back to her suitcase. She combed her fingers through her hair and looked at herself in the mirror hanging above the lavatory.

She knew that she was no beauty, but she was passably pretty, or so she had been told numerous times. Her hair, dark red and curly, came from her daddy; eyes, slate blue from her mother. She was of average height, small-boned and slim, except for the rounded abdomen where she carried her baby. She was still able to wear two of her dresses if she didn't belt them.

Leaving the cabin, she locked the door and put the key in her pocket. Walking up to the house, she realized how weak she was. She'd had only crackers and cheese the day before. When the bus stopped in Amarillo, she had been tempted to buy a hamburger but chose to wait because she was only a few hours from home.

It was broad daylight when she reached the house. Cars were going by on the highway, their tires singing. Her daddy used to call it the song of the road.

Oh, Daddy, you were such a good, sweet man. You deserved so much more than you got: a drunken wife and a daughter who ran off and left you because she was tired of being ashamed of her mother.

The door was open. Mary Lee went to the kitchen thankful that both bedroom doors were closed. A deck of cards, an empty whiskey bottle and several glasses were still on the kitchen table. She resisted the impulse to crash the whiskey bottle against the sink that overflowed with dirty dishes. Instead she left it where it was and opened the door of the icebox to find only a small chunk of ice. The smell that came from the interior told her that it hadn't been washed out in weeks. The only things in it that she could use were eggs and butter. She went to the front room and turned the ice card so that when the iceman passed, he would know to stop and bring in fifty pounds.

After washing a skillet, she buttered two pieces of bread, pan-fried them, then scrambled three eggs.

She felt much better after she had eaten.

Mary Lee had changed her dress in the living room, added a touch of lip color and was putting on a blue cloth-crowned hat with a stiff brim when her mother came out of the bedroom. She was barefoot and wearing a thin voile nightgown that came down to just past her knees. She cupped her hand over her eyes to shield them from the light.

"You goin'?" she asked on her way to the kitchen.

"Just to town. I'll be back." Mary Lee followed and watched her mother pick up the whiskey bottle then slam it down when she saw that it was empty.

"Son of a bitch!" Completely ignoring her

daughter, Dolly Finley pulled open the door to a side cabinet and swore again.

As she had done so many times before when her father had hidden it, Mary Lee watched her mother search for the whiskey.

"Go back to bed, Mama, until you sober up."

"You think I'm drunk? A hell of a lot you know."

"No, I think you're hungover. You'd better get yourself straightened out, because we're going to have a talk as soon as I get back from town."

"'Bout what?"

"About getting your friends out of my room, for one thing."

"Pearl's got nowhere to go."

"Neither have I. That's why I'm here."

"Shit!"

"It wouldn't hurt to tell her to get in here and help you clean up this mess." Mary Lee went to the door. "I'll be back in a little while."

Chapter 2

Cross Roads was a pleasant little town, considered a good place to live by the slightly more than five thousand residents. The businesses were nearly all located along Main Street. Branching off it were ten streets of homes, most of which were small, some with ample space for a garden and chickens. On the outer edge of town were acreages with barns and pastures. This was ranch country, and almost everyone who had a place to keep a horse had one or two.

Not all the houses in Cross Roads were small. As in every place where people settle, there were those who had more than their neighbors. The banker's house and several others would have looked quite at home in the affluent sections of Amarillo or Albuquerque.

There were three churches in town, a school with grades one through twelve, one hotel, two barbershops, a five-and-dime, two dry-goods stores, a shoe repairer, a hat shop, a pawn shop, hardware/lumber yard, feed store and four beer joints. There were no known whorehouses, but circulated among the men were names of women who would, for a price, scratch any particular itch they happened to have.

The business area of Cross Roads was large because it served ranches that were spread across two counties. The town was justifiably proud that its bank had remained solvent while banks all over the country had gone broke.

One overworked doctor cared for the sick and injured. Three lawyers, one of whom Mary Lee was on her way to see, took care of the citizens' legal problems.

She took her time, knowing that Mr. Morales might not reach his office until eight o'clock. In front of the post office, she stopped to speak to Miss Watson, one of her high school teachers.

"Mary Lee! It's good to see you."

"It's good to see you, Miss Watson."
Mary Lee was sincere. The teacher had
been a good friend while she was in school.

"Are you here on a visit, or do you plan to
stay?"

"I'm staying . . . awhile."

"And heavens! You're going to have a
baby. Poor little thing. I know you'll handle
being without your husband just as you've
handled everything else in your life." She
gave Mary Lee a hug. "You'll make a wonderful mother."

"Thank you, Miss Watson."

"I was sorry to hear about Bobby."

"It was a shock."

"I imagine it was. Come by and see me.
You were one of my favorites, you know."

"I'll do that. Good-bye, Miss Watson."

Mary Lee continued down the street. She
knew perfectly well to what Miss Watson
was referring. Not only had her mother's
drinking been an embarrassment to her, she
had married a weak, shiftless man. She had
known almost from the start that her marriage had been a mistake. She couldn't
undo a lifetime of the undermining of
Bobby's self-confidence. But the time she
had been with him had not been for naught.

It had given her a baby to love and to work for.

A few of the men she met on the street nodded and tipped their hats. One woman looked at her curiously, and another turned her head and pretended to be looking in the window of the hat shop until Mary Lee passed.

Even in a town the size of Cross Roads there were class distinctions. Because her mother had made a spectacle of herself more times than Mary Lee had fingers and toes, she wasn't welcome and, at times, not even acknowledged by those in the higher social circle, even though her father had been a respected businessman. Such discrimination didn't hurt as much now as it had while she was in school. She no longer had an interest in hobnobbing with a bunch of snobs.

At eight o'clock according to the clock in front of the barbershop, Mary Lee climbed the stairway that separated the dry-goods store from the billiard parlor. In the upper hallway she paused when she reached a frosted-glass door. On it, printed in fancy gold lettering, was the sign: SIDNEY MORALES, ATTORNEY AT LAW.

After a moment of hesitation, she opened the door. Mr. Morales was sitting at a paper-strewn desk. He looked up over glasses perched low on his nose, then got to his feet.

"Morning, ma'am."

"Morning, Mr. Morales." Mary Lee held out her hand. "Do you remember me? Mary Lee Clawson, Scott Finley's daughter."

"I thought you looked familiar. I just couldn't place you for a minute. It's been some time since I saw you."

"I've been away for a while."

"I'm sorry about your husband. The whole town was shocked."

"It was a shock to me too."

"Sit down, Mrs. Clawson, and tell me what I can do for you. I sent you a copy of your father's will. When I didn't hear back, I presumed that you understood the conditions."

Mary Lee gave him a blank stare. "I never received a copy of Daddy's will. I'd no idea he even had one."

The lawyer looked at her steadily for a minute, then said, "I mailed it a week after Scott passed away. Let me see"—he pulled open a file and took out a folder—"it's right here. I mailed it on the third of January and sent it registered. According to the post office, Bob Clawson signed for it."

"Mr. Morales, I've not seen it. I came to ask you if I had any authority at all to make some changes out at the motor court. Things out there are in a mess."

"You have all the authority you need, Mrs. Clawson. Your father left all his possessions, including the motor court, to you with the request that you take care of your mother."

"He . . . did?"

"Yes, he did. I've a copy of the will right here."

"I wonder why Bobby didn't tell me."

"I've no idea."

He was afraid that if I knew, I would leave him and come home. He couldn't stand the thought of being alone, and he'd rather be anywhere in the world than in Cross Roads, so he didn't tell me about the will. The . . . weasel!

While these thoughts were going through Mary Lee's head, she looked away from the lawyer, lest he see how embarrassed she was that her husband would keep such important news from her.

"Frankly, Mrs. Clawson, I've been disturbed by the conditions out at the motor court and wondered if you were aware of how it was being run. Scott took out a small loan to do some painting and minor repair about a month before he died. I don't think he had time to do the work."

"I'm sure he didn't. The place is terribly run-down, and Mama has rented at least one cabin by the month."

"I don't mean to be unkind, but it's common knowledge that she has some unsavory hangers-on out there."

"Do I have the authority to clear them out?" Mary Lee asked bluntly.

"The place is yours, lock, stock and barrel. Your father *requested* that you take care of your mother. He knew, and I'm sure you know, that she has a drinking problem."

"I've known it all my life. It's one reason I wanted to get away from here. I should never have left him—"

"Now, now. Your father understood that you had a right to a life separate from your parents."

"He told me that. But I . . . jumped out of the frying pan into the fire," she admitted. "I

exchanged one set of problems for another."

"Have you seen Bobby's father?"

"I just got here last night."

"He'll probably be interested in your . . .
ah . . . condition."

"Why is that? He kicked Bobby out. Disinherited him. He'll have no claim on
Bobby's baby."

"Well, I could be mistaken." Mr. Morales
made busy work straightening the papers
on his desk. "But after all, Bobby was his
sole heir, and now that he's gone—"

"Bobby wasn't and never was going to
be Mr. Clawson's heir. He made that plain
enough. He didn't even acknowledge the
wire I sent him when Bobby was killed. The
county had to bury the son of a rich man!"

"Perhaps he would have changed his
mind."

"It doesn't matter," Mary Lee said heatedly. "He's partly responsible for the way
Bobby . . . was."

After a small silence, Mr. Morales said,
"Would you like to see a copy of Scott's
will?"

"Yes, please."

Mary Lee turned slightly to the side so

that the light from the window fell on the document. She quickly glanced over the legal heading. Tears dimmed her vision as she read: *To my beloved daughter, Mary Lee Finley Clawson, I leave the total sum of my worldly goods . . .*

The lawyer accepted the document when she returned it. "You should see Mr. Rosen over at the bank and find out if anything has been paid on the loan."

"I'll do that."

"And, Mrs. Clawson, it might be a good idea to have your mother's name taken off the bank account . . . if there's anything left in it."

"Thank you for the advice, Mr. Morales."

"One more thing, Mrs. Clawson. I'm sure you know that nothing goes on in a town this size that isn't gossiped about. Jake Ramero has been staying out at the motor court. He got out of the pen a few months ago and has been working out at the Quitman ranch and doing some steel work on a bridge now and then."

"What was he in prison for?"

"Cattle rustling. Ocie Clawson accused him of stealing fifty steers. The judge gave him two years. I'm surprised he came back here."

Mary Lee frowned. "Bobby talked about him a time or two. He didn't like him. He said he would steal the pennies off a dead man's eyes."

"I don't think he's quite that bad, but I understand why Bobby would say so."

The lawyer swung his chair around to the file cabinet, clearly ending the conversation about Jake Ramero. Mary Lee went to the door.

"Is there anything I need to sign?"

"No. It's been taken care of. The deed has been registered in your name."

"Thank you. Do I owe you anything?"

"Scott paid for my services when the will was drawn up. I wonder if he had a premonition that something was going to happen to him."

Mary Lee walked down the stairs holding tightly to the railing. The shock of what she learned in Mr. Morales's office had made her weak.

"I would like to speak with Mr. Rosen."

"I'll see if he's busy."

The teller had been polite and businesslike, but had not acknowledged knowing her. He had been several grades ahead of her in school. Mary Lee remembered vividly the night he and another boy had followed her home from play practice, scaring her with their lewd remarks. Holding her head high, she looked him in the eye when he returned to say the banker would see her in a few minutes.

Mary Lee waited in the bank lobby for twenty minutes, sitting on a hard bench, before she was ushered in to see Mr. Rosen.

"Come in, Mrs. Clawson. Have a seat."

"Thank you. I'm here about the motor court. I was told my father took out a loan just before he died."

"He did. Three hundred dollars."

"Has any of the loan been paid?"

"Not a cent."

"When is it due?"

"October first."

"Is there a balance in the checking account?"

"Not a cent," the banker said again. "There has not been a deposit made since Scott died."

"That will be changed now. I was unaware that my father had left the motor court to me."

"Unaware? How can that be?"

"A slipup in the mail." Mary Lee kept her eyes on his and refused to say more.

"May I make partial payments so the loan will be extended?"

"No. It must be paid in full," he said briskly. "I may have a buyer for the court."

"It isn't for sale."

"My advice would be that you sell before it's run completely into the ground."

Mary Lee stood up. "Thank you for the advice. I have four months to pay the three hundred dollars, is that right?"

"That's right."

"And if I don't?"

"The bank will take over the property and sell it. We protect our stockholders."

"You would sell it out from under me for a three-hundred-dollar loan?"

"Business is business. We're a bank, not a charity institution." He stood up and looked her over as if she had come riding into town on a freight train.

"I wasn't asking for charity. Just a reasonable amount of time to pay the loan."

"October first, Mrs. Clawson."

"Good day, Mr. Rosen."

"Good day, Mrs. Clawson."

Mary Lee left the bank with questions floating around in her mind. Her father hadn't had time to spend the money he borrowed on repairs. And he always kept a small balance in a checking account. Her mother had either blown the money on booze or had let her worthless friends take advantage of her.

More determined than she'd been in all her life, Mary Lee headed home, forgetting that she had planned to buy tooth powder until she was a block past the drugstore. Her future and that of her unborn child depended on her making the motor court pay. Her father had done it, and so could she.

It was a warm May day, and Mary Lee was hot when she stepped up onto the back porch and entered the kitchen. Her mother, Pearl, and the man they had called Jim sat at the table. Mary Lee could smell bacon and fried potatoes. The sink was still full of dirty dishes, and the sheets she had brought up from the number four cabin were still on the floor in the corner.

"Where you been?" Dolly asked as if she really didn't care.

"To see Mr. Morales."

"What for?"

"To find out about Daddy's will. He sent me a copy, but it must have gotten lost in the mail. Daddy left everything to me, Mama. The house, what's in it, and the cabins are in my name."

"Ah, he didn't. Frank said that will wasn't worth the paper it was written on."

"Frank Pierce is a lazy, no-good deadbeat who doesn't know beans. I want him out of here."

"Now, see here." Dolly stood up. "He paid for a month."

"When?"

"A couple of weeks ago."

"Does he have a receipt for his money?"

"I don't . . . remember."

Mary Lee looked at Pearl and then at Jim. "I want you to leave too. We're having no more freeloaders around here."

"Now, wait a goddamn minute!" Dolly yelled. "You got no right comin' back to my house telling my friends to get out. Who do you think you are?"

"*My* house, Mama. I'm the owner here. Lock, stock and barrel. The attorney said so. What I say goes. I will not have your drunken friends here!"

"I've been helpin' Dolly," Pearl said lamely.

"We don't need your help, and I need my room."

"You don't have to go, Pearl. You can sleep with me." Dolly glared at her daughter. "It ain't right that Scott left it to you."

"Daddy knew that you'd do just what you've been doing. In six more months everything would be gone."

Jim got to his feet. "I've not been stayin' here. I only come once in a while to visit Pearl."

"I see," Mary Lee said, tight-lipped. "Well, the whorehouse is closed as of this minute. Don't come back."

"Jim, where'll I go?" Pearl whined.

"You figure it out. You've no strings on me." He pulled out his wallet and threw a five-dollar bill on the table, turned and walked out the door.

"You son of a bitch! You horny bastard! You got what you wanted. . . ." Pearl burst into tears.

"Mama, we've got a lot to do. Why don't you clean up this mess in here while Pearl gets her things out of my room. I'll change my dress and start the washing so we can put clean sheets on the beds in the cabins."

When Pearl went to the bedroom, Dolly slumped down in a chair and covered her face with her shaking hands. It was hard for Mary Lee to remember the young and pretty mother she'd been so long ago. Dolly's hair was streaked with gray; her eyes were dull and sunken. Her print dress hung from her shoulders, scarcely touching the rest of her thin body.

"Have you eaten anything today, Mama?"

Dolly didn't answer, and Mary Lee hadn't expected her to. In the living room, Mary Lee took off the jersey skirt and overblouse, the only thing she owned that did not wrinkle, and put on a print dress that was snug but still wearable without the belt. She put on her everyday shoes and went back to the kitchen. Dolly was still sitting at the table.

"Mama?" Mary Lee put her hand on her shoulder and shook her gently.

"Get away from me! Why'd you have to come back?"

"Because this is my home."

"That shithead Scott always cared more for you than he did me."

"That's not true. He put up with your drinking all these years, and he never had a harsh thing to say about you. He left me everything because he knew that you'd do just what you've been doing. He left it to me knowing that I'd take care of you."

"He never wanted me to have any friends or—"

"Where's Daddy's car?"

"Sold it. Wasn't doing no good sitting here. The stingy fart wouldn't teach me how to drive it. He was afraid I'd run off, and I would've."

"Hush!" Mary Lee shook her mother's shoulder. "Don't you say a bad word about Daddy. He loved you, put up with you, and it probably killed him."

"You always took his side."

"What did you do with the money from the car and the three hundred dollars Daddy got from the bank? He didn't have time to do the repairs."

"I don't have to account to a snot-nosed kid about what I do with my money. You went off with that brat of Ocie Clawson's and got yourself knocked up, then come crawlin' back here to take over."

"Bobby and I were married. I can show you the marriage certificate. I want you to understand that things are going to be different around here. I'll have no more hangers-on here. Anyone who stays in one of those cabins will pay for it. You're going to have to help me."

"Maybe I'll just go with Pearl and leave it to ya."

"If that's what you want to do, go right ahead." Mary Lee had heard her mother threaten to leave a hundred or more times and knew that she never would.

"You don't care what happens to me. I'm . . . sick—"

"I care. You're my mother. And it's no wonder you're sick. You drink that rotgut whiskey and don't eat. Fix yourself something to eat, then clean up in here. I'm going out to light the hot water tank so I can do the wash."

Mary Lee opened the door to her old room. Pearl was bending over an open dresser drawer. She looked up with pure malice on her face.

"I didn't hear a knock."

"Why should I knock? It's my room."

"You could wait till I get out. I worked for this room."

"It doesn't look to me like anyone has worked around here for quite some time."

"I cleaned cabins and this is the thanks I get."

"I imagine you were well paid—in whiskey. But I'll not argue with you. Clear out or I'll call the sheriff."

When Mary Lee pulled the sheets off the bed, she smelled the sickening odor of cigarettes and sex. Gathering the sheets into a roll, she took slips off the pillows and went into the bathroom that connected the two bedrooms, to collect the towels. It had been a while since the room had been cleaned.

Why wasn't she surprised?

She closed her eyes for a moment and wondered how she was going to do all that had to be done.

Chapter 3

The noon whistle blew while Mary Lee was hanging the wash on the line. In the storage building behind the house, where supplies for the cabins and the washer were kept, Scott had built in a long line of shelves for storing the sheets, towels and other necessities for the cabins. Today the sheet and the towel shelves were empty.

The oversize washing machine her father bought from Sears Roebuck two years ago would hold six sheets and six pillowcases at one time, or two dozen towels. It was hard work to lift the wet sheets out of the washer, run them through the wringer to the rinse water, then back through to the basket to take to the line.

Mary Lee's back hurt, and her arms felt

as if lead weights were tied to them by the time she finished hanging the wash on the lines. She went to the kitchen, poured herself a glass of tea and sank down in a chair. The dishes had been washed, but that was all. The door to Dolly's room was closed. There was no sign of Pearl.

Knowing that every minute counted if she was going to get the three available cabins ready for renting, she rested a minute or two, then fixed herself a bread and jelly sandwich. After she ate, she went down to number four cabin with a broom and a bucket of cleaning supplies. She worked in the cabin steadily for an hour. When she left, it was clean-smelling again. She took her sheets off the bed and carried them back to the house.

An hour later she had cleaned another cabin. She made up the beds in the two clean cabins with the sheets she took off the line. Two of the three rental cabins were ready when she started on the third. The work went slowly because she was so tired. When she finished, she wanted to sit down and cry. Instead she made sure the doors were locked and the keys were in her pocket, and headed back to the house.

It was getting along toward evening and time when travelers stopped for the night. Mary Lee allowed herself a moment to watch the cars speed past on the highway.

Where are you going and what will you do when you get there? I hope that you have a better life than the one you left behind.

She had one more thing to do before she could go to the house: put on a clean dress and make herself presentable. She looked at the mattress with the hole burned in the center. Lying there, it was an eyesore. It made the court look trashy. The only way to get it out of sight was to drag it behind the washhouse.

She grasped a corner of the mattress with both hands and dug in her heels. She was able to drag it only a few feet before she had to stop and rest. By the time she had dragged it ten feet, she was breathing hard and sweating profusely; her hair stuck to her cheeks and to the back of her neck.

Unaware that anyone was near, she was startled when a big hand reached down and took hold of the mattress. She looked up at a stern-faced man in a black hat. Her eyes met his. She felt the blood drain from her face.

She had looked into those sea-green eyes before. But where? When?

"You tryin' to kill that kid you're carryin'?" She heard him speak over the roaring in her ears. "Where do you want this?"

"Behind . . . the shed." Mary Lee was so out of breath she could hardly talk.

The man walked off dragging the mattress as easily as if it had wheels. Mary Lee hurried to where she had left her cleaning pail and broom, then followed. He had dumped the mattress on a pile of trash and was on his way back when she met him.

"Thank you." It was all she had time to say.

He tipped his hat and went on by. At the door of the washhouse she turned to watch him until he disappeared between number five and number six. He was the tenant who rented by the month. Jake Ramero. She shook her head to rid it of the thought that she had met him before.

It was nice of him to help her; she had to give him that. But if he didn't have a receipt for the money he gave Dolly, he had to go.

Mary Lee didn't have time to think about him now. She washed, put on a clean dress, brushed her hair and tied it back with a ribbon. Her father had always made sure that he was neat and clean, even if working, when folks came off the highway to rent a cabin. In the drawer of the library table she found the ledger where he registered the guests who stayed at the cabins. She felt a flash of anger when she saw that the last entry made was in his handwriting.

She knocked on Dolly's door, then opened it. "Mama, are you all right?" Her mother was lying on the bed, her arm over her eyes.

"What'a you care?"

"Are you going to fix supper?"

"You fix it; you've taken over everythin' else."

Mary Lee closed the door. A car had turned into the drive and stopped in front of the house. She went out onto the porch.

"Good evening," she said to the man who got out of the car.

"I'm lookin' for a place to stay the night."

"You've come to the right place. Would you like to see one of the cabins?"

"If it's got a bed and it's clean it'll be all right. How much?"

"Dollar fifty," she said, and held her

breath. Her father had charged a dollar twenty-five.

The man dug into his pocket and pulled out the money.

Thankful he had the correct change, Mary Lee said, "Thank you. I'll get the register."

She came out of the house and sat down on the step.

"Your name for the record, please. The law requires it."

"John Hardy, Kansas City, Missouri."

After carefully making the entry and noting the amount paid, she laid aside the ledger.

"Follow me down to number four."

She waited at the door while he parked. "There are towels and soap in the bathroom. In the morning, leave the key on the table." She smiled. "When you pass this way again, we'd be happy for you to stay with us."

"I just might do that. I'll be back about this time next month."

Without a moment of hesitation, Mary Lee went straight to the last cabin and knocked on the door. She had to see Jake Ramero again to rid herself of the creepy feeling that she had known him before. She waited and was about to knock again when the door opened. The man's chest was bare, and a towel was flung around his neck. His look said, "What'a ya want?" but he remained silent, the quiet broken only by the radio playing inside the cabin.

Mary Lee drew in a deep breath. Oh, Lord! His face was familiar. *How could that be?*

"I'm Mrs. Clawson, the owner of the motor court."

"Hello, Mary Lee Finley."

His voice came to her as if he had said her name a million times. It took her a minute to bring herself back to the business at hand.

"I'm giving you notice, Mr. Ramero, that unless you want to pay by the day you'll have to move out."

She had to look a long way up to see his face. He had been shaving when she knocked. Streaks of shaving soap were visible high up on his cheek. His eyes were a piercing green with gold flecks, sunlight-squinted, and seemed endowed with the ability to look a hole through anyone. His age was somewhere around thirty, maybe less. Wet black hair looked as if he had been rubbing it with the towel.

"You were on the bus last night." She said the words even as they came to her.

"No crime in that."

At the sound of his low, husky voice she moved her eyes away from him.

"You'll have to move, Mr. Ramero."

"Not for three months."

"Three months? Did my mother rent this cabin for three months?"

"Four. But I've been here a month."

"And how much did you pay her?"

"I paid forty dollars in advance for four months."

"The cabins rent for one fifty a day."

"Is that right?"

"That's right. You got a bargain."

"She got ready cash. It's what she wanted."

"I don't doubt that for a minute. She was out of boo—" Mary Lee cut off the word. "Do you have a receipt for the money you gave her?" She was angry at him because his face was familiar, and at herself because it was stuck in her memory.

"Yes, ma'am, I do."

"Keep it handy. When the sheriff comes you'll need it."

"I paid her price."

"I can't just take your word on it."

"Unless you give me my forty dollars back, I'm staying. And don't tell me that I took advantage of her. I thought I was doing her a favor."

"I don't doubt that she gave you a pitiful story. When she gets to a certain . . . ah . . . state, she'll do anything." Mary Lee turned and, as fast as her tired legs would carry her, headed back to the house. It was all she could do to keep her head up and her shoulders straight.

Jake Ramero watched Mary Lee until she reached the house. He felt the same flutter deep in his gut as when he had caught a glimpse of her on the bus. Last night he had been tempted to wait until he was sure someone was meeting her; but when he saw her get back on the bus, he had taken off through the back streets to the motor court.

When the bus stopped and let her off in front of the court, he was unlocking his door. He had known immediately that she was Scott Finley's daughter.

Of course, everyone in town knew that her mother was, and remained, a drunk. That would limit her opportunities with any of the high-tones in town. Hell, after his two-year stint in the pen, he doubted he'd ever be invited to dine with the banker. His chuckle was dry and without humor.

Good Lord. Surely she could have done better than a loser like Bobby Clawson.

If she thought old Ocie Clawson was going to give her something because she was carrying Bobby's kid, she'd better think again. If the old bastard did anything, he'd take the baby and tell her to get the hell out.

Jake closed the door. It had angered him when he saw her tugging on that old mattress. She shouldn't be doing things like that in her condition. Hell and high water! It irritated him that she stuck in his mind. He had enough problems without taking on hers. He had come back here for one reason only; and as soon as he took care of that matter, he'd be long gone.

Mary Lee stopped on her way to the house and rattled the doorknob on number one. It was closed up tight. Frank Pierce had made himself scarce since last night.

Well, he had to come back sometime.

An hour later the light over the Vacancy sign was turned off. The three cabins were rented. Mary Lee had four dollars and fifty cents in her pocket. Tomorrow she would pay down on a mattress to go in number three; and when it was paid for, she would see about getting the telephone turned back on. Thank goodness her mother had paid enough on the electric bill so they still had electricity.

Mary Lee was too tired to eat but knew that she had to for the baby's sake, which reminded her that she had to see Dr. Morris sometime soon. That was another thing. When was she going to find the time to hem diaper material and line a basket? She had secreted away ten dollars to spend on things for the baby. So far all she had was the diaper material and two gowns.

The baby was a miracle that she had at first resented because of the way it had been conceived. She had hated every minute she spent in bed with Bobby, trying to give him satisfaction. During the first weeks of their marriage he had tried to penetrate her almost every night and succeeded only a couple of times. As the months went by, his obsession with gambling grew, and he initiated sex less and less.

One night during an argument about his gambling, he slapped her, then threw her down and penetrated her with more gusto than he'd ever shown before. He was immediately sorry, wept, and begged her not to leave him. He said it would never happen again, and it hadn't. Bobby never knew that the result of that one act had left the only positive thing to mark his time spent on this earth.

It didn't matter now how her baby came to be. She already loved it with all her heart and was determined that it would grow up knowing a mother's care.

Mary Lee scrambled eggs and toasted bread beneath the burner in the oven. She was sitting down to eat when her mother came out of the bedroom. She had changed into a sleeveless sundress that revealed her bony shoulders. She had crimped waves in her hair by using the curling iron, heated in the chimney of the coal oil lamp. Her cheeks were rouged and her lips smeared with bright red lipstick. To Mary Lee she was a pitiful sight.

"Want to share my eggs?" Mary Lee asked.

"No."

"Have you eaten today?"

"Listen. I don't need you nagging me."

"I don't mean to nag, Mama. I don't want you to get sick."

"If you're so concerned, why did you run off my friends?"

"Mama, don't let's fight. Help me get this place running again like it was when Daddy was here."

"Scott didn't nag me."

"No. He probably knew it wouldn't do any good," Mary Lee snapped irritably. Then, when Dolly went to the door, "Where are you going?"

"None of your business. If I can't have my friends in my home, I'll go to theirs."

"I didn't say you— Oh, never mind." Mary Lee realized that her mother was not in a reasonable mood.

Without a look or another word, Dolly walked out the back door. Mary Lee placed her fork on the edge of her plate. The eggs suddenly tasted like sawdust. Her mother was showing her dislike for her more than she ever had before.

Mary Lee wished that her attitude didn't hurt so much.

She still had her suitcase to unpack before she went to bed. Tomorrow she would find time to clean the room. All of that left her mind when she looked out the window and saw a light in cabin number one.

Frank Pierce was back.

Mary Lee hurriedly left the house and went to the cabin. She lifted her hand to rap, then paused when she heard her mother's voice, then the low rumble of a male voice. Anger erased her tiredness and stiffened her back. She rapped on the door, hard and insistently. When it opened, Frank stood there, blocking her view.

"What'a ya want?"

"You to leave."

"I told you I rented by the month."

"Show me the receipt or I'll call the sheriff."

Dolly crowded in, holding on to Frank's arm with one hand and the neck of a bottle with the other. "He paid for a year, Miss Nosy. I gave him a receipt."

"You'll have to swear to that, Mama," Mary Lee said calmly.

"Go on back in the house," Dolly said.

Mary Lee's eyes moved past Dolly to see Pearl sitting on the bed. "Has she been here all day?"

"I told her she could come out here."

"It's none of yore business who's in my room," Frank said in a booming voice. "Now, unless you want to join the party, get the hell away from my door. I'll take ya on even if ya do have a bun in the oven." He gave her a wolfish leer.

"You're an insult to the human race. I'll go see Mr. Morales in the morning and see what can be done about getting you out of here."

"Do that, and while yo're at it, tell him 'bout the jailbird ya got down in number six!"

"Mama rented to him and took his money. But that has nothing to do with you. Have your receipt handy. You'll need it."

"And ya can kiss my ass, bitch!" he yelled, and slammed the door.

Disappointment in her mother kept Mary Lee rooted to the spot. Blood rushed to her face, and her heart beat so fast she could hardly breathe. Her knees were weak when she turned to go back to the house. When she stumbled on a clump of dirt, she felt a hand on her arm. She let out a small shriek of alarm.

"Don't be scared. I don't want you to fall and hurt the kid." She recognized the distinctive voice of the man in number six.

He had witnessed her humiliation!

"I'm all right."

"You don't feel all right. You're trembling like a scared rabbit."

"You heard?"

"Yeah. Passing by on my way to town. Couldn't help but hear."

"I've got to get him out. Mama will never straighten up with him here," she said, as if talking to herself. They reached the porch steps. "Thank you." She turned and sat down on the steps, not wanting him to see her stumbling into the house.

She expected him to leave, but he stood there looking down at her.

"Thank you," she said again.

"You said that. Haven't you learned that there's a time to attack and a time to back off?"

"What do you mean?"

"You'll get nowhere with a man like Frank Pierce, especially when he's drinking. Talk to the sheriff."

"Mama will give him a receipt. He probably paid her in whiskey."

"You'd better get some help if you're going to run this place."

"I can't afford it. My daddy ran this place without help."

"He wasn't a girl and he wasn't pregnant."

Ashamed that she had revealed so much to this man who was a stranger yet not a stranger, she got shakily to her feet, afraid that she would burst into tears before she got in the house. "Good night."

She didn't know if he answered or not. She hurried to her room and threw herself down on the bed. Something seemed to give way inside her. She was too depressed even to cry.

Jake Ramero headed once more for town, telling himself that he had no business getting involved with the girl or her problems. But dammit to hell. Frank Pierce was a lazy loudmouth and as mean as a rutting moose when he was drinking. Mary Lee would have a hard time getting rid of him.

How in hell was a pregnant woman going to keep the motor court going by herself?

Weeds needed to be cut, holes in the road-
way filled, trash hauled away. Even the
signs along the highway needed to be re-
painted. She had her work cut out: doing
the washing, keeping the cabins clean and
her mother out of sight.

He had seen cars drive in and leave after
being greeted by Mrs. Finley. In the month
he'd been here, he'd seen the floozy who
stayed there clean a cabin a time or two,
but he'd not seen a wash on the line. After a
couple of weeks, he'd bought himself a set
of sheets and a few towels.

With his thoughts to distract him, Jake's
long legs covered the distance to town before he knew it. At the post office he
dropped a letter in the mail slot, then went
down the street, turned in at Red Pepper
Corral and straddled a stool at the bar.

"Hi-ya, Paco."

"*Hola,* Jake. Bottle or draw?"

"Draw."

"Quiet tonight." Jake drank deeply and
wiped the foam off his lips with the back of
his hand.

"It's early. You still out at Quitman's?"

"Part-time, breaking stock horses. He

gives me time off now and then to do some bridge work."

"Heard you came in on the bus the other night."

"Does anything happen in this town you don't know about?" Jake growled. Paco was one of a few men in Cross Roads he called a friend.

"Very little, *amigo*." Paco grinned, showing the wide space between his front teeth. He was a short man with broad shoulders and long arms. His family had been in northern New Mexico since 1826. He and Jake had become friendly when they learned that both their great-grandfathers had fought in the Battle of Glorieta in 1862.

Jake's mother had been the granddaughter of Luis Gazares Callaway, who was considered a hero in that battle. With his half brother, Burr Macklin Calloway, Luis had owned a large parcel of land called Macklin Valley in central New Mexico. Jake's mother had told him that although Luis Gazares had died when she was a little girl, from what she could remember of him, Jake was his image.

"I went to Amarillo to buy a pair of boots."

"Horse hockey! Ocie was in here earlier. You just missed him."

"My lucky day."

"He was nosing 'round. Wanted to know about Bobby's widow. Rosen, over at the bank, had told him she was back. I never understood why that girl married Bobby in the first place. Her daddy was as nice a man as I ever met." Paco moved down the bar and filled a glass for another customer.

"Didn't know you let jailbirds in here or I'd not a come in." The rough-looking cowboy turned on his stool to look at Jake.

"Bet that jailbird didn't know I let braying jackasses in here either. You can leave anytime ya want. I'll not go broke missing your business." Paco scooped up the cowboy's money and came back to wipe the counter in front of Jake.

"One of Lon Delano's bigmouth flunkies," Paco said loudly enough for the cowboy to hear. Then in a lower tone, "Hangs out with Lon. That son of a bitch is awfully interested in what you're doin'. Now that Bobby's gone, he figures that he's next in line to get Ocie's ranch."

"If he lives that long."

"Talk is, Bobby's widow came back pregnant. I don't think Lon knew that when he was in here. I'd think Ocie'd favor a grandchild over a nephew. The young lady'd be smart to watch herself."

Jake had been thinking the same thing. Lon Delano was vicious in his greed to get the Circle C. He was sure Lon had had a hand in framing him for stealing steers. He hadn't been able to prove it yet, but he would. Paco broke into his thoughts.

"Feller was in here today bitchin' about Bobby's widow. What he said wasn't pretty."

"Frank Pierce?"

"Yeah. Didn't take him long to latch on to Dolly Finley after Scott passed on. Guess he didn't expect her daughter to come waltzin' in."

"They come in here?"

"Not often. They drink whiskey, rotgut or bathtub. I don't serve either."

Jake stood abruptly, drained his glass and headed for the door. "See ya, Paco."

"*Buenas noches,*" Paco called as Jake went out the door.

Chapter 4

Mary Lee almost jumped out of her skin early the next morning when she went to the washhouse to light the hot water tank. She opened the door, and a tall boy sprang up from a pile of rags in the corner. He stood with his possessions clutched to him as if prepared for flight. She knew immediately he wasn't a man, but still it took a moment before she was able to speak.

"Who're you?"

"Eli Stacy." His voice began low and ended in a high squeak.

He was shabbily dressed and barefoot. Long brown hair hung down over his ears, and a pair of boots dangled from a heavy cord around his neck.

"What are you doing here?" Mary Lee

asked, her fear leaving as suddenly as it had appeared.

"Sleepin'."

"Are you a hobo?"

"I guess so. I didn't take nothin'," he added quickly. He looked tired, gaunt, his eyes hollow.

Mary Lee knew very little about boys, but she knew that this one was hungry. Her heart went out to him.

"Do you live around here?"

He hesitated a minute, then said, "No."

"I'm going to light the water tank. Then I'll make breakfast. Would you like to join me?"

"If there's work I can do for it. I ain't no beggar."

"Glory! There's no shortage of work around here. I'll be glad for your help. Come on in and wash up."

With a look of disbelief on his face, the boy followed Mary Lee into the house. He dropped a cloth sack beside the door and, when she beckoned, followed her through her bedroom to the bathroom.

"You can wash in here." She glanced at the cowboy boots still suspended around his neck. They were hand-stitched and polished. "Good-looking boots."

"I didn't steal 'em," he said defensively. "I worked for 'em."

Mary Lee raised her brows. "I never doubted that for a minute."

"Why not?"

"My daddy used to say, 'come easy, go easy.' The boots didn't come easy, did they? It's why you're taking good care of them. I've got biscuits in the oven. I'll go make the gravy."

Mary Lee felt strangely lighthearted. Last night her spirits had been lower than a snake's belly, she mused. But this morning, with the bright sunshine and the sweet, fresh air, she was rejuvenated. She didn't know if her mother was in her room or not, but knew that if she was, she'd not be wanting breakfast this early.

Mary Lee set the table for two while the gravy was bubbling in the skillet. When Eli came back into the kitchen, he stood hesitantly in the doorway. He had washed and smoothed his long hair back with wet palms. Before coming into the room, he lifted the cord holding the boots up over his head and set them beside the bundle he'd left beside the door.

"Sit down." Mary Lee placed a pan of biscuits on the table. "Do you drink coffee?"

"Yes, ma'am."

Mary Lee poured the gravy from the skillet into a bowl, brought it to the table and sat down. Eli sat opposite her. His hands were in his lap, his eyes on the plate of biscuits. Mary Lee nudged it toward him.

"Help yourself. Butter is in the crock and there is plum jam."

The boy took a single biscuit, split it and reached for the gravy bowl.

"You'd better have more than that. My daddy used to split three biscuits and cover them with gravy. He put a lot of black pepper on his gravy." Mary Lee continued to talk while she buttered a biscuit, hoping to put the boy at ease. "We're out of milk. I need to go to the store, but the coaster wagon Daddy used before he got the car is broken down."

"I . . . can carry them for you."

"Oh, would you? That would be a big help. How old are you, Eli?"

He looked down at his plate. "Sixteen."

"Is that right?" He was as tall as Mary Lee, but she doubted that he was sixteen.

"Where's your man?" he asked abruptly.

"I'm a widow. My husband died two months ago." Mary Lee got up to pour coffee. "Where are your folks, Eli?" she asked when she returned to the table.

"Ain't got none."

"Really? Oh, my. Where have you been living?"

"At that . . . place. I ain't going back there," he added hastily.

"To the orphans' home?"

"I ain't no throwaway kid. I'm going to get a job on a ranch. I ain't needin' nobody to mollycoddle me."

"You're a cowboy. Would a cowboy be willing to help me here while he's looking for a job? Pay wouldn't be much. You'd have a place to sleep and meals."

"I ain't washin' no dishes. I done washed a boxcar-full back at that . . . place."

"Was that your job at the orphanage?" When he didn't answer, she continued: "You won't have to wash dishes. Would you object to helping me clean the cabins? If we're going to work together we've got to put our cards on the table."

"Guess . . . not."

After the boy had eaten six biscuits and

almost the entire bowl of gravy, Mary Lee pushed the jar of plum jam across the table.

"Finish up the biscuits with this, Eli. My daddy made it."

"Where's he at?"

"He died around Christmastime."

"My mama died around Christmastime. Long . . . time ago."

"I'll put the dishes in the pan to soak. Do you have shoes other than the boots? There are plenty of cockleburs out there in the grass."

"Canvas ones, but the shoestring is broke."

"We can fix that." She went to her bedroom and brought back a pair of brown shoes. She had found her father's clothes piled on the floor in the closet and was wearing one of his shirts over a skirt.

"These would be too big for you, but we can use the shoelaces." She watched while he dug into the pillowcase he was using as a knapsack and brought out a pair of dirty white canvas shoes. "I'll be washing this morning. If you have anything that needs to be washed—"

Eli straightened up. A puzzled, suspicious look came over his young face.

"What're ya bein' nice to me for?"

"You can catch more flies with sugar than vinegar. I want you to stay and help me. To tell you the truth, Eli, I need you every bit as much as you need me. I'm trying to run this place by myself. When my father was alive, it was a pretty place. He made a good living here. He's gone now, and it's getting more run-down every day. I can't do all the work by myself."

"Who's the woman who came in last night?"

"Oh, she came in? I wasn't sure. She's my mother and she'll be no help."

"What'll she say 'bout me bein' here?"

"She'll have plenty to say, but don't pay any attention. I own this place. You and I are in the same boat, Eli. I don't have anyone either, and the end of September I'm going to have a baby to take care of. I've got to make this place pay or the bank will take it, and my baby and I will be out on the street."

He tried to tuck his ragged shirt down in his britches. "I got another shirt and pants, but I was savin' 'em."

"Can you wear them while we wash what you have on?"

"Guess so."

"Go out and change. As soon as the folks in the cabins I rented last night are gone, I'll gather up the sheets and towels and start the washer."

The boy stepped off the porch, then turned and looked at the ground. "I'm thirteen. Do you still want me to stay?"

"Sure. And thank you for telling me."

Mary Lee heard a car and hurried to the front of the house expecting to collect the key from one of her renters. It was Jake Ramero's truck.

He watched her approach from around the side of the house. Most of the pregnant women he had been around had been pale and listless. Mary Lee was beautiful and energetic. She wore a loose shirt, and her auburn hair seemed to catch fire in the sunlight. He also noticed that she didn't look so tired this morning and that she appeared to be pleased about something.

"Howdy." He put a hand to the brim of his hat.

"Morning. You leaving?"

"Sorry to disappoint you. I'm just going to work."

"Oh, well. This isn't my lucky day after all."

"I'm willing to pay extra if you wash my sheets, towels and a few other things."

"I'm surprised that you don't expect that service for your big ten dollars a month you've paid to rent that dollar-and-a-half-a-day cabin."

Jake tried not to grin at her sarcasm. "I did, at first. After a few weeks, when I wasn't given clean sheets and towels, I had to buy some or sleep on a dirty bed. Do you want the business or not? If not, I can get them washed uptown for six bits."

"I don't do ironing."

"That's all right. I'll do that myself."

"You can iron?"

"You'd be surprised what a jailbird can do."

"You sound like you're proud of it."

"I am kind of proud. I can iron shirts with the best of them." His eyes crinkled at the corners, but he didn't smile.

"A dollar is what it'll cost for two sheets, two towels, pants, a shirt and . . . a few things."

"You drive a hard bargain."

"Take it or leave it."

"I'll take it." He got out and lifted a bundle

from the back of the truck. "Where do you want it?"

"I can take it."

"I'll take it to the washhouse."

Mary Lee followed his long legs around the end of the house. Eli was coming out the door as they reached it.

"This is Mr. Ramero, Eli. He'll be in number six . . . for a while. We'll do his washing and, of course, he'll pay extra for it."

"Howdy."

Jake nodded. "I'll pick them up tonight," he said to Mary Lee, and walked away.

She looked up to see Eli staring after him. "Do you know him?"

"He's Jake Ramero, ain't he?"

"Yes. Are you afraid of him?"

"Some folks think he got railroaded."

"What do you mean?"

"He got framed for stealing steers from old Clawson. They say he's a hard dog to keep under the porch, but he ain't no thief."

"Why would someone frame him?"

"Guess him and Clawson's men don't get along a'tall."

"Ocie Clawson?"

"Lon Delano. Fella said they'd had a couple of knock-down, drag-outs, but he didn't know what it was about. Jake and his maw lived out there when he was little."

"You're just full of information. I was married to Bobby Clawson and he never told me that."

"You was married to—?"

"Ocie Clawson's son. He didn't get along with Bobby either."

"I stayed out there awhile . . . till the old man run me off."

"Did you stay in the bunkhouse?"

"Yeah. But I cleaned it—swept out the mud and emptied spit cans. I wasn't beggin'. I worked for my grub."

"I'm sure you did. Emptied spit cans? Ugh!" Mary Lee liked the boy more and more. He had pride. "What did the men think of Mr. Ramero?"

"Most of 'em didn't like him 'cause they was suckin' up to Lon Delano and the old man. Two of them did. Said he got a raw deal, but couldn't prove it. They didn't talk much in front of the others."

Mary Lee showed Eli what had to be done to clean up the months of weeds and trash that littered the motor court.

"As soon as the cabins are empty, we'll strip the sheets and towels and start the wash. Meanwhile, I'm going to walk down to the filling station and use the phone. If one of the renters leaves while I'm gone, take the key, thank them and tell them we'd be glad for them to stop again. Can you do that?"

"Don't take no brains to take a key and thank somebody."

It was a five-minute walk down the highway to the Phillips 66 station. Cars whizzed by her on the highway, some on their way to California, the land of promise. She waved back at the few who waved.

She had known Mr. Santez since she was a little girl. He had been a good friend to her father. He probably knew, as much as anyone, what had been going on at the motor court before and after her father died. The short, bald man came from the back of the gas station, wiping his hands on a greasy rag. Her father used to say that you seldom saw a bald-headed Mexican, but then, he reasoned that Mr. Santez was only half.

"Well, well. Mary Lee. I heard you were back."

"Hello." She offered her hand. "How is the family?"

"All good. Last one leaves school this year."

Four of the Santez children had already graduated from high school, an accomplishment of which the Santez family was terribly proud.

"Tell them all hello for me."

"I will. Glad yo're back, Mary Lee. It's time ya took a hand up there. Cross Roads needs for folks to have a reason to stop here."

"I know. I'm going to try to get it back to where it was when Daddy was alive."

"I'll speak plain for yore daddy's sake. Ya got to get rid of that trash yore ma's got hangin' around."

"I don't know how I'm going to do it. Mama rented out two of the cabins by the month. If I try to throw Frank Pierce out, she'll say she rented it to him by the year. The other one, Mr. Ramero, rented for four months and paid her in advance. Mama must have needed cash money pretty bad."

"Jake Ramero is a rough, hard man, all right, but he ain't as bad as some folks believe. He don't bother anybody if they don't bother him. He was in this morning a-buyin' gas. Doin' bridge work, he said."

"I won't get any money for that cabin or for the one Frank Pierce is in all summer. It means I'll have just four cabins to rent. I'll have to keep them rented every night."

"It's the only place along here, Mary Lee. Some folks don't want to turn in to town to go to the hotel. I stopped sending folks to your court when it got so run-down. Folks won't stay in a dirty place."

"And I don't blame them. It'll be different now. If I've got a cabin to rent, it'll be clean. Right now I'd like to use your phone to call Mr. Collins at the furniture store and see if I can get a mattress. Someone burned a big hole in the one in number three. I'm surprised the whole place didn't burn down."

"You go right ahead and help yourself."

"As soon as I can, I'll have ours connected again."

Mary Lee went into the station and lifted the receiver from the box on the side of the telephone and asked the operator to ring Collins Furniture Store.

"Mr. Collins, this is Mary Lee Clawson. I'm back home now, and running the motor court. I need a mattress and I'd like to pay five dollars down and a dollar a week until it's paid for."

She listened intently to the man on the other end of the line for a long while. Color came to her cheeks.

"I know all that, Mr. Collins. And no, I have not talked to Mr. Clawson and I don't intend to. It's none of his business what goes on out at the court. Being his son's widow does not give him authority over me. I want to make it perfectly clear that he is not responsible for my bills," Mary Lee said heatedly.

After a pause, she said, "There are changes being made. I have the money to pay for the mattress, but I don't think it wise not to have a little put back. I'm renting the cabins for a dollar and a half a night. I should be able to pay you more than the dollar a week."

She looked at Mr. Santez. He was motioning to her. She put her hand over the mouthpiece.

"I'll pay for the mattress and you can pay me if that penny-pincher won't give you credit."

Mary Lee's shoulders slumped with relief. "All right, Mr. Collins. I'll pay for the mattress. Fifteen dollars? Will you bring it out today? Thank you."

Mary Lee hung up the phone and leaned her forehead on the mouthpiece for a minute before she turned to her father's old friend.

"He knew about the loan Daddy took from the bank before he died. He asked me if I had paid it off."

"He and the banker are thick as thieves."

"He said the mattress was fifteen dollars cash but twenty dollars if paid for on time, and he would have to think about giving me credit."

"He's a shyster, is what he is."

"Thank you for the loan, Mr. Santez. I'll pay you as much as I can each week."

Mr. Santez dug his wallet from the bib of his overalls and gave her a ten-dollar bill.

"I'll write you out an IOU."

"No need. Scott helped me out many a time. There's not a doubt in my mind that you'll pay me back."

"Thank you." Mary Lee had to blink away the tears.

Ollie Santez watched Mary Lee walk back up the highway. The girl had had her share of trouble. Her uncaring sot of a mother was more than likely the reason she had married a man who had no more gumption than a sand hill, just to get out of town. Now she would have a babe to take care of. She had come through it all with her head held high. Surely the breaks would come her way soon.

Jake Ramero sat on the ground, his back to a tree, and ate the sack lunch he had picked up at Ruby's Diner, where he had eaten his breakfast. He hated the relentless wind that swept down the canyon. His eyes went to the top of the bridge span he had been working on, and his mouth went dry. He fought a constant battle to conquer his fear of heights. He had been successful so far; but as soon as he got the money he needed, he swore that he would never climb another damn girder.

His thoughts went back to the woman at the motor court. She was like the sprigs of mountain flowers that grew out of the rocks along the canyon walls: perky, pretty, promising life.

How would it be to walk with her, her hand in his, take care of her, make love to her in every way a man makes love to his woman—to caress the mound of her unborn child, catch the babe as he came into the world? If she were his, he would fight for her, work for her. She and the child would be his to love and to cherish.

Dear God! Where had those thoughts come from?

He didn't want to be attracted to her. He wished desperately that he had found something about her to dislike. She was not a ravishing beauty, but there was gentleness about her, an innate femininity and dignity. He didn't want even to like her, but he found himself drawn to her like a mouse to a baited trap.

Why in hell did she have to be Bobby's widow?

He closed his eyes to will the image of her away and, instead, pictured her again as she had been this morning: a man's shirt covering her pregnancy, her hair pulled back and held with a ribbon, her cheeks flushed and eyes open and honest, blue as the sky.

He threw an apple core far out into the brush alongside the riverbank. He wanted nothing to do with her. Hell, it was one thing to have a sexual need, but, Christ on a horse, not with a pregnant woman! Besides, what woman of goodness, gentleness and intelligence would have anything to do with a man who had spent two years in prison?

A bell clanged. He got slowly to his feet, steeling himself to climb the giant girder again.

Chapter 5

By late afternoon the mattress had been delivered and four cabins were clean and ready to rent. Eli had raked along the front of the cabins, and the trash had been picked up. He had helped Mary Lee feed the sheets into the wringer, carried the wet clothes basket and then held the two ends of the sheets together while she fastened them to the clothesline. He had been such a help that when the last cabin was cleaned, she had put her arm across his shoulder.

"I'm so glad you stopped here, Eli. Please don't leave for a while."

"If . . . ya don't want me to." His face turned a bright red, and he refused to meet her eyes.

The only blot on the day came at noon,

while Eli and Mary Lee were sitting at the kitchen table. Dolly came from her room. She was wearing an old wraparound robe. Her hair looked as if she had been in a tornado. Hungover from the night's drinking spree with Pearl and Frank Pierce, she was in a foul mood.

"Who're you?" She squinted at Eli.

"This is Eli Stacy, Mama. He's going to help us for a while."

"Sh . . . it. Whose kid is he?"

"Mr. and Mrs. Stacy's," Mary Lee said, and winked at Eli.

"He can get his skinny ass out of here. We ain't feedin' no tramps."

"He's staying here," Mary Lee said firmly.

"Not in my house, he ain't."

"It's my house, too, in case you've forgotten. I'm setting up a cot in the washhouse."

"Sh . . . it!"

"Watch your language, Mama," Mary Lee said sharply.

"You think a kid like that ain't never heard the word 'shit' before?"

"It doesn't matter if he's heard it or not. I hate it when you talk trashy."

"Well, la-dee-da. You sure got uppity all of a sudden."

"Is Pearl still here?"

"She left last night. Happy now?"

"Sit down and eat, Mama."

Dolly ignored Mary Lee and opened the icebox. "Not a goddamn thing in there fit to eat." She filled a glass with ice chips, poured tea from the pitcher on the table and went back to her room.

Mary Lee got up and closed the door to the icebox.

"My mother . . . isn't well," she said to Eli. "She's usually out of sorts in the morning." When he said nothing, she added, "You may as well know. She drinks."

"My uncle drank moonshine whiskey."

"Did you live with him?"

"Little while."

"When Mama goes on a drinking spree, she keeps at it until she gets good and sick. Then she'll leave it alone for a while. My daddy spent his life trying to help her. I used to think that she drank because of me. She said many times that she hadn't wanted to have me, that Daddy made her. He told me to pay no mind to what she said when she was drunk, that she was my mother and I should love her because she gave me life."

"She'll run me off." There was resignation in the young boy's voice.

Mary Lee put her hand on his arm. "No. She'll not run you off. You can stay as long as you want. I'm in charge here and I need you."

It was late evening and Mary Lee was showing a cabin to a couple from Missouri when Jake drove in. He lifted a hand in greeting. She waved back. He parked beside his cabin, then walked behind the other five to the washhouse. Eli was sitting in the open doorway, rubbing his boots with a soft cloth.

Jake's "few things" to be washed had turned out to be three shirts, two pairs of pants, four pairs of socks and three underdrawers, besides the sheets, pillowcases and towels.

Eli saw the heavy ankle-high, rubber-soled shoes first. He looked up the long legs to the dusty, whiskered face. He got quickly to his feet and placed the boots inside the doorway, out of sight.

Jake looked down at the boy. Memories came rushing back to the time when, after working an entire summer as cook's helper on a chuck wagon, he had bought his first pair of cowboy boots. Lord, but he had been proud of those boots. Then, to be ornery, a cowhand had spit tobacco juice in one. Jake had run at him, even though the man was twice his size, and butted him in the groin with his head, causing enough pain to lay him out. He'd wanted to kill him; instead he had made an enemy for life. The cowboy, a distant relative of the owner of the ranch, had been so humiliated at being bested by a boy that he swore to get even. The man developed a deep hatred for the boy that existed even fifteen years later.

"I didn't steal 'em, if that's what you're thinkin'," Eli said belligerently.

"Why would I think that?"

"It's what most folks think . . . when they see 'em."

"I'm not most folks, son. I've been in your shoes."

"I'm not your son."

"I reckon you're not, but I'd have sworn you're somebody's son."

Eli glared at him. "Well, I ain't. I ain't nobody's and don't want to be nobody's. I'm not lookin' out for nobody but me."

"Not even Mary Lee?"

"I'll get your wash."

"I'd be obliged . . . that is if you can get down off your high horse long enough."

Eli stepped inside the washhouse and came out with a bushel basket of neatly folded wash.

"Miss Mary Lee said collect a dollar."

"I don't guess Miss Mary Lee would give me credit."

"She said collect."

Jake rammed his hand down in his pocket and came out with a silver dollar. He flipped it up and caught it a time or two, then flipped it to Eli and picked up the basket.

"You stayin' here nights?"

"Plannin' on it."

"Keep an eye on that bird in number one. If he gets smart with Miss Mary Lee, come get me pronto. Understand?"

"Yeah."

Eli watched him walk away, then sat down on the doorstep and reached for his boots. Jake Ramero must have a reason for thinking the fella in number one was going to be mean to Miss Mary Lee. If he did, he'd fix him. He'd learned a lot about getting even since he'd been fending for himself. Eli figured he owed the lady a lot. His stomach was full, he was clean and he had a place to sleep. It was more than he'd had for several weeks.

Eli was still sitting on the doorstep when Jake, bathed and in clean clothes, came back on his way to town to eat. He paused.

"Do you like to listen to *Amos 'n Andy*?"

"Only heard 'em a time or two."

"I'm going uptown to eat. They'll be on soon after I get back. You're welcome to come listen."

"I'll think about it."

Jake went across the lot behind the motor court, taking the shortcut to town. The kid reminded him of himself at that age: gawky and with a chip on his shoulder as big as a boulder, but, he reckoned, not for the same reason.

When he entered Ruby's Diner, it was empty except for Frank Pierce, who sat at the counter. He glanced up, then continued with his meal.

"Howdy, Jake." Ruby, scraping the grill, paused to greet him. "You're late tonight."

"Yeah." Jake hung his hat on the rack beside the door. "Guess I am." He straddled a stool.

"What'll ya have?"

"Your thirty-cent steak."

"Golly, you must be hungry tonight."

"I could eat the rear end out of a skunk."

"You'll not have to do that." Ruby's large belly shook when she laughed. She took a slab of meat out of the icebox and slapped it on the grill.

Jake liked Ruby and counted her as one of his few friends in town. She was so homely she would have to tie a pork chop around her neck to get a dog to play with her, but she was honest and fair and hard-working. She was a tall woman, almost six feet, broad, and could be an advertisement for her own cooking. Her husband had been killed on the highway right after her last son was born. She had two daughters, one of whom helped her at the diner, and a son who wasn't worth the powder it would take to blow him up. Her other son had not been right when he was born and had needed constant care until he died at age seventeen.

Jake figured Ruby had endured enough sorrow for two lifetimes.

"I hear they're about to wind up the work on the bridge."

"Another week or two."

"Are you moving on down the highway with the crew?"

"Not planning on it. I've got horses to break for Quitman."

"Quitman isn't particular 'bout who he hires," Frank mumbled to Ruby when she passed him. "Like you ain't particular 'bout who eats here."

"No, I ain't. That's why I serve you just like anyone else, Frank."

Jake ignored the conversation and spread butter on the bread Ruby had set before him.

"You still stayin' out at the motor court, Frank?" Ruby asked.

"Yeah."

"I heard you and Dolly were goin' to get married."

"That was a while ago."

"Before you heard that Scott Finley left everything to Mary Lee?"

"Dolly could still get part of it if she went to court."

"Lawyer's fee would eat up all she got, if anything. Isn't that right, Jake?"

"I wouldn't know. How's my steak comin'?"

"Medium rare, huh?"

"Yeah, and while I'm eatin' it, stick that piece of apple pie in the oven to warm up."

"I hope you're this hungry when you're breaking horses, or do you eat out at Quitman's?"

"I eat at noon out there."

Frank put his money on the counter, slapped his hat on his head and walked out.

"Thank you, Frank," Ruby called, then chuckled. "Guess he got his tail over the line. Don't matter. As soon as his ditch-diggin' job plays out, he'll be back wantin' to eat on credit."

"Where's he working?"

"On the sewer lines the town's layin' north of town. As soon as Scott died, he was right out there playin' up to Dolly. She's got no more sense than a cross-eyed goose—never did have as long as I've known her. Frank's just the type she'd take up with. I'm glad Mary Lee is back and takin' over the court. Hear she's expecting."

Jake listened to Ruby talk while she stirred the potatoes she was frying on the grill next to the steak.

"Now, that girl's had a peck of trouble. She had a time goin' through school, bein' shamed by the way Dolly acted and everybody in town knowin' it. Then she married that good-for-nothin' Bobby Clawson, but I guess you know that. She was determined to leave town and didn't want to go by herself, is what Trudy said. My Trudy and Mary Lee were good friends in school."

This was news Jake had heard before, yet he was all ears and kept quiet hoping Ruby would continue to talk.

"Did you know that when Bobby was killed, Ocie Clawson didn't as much as telephone Mary Lee or help her bury his son? He told it himself at the pool hall, and you know that everything that's said at that place is spread all over town. It must have been humiliating to that girl to have the county bury her husband."

Ruby's mouth continued to run while Jake was eating. He didn't mind. Between her and Paco at the Red Pepper Corral he got more news than if he read the newspaper. It was as he was getting ready to leave that Ruby warned him about Lon Delano.

"Jake, keep an eye out for Lon Delano and his bunch. They were in here the other day talking about how they'd like to grease those girders you climb on out at the bridge and watch you take a nosedive into the canyon."

"Not a one of them has the guts to climb the girder to grease it. Thanks for the warning, Ruby. I'll be here in the morning. Pack me a lunch."

"Night, Jake."

When Jake neared the motor court, he noticed a light in each of the four available cabins. Mary Lee had a full house tonight. There was also a light in the one where Frank was staying.

Eli was still sitting on the doorstep of the washhouse.

"Made up your mind yet?" Jake asked, and walked on by.

"Yeah." The boy got up and hurried to catch up with him.

"After *Amos 'n Andy,* the *Texaco Fire Chief* is on."

"Never heard of that one."

"It's pretty funny." They reached the cabin. Jake unlocked the door. "Come on in and close the door. It's a little cool at night."

Eli stood hesitantly in the doorway until Jake turned on the light. The room was tidy;

the bed was made, and clothes hung on a rod stretched across a corner. A square box radio sat on a table, and an attached wire ran out the window. Jake switched the set on. Eli eased down on his heels beside the door.

"Now, ain't dat a shame. Amos, yo got no sense a-tall."

The program had already started. Next they heard Andy's most recognized line: *"Buzz me, Miss Blue."*

"Yo don' need no buzz from Miss Blue, Andy. The Kingfish is here."

"How do, Kingfish? Yo wantin' to ride the Fresh Air Taxi down to the lodge hall?"

Jake lit a cigarette and lounged on the bed. They listened to the remainder of the program without much to say to each other. When it was over, Eli got up to leave.

"Thanks." He opened the door.

"Stay for Ed Wynn's show if you like."

"Naw. Better get back. Miss Mary Lee might need me."

"Come again."

The boy left, and Jake kind of wished he'd stayed awhile. He liked the kid. He had pride and a dignity that you didn't see in some grown men nowadays. It had to be tough being on your own at that age, eating in soup kitchens and looking for a dry hole to sleep in. Jake wondered why the kid didn't try to hitch a ride to California. It seemed that everybody and his dog was going there. Folks traveled the highway every day, their cars and trucks loaded with furniture and kids, all seeking a better life.

Jake reached over and put out his cigarette. Whatever had possessed him to take the bridge job when every minute he spent on those girders was pure agony? He knew even as he asked himself the question. He was doing it for money, and when the job was over, he would be just that much closer to the day when he would have his own little spread.

He looked forward to the time when he could sit on the porch of his own house and watch his horses and cows eat the grass in his own meadows. He wanted a soft, sweet woman to be waiting for him after a hard day's work. He wanted one who would be glad to see him, listen as he told about the happenings of the day and cuddle with him in a warm bed at night. He wanted a little curly-haired girl to run to meet him, and a stout boy to teach about horses and cows—

legitimate children who never doubted who they were and who knew that their parents wanted them.

The *Texaco Fire Chief* came on and off the radio without Jake's hearing it.

"What in the world—"

Mary Lee woke out of a sound sleep and sat up in bed. Her heart pounded. She swung her legs over the side and turned on the light. It was one o'clock in the morning. The loud music from a radio spilled out into the night. She slipped her feet into her shoes, put on one of her daddy's old shirts, *hurried* to the door and out onto the porch. The music was so loud, she was sure it could be heard a block away.

A light was on in cabin number one, Frank's cabin. The windows, as well as the door, were open. The radio blared. As she stepped off the porch, lights came on in the other cabins. Anger propelled Mary Lee to the door. Frank lounged on the end of the bed with a bottle of booze in his hand. Her mother, fully clothed, lay on the bed beside him.

"Turn that radio down!" Mary Lee had to shout in order to be heard.

Frank looked at her, grinned and raised his bottle. His lips moved; she couldn't hear, but she was sure he said, "Make me."

"I said, turn it down. You're disturbing folks who want to sleep."

Dolly sat up on the edge of the bed. Ignoring Mary Lee, Frank playfully pushed her. She fell back giggling. He moved over on top of her, rubbing himself crudely against her.

Mary Lee's face reddened. "Mama, come home."

She was sure that her mother was falling-down drunk, and it made her sick to her soul to see her on the bed with trash like Frank Pierce.

"Get the hell away from here!" Frank shouted.

"Not until you turn down that radio." Mary Lee stepped up onto the doorsill.

Frank sprang off the bed, slammed a hand against her chest and pushed her back. She stumbled but regained her balance.

"This is my place. I never invited ya in."

"Don't touch her!" Eli's young voice was heard over the music. He was beside Mary

Lee, holding up a big stick, ready to defend her.

"Watch yoreself, kid, or ya'll get yore ass kicked." Frank stepped back and slammed the door.

Mary Lee backed away. "I don't know what to do, Eli. The renters will leave and demand their money back."

"I'll get Jake. He told me to . . ."

Eli took off on the run even as she was saying, "No! Don't."

A man came out of number two to see what was going on, and another came from number three.

"Turn that radio off or I'll call the sheriff," Mary Lee called, even though she knew Frank couldn't hear her.

The man from the next cabin came over. He was an older person with a head of gray hair and a lined face.

"Call the law, ma'am. We can't sleep with that racket goin' on."

"I'm awful sorry . . ."

At that moment Mary Lee vowed that she would take the money she had been saving for the baby and have the phone reconnected.

"Eli said Frank pushed you." Mary Lee

turned to see Jake Ramero. He wore only his pants and boots. He was a welcome sight.

"He was on his way here," Eli explained.

Jake put his hand on her shoulder. "Are you all right?"

"He didn't hurt me. I'm afraid my renters will leave. I'll have to give them their money back." Unconsciously, Mary Lee began to wring her hands.

Jake stepped up to the cabin and tried the door. It was locked.

"He isn't going to be reasonable. Do I have your permission to break in?"

"I don't want a fight . . ."

"It's either that or you lose your renters, and believe me, news travels down the highway."

"Break in. And if he gives you an excuse, knock his teeth out!"

Jake grinned. "Thought you didn't want a fight."

"It won't be much of a fight. He's too drunk."

Jake took a step back, raised his booted foot and smashed it against the door. It flew open. He stepped inside, grabbed Frank by the shirtfront and slammed him up against the wall.

"That was for pushing the lady. If you ever put your hands on her again you'll find your pecker in your ear and your balls hanging on a clothesline." Jake hauled him to the door and shoved him so hard he went sprawling facedown in the yard. "That was for causing the racket and waking up all these folks."

With a mere glance at the giggling woman on the bed, Jake yanked the cord connecting the radio from the electric line. There was an instant silence. He then pulled the wire used as an antenna from the window and picked up the radio.

Frank was still on the ground. Eli stood over him with a big stick. "I'll just keep this awhile to make sure you don't decide to do something foolish and turn it on again."

"I'll complain to the sheriff. They'll throw you so far back in jail you'll never get out."

"No, they won't. If anyone goes to jail it'll be you," Mary Lee said. "I'll insist on it."

"That jailbird's stealin' my radio."

"Get up," Jake said, nudging him with the toe of his boot. "Get back in there and keep your mouth shut. You're just a whisker away from me kickin' your butt up between your ears."

"You're on parole. I'll tell the sheriff—"

"Frank, honey." Dolly stood swaying in the doorway. "Ya comin' back in?"

Mary Lee went to her. "Come to the house, Mama."

"Ya can kiss my foot!" Dolly yelled. "You're just like that stuffy old Scott. Ya don't want me to have no fun."

Frank brushed past Mary Lee and took Dolly's arm. "Come to bed, sugar," he said, glaring triumphantly at Mary Lee. "We'll have us a hot time 'tween the sheets. I know a few tricks that'll give ya a duck fit."

Mary Lee felt a hand on her arm pulling her away from the door. "You're shivering. Go on back to the house." Jake walked with her back to the porch.

She couldn't hold back the tears that filled her eyes and rolled down her cheeks. They were tears of humiliation, grief and anger.

"Thank you for what you did. I hope you won't get in trouble."

"I won't unless the owner complains about me breaking down her door." Jake resisted the urge to put his arms around her.

"She won't."

"I'll take a couple of tubes out of the radio and leave it on the step over there so he can't accuse me of stealing it."

"I didn't want to bother you."

"It wasn't a bother. I told Eli to come get me if Frank got smart with you."

"The telephone is disconnected or I'd have called the sheriff."

"Go on back to bed. You've got a good lookout. Eli will let me know if there's any more trouble. I kind of wish I'd let him hit Frank with that stick."

She felt strangely disturbed and too warm. A little laugh bubbled from her lips. "So do I."

Chapter 6

"I'm . . . coming! I'm coming—" he yelled as he ran through the high meadow grass. The long blades wrapped about his feet and held him back. Mary Lee! She was holding her arms over her belly, trying to protect her unborn child. Her mouth was open in a silent scream.

Jake woke with a start and reared up in the bed. His heart was pounding. He was wet with sweat. It was dark where, seconds before, it had been bright sunlight. The cramp in his leg brought him to his feet. He put all his weight on the leg and massaged the tight muscle in his calf with strong fingers. When he was able to stand, he walked back and forth beside the bed until the muscle was relaxed.

The dream was still with him.

Lon Delano, the son of a bitch, had tried to kill Mary Lee's baby! And when he saw Jake coming, had shot him.

The room was pitch dark, but in his mind's eye he could see Mary Lee's fear-filled eyes, pain in every line in her face. She had been big with his child when Lon threw her to the ground.

His child?

Jake sat down on the bed and put his face in his hands. The dream had been so real, he was still shaking. For the first time in his life he began to doubt his sanity. Mary Lee was carrying Bobby's baby, not his. Bits and pieces of the dream kept coming back to him.

They had made love in a meadow surrounded by a thick fog. Warm and naked, she had lain on top of him so that he could feel the movement of their child. He had slipped inside her so gently she had been unaware of it. When she realized that they were joined, she laughed and laughed and kissed him again and again.

Another flash of memory presented itself. Before Lon Delano shot him, Ocie Clawson, on a big black horse, his white hair blowing in the wind, had raced toward them. At the time Jake had not known if Ocie was coming to aid Mary Lee or to help Lon Delano kill her and her baby.

Jake switched on the light long enough to see the time. It was three o'clock. He went to the small bathroom to get a drink of water. Damn, but he had to get the dream out of his mind so that he could get some sleep. He needed to be sure-footed when he climbed that girder in the morning.

It was an hour before Jake could get back to sleep, and during that time he became reconciled to the fact that any connection he had with Mary Lee Clawson had been conjured up by wishful thinking. Sure, he would like to have a woman like her. What man wouldn't?

But to save himself the humiliation when she rejected him, he would keep his distance, help her if she needed it, the same as he would do for any other woman; but that was all.

He slept, and on awakening, his first thoughts were of Mary Lee Clawson.

Frank Pierce was gone when Mary Lee awoke. Before breakfast she went out and picked up the liquor bottles and other trash he had thrown out, and snatched off the KEEP OUT sign he had tacked up on the door.

As soon as the overnight renters had left, Mary Lee instructed Eli to strip the beds and put the sheets and towels in the washer and start the machine. She put on her straw hat and walked down the highway to Mr. Santez's filling station to use the phone. She had to know how much of a telephone bill her mother had run up and if she had to pay it all before she could get the telephone connected again.

"Morning, Mr. Santez."

"Mornin', gal. What brings you down the hill so early in the mornin'?"

"I'd like to use your phone again. I need to see about getting our telephone connected. Last night I would have called the sheriff if I'd had one."

"Someone givin' you trouble?"

"Frank Pierce. He turned the radio up so loud I'm surprised you didn't hear it down here."

"I'd of bet my boots he'd cause trouble. He had hopes of marryin' Dolly and gettin' his hands on the court."

"That will never happen. Oh, he might

marry Mama. But he'll not get Daddy's court. I'll burn it to the ground first. One of my renters broke down the door and took the radio or I'd have lost my night's receipts."

"Jake, huh?" Mr. Santez went on without waiting for her to confirm his question or express her surprise. "Jake's a good man to have on your side. I'm glad he's up there."

"I told Mr. Ramero to break down the door, but Frank is threatening to go to the sheriff and have his parole revoked."

"Won't do him no good if you tell how it was. Sheriff Pleggenkuhle knows what Frank Pierce is."

"How did a man with a name like Pleggenkuhle get elected sheriff in a county where there are so many Mexicans?"

"Wait'll you meet him. Big man, loud voice, but straight as a string and fair to a fault. If he can't corral 'em by talkin' to 'em, he'll bash heads. He's been good for the county."

"I hope he'll do something about Frank."

"Rosa sent a box for me to brin' up to ya. It's stuff that we pass down through the family. Both my girls and their babies has used 'em. Rosa said they didn't need to be sittin' around waitin' for one of the girls to have another baby. Use whatever you want, and hand 'em back when you're done with 'em. Rosa'll keep 'em and pass 'em on."

Tears came to Mary Lee's eyes. "Tell Rosa that I appreciate it and that I'll take good care of everything and send them back."

"Now, now. Ain't no need to blubber 'bout it. I'll bring the box up sometime today. It's too heavy for ya to be totin' back up the hill."

"I have a boy helping me. He's going to fix our old coaster wagon. When he gets it fixed, I'll have him come get the box."

"Well, now, it's good ya got someone to help. Tramp, is he?"

"I guess so. He's only thirteen. He's good help."

"Ya got to be careful, Mary Lee. Rosa's been helpin' out down at the soup kitchens. Tramps and hobos are comin' through every day. Some of 'em are good men down on their luck. But some are just as sorry as sin."

"I'll be careful."

After Mary Lee used the telephone, she walked slowly back up the hill to the motor court. The company had refused to connect the phone unless she paid the back bill of twenty-two dollars. Her mother had not paid one bill after her father died.

Knowing that she needed advice on how to handle Frank Pierce, she had called the sheriff and asked him to stop by the court when he had time.

Disappointed, but determined, Mary Lee plunged into the day's work. She had made six dollars last night and four dollars and fifty cents plus the dollar for doing Jake Ramero's laundry the day before. She had the ten she had been saving for the baby. The water and electric bills were coming up, and she would have to buy groceries. There was no way she could have paid on the telephone bill even if they had allowed her to pay only part of it.

After the cabins were cleaned and while the sheets were drying on the line, she mixed a bucket of water and vinegar, and she and Eli washed the windows in the cabins. She was standing on a chair washing the outside of the windows in number six when the sheriff drove in. She got down off the chair and went to meet him.

"Hello, Sheriff. I'm Mary Lee Clawson, Scott Finley's daughter."

"Howdy, young lady. I heard that you were back running the place."

"I left the message for you to come by because I'm having trouble with one of the renters. Frank Pierce and my mother claim that she rented him the number one cabin. One time she said she'd rented it for a year, and one time he said for a month. He claims to have given her money, but so far he hasn't produced a receipt."

"Your mother was in charge of the court when she rented it?"

"Yes, sir. I'd like to get him out."

"I don't see how you can do that unless you give him his money back."

"Last night he turned his radio up so loud my other renters threatened to leave—"

"I heard about it. He said Jake Ramero broke down his door, assaulted him, then stole his radio."

"You believed him?"

"Let's just say I keep an open mind where Frank is concerned."

"When I asked him to turn down the radio, he pushed me, almost shoving me down. Mr. Ramero came to help me, and I asked him to break down the door and take the radio before my other renters demanded their money back."

"Jake's on parole, you know. Assaulting Frank, if he pressed charges, would be enough to get Jake sent back to serve the rest of his sentence."

"He was protecting me, Sheriff. I swear it."

"Frank said that he was held down and threatened—"

"By a thirteen-year-old boy with a stick! I need to get Frank out of here so I can clean up that cabin and rent it."

"Where does your mother stand on this?"

Embarrassed, Mary Lee looked away from the big man. "Mama has been either drunk or with a hangover ever since I came home. More than likely she'll say he paid her for a year."

"I can't see that I can do anything for you unless he causes another disturbance and I'm called."

"You can't make him move?"

"Not if Mrs. Finley says he paid her rent."

"What about Mr. Ramero?"

"I'll have to have witnesses before I make

a report to his parole officer." Sheriff Pleg-genkuhle grinned.

"You'll not get any witnesses from here," Mary Lee said stiffly.

"I didn't think so. Tell you what: I'll have my deputy swing by here a couple times a night for a while."

"Couldn't you put Frank in jail or something?" Mary Lee asked desperately.

"Not unless I have something to charge him with."

"I could file charges saying he's wrecked one of the cabins. He has. It's filthy."

"Has he broken any windows?"

"No."

"Well, tell Jake to be careful. I'd hate like hell to have to take him in. If you have any trouble, call me."

"I don't have a phone, Sheriff. But I have a boy helping me. He can run up to the telephone office."

Mary Lee's shoulders slumped as she watched the sheriff drive away. She couldn't get rid of Frank Pierce, but she had set the sheriff straight on Jake's involvement. Lord, she'd hate it if he had to go back to prison because of her.

*   *   *

It was late in the afternoon when Eli proudly showed her the coaster wagon. He had nailed a board across the front and attached the wagon tongue. Mary Lee made a big to-do about how handy he was, then asked him to go to Mr. Santez's gas station and get a box.

She washed, combed her hair, put on one of her daddy's clean shirts and sat on the front steps. Her mind wandered as she watched the cars go by on the highway, listened to the sound of the rubber tires meeting the concrete and the purr of passing engines. Route 66, the Mother Road, was carrying thousands of families fleeing the dust bowls of Oklahoma and the arid lands of Kansas and Texas westward to the fertile fields of California.

Had things been different, Mary Lee would have reveled in the adventure of traveling the road through the wind-blown plains, deep forests and high mountain passes. But her place was here, beside the road, watching those who passed by and wishing them Godspeed.

Eli returned with a cardboard box in the wagon bed. She followed him around to the back of the house.

"Mr. Santez said you hadn't ought to be liftin' heavy stuff. Said it would be hard on ya when your baby came."

"He's a nice man." Mary Lee couldn't get used to speaking so frankly about her condition to men and boys, but Eli evidently thought nothing about it.

"I'll carry the box to your room."

"Thanks. Oh, there's a car turning in. If they take the cabin, we'll be full up." Mary Lee hurried to greet the man stepping out of the car.

It wasn't until the four cabins were rented and the light turned off over the No Vacancy sign that Mary Lee had time to open the box from Rosa Santez. Tears rolled down her cheeks when she lifted out baby gowns, bands, booties, and several small flannel blankets. There were three maternity dresses with drawstrings at the waist, and a nice skirt with matching overblouse. Everything was here that she would need for the baby for the first few months.

Mary Lee opened the bottom drawer of her chest to put away the baby clothes and saw the strap on her handbag sticking out from the drawer above. A premonition caused her heart to sink even before she opened the purse to check her money.

The ten dollars she had tucked away for the baby was gone.

It hurt dreadfully to lose the money, but it hurt even more knowing who had taken it. She stood for a long moment, holding her purse to her chest. How could her own mother do this to her? She fought back the storm of tears that threatened to sweep over her. *She could not break down. She could not let go.* The words repeated themselves over and over in her mind. She had to cope. There was no one to help her. She thanked the Lord she had locked the rent money in her suitcase.

Hurt gave way to anger. She went through the bathroom to her mother's room, but the door wouldn't open; something was wedged against it. The door going into the bedroom from the living room was locked. Mary Lee hurried out the back to where Eli sat on the step of the washhouse.

"Eli, have you seen my mother?"

"She left before I went to get the box."

"Did she go to town?"

"She went that way."

Mary Lee was not only angry, she was

heartsick. She had no doubt that the ten dollars she had saved for her baby would be spent on booze at one of the dives in town. Dolly would be the big spender tonight and treat her cronies.

The jukebox was blaring. The Texas Playboys were playing "San Antonio Rose" when Jake, after eating at Ruby's, walked into the Red Pepper Corral and took a seat at the bar. Paco was busy drawing beer in the heavy mugs and handing out bottles from the cooler. A few couples were dancing on the small floor. He was smiling when he came down the bar with a mug of beer for Jake.

"Business is good tonight."

"I could tell by the grin on your face."

"Lon Delano and a couple of pals are over there in the corner with Frank Pierce and Dolly Finley."

"I saw them when I came in. Started to back out, but what the hell—I didn't come in to prove my dick is bigger than theirs. I've as much right to come in here as they have."

"Frank's in a mean mood."

"I'll not start trouble if he doesn't."

"He's brayin' about you takin' his radio and how it took you and a kid with a ball bat to get it away from him."

Jake grunted and took a deep drink from his glass.

"Dolly's treatin' tonight."

"Where'd she get the money? They can't even connect their telephone."

"She bought several rounds for the whole bunch."

"If she messes around with that trash she'll get more than she bargained for."

Paco wiped the bar vigorously. "They're making a fool of her."

"What do you care?"

"I hate to see any woman, even an old drunk like Dolly, being used by horseshit like Delano and Frank."

"She wouldn't thank you for those thoughts." Jake emptied his glass.

"I hear her girl is cleaning up the court and it's looking presentable again."

"She's working her tail off. I've not seen Dolly lift a hand."

"What happened 'tween you and Frank?"

"The bastard had his radio turned up so loud you could hear it a block away. Mary Lee asked him to turn it down and he shoved her. I stepped in so her overnighters wouldn't demand their money back and leave."

"Careful you don't give anyone cause to send you back to the pen."

"If I think there's a chance, I'll be long gone. I'm not going back to that hellhole for something I didn't do!"

Lon Delano, a thick-chested man who tried to make up for the loss of hair on the top of his head by wearing his sideburns long and growing a thick mustache, led Dolly onto the dance floor. It was a pathetic sight. Her scrawny arms were around his neck. Soon the fingers of the hand cupping her buttock were pleating her dress. The hem came up the backs of her thighs and had almost reached her bottom. Dolly was either unaware of it or didn't care.

Paco growled his disapproval. He reached under the counter and brought out a heavy leather strap with a weight on the end. He slapped it on the counter.

"That's gone about as far as it'll go on my dance floor."

"She's drunk."

"He isn't." Swinging the sap by the end, Paco walked from around the counter and out onto the floor. He tapped Lon on the shoulder. "If you're wantin' to get in her drawers, take her outside."

"What's he sayin', honey? What's he sayin'?"

"He's sayin' you're the prettiest gal in here tonight." Lon winked at Paco. "Let's go sit awhile." With an arm around Dolly, he urged her back to the booth.

"What was that about?" Frank asked belligerently.

"Nothin' important."

"I've seen him swing that sap. It'd break a man's jaw."

Lon sat close to Dolly.

"She shore don't look like she's goin' to be a grandma, does she, Frank?"

"Hell, she don't act like she's goin' to be a grandma, either."

"When is your gal goin' to pop out that youngun?"

"Haven't asked her."

"She goin' to get Ocie to help her raise the kid?"

"She'd better get somebody to help her. I sure ain't."

"Don't blame ya, honeybunch. You're too

young and pretty to be tied down to a squalling kid."

"Ah, pshaw. Ya don't have to butter me up."

"I'm not butterin' ya."

"What'a ya call it, then?"

"Tellin' a pretty woman I'd like to come callin' on ya."

"Hey, wait a minute," Frank said. "Dolly's my girl."

"You boys goin' to fight over me?" Dolly asked coyly.

"Damn right," Frank said, and winked at Lon.

Lon gritted his teeth and looked away. *Ugly old bitch! Frank can have her. I wouldn't piss on her if she was on fire, if it wasn't for her girl and the brat in her belly.*

"You're welcome to come anytime." Dolly dug into her pocket and put some money on the table. "I'm ready for another drink. How about you, sugar?"

Chapter 7

The light of dawn was coming in through her bedroom window when Mary Lee heard Jake's truck go by the house. She swung her legs off the bed and sat on the edge, letting her head clear before she stood and went to the bathroom. Her back and shoulders ached as they had each morning since she returned to the motor court. Thank goodness she was past the period of morning sickness.

Mary Lee washed her face and hands, and as she dried them, she looked at herself in the small mirror over the sink. She had never considered herself pretty, merely pleasant-looking. Now she looked . . . haggard. Dark smudges underlined her eyes, and because her face was thinner, her nose appeared sharper and her cheekbones stood out.

She had to take the time to go see Dr. Morris.

After scrubbing her teeth, she brushed the thick hair back from her face and looped it behind her ears. It was getting too long. One of these days soon she was going to have to cut the ends. Maybe she could get Eli to do it.

In the kitchen she filled the teakettle, set it over the kerosene burner and took down the heavy crockery pitcher to make tea. She hadn't been able to drink coffee since she had become pregnant. Mary Lee wasn't in the mood to eat, but knew that she must and that Eli would be hungry. Fifteen minutes later biscuits were in the oven.

As the morning progressed, she buried herself in the work and tried not to dwell on her mother's betrayal. She had been awake when Dolly came in last night, or rather early this morning. Someone had helped her, because later Mary Lee had heard heavy footsteps leaving the house.

Mary Lee had gone over and over in her mind what she was going to say to Dolly when she sobered up. Finally she decided that, other than letting her know that she was aware who had taken her money, she wouldn't distress herself by saying more. Her mother hadn't paid attention to her husband, so why would she pay attention to what her daughter had to say?

Mary Lee's problems seemed to multiply later in the morning when a big black car drove in off the highway as she was coming out of a cabin with cleaning supplies. The car moved slowly toward her and stopped. She made no attempt to greet the man who got out, but proceeded on to the last cabin to be cleaned.

Anger, fear and resentment set her heart hammering when Ocie Clawson came to the door.

"Come out here, girl," he demanded gruffly.

"What do you want?"

"What are ya hidin' for? Are ya ashamed to face me?"

The harsh words brought Mary Lee out the door. She stood with her hands on her hips.

"You've got a nerve to come here and face *me,* you coldhearted old . . . toad!"

"Well, now, that's more like it. Is that Bobby's kid in yore belly?"

Mary Lee's face went hot and cold by turns. She stared into sharp blue eyes that stared back at her from beneath shaggy white brows. Ocie Clawson was a big man, long in the body, with broad shoulders and deep chest. Age had thickened his middle and thinned his hair. A stained white mustache curved down on each side of his mouth. He wore a five-dollar Stetson and hand-tooled boots.

"It's none of your business who fathered my child." Amazement and anger that he would ask such a question warred in her chest.

"I think it is. If it's Bobby's kid, it's a Clawson and I'll see that it's reared right!"

"Well, it isn't Bobby's. So you can forget that. I had so many men I don't know who the father is."

"Yo're a liar!" His hamlike fists clenched as if to strike her. "I know what ya was doing in Oklahoma. I knowed where ya worked, knowed where ya lived, knowed ya didn't get no help from that lazy whelp ya married up with. Ya didn't have no other man then. I ain't knowin' 'bout while ya been here."

"You knew where we were, yet when your son was killed, you let the county bury him in a pauper's grave. You miserly, miserable old buzzard! You should be very proud of yourself."

"He was no son to me!" he roared. "He stole money from his own pa and gambled it away!"

Mary Lee took a deep breath. His words so closely paralleled what her mother had done to her that, despite herself, she felt a twinge of compassion for him that faded as soon as he spoke again.

"Ya married him thinkin' ya'd get money out of me and be livin' on easy street. It didn't work, did it?"

"I never wanted anything from you then and I don't now. I felt sorry for Bobby. You ran him down all his life, eroded his confidence, made him feel worthless. He wasn't up to what you thought a man should be, so you ran him off."

"Ya know nothin' about it, missy."

"I know plenty. During the year and a half I was married to him he cried many times and told me how you had humiliated him in front of the men who worked for you by telling them he wasn't man enough to bed a woman and how you beat him when he couldn't stay on a bucking horse!" Mary Lee's angry voice was evidence of the hatred and disgust she had for this man. "When he fought you for taking a horsewhip to one of the Mexican women, you disowned him, threw him out."

"Lies! All lies! He was a liar and a thief!"

"And whose fault was that? All his life he tried to please you but never quite made the grade."

"Christ, woman! Ya swallered his lies hook, line and sinker. But I ain't carin' what ya think. I intend to have a say 'bout that kid in your belly. You can count on it."

"*You* can count on this, Mr. Ocie Clawson. You're a bullheaded, narrow-minded know-it-all and you'll have nothing to say about my child. Get off my property and don't come back. I don't want my baby to ever set eyes on your face."

"Right sassy, ain't ya? We'll see. What're ya goin' to do when Bob Rosen throws ya out of here for not payin' yore pa's loan? Ya ain't takin' my grandson to no hobo camp or soup kitchen. Ain't no Clawson—except that weak-kneed milksop ya married—been so down and out that they had to beg, and even he had enough sense to get a woman to work and support him."

"Get off my property, you big fat cockroach! You're not worth the energy it would take to squash you!"

"'Nother thin'," he said, ignoring her outburst. "I hear ya got Jake Ramero livin' out here. Get rid of him!"

"I'll do no such thing! He's paid his rent."

"He's a damn thief."

"A lot of people think he was framed."

"Bullfoot! He had my steers in a blocked-in canyon, the brands newly changed. The sheriff caught him."

"Did you see Jake take them?" Mary Lee had no idea why she was defending Jake Ramero.

"The law said he was guilty."

"You saw to it, didn't you?"

"Damn right I saw to it!"

"I'll not make him move on your say-so."

"So that's the way the wind blows, huh?"

"What do you mean?"

"Lon said he'd be gettin' in your drawers. Wal, yo're already knocked up, so it makes no never-mind to me as long as he don't jar my grandson outta ya."

"You nasty-minded old . . . old . . . devil." Mary Lee was so angry her ears were pounding. She came within a whisker of hitting him with the broom she was holding. "Get away from me."

"Take care of that youngun. Hear?" Ocie Clawson made his way back around the car. He paused before he got in, and looked at her over the top. "Ya needin' anythin'?"

"If I did, you'd be the last to know!" Mary Lee shouted.

He snorted, got in the car, backed up and turned out onto the highway.

Angry tears blurred Mary Lee's eyes. She didn't see Eli until he was there taking the broom out of her hand.

"I thought it best to stay outta sight. Old Clawson don't like me none a-tall."

"What did you do to him?"

"Nothin'. He told his ramrod to run me off."

"I'm surprised he didn't do it himself. Throwing a thirteen-year-old out to starve wouldn't bother him."

"I'm glad he did . . . now."

"So am I. Oh, Eli, I don't know what to

do." She turned and leaned her forehead on the boy's shoulder. "Money isn't coming in fast enough to pay the bills much less pay on the mortgage. I've got to have three hundred dollars by the first of October or the bank will take the motor court."

Eli patted her back gently. "We'll just have to figure out a way to make more money."

"I can't raise the price. One man turned away because I wouldn't rent for a dollar. And I feel guilty about not paying you anything."

"You're feedin' me, and I don't need any cash money right now."

"You've been a godsend. I don't know what I would have done without you."

"You'd a done somethin'. You ain't no quitter." The boy seemed embarrassed but pleased. "Speakin' of eatin', have ya thought about givin' breakfast to the folks? I stopped by a place over near Albuquerque that charged two dollars a night including breakfast. 'Course I didn't stay there. I slept in the shed."

"Lordy mercy, Eli, I've only got two hands. I couldn't depend on Mama to help."

"I can do more. I can't make biscuits, but

I can do all the wash and most of the cleanin'.' "

"Do you think we could get two dollars?"

"There isn't another motor court within twenty miles in either direction. If we painted some signs, I bet I could get Jake to drive me down the road to put them up."

"No. I don't want to be obligated to him."

"I could ride with him when he goes to work and walk back."

"If I rented the four cabins every night, which I probably won't do, it would bring in eight dollars a day. That's two hundred and forty dollars a month. If I could put back a hundred of it, I'd have the money to pay off the bank . . ."

"See there, things will work out."

"—only if I can keep the cabins rented."

"We'd have to get signs up five miles down the road in both directions."

"Mr. Santez will let me put a sign up at the filling station."

"There's some boards on the trash pile behind the washhouse. I could paint them white, but I'm not good at lettering."

"I'm not either, but I know someone who is. Trudy Bender printed all the signs when we were in school."

"We'll need something that says: ROUTE 66 COURT. ROOM AND BREAKFAST—TWO DOLLARS."

"Oh, dear. What would I give them for breakfast?"

"The same thing every morning. Biscuits, gravy, bacon, butter and jam."

"Mama doesn't get up until almost noon, so she wouldn't be a bother." Mary Lee voiced her thoughts aloud. Then: "I wonder if I could get Trudy to come help a couple days a week."

"You won't know till you ask."

"Oh, Eli, do you think it would work?"

"You won't know till—"

"—you try," Mary Lee finished, and they both laughed. She hugged the blushing boy. "Thank you for the idea, Eli. I think I'll try it. It'll be sink or swim. This afternoon I'm going to talk to Mr. Morales, the lawyer, about Frank Pierce and I'll go see Trudy."

Dolly came out of the bedroom while Mary Lee was getting read to go to town.

"What's there to eat?"

"Eli and I had fried mush left over from breakfast."

"Sh . . . it." That seemed to be her mother's word for everything. Mary Lee looked at her haggard face. Her mother was killing herself, and there wasn't a thing she could do about it.

"Mama, I know you took ten dollars from my purse. I was saving the money to buy things for the baby and—"

"Shit. You've been gettin' money every night for the cabins. I took my share."

"You've done none of the work."

"I don't have to. I helped Scott get this place goin'."

"If I remember right, you did nothing but cause him trouble and heartache."

"Sh . . . it. I'm tired of your preachin'. Ain't there no coffee?"

"There's tea in the icebox."

With hands that shook, Dolly chipped ice, then filled a glass with tea. She headed back toward her bedroom.

"I'm going to town, Mama."

"Go on. Ain't no skin off my butt where you go."

Mary Lee was beyond being hurt by her mother's words. She slipped on one of the maternity dresses Rosa had sent. It hung from the shoulders, fit loosely, and had a drawstring at the waist. It was a little short for her taste, but not enough to make her uncomfortable. She put on her straw hat and picked up her purse.

On her way to the vacant lot behind the court and the shortcut to town, she stopped to speak to Eli, who was sorting through the wood in the scrap pile behind the washhouse.

"Have you found anything?" Mary Lee asked.

"Yeah. Several boards that ought to do. I'll get them ready to paint."

"If someone comes in, see to them before Mama does, or she'll take the money and we'll never see it."

"I'll keep an eye on things. You ain't ort to be totin' much. Leave what you get at the store. I'll get it with the wagon."

"Yes, Papa." Mary Lee laughed and kissed him on the cheek.

"Now, why'd you go and do that for? I'll get ya all dirty." His voice scolded, but she knew he was pleased.

"If my baby is a boy, I want him to be just like you."

"You want him to be a bum?"

"You're no bum! And if you say that one more time, I'll . . . I'll kiss you again . . . right in front of . . . of Jake Ramero." It was her parting shot. She waved, crossed the vacant lot and headed for town.

Mr. Morales listened while she explained the problems she was having with Frank Pierce.

"He may have given Mama a little money, but I know he didn't pay for a year. He wouldn't have that kind of money if she rented the cabin for fifty cents a week."

"If she says he did, your hands are tied. She was in charge of the court at that time."

"What if he runs off my renters?"

"Call the sheriff. You'd have grounds to put him out."

"Some of them would have left the other night if not for Mr. Ramero."

"I heard about it. Jake will have to be careful. I'd hate to see him sent back to prison."

"Why does nearly everyone dislike him? Is it because he was convicted of stealing cattle?"

"I don't know. It may be because he kept to himself and took no guff from anyone. He and his mother lived off and on at Ocie's ranch. She worked in the house. He turned out to be a top-notch horse trainer. It's said that he can teach a quarter horse to spin on a dime."

"Bobby had nothing good to say about him."

"I can see why. Ocie may have compared the two boys. Jake was a few years older, but they went to the same country school."

"Did Jake's father work there too?"

"No. His father wasn't in the picture at all as far as I know."

"Mr. Clawson came to the motor court this morning. He told me to get rid of Jake."

"Ocie is a stubborn old fool."

"I'll not do anything on his say-so anyway." Mary Lee went to the door.

"When is your baby due, Mary Lee?" Mr. Morales got up from behind his desk.

"The last of September. I'll have the bank loan paid off by then."

"If you need anything . . . something to tide you over, let me know."

"Thank you. I'll remember that."

Mary Lee went down the steep stairs to the street. The sun was so bright it almost blinded her, and she didn't see Frank Pierce until he was in front of her. She backed up to go around him, but he sidestepped to block her way.

"Get out of my way."

"Make me, Miss Prissytail."

"Move, or I'll scream so loud everyone in town will hear me."

"Go ahead, but first ya better know ya ain't gettin' away with takin' the court away from Dolly."

"I didn't take it away from her. My father did. Now get out of my way."

"Tell that jailbird you're screwin' that the next time he puts his hands on me he'll go back to the slammer."

"If you're referring to Mr. Ramero, tell him yourself if you've got the nerve."

"Don't get smart with me, you prissy-tailed bitch."

Mary Lee took a firm grip on her purse handle and was ready to swing it when a big woman with a well-worn Stetson crammed down on her head dug an elbow in Frank's ribs and pushed him aside.

"Get goin' 'fore I stomp you into dog meat."

"Hello, Mrs. Bender. I was just on my way to the café," Mary Lee said.

"Howdy, child. I been to the store to put in an order. Let's get on down to my place and have a glass of tea." Ruby Bender looked over her shoulder. "Frank been bother-in' you?"

"Now and then. Nothing I can't handle."

"If he gets too frisky, let Jake know. He'll take care of him."

"I don't want to do that. I'm afraid Mr. Ramero will get in trouble."

"Jake won't hold back 'cause of a little trouble."

"How's Trudy?" Mary Lee asked, not wanting to talk more about Jake Ramero.

"Chipper as ever. You'll see in a minute. She's at the café."

Mary Lee was greeted by her girlhood friend with hugs and squeals.

"You're still just so pretty," Trudy ex-claimed, hugging her again.

"And you've gotten blind as a bat." Mary Lee smiled at her friend, who was barely five feet tall. It used to make Mary Lee an-gry when the kids in school called her Runt. Trudy's bottom was large, her legs short and slightly bowed. She had big brown eyes, short curly hair and a sweet smile that showed dimples in both cheeks.

"My sister, Ardith, had a baby. I've been out at the ranch helping out or I'd have been out to see you. Oh, and I'm sorry about Bobby."

"Thank you."

"I heard you were going to have a baby." Trudy's large brown eyes darted down to Mary Lee's stomach. "Are you excited?"

"Excited and worried about how I'm going to support it. Thank you." Mary Lee accepted the glass of tea Ruby brought to the long table at the back of the café.

The two friends spent a pleasant half hour reminiscing before Mary Lee mentioned that she wanted to start serving breakfast to the guests who stopped at the motor court.

"I'll not do it if it means taking business away from you, Mrs. Bender."

"Pshaw! I don't get much breakfast business off the highway. You go ahead and do it." Ruby wiped her hands on her apron and added a dash of hot sauce to the chili she was cooking.

"Do you work here every morning, Trudy?"

"Only once in a while. I work mostly at suppertime."

"Would you consider coming out to the court a few mornings a week to help me get started?"

"I don't even have to consider it. I'd love to."

"I can't pay you much."

"*That* we'll talk about later."

"You know that Mama . . . will be difficult. I'll be worried sick that she'll come out of her room and be nasty."

"Between the two of us we should be able to handle her. When do you want to start?"

"Tomorrow? We have signs to paint and put up, the kitchen to clean and rearrange."

"I can help you until noon. How's that?"

"Oh, Trudy, you're the best friend I've ever had."

Chapter 8

Late in the afternoon, a half mile from the motor court, a car went out of control and flipped over on its side, spilling household goods along the highway. The two people in the car were taken to the doctor in Cross Roads. A deputy sheriff came out and stopped the traffic.

Cars and trucks and even a bus were backed up as far back as the motor court. Some of the people got out of their cars as they waited for the wreck to be hauled off the highway, and walked up to the motor court for a drink of water.

Mary Lee stayed in the house. Eli talked to the travelers while pumping a bucket of water from the deep well that had been on the place as long as she could remember.

He seemed to be more sure of himself, not quite as shy as when she first found him in the washhouse.

After the four cabins were rented for the night and the No Vacancy sign turned on, Mary Lee washed her hair. She was sitting on the back steps, combing out the tangles and enjoying the evening, when Jake's truck turned into the lane in front of the cabins. He lifted his hand in greeting. Mary Lee nodded.

"Trudy will bring her sign-painting brush when she comes out tomorrow," she said to Eli, who was painting the boards he had selected for the new signs.

"The background paint should be dry by then."

"She's going to help me clean and rearrange the kitchen. We have six chairs. We may need to use the old chair in the washhouse. We'll have to scrub it down and get it ready."

"It's wobbly, but I think I can fix it."

"Trudy's mother suggested that we charge ten cents extra for two breakfasts if it's for a husband and wife. For two men, twenty cents each. Do you think that's too much? You can get a steak dinner for thirty-five cents."

"I don't think so. They couldn't get two meals uptown for that."

"It's what Ruby said. We can try it and if it doesn't work we'll have to stop. Oh, Lord. I hope it works. That three hundred dollars hanging over my head is driving me crazy."

"What's driving you crazy?" Jake appeared at the corner of the porch.

"Eli is painting boards for our new signs; then I'm going to talk him into cutting my hair." Mary Lee fumbled for a plausible answer.

"Cut your hair?" Eli stopped painting. "I can't cut hair."

"Why are you cutting it?" Jake squatted down on his heels beside the steps and pushed his hat back off his forehead. His brows puckered; the eyes beneath them held a quizzical expression.

"I like it shoulder length. When it's longer than that, it's too hard to take care of."

"It's pretty. It'd be a shame to cut it," he said slowly.

"Let Jake cut it," Eli said, and dropped his brush in a can of kerosene. "It'll take me half an hour to get all this paint off." He held his paint-splattered hands out for her to see.

"I'm in no hurry." Mary Lee was flustered by Jake's presence.

"Are you afraid I'll scalp you?" He cocked his head to one side. She could feel the intensity of his gaze on her flushed face.

"Nooo . . . I only want about this much off the ends." She held her thumb and forefinger a couple of inches apart.

He stood and reached for the comb. Mary Lee automatically got to her feet.

"Get the scissors—or do you want me to use my knife?" Mary Lee saw the teasing glint in his eyes. His firm lips were tilted in a grin.

"Oh, you!" She stepped up onto the porch and went into the house. Seconds later she returned with the shears and paused on the steps. "Maybe I should wait for Eli. I don't like that look in your eye."

"Don't worry. If I had the right to say so, I'd forbid you to cut off even a smidgen. Stand there on the steps and turn around. It'll put me about eye level with the back of your head."

Mary Lee stood as still as a stone, praying that he didn't know that her silly heart was beating like the wings of a wild bird caught in a snare. It seemed to her that he ran the comb through her hair for a long time before he spoke.

"I don't know why you want to cut it. It's thick and wavy and . . . awfully pretty," he said on a breath of a whisper. He ran forked fingers up from her nape and through her hair.

"Just trim the ends." Then she said lightly, "I suppose you'll want a quarter. It's what the barbers uptown get."

"I was thinking about paying you for letting me comb it," he murmured.

Mary Lee's head jerked around so she could look at him.

"Now you've got it messed up. I'll have to comb it again," he said.

Eli watched from the door of the washhouse, and the thought came to him that Jake liked Mary Lee, really liked her, in the way that a man wanted a girl to be his sweetheart. Eli didn't know how he felt about that. He had taken to Jake instinctively, knowing that he was a good guy, but his mind questioned. Mary Lee deserved a man who would take care of her so that she wouldn't have to work so hard. How would

Jake feel about raising another man's kid? His uncle hadn't wanted him when his folks died, and he was blood kin.

Jake finished cutting the tip ends of her hair and asked, "What about the new signs? Where are you going to put them?"

"On the highway. We're going to serve breakfast between six and eight every morning after the signs go up."

Jake waited a minute before he spoke. "Is your mother goin' to do the cookin'?"

"Heavens, no! She'd never get up in time. Trudy Bender, Ruby's daughter, is going to help me get started. Then I can do it. Eli says my biscuits are as good as any he's ever had."

He was still for a minute, then took her by the shoulders and gently turned her around. His face was level with hers.

"You can't take on more work." His voice was deep and soft. He gazed at her for so long that a swift new wave of color filled her cheeks. "You're already doing too much."

"I have to. I've got bills to meet." She wanted to press her hand to her heart to stop its mad gallop.

"You need to rest more." His thumb and

forefinger circled her wrist. "When is your baby due?"

"The last week in September." *The bank note is due the first of October!* her mind screamed. She tugged on her hand and succeeded only in pulling her wrist from his fingers to have them interlace with hers. "Women have been having babies for years, you know," she said when she finally got enough air into her lungs.

"I know."

"Back in the olden days an Indian woman squatted behind a bush, had her baby, then caught up with the rest of the tribe." She didn't know why she told him that, and wished that she hadn't. Suddenly embarrassed, she glanced at Eli leaning against the washhouse, hoping he would say something. When he didn't, she said quickly, "It's nice of you to be concerned about me, but . . . it really isn't necessary."

"I think it is. Have you seen a doctor?"

She laughed nervously. "For goodness' sake. You sound like . . . like . . ."

Good Lord, she had almost said, "my *husband!*"

But Bobby wouldn't have been concerned. He would have been angry because she couldn't work and that the baby took time away from him.

"You haven't left this place since you came here, have you?"

"I went to town today." Her voice quavered thinking of what she had almost said.

"Would you like to go for a ride and see how the work is coming on the bridge?"

"No, but thanks. I can't leave. Mama could act up or . . . if Frank Pierce discovered I wasn't here, he'd cause trouble."

"Eli will be here. The cabins are rented. Frank couldn't do much harm in an hour."

She shook her head.

"I doubt that anyone will see you with me," Jake said. "If that's what's worrying you."

"That's not it," she said forcefully.

"Go for a ride, Mary Lee," Eli urged. "Pick out places to put up the new signs. They'll be ready the day after tomorrow."

Mary Lee's eyes went back to Jake's. "You haven't cut my hair yet."

"I trimmed the ends." He caught a strand between his thumb and forefinger and traced its length. "I hate cutting off more of it."

"I guess I'll just have to put it up in a granny bun on top of my head."

His eyes crinkled at the corners when he grinned. For the first time she noticed that his teeth were exceedingly white and even.

"Put away the shears and walk down to the truck. I'll hide you until we're out of sight. Your mother and Frank won't even know you're gone."

"Frank isn't here. Mama is sitting by the window. I suppose she's looking for him." Mary Lee reached over and took her comb from the pocket of his shirt. She looked away from him toward Eli. He could tell that she was pondering whether to accept his invitation. Her face was so expressive that he knew the instant she had decided, and he was smiling when she said, "I'll be down in a few minutes."

"What do you think, Eli?" Mary Lee waited until Jake had almost reached his cabin before she spoke.

"'Bout what?"

"About me going with Jake."

"You'll be all right with him and we need to know where to put up the signs."

"Yeah, we do, don't we?"

*   *   *

Jake couldn't believe what he was doing. Just last night he had decided to stay as far away from her as possible. He knew that it was dangerous to his peace of mind to get involved with Bobby Clawson's widow, but, dammit to hell, he couldn't help himself. He just wanted a little time alone with her; then maybe he'd get her out of his system. He seemed to lose his common sense when he was with her. She had no idea how sweet she looked with her hair all soft and shiny, her mouth smiling and her little round belly poking out.

He hurried inside the cabin and yanked off his shirt. He washed quickly, pulled off his boots and pants and put on a clean pair of jeans and the blue shirt she had washed a few days before. Rubbing his fingers over his rough cheeks, he wished that he had time to shave. He combed his hair, picked up a blanket and went out to the truck. After taking out a pair of moccasins and his water jar, he carefully spread the blanket over the seat.

Jake waited beside the car for so long he began to think she wasn't coming. Disappointment was beginning to eat a hole in his chest when she came out of the back of the house and hurried along behind the cabins.

"I had to wait until Mama went to her room." Relief set Jake's hands trembling as he opened the door and helped her up into the truck. "I don't like sneaking around," she said after he slid under the wheel.

"Slide down in the seat if you don't want her to see you when we pass."

She bent sideways until her head almost touched his thigh. "Is she in the window?"

"No, but stay there until we pull out onto the highway."

When Mary Lee felt the tires hit the pavement, she sat up. "I hate having to do that."

He grinned at her. When he looked back toward the road, she felt free to look at him. Without a hat, he appeared to be younger.

"How old are you?"

Startled by the question, he glanced at her. "Almost twenty-six."

"Then you're twenty-five."

"I'll be twenty-six tomorrow."

"Tomorrow is your birthday?"

"Yeah. It just occurred to me this morning." His smiling eyes met hers. Happiness sang like a bird in his chest. It was such a miracle that she was here in his dirty old truck with him.

"My daddy always made a big to-do over my birthday. I always had a birthday cake and a present, even if it was just a little something."

"What's a birthday cake?"

"You've never had one?"

"Not that I know of."

"It's a cake made especially for the birth-day girl or . . . boy. A candle is put on for each year. After they are lighted, you make a silent wish before you blow them out. If you blow them all out without taking an-other breath, your wish will come true. After that everyone sings the birthday song."

"I guess I've heard of it, but just never saw one."

"You were just a little older than I am when you went to prison."

"I soon learned how to take care of my-self." He spoke as if he didn't mind talking about that time in his life. "There are a lot of hard men in there, and a few decent ones. I put in my time and got by." There was a bit-ter tone to his last words.

"Mr. Clawson was here today. He said

you had his cattle penned and had changed the brand."

"Why did he tell you that?"

She evaded the question. "I asked him if he saw you do it. He didn't give me an answer."

"He was in Arizona at the time. His foreman and a couple others took the sheriff out to where the cattle were penned. Are you going to ask me if I stole them?"

"No."

"Why not?"

"I guess I don't want you to . . . tell me you did."

"If I had stolen the cattle, I'd not be dumb enough to pen them up where they would be easily found and I'd not spend a couple days changing the brand. I'd have driven them as far away as possible and sold them to a slaughter house."

"Someone wanted to get you in trouble with the law."

"I think I know who, but I don't know why."

"Today is the first time I've seen Mr. Clawson since I married Bobby." Mary Lee's hands were clenched tightly together. "He seems to think he'll have a say in how my baby is raised. I've news for him. I'll take my baby far away before I let him have anything to do with it."

"He didn't take a hand in raising Bobby until he was already set in his ways. Bobby's mother spoiled him. She was at odds with Ocie and took pleasure in bucking him every time he tried to make a man out of Bobby."

"You knew Bobby when he was a kid?"

"We went to the same school."

Mary Lee and Jake had gone a distance in companionable silence before he spoke again.

"There's no sky as beautiful as New Mexico sky at twilight."

"Have you been to a lot of other places?"

"I worked for a year on a ranch in Oklahoma. I liked it there. The Fleming people were good to work for, but New Mexico is my home."

"Where exactly is your home?" Mary Lee drew in a deep breath. "Oh . . . oh—" Her eyes met his when he turned at the sound. "I'm sorry. I seem to be asking a lot of questions."

"It's all right. My home is anywhere within a radius of fifty miles north of Cross Roads.

There are little villages in the mountains you've never heard of. My mother was from one of them."

Jake turned off the highway and onto a graveled road. The steel structure of the bridge was outlined against the darkening sky. He pulled over and stopped.

"It's two hundred feet long and spans a gorge that's a hundred feet deep."

"Oh, my. Is it about finished?"

"My part of the job will be done in a couple of days."

"What did you do?"

"See that girder that slants up to the top and levels off? I put in the bolts, then welded the joints."

"Not . . . up there on top?"

"Yes, up there on top. Some days the wind was so strong, I couldn't go up."

"Oh, Jake . . ." Unaware that she was doing so, she clutched his arm. "It gives me the shivers to think of you up there."

"At times it gave me the shivers to be there." *Especially after two men plunged to the floor of the canyon.* He put his hand over hers for the brief instant before she withdrew it.

"Then why do you do it?"

"It's good pay."

"It should be for the risk you're taking."

"It'll be over soon. I'll take my money and break horses until another job comes along."

"Are there more bridges to be built around here?"

"One more that I know of. This bridge will take a big kink out of the highway and shorten the route between here and Sante Fe by at least five miles."

"I hope they don't decide to bypass Cross Roads. I'd be sunk."

"There's no danger of that. They won't bypass a strip that's already paved."

A few stars were appearing in the sky. Jake didn't want to start the truck and head back to the motor court. The ride would be all too short. He glanced at her. She was relaxed and comfortable with him. He wanted to ask her why she had married a no-good like Bobby, but was afraid to risk the possibility of her resenting his question about her personal life.

"A friend of mine will be coming in a few days," he said, wanting to keep the conversation going. "I worked with him on the Fleming ranch in Oklahoma."

"Is he a cowboy?"

"No, he's a mechanic. He can fix a motor if it's at all fixable. He kept the machinery on the ranch going while I was there. Later he bought a garage on the highway. He's right fond of motorcycles and will be riding one when he gets here."

"Is he coming for a visit?"

"I don't know how long he'll stay. A couple of other fellows took over his garage after his mother died, so I guess he's foot-loose. He said something about visiting a friend up in Colorado. You'll like Deke. He's a funny-looking little man, but you don't notice it after you get to know him." Jake was smiling broadly. "He's not any bigger than you are, and that's not saying much."

"Well, thank you, Mr. Ramero. I'm not so small. Especially now."

"You're not much bigger than a mosquito," he teased.

"A mosquito after a full meal?"

Had she stopped to think about it, she would have been surprised at how comfortable she was speaking to him and to Eli about her pregnancy. Talk of having babies was not a subject mentioned between a

woman and a man who was not her husband or close relative.

She felt warm and giddy, basking in his
teasing smile.

"You'd better start this truck and head
back to the motor court before this skeeter
bites you."

"Yes, ma'am. Nothin' I hate worse than a
skeeter bite."

When they were back on the highway,
she said, "We didn't look for places to put
up the signs."

"How many signs will you have?"

"Four. Two on the east side of the court
and two on the west."

"I'll take care of it. You want the first one
about five miles out?"

"And the second one about a mile out,
but you don't need to do it. Eli thinks he can
get a ride out with someone and walk
back."

"I'll do it. Eli shouldn't leave you alone at
the court."

"He's just a boy."

"He's more of a man then you think he is.
He didn't let Frank back him down."

"He's only thirteen."

"Hard knocks have made him older."

"I don't know what I would have done these past weeks without him. If I could, I'd keep him with me always."

"Does he have folks?"

"An uncle who doesn't want him and sent him to the orphanage."

"Bastard," Jake muttered under his breath. Aloud he said, "There it is. The court is still there."

"So is Frank. There's a light on in number one."

"He'll not be playing a radio unless he's got a new one."

"I thought you only took out the tubes."

"I broke a little something taking them out." She saw the flash of white teeth as he grinned at her. "Do you want me to let you out at the house?"

"Go on down. Frank might be watching."

Jake parked the truck beside his cabin. She had opened the door and slid out by the time he got around to help her.

"Thank you for showing me the bridge."

"My pleasure." He took her hand, and she didn't pull it away. "Will you go with me to look at another bridge . . . if I can find one?"

She laughed up at him, pulled her hand

free of his and looped her hair behind her ears. "I think I've seen the only bridge worth seeing within fifty miles."

"Mary Lee." He liked saying her name. "At the end of the week, I will have been here two months. I'll move out and get a room uptown so you can rent this cabin by the night." They were walking behind the cabins toward the house. "Two months for forty dollars is still a bargain."

"Mama rented to you for four months and you have the receipt. The law says you can stay."

"The law may say so, but your mother wasn't playing with a full deck when she rented to me. You could be getting another twelve dollars a week from my cabin and afford to hire some help."

She stopped, turned and looked up at him. "Why would you do that?"

He looked down at her for a long time, his eyes roaming her face. Her mouth was soft and sweet, her expression troubled. All her doubts and hurt were there in her eyes.

"Why, Jake?"

"Because . . . I . . . want to help you and this is one way I can do it."

"Don't move out." The words burst from

her. "With you here, Frank won't try anything."

His hands came up to grip her shoulders. "I know about the note the bank holds. You need every dime you can get."

"How come you know about that?" Her hands came up to hold on to his forearms.

"Frank, trying to be a big dog, told Paco at the Red Pepper Corral. He said after the bank takes over, he and Dolly will run the place."

"I'll burn it down first!" Tight-lipped, she glared at him.

"I'll help you."

"I suppose everyone in town is waiting to see me lose the motor court."

"You won't lose it. You'll make it and we'll celebrate. You and me and Eli will go to Sante Fe and have a barbecue dinner."

"You sound sure."

"I am sure."

"Well, then, what's there to worry about? I'd better go in. Mama's probably out there with Frank. She'll be drunk if she isn't already. They might come in the house." Her hands dropped from his arms, and she turned away.

"Mary Lee." She stopped. He was still

standing where she'd left him. "Do you really want the baby?"

"Of course I do. Whatever gave you the idea I didn't?"

"Do you want it because it's Bobby's?"

"No! I want it because it's mine." She brought her hand up and slapped her chest. "Bobby merely sowed a seed in the wind."

Jake lifted his hand, turned, and went back toward his cabin.

Mary Lee stepped up on the back porch. Her opinion of Jake had changed drastically. When she first met him, she had thought the look in his cold green eyes was possessive and ruthless. After getting to know him, she saw him as being both gentle and protective, and genuinely concerned about her, the baby, and the motor court.

Eli was sitting at the kitchen table playing a game of solitaire.

"Is Mama over with Frank?"

"Yeah. I didn't come in till she left. I looked in the window and saw her tryin' to get in your suitcase."

"She wouldn't find anything there. I put all the money in a fruit jar and hid it."

"Did you decide where to put the signs?"

"Jake said he would take care of it. He insisted."

"Are you going to let him?"

"It would be rude to turn down help when it's offered."

Eli ducked his head and grinned. "Yeah, it would."

Chapter 9

Mary Lee had a lot to think about and was glad that her mother was out of the house. As soon as Eli finished his game and went to his cot in the washhouse, she kicked off her shoes and sank wearily down on her bed.

She had enjoyed being with Jake. There was a sadness about him that reminded her of a small, lonesome little boy. Tonight he had shown none of the animosity he had displayed the first time they met. She had felt safe with him, as if nothing in the world could hurt her. Bobby had said that he was mean, a womanizer and a thief. The steers he rustled were not the first thing he'd stolen from the Circle C ranch, according to Bobby. He also said that he fornicated with every woman under forty he could get his hands on from a little village of Mexican workers and their families on the ranch.

She had believed Bobby until now. Knowing that Bobby was a convincing liar, she felt a trifle ashamed because Jake didn't seem to fit that pattern at all. Jake had said that he and Bobby went to the same school. Alongside Jake, Bobby would be weak by comparison. Was jealousy the reason for Bobby's animosity toward him?

She didn't want him to move out. Without being aware of it, she felt a measure of security with him there.

Her thoughts turned to her mother, who was more than likely out in number one cabin with Frank Pierce. She had been home three weeks, and during that time her mother had not done one thing to help her in the house or with the cabins. She hadn't washed one dish or fixed a meal, except for herself. She was on a fast road to destruction, and Mary Lee didn't know what to do about it.

When she was little, her father always explained that her mother was sick when she went on one of her binges. The first time Mary Lee became aware that something other than being sick was wrong with her mother was when she was about eight years old. Before that, she knew to stay out of her way when the woman laughed too loudly or hugged her too hard, and when she talked nastily to Daddy. Sometimes Dolly would disappear, and Daddy would walk the floor and wait for her to come home. When Mary Lee was older, he would leave her and go look for Dolly, oftentimes bringing her home screaming obscenities at him.

One time she had crawled up into her daddy's lap and asked, "Why isn't Mama like other mamas? I don't want her to come to school. The kids call her names 'cause she acts funny."

"Your mama's got a craving for liquor, honey. It's like she can't live without it. We wouldn't turn our back on her if she was sick with the measles or whooping cough. We can't turn from her because she has this other sickness. She's nice some of the time, now, isn't she?"

"Sometimes. But . . . I want a mama who brings cookies to school on my birthday like Trudy's mama does."

"Cookies on your birthday? Why didn't

you tell me, love? You'll have cookies on your birthday . . . big ones with your name on them."

"Really?"

"Really. I'll see to it."

Her daddy had brought the cookies, and they were special because he'd had a lady at the bakery bake them. The kids had enjoyed them, and for a while she had basked in their goodwill; but later one of them asked if her daddy had to get them at the bakery because her mama had been too drunk to bake them.

During high school she had been excluded by her classmates from private parties and sleepovers. It had hurt, but she had endured and earned the highest grades in her class. But even that had not won her election as class president. At the time she was terribly disappointed. Now, as she looked back on it, she wondered if perhaps she hadn't benefited from the snobbery of her classmates. It had made her self-reliant and more able to take care of herself.

The last time she had seen her daddy was after she had married Bobby.

"Go, honey. Go and make a good life for yourself with Bobby."

"But I'll worry about you—"

"Pshaw! I'll be just fine." He put fifty dollars in her hand. She knew it was all he could spare.

"Daddy, I don't need this. Bobby and I will get jobs."

"Take it. I have to be sure you'll be all right. Now, go tell your mama good-bye."

Remembering, tears rolled from Mary Lee's eyes and soaked the pillow. That was the last time she had seen her daddy.

The air was cool and pleasant, with a smell of pines and wood smoke from the fire, where a steer was being prepared to feed the workers who could come in for the annual Fourth of July feed. Ocie Clawson sat on his porch, his eyes on a scene he had viewed all his life and had never grown tired of.

When he was a boy, the mountains seemed a hundred miles away and a hundred miles high. When he grew older, he had ridden to the top in less than a hour and discovered they were merely foothills. Once lightning had started a fire that had burned a patch of trees, and the brown spot left on the side of the "mountain" changed the scene. It had been a source of dismay to him until the following spring, when the green grasses and purple and yellow flowers had sprouted up to cover it.

The mountain was his. This place was his home. He had fought to keep every square foot of it, as had his father and grandfather before him. The grandfather who had built this house was fond of saying that when he first came to this country, he'd had to comb Apaches and Mexican renegades out of his beard. Ocie, his father and his son were all born in the same bed in the big room upstairs.

Temple Clawson had still been alive when Ocie brought his bride home to the Circle C. Edith had not liked her father-in-law. He was too crude for her taste, but she was impressed with the big ranch and the big house. After growing up as the daughter of a bank clerk who had scarcely been able to support his family, Edith had enjoyed having two servants to do her bidding: a cook and a young Mexican girl who did the housework. She was especially hard on young and pretty Juanita, who went about her work quietly taking Edith's verbal abuse stoically.

When it became obvious that Juanita was pregnant and unmarried, Edith was enraged. She summoned up every dirty, backbreaking job she could find for the girl to do. Juanita did them all without complaint.

One day, angry over a trifle, she called the girl a slut and slapped her, not knowing that her husband and her father-in-law were nearby. Ocie had been embarrassed, but Temple Clawson was infuriated.

"We do not treat those who serve us in that manner. Don't ever strike that girl or any other woman working in this house again, missy, or, married to my son or not, you will be out of here."

From that day on Edith had been careful to chastise Juanita when she was sure the men were out of the house, but her hatred for the girl grew, as did her suspicion that the child she carried was Ocie's.

One day Juanita disappeared from the house. An older woman came to take her place. After that, neither Ocie nor his father mentioned the girl's name.

A year went by, and Edith bitterly discovered that she was pregnant. She had allowed her husband to visit her room only once a month to fulfill her wifely duties, as her mother before her had done. She hated the act of copulation. She hated every day that she was pregnant, and vowed that it would never happen again.

Edith discovered that Juanita and her son lived in a small house not more than half a mile away. They never came near the ranch house, but Edith was sure that her husband kept his whore there to humiliate her. For several years she was obsessed with trying to catch Ocie with Juanita. She never did, and soon discovered another way to punish him: She completely took over the raising of their son and taught him disrespect and total contempt for his father.

Temple Clawson spent more time in the homes of his Mexican workers than he did in the house, where Edith ruled supreme. Bobby was fourteen and a dire disappointment to his grandfather when Temple died suddenly. He was mourned by everyone on the ranch except Edith and Bobby.

Now, sitting here on the porch with his feet on the railing, Ocie wondered how he had arrived at this time of his life so fast. Edith had sickened and died two years after Temple. By then, due to her influence, Ocie and his son had been at loggerheads.

Bobby loathed working on the ranch and always had excuses for getting out of work. His passion was gambling. He was so good with cards that the ranch hands refused to play with him. Bobby was also an accomplished liar and had stirred up fights among the cowboys. One of Bobby's lies had sparked a fight that had left one man permanently injured.

Ocie had never even come close to remarrying. Once burned, twice shy. Marriage to Edith had left him badly disillusioned. He'd not make the same mistake twice. There were a couple of women he used to relieve his sexual tension during the few peaceful years since Bobby left home. He paid them well, and they understood that sex was all he wanted from them.

But now, although he was only sixty years old, he had begun to wonder who would take over this place when he was gone. Certainly not Lon Delano, who was fond of calling himself a cousin, even though he was the grandson of Ocie's mother's sister. Lon was all right in his place, a hard worker who handled the men with a strong hand; but given free rein, he would run this place into the ground within a few years' time.

Ocie's thoughts went back to the girl at the motor court. She had grit. He grinned, thinking how she had gotten her back up and yelled at him, calling him a "cold-hearted old toad." Bobby had really sold her a bill of goods. He hoped to God that her grit was passed on to Bobby's kid.

If the boy turned out to be a mewling calf like Bobby, by God, he'd leave the property to the government and let Roosevelt turn it into a CCC camp. He had hoped to pass this ranch down to a Clawson with enough guts to hold on to it and see to it that Clawsons would be here for another hundred years.

Lon Delano pulled up and stopped at the big red gas barrel beside the barn, intending to put gas in the tank of his car. When he spotted Ocie coming out the back door, he sat in the car and waited. It irked him that Ocie lived in that big house all alone while he had to be content with a room built onto the bunkhouse. After all, he was family. It would lift his prestige with the hands if he lived in the house. He had mentioned it once to Ocie. All he got in return was a cold stare.

"Need anything from town, Ocie?" Lon called as his boss approached.

"Ain't Dolly Finley a mite used up for you?" Ocie ignored Lon's question and came right out with what was on his mind.

"What makes ya say that?" Lon was instantly alert.

"Heard ya was rubbin' her ass on the dance floor the other night."

"Then you heard wrong. I danced with her. What's a man to do when a lady asks him to dance?" Lon was containing his temper.

Ocie snorted. "Dolly ain't no lady. She's an old drunk! And if she was a lady, I can't see her draggin' you around by the balls." His shaggy brows drew together, and he stabbed his foreman with ice cold eyes. "Screw around with Dolly all ya want, but stay away from the motor court. I ain't wantin' nothin' to happen to that girl of hers. Hear?"

"What's so special 'bout her?" Lon asked, although he knew it was the kid she was carrying.

"She's goin' to birth a Clawson; that's what's special!" Ocie bellowed.

"Ha! Ya believe that?"

"I've no reason not to."

"I'd not take her word for it. She's got a kid in her belly and come back here thinkin' ya'd think it was Bobby's."

"Keep yore mouth shut. I don't want to hear of such talk bein' spread around."

"Hell, Ocie, we both know that the only way Bobby could get it up was to draw four aces or a full house."

"Are ya sayin' he was queer?" Ocie asked, tight-lipped.

"No, I ain't sayin' that. I'm sayin' he wasn't usually . . . hot for women," Lon stammered.

"Yo're sayin' he warn't a man 'cause he didn't rut with ever' ready bitch that crossed his path?"

"I ain't sayin' that either."

"Frank Pierce is out talkin' nasty about the girl. Put a stop to it, or it'll go hard with both of ya. She's to be left alone."

"Ain't you forgettin' 'bout Jake Ramero stayin' right under her nose?" Lon sneered. "He's a cattle rustler, for God's sake. Prison made an animal out of him. He'd screw the Virgin Mary if he got a chance. I had to talk Frank outta filin' charges against him after Jake roughed him up."

"I heard he roughed Frank up 'cause he shoved Mary Lee. If she had lost that kid, I'd have done more than rough him up. I'd have shoved a hot poker up *his* ass. Tell him to keep his hands off her."

"You'd better be tellin' Ramero. He's a troublemaker."

"Says who? The charge of rustlin' my cattle was pretty thin. I went along with it 'cause you and two others swore you saw him brandin' the cattle."

"Goddamn! Are ya backtrackin' on that jailbird?"

"I ain't backtrackin' on anythin'. I'm sayin' he done a good turn puttin' Pierce down when he was messin' with my daughter-in-law and I ain't forgettin' it. Leave him alone." Ocie turned and went back into the house.

Being careful not to stir up a dust cloud in the ranch yard, which was one of Ocie's pet peeves, Lon drove away from the ranch house. As soon as he was half a mile down the road toward town, he slammed on the brakes, came to a stop and pounded his fists against the steering wheel.

"Damn her to hell!" he yelled.

He'd be damned if he'd let the kid of that wimpy, spoiled mama's boy have what he'd worked for, put up with Ocie's insults for, and what should be his.

By God, he didn't want to have to do away with Ocie, but he would before he'd let the ranch slip away from him. If Ocie died without a will, he, as next of kin, distant as it was, would inherit—that is, if that shitty girl hadn't given birth yet and Ramero was back in the hoosegow where he couldn't cause trouble. He'd work on that, but how in hell was he going to find out if Ocie had made a will?

Lon drove into town and began looking for Frank. He found him in Pedro's, a hole-in-the-wall on a back street. Lon stood in the doorway until he caught his eye, and jerked his head. Minutes later Frank joined him in the alley behind the barbershop. He looked anxious.

"What's up?"

"I thought you were goin' to see to it that Ramero broke his parole and was sent back to the slammer. You haven't done doodle-dee shit."

"I told Pleggenkuhle about him attackin' me."

"Yeah, and it's all over that the reason he slammed into ya was because you shoved a pregnant woman. Ain't ya got no more sense than that?"

"You a-wantin' her to have that kid?"

"No, you dumb-ass, but you don't try to rid her of it in front of folks."

"Ramero wasn't there when I pushed her."

"Never mind that now. You rile up that bastard until he does somethin' to be sent up for."

"Like him bustin' my head, I suppose," Frank said sarcastically.

"If ya have to. Ya'll get paid plenty. How're ya comin' with Dolly?"

"I ain't knowin' how much longer I can stomach that old drunk."

"Yo're screwin' her, ain't ya?"

"Yeah. She's so damn skinny it's like pokin' it in a knothole."

"Keep her on the string. Keep yore eyes open and work on gettin' rid of Ramero. If the girl has that kid, there'll be no chance of me gettin the Circle C, and there'll be no job for you."

"I'm short of money . . ."

"Here's a couple dollars. It's all I've got on me."

"Hell—"

"Take it or leave it," Lon said impatiently.

Frank snatched the bills from his hand and walked back down the alley toward Pedro's.

Chapter 10

Within an hour after they met, Trudy and Eli were laughing and talking as if they had known each other forever. At first, Eli was a little put out, thinking that Trudy was there to take his place; but she soon won him over with her teasing requests for him to do this or that because he was tall and she was just a short stack.

"It's not fair that you got them nice long arms and legs and can reach everythin'," Trudy fussed while climbing up onto a chair to reach the windowpane she was washing.

She had arrived at seven, and by mid-morning the kitchen cabinet, the work counter and sink had been scrubbed, as well as the stove and icebox. She had sug-gested that the table and chairs be moved nearer to the back door so that the guests didn't have to cross the kitchen to get to the table. The window curtains were drying on the line. Now all that was left to do was wash the windows and scrub the floor.

"Leave the high ones. I'll wash them after we clean the cabins." Eli had come into the kitchen after hanging the last of the morning wash.

Before Trudy could answer, Dolly came from her bedroom and stood looking around with a frown on her haggard face.

"What's goin' on? Who's been makin' all that racket?" She looked accusingly at Eli. "It was you. I told ya not to come in the house."

"Yes, ma'am." Eli grabbed up the extra bucket and headed for the door.

"Mornin', Mrs. Finley," Trudy said cheerfully. "Sorry if we woke you up."

"What're ya doin' here?"

"Helpin' out a little."

"I didn't hire ya on to work here."

"I did." Mary Lee came in the door as Eli passed through it. Then, ignoring her mother, she spoke to Trudy. "Will you have time to paint the signs?"

"What signs?" Dolly demanded.

"Signs saying that we serve breakfast."

"Sure." Trudy climbed down off the chair. "I'm finished in here except for scrubbing the floor. Eli said that he'd do that tonight."

"What are ya hatchin' up?" Dolly demanded, and retied the sash on her old housecoat.

"Like I said, Mama, we're going to serve breakfast to the people who rent our cabins for the night."

"What're ya doin' that for? For God's sake! Ya get a wild hair and there ain't no stoppin' ya. Ya just bulldoze yore way ahead and don't say shit to nobody."

"I'm doing it so that I can pay back the money Daddy borrowed from the bank. The money you spent after he died."

"Piss on the bank. They got enough money." Dolly went to the icebox and threw open the door. With it open, she looked around the kitchen. "I don't like the table over there." When Mary Lee didn't answer, she said, "I ain't hirin' no stunted runt to work here either."

Mary Lee's face reddened with anger. "Go back to your room until you sober up," she said sharply.

Her mother glared at her with pure hatred

in her eyes. "Ya've got to be right bossy, girl. No snot-nosed kid is tellin' me what to do."

"I'm telling you what *not* to do. Don't insult my friends."

"You insult mine. You run off Pearl and . . . Frank."

"They were trash, both of them."

"You shore did get uppity after you married that Clawson pup."

"No, Mama. I grew up in a hurry. But that's got nothing to do with now."

"Ya come back here and took over—"

"I had to or you'd have lost it. I'm doing all I can to make a living for us and you're not helping a bit."

"If yo're set on givin' breakfast to renters, I'll tell Frank. He's a renter."

"He's a leech, a freeloader. I'll not have him in this house. Only those who rent by the night are entitled to breakfast." Mary Lee took out a slice of bread, buttered it and spread it with peach preserves.

"How about that jailbird? Ya feedin' him?"

"Only if he pays extra."

"Sh . . . it. Frank said he'd be in your drawers quicker than ya could shake a stick. Guess it don't matter none. Yo're already knocked up."

Seething with anger, Mary Lee shoved the plate with the bread in her mother's hands. Her patience with her was threadbare. She was too angry to feel shame.

"Take this and the tea back to your room and stay there if you can't keep a civil tongue in your head." Mary Lee followed her mother to the door of her room. "You haven't changed your bedding since I've been here. Take off the sheet and I'll bring you some clean ones."

Dolly gave her daughter a contemptuous look and slammed the door in her face.

With slumping shoulders, Mary Lee went back to the kitchen. "I'm sorry, Trudy. I don't remember her ever being this mean."

"Does she stay in that room all day?"

"Some days she does. Sometimes she sits on the porch and waits for that nogood Frank Pierce. She keeps herself clean enough, but her room stinks."

"When she leaves, go in and take the bedclothes and leave clean ones."

"She locks the door when she leaves. I may be making a mistake having folks come in here for breakfast. What if she comes out and makes a scene?"

"If she doesn't get up until ten or eleven they'll be gone by then." Trudy slipped an arm around Mary Lee. "Don't borrow trouble. Come on out and tell me what you want on the signs."

While Trudy was painting the signs, Mary Lee confided, "As soon as the cabins are cleaned, I'm going to bake a cake. Today is Jake's birthday and he's never had a birthday cake."

"Fun." Trudy looked up with a broad smile. "I like Jake. When will you give it to him?"

"Tonight. After supper. Can you come back out?"

"Hummm . . . we'll see."

"I wish I had candles to go on the cake."

"We've got candles. I don't know if there's enough. How old will he be?"

"Twenty-six. There'll only be me and Eli at the party unless you can come."

"It would have to be after the supper rush at the diner is over. But then it'll be dark when I go back home. Mama's had trouble with a couple of hell-raisers, and she doesn't want me out after dark by myself."

"If Jake doesn't offer to take you home, Eli and I will walk with you."

"I won't mind asking Jake to take me."

"Does that mean you'll come?"

"It'll be after eight and I'll bring the candles."

"This will be his first birthday party. I'm going to give Eli a dime to go uptown and get a red bandanna handkerchief for a present."

"Why are you doing this for Jake?"

"Because he went out on a limb to help me when Frank was about to run off my renters."

"Is that the only reason?" Trudy teased. "He's awfully good-looking. Has he been flirting with you?"

"Oh, Trudy. You've always had a gigantic imagination. In my present state he'd as soon flirt with a hedgehog. He's been nice and I want to pay him back, that's all." And to change the subject, she said, "Did I tell you that Ocie Clawson came out yesterday?"

"What did he want?"

"He wanted to know if I was carrying Bobby's baby. He said, in not so many words, that sorry as Bobby was, my baby was a Clawson and he wanted a hand in raising it."

"He can't take the baby away from you."

"He could have me declared an unfit mother and, as next of kin, take it. Oh, Lord. I don't think I could bear it."

Voicing her fear to Trudy made it more real in her mind. The thought had been hiding there since Ocie's visit. Should he try that, she would hide herself and her baby away in one of the little villages in the mountains that Jake had talked about.

"I suppose he could get someone to trump up charges like he did when Jake was accused of stealing his cattle."

"Sometimes I wonder why I don't take what little money I have and leave here."

"Leave your daddy's court for Dolly to run into the ground? I think not."

"I get awfully discouraged."

Trudy finished the last sign and stood it up against the washhouse to dry and turned to her friend.

"Now you listen to me, Mary Lee Finley Clawson. You've put up with a lot up to now, and you can put up with this. That baby you're carryin' can't help it that it's a Clawson. It's gonna depend on its mama to take care of it and see that it has a start in life. Now, buck up. Get in there and bake a cake for Jake. I'm goin' back to the diner, but I'll be here for the birthday party."

Mary Lee stared at the small girl with the short, bowed legs and wondered how she could be so upbeat all the time. Feeling something like shame for whining, she went to Trudy and hugged her.

After the cake was iced with fluffy white icing made from sugar syrup and egg whites, Mary Lee had Eli take it out to the washhouse in case her mother came out of her room. Eli returned grinning from ear to ear.

"I set a box over it to keep off the flies."

"Good idea. I've got some green tissue paper we can use to wrap the bandanna in. I wish we had some ribbon."

"Use one of your hair ribbons, then ask for it back."

"Oh, shoot, Eli. Why didn't I think of that?"

"You can always tie it with a twine. He won't care. I got to go. I'm making my present."

"What are you making?"

"It's a surprise . . ."

"It should be a surprise to Jake, but not to me."

"I'm not exactly makin' it. I'm fixin' it." Eli's eyes danced with excitement.

"All right, then, I guess I can wait. When is your birthday, Eli?"

"The last day in October."

"We'll have a party for you." She tilted her head and gave him a bright smile before she sobered. "If you're still here, Eli; you should be in school. When my baby grows up I want him to be able to say that his Uncle Eli is a teacher, a lawyer, a banker—"

"Whoa, now. You'll not want me hangin' around . . . *that* long." There was a nervous hesitation in his voice.

"I want you as long as you want to stay. I've always wanted a brother, and you fit the bill perfectly." The smile on Mary Lee's face wavered.

"You'll marry . . . someday—"

"I doubt that. But if I do, if he doesn't want you, he doesn't get me."

"Well . . ." The boy's lips quivered. "I'd better get my present ready." He hurried out the door, and Mary Lee wiped the tear that leaked from the corner of her eye.

It was late when Jake drove in. All the cabins were rented but one. Mary Lee was beginning to worry that for the first time in a week they would have a vacancy. Then a roadster came in and stopped. A woman was nestled close to the driver. The man kissed her before he got out. He was middle-aged and starting to bald. His face was slightly flushed, and he was hastily pushing his shirt down in the waist of his britches when Mary Lee met him on the porch.

"Do you have a vacancy?"

"Yes. Would you like to see it?"

"No." He dug into his pocket for his wallet. "How much?"

Without hesitation Mary Lee said, "Two dollars."

He pulled two dollar bills from his wallet.

"I'll need your name for the record."

"George Swanson. Dallas, Texas."

"Here's the key to number five. We ask that you be out by ten in the morning."

He took the key and hurried back to the car. The woman sat the entire time with her back to the door. Mary Lee only saw bleached blond hair and wondered if they would stay the entire night or just an hour or two. He hadn't batted an eye when she asked for two dollars. He was probably cheating on his wife. She wished she'd asked three dollars.

It was almost dark when Trudy returned. She was out of breath when she stepped up onto the back porch.

"I had to stay a little later than usual," she explained. She waved an envelope. "Mama sent Jake a little present. Where's the cake? I brought the candles."

"The cake is out in the washhouse. We can bring it in. Mama just went uptown with Frank."

"My, you look pretty. You even put a bow in your hair."

"It's a party. Want one in yours?"

"Naw. I'm afraid I'd outshine you."

"Trudy! You've not changed a bit."

"Open the door," Eli called. "I saw Mrs. Finley leave."

He set a box on the table, and they all peered in at the cake.

"Put the candles on, Trudy. We can't light them until we get down there. Have you got matches, Eli?"

"Right here." He patted his shirt pocket. "I've got to go get my present."

"Hurry, then—we don't want to take the chance that Jake'll decide to go some-place."

With Eli carrying the box with the cake, they walked behind the cabins to number six. The door was open when they reached it. Jake, shirtless and barefoot, lay on the bed listening to the radio. He jumped up and grabbed his shirt when he heard Mary Lee's call.

"Anybody home?"

"Yeah."

"May we come in?"

As soon as they were crowded into the small room, Mary Lee and Trudy began to sing: *"Happy birthday to you, happy birthday to you. Happy birthday to Jake, happy birthday to you."*

Jake was speechless. Finally he managed to say, "Well, now. What's all this?"

Eli held the box while Mary Lee lifted out the cake and set it on the bureau. Her eyes were shining, her lips smiling when she looked at him. Jake felt as if his heart would gallop right out of his chest.

Trudy placed the plates and forks beside the cake.

"Eli, light the candles," Mary Lee said.

Then to Jake, "Think of a wish. If you blow out the candles with one puff it'll come true."

"That's not quite right," Trudy said. "If you blow them all out with one puff you get a birthday kiss . . . from everyone. Even Eli."

"I like that idea. But they're too pretty to blow out." Jake's blood was pounding his eardrums, and he wasn't sure if he had spoken loudly enough for them to hear him. His eyes swept over the faces smiling at him over the burning candles, and he knew that he would remember this moment forever.

"I ain't givin' ya no kiss," Eli said.

"Then I get two each from Mary Lee and Trudy." Jake's smile grew even wider.

"You won't get any if you don't hurry up."

Mary Lee was grateful that Trudy could speak, because she couldn't.

"All right. Here goes." Jake took a deep breath and blew out all the candles. When he raised his head, his eyes, dancing as brightly as the candle flames, caught and held Mary Lee's sparkling ones.

"What'd ya wish for?" Eli asked.

"He's not supposed to tell," Trudy said quickly, and pulled on Jake's shirt so he'd bend down. She placed a kiss on his cheek. "Your turn, Mary Lee."

Dark lashes momentarily screened Mary Lee's eyes. A blush covered her cheeks. Her mouth went dry as a bone. Jake's thick brows now lowered over eyes sparkling with mischief.

"Your turn, Mary Lee." His words echoed Trudy's.

When her upraised eyes took in the flushed, happy look on his face, her heart leaped in her throat and her body shook with a slight tremor. He was within inches of her now, forcing her to lift her face to kiss his cheek. He lowered his and, at the last second, turned it slightly so that her kiss landed on the corner of his mouth.

She backed up quickly to put space between them. Trudy and Eli didn't seem to notice her sudden, jerky movement. Eli was removing the candles from the cake and dropping them in a paper sack. Trudy took an envelope from her pocket.

"You've got presents to open before you can have cake."

"Presents?"

"Birthday presents." Trudy handed the envelope to Jake. "From me and Mama."

Jake backed up and sat down on the bed, then hurriedly got to his feet.

"Ladies . . ." He indicated that they sit on the bed. "I'm short of chairs. Eli and I can sit on the floor."

"Quit stallin' and open the envelope," Eli said.

"It isn't often I get presents. I'm going to make it last as long as possible."

"You got two more after that one."

"Well, in that case . . ." Jake pulled a slip of paper from the envelope and read, "'This ticket is worth one steak dinner at Ruby's diner.'

"By Golly! A steak dinner at Ruby's. I'll sure collect that." He carefully returned the ticket to the envelope and put it in his shirt pocket. "Thanks, Trudy. I'll thank Ruby when I go to collect."

Mary Lee shyly handed him a small tissue-wrapped package.

"What's this?"

"Open it and see."

He carefully untied the ribbon, folded back the paper and lifted out the red bandanna.

"How did you know I needed one of these?"

"I didn't think you could have too many handkerchiefs."

"Thanks, Mary Lee. This is so new and bright, I'll wear it on Sunday." He folded the cloth and tied it around his neck.

"I told her you'd give the hair ribbon back," Eli said.

"I don't know if I'll part with it." Jake grinned at Mary Lee's red face. "I just might want to wear it around my neck too."

"Give him your present, Eli," Mary Lee said. Then to Jake, "He wouldn't tell me what it was."

Eli produced a package wrapped in the colorful Sunday funny paper that had been left in one of the cabins and tied with twine.

"That's a good idea, Eli," Trudy said. "I'd never have thought to use the funny paper for wrapping."

Pleased by the praise, Eli watched closely as Jake unwrapped the small copper box he had found on the trash pile behind the wash-house. After pounding out the dents and straightening the lid so that it would close, he had spent a couple of hours polishing it.

"It's to put your razor in."

"Or anything of value," Jake said. "It's so

shiny I could almost use it for a mirror. Thanks, Eli. You put in a lot of work on this."

"I polished it up with vinegar and soda. One of the few things I learned at the orphans' home."

Mary Lee said, "That's a new one on me. I didn't know vinegar and soda would shine copper."

Eli basked in their admiration until Trudy produced the cake knife. "Now it's time to cut the birthday cake."

Chapter 11

"Take this last piece, Jake."

"I've had three pieces. Give it to Eli." Jake sat cross-legged on the floor with his empty plate in his hand.

"How about it, Eli?"

"Well, sure, if nobody else wants it."

"Just eat it off the plate." Trudy handed him the cake plate. "I think he's got hollow legs," she said in an aside to Jake.

"I didn't know cake could be so good. Pie is the usual dessert in diners."

All this was almost more than Jake could take in at one time. He was still in a daze. He had been alone for so long, he hadn't known another way of life. That Mary Lee had remembered today was his birthday and had gone to such lengths to make it special for him was little less than a miracle.

"It was just plain old everyday cake. I fancied it up with white mountain icing." Mary Lee went to the door, looked out, and was relieved to see that the cabin Frank Pierce occupied was still dark.

"One thing is sure—I'll never forget my twenty-sixth birthday." Jake stood. Trudy took the plate from his hand.

"I hate to break up the party, but I've got to be gettin' home." Trudy put the plates back in the paper sack. "Jake, how about you and Mary Lee givin' me a ride home? Mama don't want me walkin' by myself after dark."

"I've got to get back to the house," Mary Lee said quickly.

"How would it look if folks saw me out at night alone with Jake?" Trudy replied. "Tongues would start waggin' about a romance brewin'."

"What would be so bad about that?"

"Maybe I've got my eye on another fella," Trudy retorted sassily. "Bein' with Jake would blow my chances."

"You never told me."

"I'm keepin' it a secret." With her back to Mary Lee, she winked at Jake.

Trudy was sure that Jake had fallen for Mary Lee. Being careful not to let Trudy catch him, Jake's eyes had followed her friend since the moment they stepped in the door. She hoped that Mary Lee could see the real Jake behind his jailbird reputation.

Just before he went out the door, Eli picked up the sack with the soiled dishes and forks. "I'll keep an eye on things until you get back."

"Oh, but—"

"We won't be gone fifteen minutes. Come on, half-pint," Jake said to Trudy. "Mary Lee'll be gettin' antsy."

"I'm washing the cake plate. It was sticky." Trudy worked at the small sink, then wiped the plate on one of Jake's towels. "You'll have to scald this plate before you use it," she said to Mary Lee. "Jake's probably dried his feet on this towel."

When the three of them got into the truck, Mary Lee was hugging the cake plate to her as if it were a shield. She moved over into the middle of the seat to make room for Trudy. Her arm and shoulder were behind Jake's; his hip and thigh, warm and hard, against hers. When he reached to shift the gears, his fingers brushed her knees, and she felt the touch to the tips of her toes.

The ride to Trudy's house was no longer than five minutes. Trudy chattered all the way, seeming to know that she was needed to fill the silence.

"I won't be over tomorrow, Mary Lee, unless you need me. But I'll be there the next morning. If I get there at five, it will be soon enough to get breakfast ready by six. Eli said you were going to put up the signs in the morning, Jake. So the price for lodging goes up tomorrow? Mary Lee, are you going to charge two dollars if they eat or not?" Without waiting for an answer, Trudy said, "I would. Don't give them a choice. Mama says that folks will dilly around if they have to make a choice. She only has four things on the menu at the diner. She said that if she had something fancy like green bean casserole with mushroom topping, most folks would still order steak and potatoes. Maybe they would order the casserole at a place like Daytonas in Santa Fe, but not at Ruby's Diner in Cross Roads. The only traveling men who come here stop at the motor court. Oh, maybe a few of them go into town to the hotel." Trudy paused and took a breath, then said, "I'm about to run out of anything to say."

Both Mary Lee and Jake laughed. "I was wondering when you were going to run down," Jake said.

"Well, you weren't helping me none a-tall."

"I couldn't have gotten a word in edge-ways."

"I've stopped now. What did you want to say?"

"I wanted to say thank you for the party and ask you to tell your mother thanks for the present. I'll cash in my ticket one night soon."

"Are you finished at the bridge?" Mary Lee asked.

"I go back tomorrow to get my pay. After I put out your signs, I'll go out to see Quitman and find out when he wants me to start out there."

Jake stopped the truck in front of a small house with a long front porch. A dog came out and barked.

"Oh, be quiet, George," Trudy scolded as she hopped out of the truck. "Thanks, Jake. See you day after tomorrow, Mary Lee."

Jake waited until Trudy was inside the house before he moved the truck down the street. Still holding the cake plate clutched against her breast, Mary Lee moved over to the far side of the seat. He missed the warmth of her body against his. The smell of her was in his nostrils. He longed to reach out, put his arms around her and draw her back against him.

"Trudy is a chatterbox." It was the first thing that came to Mary Lee's mind to say. "Even when we were in school, she always had something to say."

"And you were the shy one."

"How did you know?"

"You're shy sometimes now, and at other times . . . wow!" He looked at her and grinned.

"Like the night Frank Pierce had his radio on so loud? You should have heard me yelling at Ocie Clawson. I'm sure that Mr. Santez down at the filling station heard me."

"Ocie Clawson? Was he here?" Jake asked sharply.

"Yesterday."

"Was he wanting you to get rid of me?"

"He mentioned it. Mostly he wanted to know if the baby was Bobby's."

"Why the . . . low-down, dirty polecat!"

"If it was, he wanted to have a hand in raising it."

Jake was quiet for a minute, then asked, "Are you going to let him?"

Mary Lee's brows drew together, and she looked at him as if he were crazy for even asking the question.

"I'll hide away in one of the little mountain villages you told me about before I let him have a hand in raising my child."

"In his defense, I'll have to say that Ocie didn't have much of a hand in raising Bobby. It was all his mother's doing."

"You said once that you went to school with Bobby."

"My mother and I lived on the ranch. I rode fence when I wasn't going to a one-room school. Even then, Mrs. Clawson thought Bobby knew more than the teacher."

"How old were you then?"

"About Eli's age, I guess. I was fifteen when my mother died. The only friend I'd had there had been Temple Clawson. He died a few months before my mother. There was nothing for me at the Circle C after that, so I took off."

"That was ten years ago."

"Thereabouts. I've learned a lot during those ten years."

Mary Lee wanted to keep him talking. "You liked the older Mr. Clawson?"

"Yeah. I did."

"Bobby didn't like him. Called him crude and ignorant."

"Mrs. Clawson didn't like him, and what Mrs. Clawson didn't like, Bobby didn't like."

A light was on in number one cabin when they reached the motor court. Jake drove past it and parked the truck beside his cabin.

"I hope Frank hasn't caused any trouble."

"Things seem quiet. Sit with me a minute. Eli will know that we're back, and will come for you if you're needed." He turned and rested his arm on the back of the seat.

"The people in number five have left already. They didn't even bother to close the door."

"They may be back."

"I don't think so."

"One of those, huh?"

"I used to ask Daddy why people rented

and didn't stay the whole night. He never gave me a good answer. Now I know." Mary Lee was so comfortable with him here in the darkness that she wasn't the least embarrassed by the topic of their conversation.

There was a long silence while all sorts of wild thoughts floated through her mind. Bobby had been dead only a few months. How could she so completely forget a man she had lived with for more than a year? What was she doing, sitting in the dark with a man she had known only a few weeks, a man who had been in prison, a man who she had thought was a dangerous crook.

She turned her head and saw that he had leaned slightly toward her, his eyes warm on her face. Suddenly his hand was on her arm, moving down to clasp her hand. He lifted it, held the back of it to his mouth and kissed it. The warmth of his mouth caused a lovely feeling to unfold in her midsection. It was strange to her. She tugged on her hand. He held it between both of his.

"Mary Lee . . ." His voice was a mere whisper. "Don't be scared. I'm trying to tell you how much this evening has meant to me. I've had my first birthday cake, my first birthday present, and all because of you."

"The . . . presents were not much."

"To me they were very special. Do you really want the hair ribbon back?"

"Did you plan to wear it?" she asked, and couldn't hold back the giggle that bubbled up.

"Now, wouldn't I be a bird with that ribbon in my hair? I may wear it around my neck under the bandanna."

Suddenly, and unexpectedly to both of them, the hand on the back of the seat slid down to cup Mary Lee's nape and pushed lightly. He bent his head; his mouth found hers and moved softly, gently over it as if she were the most precious thing in the world. She was too shocked to move. His lips pressed upon hers again, kissing her tenderly. Her mouth trembled under his. He released the pressure slightly.

"Have I ruined things?" he breathed against her lips.

Mary Lee felt her insides warm with pleasure as she looked into his quiet face and green eyes now anxiously waiting for her answer.

"Isn't that carrying gratitude a little too far?" she managed to say.

"Gratitude had nothing to do with it. I

wanted to kiss you because you're pretty and sweet and spunky. If another man ever takes advantage of you like I have just done, I'll beat him to a pulp."

"You don't have to worry about that. Men aren't exactly standing in line to kiss me." She pulled away from him. "I must go."

"Have I ruined things between us?"

"There's nothing between us."

"No, of course not. I understand."

"No, you don't. You think it's because you've been to prison. That's not it at all. I'll be having a baby in a few months. No man in his right mind would see me as anything but a pregnant woman waddlin' around—" Her eyes were bright, and her lips trembled when she spoke.

Jake's fingers came up to cover her lips. "Then I don't have my right mind. I see you as soft, pretty and sweet as a woman is meant to be." His palm slid down to lie gently against the mound of her stomach. "This baby will be so lucky to have you for its mother." He moved away from her quickly and opened the door. By the time he got around to the other side of the truck, she was out.

"You don't have to walk with me—"

"I'm going to." His hand cupped her elbow and pulled her close to his side. "You could stumble in the dark."

They didn't talk as they walked behind the cabins to the main house. Mary Lee's mind was filled with what had happened in the truck and the joy she had felt when he placed his hand on her stomach. It was almost as if he wished that the baby growing inside were his.

She wasn't aware that a man had come from between the first two cabins and stood waiting for them, until he spoke.

"Well, well, if it ain't the jailbird and the bitch," Frank Pierce said loudly.

Mary Lee felt Jake tense. "Don't pay any attention," she said quickly. "He's goading you."

"Got nothin' to say, jailbird?"

"I'll have plenty to say . . . when the time is right."

"No guts, huh?"

Mary Lee kept a tight hold on Jake's arm.

"You'll find out when yours are strung between here and Sante Fe."

"Once a jailbird, always a jailbird. It's what ya'd expect from a breed . . . Indian or Mex."

"You're not half the man Jake is." Mary Lee's voice was rising with her temper.

To her astonishment, Frank unbuttoned his pants, pulled out his penis, and in the light from the window, began to urinate against the back of the cabin.

"You . . . crude son of a bitch!" Jake lunged. Mary Lee managed to get in front of him.

"Don't, Jake! Please . . . please . . ." She put a hand on his chest to hold him. "Can't you see it's what he wants?"

As soon as she stopped his forward motion, Mary Lee spun around and, quick as a cat and with all her might, brought the edge of the cake plate down on the exposed part of Frank that was protruding from his britches.

He screamed and fell to his knees.

"You nasty old buzzard, I hope I broke it off!" she yelled.

"Oh, God! Oh, God!" Frank flopped over on the ground, clutching himself and yelling with pain.

"You're trash! Plain trash. A hog's got more manners than you've got. You thought to get Jake to fight you so you could call the sheriff. I'll call him. I want him to see you, you slimy toad!"

"You fixed him. He'll not be able to do anything for a while," Jake said, a chuckle bubbling up out of his chest. "Serves him right."

"He did it so you'd hit him."

Frank lay moaning and crying. "Oh, Jesus—God in heaven—you bitch! You broke it."

"Call her that again and I'll stomp you where you lie," Jake snarled. Then to Mary Lee, "He's lucky it was you who hit him. I came within a whisker of it. I was mad enough to kill him." Then with laughter in his voice, "Remind me not to make you mad at me."

"To do that in front of us was so . . . nasty!"

"Gosh, Mary Lee, you really whacked him. I was hopin' I'd get in a lick or two." Eli moved out of the darkness with a big stick in his hand.

"Too late, Eli," Jake said. "Unless you want to hit him while he's down."

"I'd rather he was on his feet."

"What's the matter with Frank?" Dolly came from the cabin followed by a man in bib overalls. Her voice was slurred, and she reeked of cheap whiskey. She squatted down beside Frank, then looked up at Jake and demanded, "What did ya do to him?"

"He didn't do anything, Mama. I hit him with this plate. Eli, I think Mr. Santez's station is still open. Will you go call the sheriff?"

"Ain't you that jailbird?" the man said to Jake as soon as Eli took off on the run.

"You know who he is," Mary Lee answered. "You and this no-good, trashy polecat were waiting for him."

"Ya lettin' a split-tail do yore talkin'?" the man asked Jake with a sneer.

"The lady is doing a pretty good job of it, and watch your mouth."

"Or what?"

"Or sometime when you least expect it, you'll find yourself with a couple broken legs and a mouth without teeth."

"Help me," Dolly said to the man with her. "We've got to get Frank to a doctor."

"Leave him right where he is until the sheriff gets here," Jake said with authority.

Dolly turned on him. "You ain't tellin' us what to do. You ain't nothin' but a jailbird."

"He's more of a something than that trash

there on the ground," Mary Lee said in a brittle tone. "Leave that skunk right where he is."

"You takin' up with this jailbird?"

"When did you ever care who I took up with?"

"Sh . . . it. First you take in that shitty kid, then this cattle thief. I want him arrested."

"We'll let the sheriff decide who should be arrested."

"Oh, God. She ruint . . . me—" Cradling his privates in his bloody hands, Frank curled up in a ball.

Lights from an automobile lit up the area.

"If that's the sheriff, he was close."

A car door slammed; then Eli and Sheriff Pleggenkuhle approached the group at the back of the cabin.

"What's going on here?" The sheriff was a big man with a big voice.

"He was at the station," Eli said in an aside to Mary Lee.

"They jumped him," said Dolly.

"I hit him." Both Mary Lee and her mother spoke at the same time.

"Help me, Sheriff. They've . . . ruint me—" Frank rolled over but didn't sit up.

Sheriff Pleggenkuhle knelt down. "Let me see what happened."

"They broke . . . it." Frank moved his hands so the sheriff could see the damage to his private parts.

"I don't know if it's broke or not. It's a bloody mess." The sheriff stood. "Now, tell me what happened."

"That jailbird did it," Dolly said shrilly. Her thin shoulders were hunched; the front of her dress gaped, showing her sagging breast.

Mary Lee was mortified. "You weren't out here, Mama."

"What happened, Mrs. Clawson?"

"I went with Jake to take Trudy Bender home. He was walking me back to the house when Frank Pierce came out and tried to start a fight with Jake by saying nasty things to me. When that didn't work, he . . . he exposed himself and began to . . . you know . . . against the cabin. I lost my temper and hit him with this plate. Jake didn't touch him."

"Did you walk up on him while he was doing it?"

"No, he deliberately unbuttoned his pants and moved over into the light from the window so I would see it."

"Is that the way it was, Jake?"

"That's the way it was."

"That's a lie. He did it." Dolly pointed a finger at Jake. "They're trying to make Frank move out. But he paid rent—"

"Mama, hush. You weren't out here."

"I saw it, Sheriff. Jake didn't touch him." Eli spoke from beside Mary Lee.

"Don't believe what that lying, snot-nosed kid says. He'd jump in the fire if she told him to."

"Oh, Mama, please. You're making a fool of yourself."

"Have you been drinking tonight, Mrs. Finley?"

"One drink. Ain't that right, Yancy?"

The sheriff ignored the man and spoke to Jake. "Got anything else to say?"

"No. I'd have wiped the ground with him, but she beat me to it."

"Are you going to arrest her?" Yancy asked.

The sheriff gave him a disgusted look and spoke to Frank. "Can you get on your feet? I'll take you to the doctor before I take you to jail for exposing your privates to this lady."

"Why're you takin' Frank? He didn't do

nothin'." Dolly stood protectively over the man on the ground.

Sheriff Pleggenkuhle ignored her and took Frank's arm to help him up.

"Leave him alone." Dolly tried to push the sheriff.

"Go in the house, Mrs. Finley, unless you want to go to jail for being drunk and interfering with an officer."

"I ain't either drunk!"

"I say you are. You smell like you've been swimming in a barrel of home brew."

"It's her fault. She come here . . . and took over. She hides the money and don't give me any." Dolly pointed a shaky finger at Mary Lee and began to cry.

Humiliated by her mother's actions, Mary Lee turned her back and closed her eyes. Jake's hand on her arm was all that kept her from reeling.

The sheriff told Yancy to take Frank's arm. The two men lifted Frank to his feet and between them led him to the sheriff's car.

After they had rounded the building, Dolly turned on Mary Lee. "Guess you're satisfied now. You've been a pain in the ass and a thorn in my side since the day you were born. Scott couldn't see anything but his *precious* little girl. You turned him against me. Now you're gettin' Frank sent to jail with your lies."

"They were not lies, Mama."

"You didn't like him 'cause he didn't bow and scrape to you like your daddy did. You ain't goin' to be satisfied till you take everything I got . . . my friends, my cabins. And ya got that jailbird helpin' ya. I hope that damn kid you're carryin' comes out cross-eyed and bowlegged and gives you as much hell as you've given me." Dolly spit out the words with pure hatred in her eyes as she looked at her daughter.

Mary Lee stood still as a stone after Dolly turned to follow the sheriff and Frank. Vaguely she heard the sheriff's car leave. Eli reached out and took the plate from her hands. Tears that she couldn't hold back blurred her vision as she stumbled toward the back porch. Jake, steady as a rock, was there, his hand clasping her elbow to keep her from falling.

Chapter 12

"Don't let what she said bother you." Jake's voice, smooth and confident, came out of the darkness.

"She . . . she hates me . . ." Mary Lee's words reflected the misery in her soul.

"You're wrong, honey. She was drunk and upset over Frank. She doesn't hate you." His voice vibrated with tender concern. "No one in their right mind could hate you."

Mary Lee squeezed her eyes tightly shut as tears welled and glistened on her lashes. Her heart swelled, and she thought she would choke with the effort of keeping the sobs from her throat.

"Not *you*," he whispered.

On hearing his tender, sincere words, the flood of emotion she had kept in check for so long broke. She turned to him, buried her face against his chest and cried as though her heart would break. Jake's arms went around her. He held her tightly against him and stroked her hair. She wrapped her arms around his waist, clung to him and sobbed.

"Don't cry, little love." The whispered voice was against her ear. "She didn't mean what she said." He held her close, his head bent over hers, his hand caressing her back.

"Yes, she . . . did." Mary Lee had not felt such crushing grief since she received word her daddy had died.

Her tears soaked Jake's shirt. He cuddled her to him, feeling her hurt, wanting to take it away and knowing there was nothing he could do.

Suddenly, he felt the movement of her child against his lower abdomen. He caught his breath. He thought his heart would stop beating. The fluttering continued for a minute or two. It was electrifying to feel the movement of the baby within her, even if it wasn't his own. He closed his eyes, savoring the moment.

"*Querida,* don't cry!"

"I . . . can't help it . . ."

"Where's that spunky girl who hit Frank with the plate?"

"I'm . . . tired of being . . . spunky. I'm tired of . . . being alone . . . having to do everything—"

"You're not alone, little *amante*. You've got me and Eli and Trudy," he whispered against her ear.

"They're goin' to keep at you till you're sent back to jail . . . and I might lose the court. That damn old Ocie thinks he has a claim to my baby—"

"Don't worry about him, *querida*. He'll have nothing to say about your baby if you don't want him to. I swear it."

"Everything has piled on all at once. I'm just so . . . scared."

"Don't be scared. I'll be here. It was the thought of going back to jail, leaving you, that kept me from beating the hell out of Frank." His lips were against her wet cheek.

"I worried that you'd fight him and get in trouble." Mary Lee opened her eyes, but tears blinded her. She tried to wipe her cheeks with the back of her hand, but he moved her hand away and held it in his.

"It's been a long time since anyone worried about me." He lowered his head, and his warm lips caressed her forehead. "Feel better now? Eli is standing over there ready to take on the world with a willow switch for making you cry."

"I'm . . . sorry. I don't usually let go."

"After what you've had to put up with, you're entitled to let go once in a while." Jake took the new bandanna from around his neck and wiped the tears from her cheeks.

"Thank you."

"I'll be glad to hold you if you want to cry some more," he teased.

"I'm all cried out." Mary Lee moved back; his arms dropped from around her, but his hands moved down and clasped hers. "Thanks for the loan of your shoulder," she said.

"It's available anytime."

Mary Lee's hands slipped from his. She stepped up onto the step and turned to look at him.

"Jake, have we ever met before?"

"Why do you ask?"

"I just feel like I know you. Something about your eyes and your . . . face strikes a chord in my memory."

"It was a long time ago when you were a little girl." He reached for her hand again as if he needed to touch her.

"Then you must have been a little boy."

"I was eleven or thereabout."

"I would have been seven or eight?"

"I thought you were the prettiest little thing I'd ever seen."

"You couldn't have thought that! I was ugly . . . all arms and legs, snaggletoothed and freckled."

His laugh was low, a soft intimate sound that came out of the darkness.

"You don't remember being kind to a tired, hungry kid with sore feet?"

She squinted her eyes and looked at his face. Smiling softly, she said, "I remember! You came off the road and went straight to the well but didn't drink until you'd asked for the water."

"My tongue was so swollen I'm surprised I could talk."

"A cowboy had taken you out in the hills and dumped you . . . without your shoes. Your poor feet—were bloody."

"You cried and held my hand while your daddy cleaned them. He smeared them with salve and wrapped them."

"You didn't let out a peep while he was doing it. I thought you were brave . . ."

"I wasn't going to cry while a little girl with big blue eyes watched me, no matter how much it hurt."

"I had never noticed green eyes before. I asked Daddy why yours were green and not blue like mine. He said God made them green so you could see better in the mountains where you came from."

"That was fast thinking."

"You stayed two days. Then a man came to get you in a wagon. Who was he?"

"Temple Clawson."

"What happened to the cowboy? Did he get fired?"

"I never told who did it."

"Why not?"

"I didn't want to cause more trouble."

"When you helped me with the mattress I was sure that I'd met you before. You knew who I was, didn't you?"

"Of course. I'm sorry about your father."

Standing on the step, her eyes were level with his. She looked searchingly into them for a long time, then turned to open the screen door.

"Good night, Jake."

"'Night, Mary Lee."

Sleep didn't come easily for Mary Lee despite her tired and aching back. The baby was restless and seemed to be constantly on the move. She pressed her hand to her abdomen.

"Be still, baby. You're going to be all right."

Her mind was filled with memories of a quiet, dignified boy. She could see his face as he struggled to keep from crying as he hobbled to the well to get a drink of water. That face with the leaf-green eyes had stayed in the back of her mind all these years. It was no wonder that she was startled when she saw the man he had grown up to be.

Was it possible that she had fallen in love with Jake Ramero, accused cattle rustler, prison parolee? He had been kind tonight, letting her cry on his shoulder. She knew enough Spanish to know that the endearments he'd murmured were merely comforting words.

Earlier, she had sat in his truck, as still as a stump, and let him kiss her. Good Lord. She had made it easy for him, and what's more, she had enjoyed it. She'd not have protested if he had done it again and again, hadn't even protested when his hand moved down to rest on her rounded stomach.

She could still see the wonder on his face when he saw the cake. Gratitude. *That was why he had kissed her.*

Other questions formed in her mind. Why had she let what her mother said about her always being a pain hurt her so? Was it because she had said it in front of Jake? She had known for years how her mother felt about her, but she had not really put it in words before.

Mary Lee doubted that her mother had drawn a dozen sober breaths since she'd returned home. Oftentimes drink made people brave enough to say what they really thought about things. Thinking about the hatred she had seen in the eyes of her mother's friends, she shivered.

She had never been afraid before, but tonight she was aware of every sound. Cars passed on the highway; one of the cabin doors slammed. In the distance a dog sent up a howl.

Mary Lee got out of bed and brought a chair from the kitchen, shut her door and wedged the chair's back beneath the door-knob. It wasn't much protection, but she would hear if someone tried to enter her room. The door to the bathroom opened in-ward. All she could do was drag her trunk across the door and set her shoes on top. If someone tried to come in that way, the shoes might fall off and wake her.

Back in bed, she huddled beneath the sheet and wished that Jake were in number one instead of the farthest cabin. Although Jake was a big man, there was something vulnerable about him, something that made her want to protect him.

Oh, heck! she groaned. She was devel-oping a crush on him. And he thought of her as merely the daughter—pregnant daugh-ter—of a man who had once befriended him.

Her last thought before sleep overtook her was that she hoped Frank stayed in jail for a long, long time and that that *thing* he had so proudly displayed would never work properly again.

Mr. Santez knocked on the back door while Mary Lee was cooking breakfast.

"Ya all right?" he asked through the screen door.

"I'm fine. Come in and have coffee."

"Can't." He opened the door and stepped inside. "Got to get back to the station. Rosa was worried after what happened last night and wanted to be sure that lout hadn't hurt you."

"Is it all over town already?"

"Not yet. When the boy came to call the sheriff, he just happened to be there to get gas. He took right off and when he came back, he had Frank Pierce with him. Frank was yellin' and cursin' and callin' ya nasty names. The sheriff got gas and told him to can it or he'd put a gag in his mouth. Guess they was headed for Doc Morris."

"I hit him with the edge of a plate."

"He was blabbin' that ya broke some-thin'."

"I hope I did and it falls off," she blurted. Her face turned scarlet when she realized what she had said.

"Take care, girl. Frank's mean and he runs with a mean bunch."

"I will, and thank you for thinking about me. I'll get over to see Rosa one of these days."

"Will Jake be stayin' on now he finished his bridge job?"

"I think so."

"Glad to hear it. If ya get in a bind and need help, and Jake ain't here, send the boy down. I'll lock up and beat it up here. The boy 'pears to be right sensible, by the way."

"He's been a big help."

Mary Lee was taking the biscuits out of the oven when Eli bounded up onto the porch and snatched open the door.

"What'd Mr. Santez want?"

"Nothing. Just wanted to know if things were all right here. Where have you been?"

"Down with Jake. He's getting ready to take the new signs out."

"Has he left yet?"

"No. He's loadin' up."

"The least we can do is give him breakfast. Go tell him to come in and have biscuits and sausage gravy before he goes."

Mary Lee flinched when the screen door slammed behind Eli. She hoped that the sound hadn't wakened her mother. She strained her ears for a sound that didn't come.

Eli returned and took his place at the table. Jake stood hesitantly in the doorway.

"You don't have to feed me."

Mary Lee looked at him and grinned. "I'm not going to. You'll have to feed yourself. I'm merely supplying the biscuits and gravy. It's a trial run to see how we'll do tomorrow morning when we feed the overnighters . . . that is, if we have any after we raise the price."

He smiled. It changed his quiet face, making him look younger than his twenty-six years.

"That gravy smells good . . ."

"Come take a seat. Go ahead and help yourself before Eli gets up to full speed or you might not get anything. I'll pour your coffee."

"I'll pour it." Eli jumped up and beat her to the pot. While he poured into the three cups, Mary Lee brought a jar of peach preserves to the table and sat down.

"You mean I'll have to wrestle this kid for a biscuit?" Jake teased.

He put his hat on the floor under his chair and sat at the end of the table. His eyes followed Mary Lee. She was wearing a man's shirt. The collar had been cut off and the

sleeves cut short. Her face was flushed
from the heat of the oven. Damp wisps of
hair stuck to her cheeks. She had made no
attempt to pretty herself up, but she didn't
need to. She was pretty and soft and wom-
anly.

Jake wondered how he should approach
her about paying for his breakfast, not only
this morning but every morning. He had
tried to think of ways he could help her
without stepping on her pride. It had not
been a surprise to him that Rosen at the
bank was eager to get his hands on Mary
Lee's motor court, and she needed all the
money she could get to pay off the loan.

*She wouldn't lose this place if it took
every cent he had saved to start his cattle
operation.*

"If my overnight guests eat as much as
you and Eli, I'll have to raise the price,"
Mary Lee teased after they had finished the
meal.

"You shouldn't have such good biscuits,"
Jake said. "And . . . Lordy, but that gravy's
good too."

"It's a good thing biscuits are cheap to
make."

"I know what you can do," Eli said, smiling

broadly. "You can make the biscuits lumpy and doughy. They'll not eat so many."

"And never come back."

"Not many of them do anyway. They're one-timers mostly."

"There's a problem with that." Jake stood and hit Eli on the back with his hat. "I'll not be a one-timer if it's all right with Mary Lee."

"Ya signin' up to eat with us?"

"It would be handy." His eyes snagged Mary Lee's. He dug into his pocket and placed a twenty-five-cent piece on the table.

"No. I invited you." She picked up the quarter and put it back in his hand. "I should pay you for putting up our signs."

"Don't even mention it." Jake went to the door and turned to catch her with her hand pressed to the small of her back. She dropped it to her side when she realized he was looking at her. "Do you keep the doors locked at night?"

"Mama's room is the only one with a key."

"I can put a drop bar across your door."

"Well . . . if you want to."

"Stick close to her while I'm gone, Eli. And if you have to use . . . ah . . . what I gave you, use it where I told you to."

"Don't worry." Eli followed Jake out the door.

Mary Lee was taking the dishes from the table and piling them in the dishpan when she heard Jake's truck start up and drive away. Shortly after that, Eli came back in the kitchen.

"What did he give you and what are you going to do with it?" she asked with her back to him. When he didn't answer, she turned. "Eli?"

Reluctantly he pulled an object from his pocket.

"What is it?"

"They're called brass knuckles, but they're iron." Eli fitted the contraption on his hand. "Jake thought I needed somethin' besides a stick. He said if I could get up close and hit 'em with this . . . they'd fold like Frank did when ya hit him with the plate."

"Well, for goodness' sakes! You're just a boy. I won't have you fighting—"

"I won't, unless I have to."

"Oh, Eli." Mary Lee went to him, put her arms around him, hugged him, then leaned back and smoothed his hair off his forehead with her fingertips. "You're so dear to me. I couldn't bear it if you got hurt. Why did Jake think you even needed them?"

"That friend of Frank's is still out in his cabin. I'm to stick to you till he leaves. I told Jake I would. He's depending on me."

"So am I, Eli. I couldn't have stood it here these last weeks without you."

"Nobody'll touch ya while I'm here." His arm went across her shoulders for a brief minute.

"Is Mama out there?"

"He brought her as far as the porch sometime after midnight. I helped her to her room. She didn't even know it was me."

"I didn't hear a thing. Oh, I hate that. Someone could carry off the house and I'd not wake up."

"I've been thinkin' I'd bring my cot up to the back porch."

Mary Lee turned away before he saw the tears in her eyes. Damn! It made her so mad! Lately she bawled at the drop of a hat.

"The iceman's here. How much did you want?"

"The card's in the window. Fifty pounds, I think." Mary Lee hurried and dried her eyes before she heard the heavy footsteps on the back porch. "Hello, Mr. O'Riley."

"Howdy, ma'am."

While he was putting the ice in the box, Mary Lee went to her suitcase and took out the envelope marked ICE. After taking out the change, she locked the suitcase and went back to the kitchen.

"Heard you had a little trouble here last night. You all right?"

"I'm fine."

"That's good. Nice woman like you ain't ort to have to put up with no-goods such as Frank Pierce. Drunken deadbeat is what he is. Ever'body knows that."

"Unfortunately not everyone, Mr. O'Riley."

"Ya've done a good job turnin' this place around."

"Thank you."

"Well, this ort to last ya till Monday. I'm leaving ya a new ice pick here in the other holder."

"Thanks, Mr. O'Riley."

Shortly before noon Ocie Clawson walked into the sheriff's office. Pleggenkuhle was talking on the phone. He motioned for Ocie to sit down and continued his conversation.

"Ma'am, do you know for sure that she's takin' onions from your garden?" The sheriff paused to listen, his eyes on his boots propped up on the end of the desk. "Did you see her pull them up?" He lifted his eyes to watch a fly on the ceiling. "I realize you can't see the garden from the house, ma'am." The voice on the other end became loud, almost shouting. "Tell you what . . . find a good comfortable place outside tonight where you can see the garden. If you see anyone out there pulling your onions, call me and I'll be there pronto." Then, "Yes, I will. But I can't arrest her and fine her unless we catch her red-handed. All right? Bye, ma'am."

The sheriff hung up the phone and let his feet plop off the end of the desk. He eyed Ocie as he ran forked fingers through his hair.

"I wish that all I had to worry about was someone stealing onions out of a garden. What's on your mind, Ocie?"

"I hear ya got Frank Pierce in your jail."

"News travels in Cross Roads."

"Heard he got hurt out at the motor court."

"Yeah, he did. He'll be a-walkin' bow-legged for a while." Sheriff Pleggenkuhle could barely suppress a grin. "Serves him right, I'd say."

"Yancy Hummer is tellin' folks uptown that Jake Ramero and my daughter-in-law attacked him, hurt him bad, and that you took their side."

"Yancy Hummer doesn't have as much sense as a cross-eyed polecat."

"Well . . . what happened?"

"I'm not obligated to tell you what happened, but I will. Frank tried to draw Jake Ramero into a fight by talkin' nasty to Mrs. Clawson so I'd arrest him and he'd go back to jail. Jake didn't bite. So Frank pulled out his pecker right in front of Mrs. Clawson, moved over under the light from the window and pissed on the cabin wall. Mrs. Clawson had a cake plate in her hand. She whacked him a good one with the edge of it and did real damage to his pisser. Doc says he'll not be using that pitiful pecker of his for anything but to pee out of for a good long time, if ever."

By the time the sheriff finished, Ocie was laughing so loud he could be heard a block away.

"By God, that girl's got grit," he said when he finished laughing. "Tell Frank that if he goes near that girl again, he'll not only be unable to use his pecker, he'll have a fence post shoved up his ass."

"Go back there and tell him yourself. He's ripe for some good news."

"I will." Ocie got to his feet.

"Somebody wants Jake sent back to prison. Is it you?"

"Hell, no. But I ain't wantin' him hangin' around Mary Lee either."

"You better hope he stays. She needs someone out there to keep an eye on things. That mother of hers isn't worth the lead it would take to shoot her, and she's hangin' with a bunch of trash that took her for every dime she had."

"Rosen will take over the court in a few months, sell it for what's mortgaged against it. They'll get a little money out of it."

"You'll stand by and let that skinflint banker take that girl's home?"

"It's what I'm countin' on."

"Godamighty, Ocie! I'd of never thought it of you. She's goin' to have your grandkid."

"I want her and the kid at the ranch. There isn't a snowball's chance in hell of her coming out there if she's got that motor court." Ocie paused and waved his head from side to side working out a kink in his neck.

"Now, how do I get back to the cells to say my piece to that shithead ya got back there?"

Chapter 13

Lon Delano waited in the alley behind Pedro's for Yancy. He had given him the nod to come out ten minutes ago. The fool was enjoying being the center of attention as he related how Jake Ramero and the Clawson woman had come upon Frank taking a piss behind the cabin. He figured Jake had held Frank while the woman whacked at his pecker with the broken edge of a plate.

Yancy described in vivid detail to the avid listeners how he had come running when he heard Frank screaming and discovered him holding his bleeding pecker and rolling on the ground.

"From what I could see, it was cut almost completely in two. Poor Frank was holding it together the best he could."

"Goddamn!" the bartender exclaimed. "I almost puked thinkin' about it."

"Sure was a sight," Yancy said. "That woman out there would put Bonnie Parker to shame. She'd stand up to a parcel of wildcats. Now she's tied up with that thievin' jailbird. He stands back and lets her take the lead, but he's egging her on all the while. Threatened me, he did, when I mouthed back at her. Said he'd sneak up on me in the dark, break my legs and knock out my teeth. Next thing we know, that gal will be kickin' Dolly out to root-hog-or-die and he'll be movin' in the house with her. She don't give poor old Dolly the time of day and keeps every cent the cabins bring in."

"If Dolly ain't gettin' any money, how'd she have money to treat the crowd the other night at the Red Pepper?"

"She told Frank it was money she'd hid back." Yancy set his beer mug down on the bar. "Got to be goin' fellers. Got business to tend to."

He went out the door, hesitated to see if anyone followed him, then darted around the building to the alley.

"What the hell took ya so long? I ain't got time to be hangin' 'round waitin' for you."

"I couldn't just walk out. The fellers wanted to know what had happened to Frank."

"Well . . . ?"

"I told 'em. Spread it on thick."

"Jesus. I send you two to pick a fight with Ramero. One of ya gets his pecker all tore up and the other'n gets to runnin' off at the mouth. Now, goddammit, how hard is it to pick a fight with one hair-triggered ex-con?"

"That bloated-up cow twists him around her little finger. She says do this or that and he does it."

"Are ya stayin' out there?"

"No, I ain't. I ain't aimin' to get my head bashed in and I ain't aimin' to screw an old drunk."

"Why not? When've ya ever screwed anythin' else?"

"Now see here—"

"You see here, you shithead. Yo're workin' for me, or have ya forgot it?"

"I don't have to take that talk from you. I ain't one of yore piss boys—"

"Ocie'll fire ya in a minute if I say the word. Ya want a job, don't ya?"

"Am I fired if I don't stay out there and screw old Dolly?"

"No, of course not." Lon softened his voice. "We got to see to it that that girl flushes the kid before its time. Ocie is all puffed up 'bout bein' a grandpa. Ya got to understand that if he passes the Circle C on to her and her kid, we'll all be out of a job."

"Ocie don't 'pear to me to be on his last legs."

"No, he don't, but accidents can happen. I need someone out there at that court keepin' an eye on thin's. Frank ain't the smartest, ya know. Takin' his pecker out in front of that woman showed him in a bad light. The sheriff ain't goin' to forget it."

"How long's he in for?"

"I don't know. Ocie's over there now. As soon as he heads back to the ranch, I'll go over and find out. You'd better hightail it out to the ranch so he'll see ya around, but be back here tonight. We got to keep someone in that cabin to let us know what's goin' on, and keepin' close to Dolly is the only way to do it."

"Ya want me to stay out there tomorrow? What'll Ocie say 'bout me bein' gone?"

"Hell. Ya think he comes 'round lookin'

for ya? If he asks, I'll tell him I sent ya out lookin' for a lobo that brought down a couple of calves. Get on back, now."

"I ain't got a ride."

"Go down to the livery stable. There's two Circle C horses down there. Tell Smitty to give you one. Go cross-country. I don't want Ocie passin' ya on the road."

In late afternoon, after the cabins had been cleaned and readied for occupancy, Mary Lee took a quick bath and, confident that Eli would look after the court for an hour, walked uptown to see Dr. Morris. After she had endured the embarrassing examination and was anxious to get back to the motor court, she paused beside the desk of his nurse.

"Doctor wants you back August fifteenth, Mrs. Clawson. Then every two weeks after that."

"What do I owe for the office visit?"

"The office calls are included in the delivery fee."

"And how much is that?"

"You'll have to discuss it with the doctor."

"Does he know that I'll have to pay in installments?"

"I'm sure he does. Don't hesitate to call or come in if you feel anxious about anything. And don't forget to take the iron pills the doctor gave you."

"I won't, and thank you again."

Mary Lee was smiling as she walked out onto the landing at the top of the iron steps attached to the bank building. The doctor had said that her pregnancy was progressing normally; her baby had a strong heartbeat and was in the correct position. He could see no reason why she would have any difficulty in birthing. Holding on to the railing, she hurried down the open iron stairs, her heels clicking on the steps.

It happened so fast that she had no time to do anything but hold desperately on to the railing. Something closed around her ankle and jerked her foot back through the opening in the stairs. She screamed. Her purse went flying out into space. Her knees hit the steps with a jarring force. Fear consumed her. She didn't even feel the pain as the rough iron of the steps scraped the skin from her shin and her knees. Her one thought was to keep from landing on her stomach.

With all her strength she clung to the railing. Her hat was tilted down over her eyes. She was unaware of the frightened sounds that came from her, or the man who had raced up the stairs and was lifting her with his hands beneath her arms.

"*Madre de Dios!*" Mother of God. The words burst from him. "*Señora,* are you hurt?"

Mary Lee burst into tears.

"You can turn loose of the rail, *señora.* I won't let you fall."

On hearing the commotion, the nurse from the doctor's office hurried down the stairs. "Is she hurt?"

"I'll lift her if you can pull her leg up."

"Careful of her knees. How in the world did her leg get back there?"

With cautious maneuvering, Mary Lee was lifted and set on the steps, her skinned and bloody legs stretched out in front of her. She was too hurt and shaken to be embarrassed at the scene she had created. She cradled her stomach with her two hands while the nurse lifted her skirt to look at her knees. She hurt so bad she was unaware of the attention she was getting.

"Can you stand?"

"I think so."

"Come back into the office. The doctor will want to see you, and I can take care of your skinned legs."

"What happened, Paco?" Several men had come up the stairs. One of them was carrying Mary Lee's purse and one shoe. Another picked her hat up off the steps.

"I was passin' by and heard the lady yell."

"How could her foot slip backward through the open stair?" The nurse had a puzzled frown on her face. "Would someone get her other shoe? It fell off when her leg went through the opening."

Paco said, "I thought I saw someone under the stairs. He dodged around the building."

"Someone grabbed my ankle." Mary Lee wiped her face on the handkerchief she took from her pocket. "Someone wanted me to fall."

Paco lifted her to her feet and held her while she steadied herself then limped up the steps to the doctor's office. He helped her to a chair.

Mary Lee looked up with tear-filled eyes. "Thank you."

"You very welcome, *señora*."

"What's happened here?" Doctor Morris

came from the back room. After being told, he listened to her heartbeat and that of her baby, then moved his knowing hands over the mound of her stomach. "Young lady, you're lucky you didn't go tumbling down the steps. I don't think any damage was done by the fall. You'll have to be more careful."

Mary Lee's shin was skinned, her knees cut and bruised. After a thorough cleaning, the nurse swabbed them with iodine.

"I felt my foot being jerked backward, Doctor. I know I'm not imagining it."

"You don't say? Hummm . . ."

"I couldn't have slipped backward."

"Then someone was deliberately trying to hurt you. You should tell Sheriff Pleggen-kuhle."

"Her shoe was yanked off, Doctor." The nurse knelt down and slipped the shoe on Mary Lee's foot and tied the laces.

"If you see any spotting, call me or come in at once." At that moment a baby began to cry in the examination room.

Paco spoke to the doctor. "I must go to the bank; then I will get my car and take her home."

"Oh, but I can't let you do that," Mary Lee protested.

"Yes, you can. Sit right here and wait for Paco. He'll see that you get back home. I'd take you myself, but I've got a full schedule this afternoon." The doctor left them.

"I don't like being so much trouble."

"None of us do," the nurse said. "But sometimes we have to be gracious and accept help when it's offered."

"The man who helped me is Mr. García, isn't he?" Mary Lee asked when they were alone. "I haven't seen him for a long time."

"Yes. You'll be all right with him. I'd heed the doctor's advice if I were you and tell the sheriff you think someone grabbed your ankle. I can't imagine why anyone would do such a thing."

After the doctor called the nurse into the examination room, Mary Lee got to her feet holding on to the back of the chair. Her knee was so sore, she winced when she put her weight on it. She walked back and forth, her mind going back to what had happened on the iron stairs. She had been halfway down the stairs when she felt something close around her ankle. Now she knew that it was a hand. It had jerked and pulled her foot back between the two steps.

She shuddered to think of what would have happened if she had not been able to hold on to the railing. She would have gone facedown, down the stairs, and surely her baby would have been injured or killed.

Who besides Frank Pierce would want to hurt her? He was in jail; and if he wasn't, he was in no condition to be lurking beneath the stairs. Ocie Clawson wanted her baby. He would not hurt it. Could it have been the man her mother called Yancy? With her gone, the court would go to her mother . . . until the bank took it away from her.

A wave of fear traveled down her spine.

Her legs were trembling as Paco helped her down the stairs. She held on to the stair railing and leaned heavily on his arm. People passing gawked as he helped her into his car. She held her head up and didn't look at any of them.

Jake and Eli were in front of the washhouse when the car stopped in front of the house. Before she could open the door and get out, Jake had charged around the building. His dark face held a worried frown. Eli was behind him.

Paco was getting out of the car as Jake pulled open the door. "What happened? Are you all right?"

"I'm all right."

"*Hola,* Jake," Paco said casually.

"What happened?" Jake demanded again. "Why'd you bring her home? I was about to go to meet her."

"I fell on the doctor's stairs and Mr. García was kind enough to give me a ride home." Mary Lee turned and put her feet on the running board so she could step down.

"Fell on the stairs?" Jake echoed her words. His eyes went to her skinned legs, now dark red with iodine. He clenched his teeth until a muscle danced in his jaw. "Son of a bitch," he whispered beneath his breath.

She tried to push his hands away when they grasped her under the arms, but he refused to be hindered and lifted her out of the car.

"Everything all right here, Eli?" she asked.

"I've rented number five. I don't think they'll stay long. We may be able to rent it again." Then, as he realized what his words indicated, his face turned brick red. "Charged 'em the two dollars too," he finished lamely.

"Has my mother been out?"

"She came out, cooked somethin', then went out to number one."

"Did the man who was there last night come back?"

"I've not seen him."

Paco, watching Jake, muttered, *"Yi, yi, yi."* His friend hadn't taken his eyes off Mary Lee.

The man was down, gravel-smitten with the little widow.

"Thank you, Mr. García, for the ride." Mary Lee took off her hat. "Excuse me. I need to change my dress."

Jake didn't say anything, but he was at the steps with his hand beneath her elbow. Eli was on her other side and followed her into the house. Jake came back to the car.

"Did the doctor see her after she fell?"

"Yeah, *amigo.* He look her over."

"Where'd she fall?"

"On the steps comin' down from Doc Morris. She thinks someone grab her foot and pull it back through the stairs. I was passin' and heard her yell. *Yi, yi, yi.* She was holdin' on to the rail."

"The hell you say! Jesus, Paco! Did you see anyone under the steps?"

"Thought I did, but not sure."

"By God, Paco! They're not wantin' her to have the baby. They're afraid Ocie will make it his heir."

"I ain't heard Ocie's so all-fired fond of Lon."

"She'll not go to town alone again."

"You her protector, *amigo*?"

"Someone should be lookin' out for her," Jake said belligerently. "Her mother isn't fit to shoot."

"Yo're it, huh?"

"She's got no one but me and a thirteen-year-old kid. If Lon's behind this and hurts her, he'll wish he'd never set eyes on her."

"Ya got to be careful, *amigo*. Let the sheriff handle it."

"I'll be careful. If I learned one thing in prison it's that it doesn't always pay to fight fair."

"It's bein' spread around town that you held Frank while the girl whacked his pecker with a broken plate."

Jake's green eyes glinted at that; his mouth spread in a grin.

"I didn't touch him and one whack was all it took. I had no idea what she was going to do until she did it. She took the sap outta old Frank. He'll not be pissin' in front of a lady anytime soon."

Paco chuckled. "I'll do what I can to set the story straight." He got into the car. "It could be Frank and his cronies who have it in for her because she took over the court."

"Frank's a stupid son of a bitch."

"Gotta be gettin' back. How're ya goin' to keep an eye on that girl and work too?"

"Trudy Bender is comin' out tomorrow. Between her and Eli, she'll have someone with her when I'm not here."

Jake stood back and watched Paco drive away. He wanted to go in the house and make sure Mary Lee was all right, but he wasn't sure of his welcome. At that moment a car came in off the highway, and Mary Lee came out onto the porch to greet a heavy-set man with a head of thick gray hair.

"Hello," she said pleasantly.

"Sign says you get breakfast with the room."

"We serve breakfast between six and eight here in the house."

"Price is kind of steep, isn't it?"

"I don't think so. You get what you pay for."

"I'll give you a buck seventy-five. Take it or leave it."

"I'll leave it. Good day." Mary Lee turned to go back in the house.

"Hold on, sister. I was just funnin' ya."

"It wasn't funny and I'm not your sister."

"Can I see the room?"

"Sure—"

"Give me the key, Mary Lee." Jake stepped forward and held out his hand. "I'll show it to him."

"Number four."

"Your wife's kinda touchy," the man said as he and Jake walked down the lane to the cabin.

Jake experienced a warm thrill on hearing the man's words and didn't correct him. He opened the cabin door and stepped back. The man looked inside, then nodded.

"Looks all right."

They walked back to where Mary Lee waited on the porch. The man gave her the two dollars and his name for the register. After he drove down to the cabin, Jake stepped up onto the porch.

"Why don't you sit down? Eli or I can do your legwork tonight."

"If I don't move around I'll get stiff."

"You can walk back and forth here on the porch."

"Who, besides Frank Pierce, would want to hurt me, Jake? I felt a hand on my ankle. I couldn't have slipped backward."

"I believe you. I don't know . . . unless . . ."

"Unless who? It wasn't Mr. Clawson. He told me to take care of myself. He wants to raise my baby, not get rid of it. It could have been the man who was here last night, getting even for what I did to Frank."

"You're not going to town or anywhere else by yourself anymore."

"You think someone is really out to hurt me?"

"I don't know, but we're not taking a chance."

Their eyes caught and held. Green into blue. Something in the way he was looking at her brought back the memory of the kiss they had shared. It had been soft and sweet. She had to admit that she hadn't been kissed like that ever.

"I'll get my tools and fix your door."

Later she was to wonder why she hadn't resented his possessive attitude toward her. *You're not going to town or anywhere else*

by yourself. He had said that as if he had
the right to tell her what to do.

She had known him only a few weeks
and had been alone with him not more than
four times. She had felt a connection with
him the first time she saw him. No, not the
first. He had hung in the back of her mind
since their meeting long ago as children.
And now being close to the tall, dark serious man he had grown up to be made her
tingle in places she had believed were im-
mune to sexual stimulation.

Chapter 14

"Eli is frying potatoes and making tea."

"Are you inviting me to supper?"

"It isn't much."

"It's plenty, but I can't keep on eating your grub."

"I need to pay you back for what you do."

"Why?"

"Just . . . because I do."

"You made me a birthday cake." He smiled. He was really quite handsome when he smiled.

"We all helped you eat it."

"Will you let me take you to Ruby's for supper one night?"

"I can't leave the court, Jake. You know that."

"You could leave for an hour if the cabins were rented. Eli would be here."

"What if Frank came back?"

"He's in jail. He's not coming back anytime soon. But I get the message." He stepped down off the porch. "I'll get my toolbox. I picked up two latches to put on your doors."

"Jake? What did you mean, you got the message?"

"I understand if you don't want to be seen with me."

"That isn't it! Dammit, why do you have to say such things?"

"Don't make a big thing of it."

"I'll go with you to Ruby's."

He shook his head impatiently. "No. I don't want you to go out of obligation."

"You can make me so mad that . . . that I want to kick you!" She glared at him.

"You goin' to eat with us, Jake?" Eli stuck his head out the door. "I cooked potatoes and onions. We've got leftover corn bread."

"No, thanks, Eli."

Mary Lee watched him walk down the lane to his truck. She had hurt his feelings. She would like to go with him to Ruby's, but she really didn't think that she could leave

Eli here alone at suppertime, when folks usually stopped for the night.

Her thoughts were cut off when a big black car turned into the drive and came to a stop in front of the house. Her hackles went up. What was *he* doing here? She stayed on the porch. Ocie got out, leaving the car door open. He wore a big black hat and a wide belt with a large silver buckle. A cigar stuck out the corner of his mouth.

"I heard that ya fell comin' out of the doctor's. You all right?"

"You sure have your ear to the ground. Does anything happen in this town that you don't know about?"

"Not when it concerns somethin' that's mine."

"I'm not yours, Mr. Clawson. I thought I had made that clear the last time you were here."

"That kid yo're carryin's got my blood. That makes you and that kid my kin."

"It does no such thing. I'd rather be kinfolk to a cross-eyed mule," she said staunchly. She saw Jake hurrying up the lane with his toolbox.

"I asked the doc if my grandkid was all right."

"You . . . you nosy old goat! You had no business talking to the doctor about me!"

"Yo're my business. I told ya so." He grinned. "I hear ya whacked Frank Pierce a good one. He had it comin'. I done set him straight. He'll not lay a hand on ya."

Jake set his tools on the porch and turned. He hadn't come face to face with Ocie since he got out of prison.

"You still here?"

"You plan to do something about it, you lyin' son of a bitch?" Jake stood with his hands on his hips, his feet spread. His green eyes were like daggers.

"Didn't prison teach ya any manners?"

"Yeah. It taught me to watch my back. It taught me that a greedy son of a bitch who has known me all my life will lie like a damn dog, send me to prison and take what little I have."

"Three of my men saw you brandin' my cattle."

"Three of your men lied and cost me two years of my life."

"The court thought otherwise."

"The goddamn court was in your pocket. You wanted me out of sight and took the word of a man who's had a grudge against me since I was ten years old. You wanted that little dab of land I'd filed on."

"Lon saw ya."

"Lon's a damn liar and you know it."

"Ya can have that patch of worthless land back. Won't do ya no good. Ya don't have nothin' to go on it." Ocie turned his attention to Mary Lee. His eyes pierced her from beneath beetled brows. "You sleepin' with him?"

"You . . . you nasty-minded old buzzard!" Mary Lee gasped. "It's none of your business what I do. Jake has been a good friend. Is it hard for you to understand that I can have a friend?"

"Ain't natural for a man to friend a good-lookin' woman less he's gettin' somethin'. But the sheriff's got more trust in the bastard than I do. Said him bein' here would keep some of the riffraff away."

"What do you mean by that?"

"Ya know as well as I do that yore mama draws trash like a fresh cow pile draws flies."

"And some of them work for you!"

"I'll fire any man who bothers ya."

"Does that go for Lon Delano too?" Jake asked.

"Damn right." Ocie looked long and hard at Jake. "I ain't carin' if yo're sleepin' with her. I ain't wantin' nothin' to happen to that kid. You see to it." He jabbed the air toward Jake with a forefinger.

"If you weren't so damn old, I'd bust you in the mouth!" Anger raised Jake's voice.

"Don't let that stop ya."

"He'd like to get you in trouble, Jake. Don't let him." Mary Lee stepped forward and put her hand on Jake's arm.

Her touch calmed him. He covered her hand with his.

"Yeah, I know."

"Good-bye, Mr. Clawson. Don't come back. There's nothing here to interest you."

Ocie went around the car and stood looking at the two of them over the top.

"Take care of her. Hear?"

When neither Mary Lee nor Jake responded, he got in the car and slammed the door. As he drove out, another car pulled in, making conversation with Jake impossible. Mary Lee greeted the man who got out, took his name and his money. Jake showed him to the cabin.

"One more to go," Mary Lee said when he returned.

Jake went into the house to look at the door where he was going to put the latches. Mary Lee left the porch and knocked on the door of number one. When she got no answer, she pushed it open to find her mother lying on the bed.

"Mama? Supper's ready. Come eat."

Dolly had sat up, but when she saw Mary Lee, she sank back down on the bed.

"You need to eat, Mama. You'll be sick."

"What'a you care?"

"I care."

"Get outta here. I'm expectin' company."

"Frank won't be coming. He's in jail."

"Frank's not the only man I know."

"Will you eat a plate of food if I bring it to you?"

"Naw. Ya'd probably put rat poison on it. Yancy's comin' and we're goin' uptown. Now get out and leave me alone."

Mary Lee backed out and closed the door. She had thought that she was beyond hurting. Jake was waiting and took her arm. She was grateful because her legs were shaky and her eyes teary. She kept her head down, hoping that he wouldn't see them.

"She's killing herself. She eats hardly anything."

"She's a grown woman, *mi bonita chica.*" My pretty girl.

"What did you call me?"

"Are you sure you want to know?" His eyes teased her.

"I'm sure."

"You won't get mad and slap me?"

"I won't promise."

"Then I'll not tell you."

"It was probably something like stubborn mule or stupid girl."

"You're close."

"Oh, you!"

"Eli's waiting for you to come eat."

"I think I'll sit on the porch. Tell him to go ahead."

"No. You've got to eat too. For . . . Gaston."

"Gaston?" She lifted a frowning face that changed in an instant to a smiling one. "Gaston?" she repeated. "How did you come up with that?"

"It's as good a name as any." He was pleased that he had made her smile.

"I wouldn't name a sick dog Gaston."

"Shame on you. The Gastons of the world will be hurt."

"Besides, who ever heard of a girl named Gaston?"

"How do you know it's going to be a girl? It could be twins."

"Twins? Wouldn't that be grand? A boy and a girl. I don't think I could handle two boys."

"Yeah. You could have Earl and Pearl, Marge and George or Bonnie and Clyde." The way his eyes roamed over her face as her laughter rang out sent her senses into pandemonium.

"Oh, Jake, you are the limit. How about Ed and Edna or Maude and Claude?"

"I like Mary and Jerry." They were standing beside the steps leading to the porch.

Mary Lee saw the teasing light in his green eyes. Deep inside, this rough man was sweet and caring; and because she was expecting a child, he was sincerely concerned with her welfare. They looked at each other for a long time before he said gruffly, "Go on in and eat."

"Jake . . ." She hesitated before she turned, her eyes probing his. "Thank you for being my friend."

He didn't know what to say. If he said anything, he was afraid that he'd put his foot in his mouth, so he said nothing, nodded and walked away.

Friend, my hind leg!

He remembered in vivid detail the day he'd helped her drag the mattress to the junk pile. Seeing her up close, after so many years, had been like a sledgehammer blow to his chest. It had sent his heart in a wild race. He had feared, as his vision focused on her, that she would hear the mad thumping of his stupid heart.

She hadn't been merely pretty. She had been spectacular. Her dark auburn windblown hair had been tumbling about her shoulders. Small nose, high cheekbones, tapered chin, and eyes the color of the New Mexico sky went perfectly with her small, almost delicately built body. The faded blue dress with the round neckline had shown her firm breasts and rounded belly where she carried her child. He had been so completely bowled over that later he couldn't even remember what he had said to her.

Jake shook his head. The fascination that he'd felt that day had increased tenfold. He was madly, crazily in love with her, and she considered him a . . . *friend*.

Mary Lee was jarred from a sound sleep when the alarm went off at five o'clock. She swung her legs off the bed and groaned. Tired and sore, she sat for a minute before attempting to stand. After running her fingers over her bruised knees, she carefully got to her feet, holding her hands to her back. The baby had been restless the first part of the night, and it had been late when she fell asleep.

Forcing herself to the bathroom, she washed, dressed and hurriedly combed her hair. This was the first morning that the Cross Roads Motor Court would be serving breakfast, and she wanted to look fresh.

Feeling as if she were being poked in the back with a pitchfork, she was now grateful that she and Eli had set the table the night before. Trudy would be arriving shortly, but Mary Lee wanted to have the biscuits made and the first pan ready for the oven by the time she got here.

It was six-thirty before the couple in number three came to breakfast. After that came the man who had thought her price was too high. He ate as if he were starved, and only grunted a good-bye when he left. The couple Eli had rented to had left in the night. After the guests had eaten, Jake knocked on the back door.

"Anything left?"

"Howdy, *amigo.* Come in." Trudy flounced around and put a clean plate and utensils on the table. "Got a pan of biscuits left. Thought I'd have to hide them from that one hog who ate everything in sight."

"He's the one who thought the price was steep," Mary Lee added. She had remained seated and looked at Jake for the first time.

"How do you feel this morning?" he asked.

"Oh, fine." She looked away from him. "Eli was in earlier. He was afraid that there wouldn't be anything left for him."

"I know. I saw him coming out of number five with an armload of things to be washed."

"Bless his sweet little heart," Trudy exclaimed. "If he was a little older, I'd marry him."

"You'd have a heck of a time getting him away from me." Mary Lee's dancing eyes went to Jake. He was looking at her with that expressionless face of his that always caused her to wonder what he was thinking.

His thoughts were about her. *Did the fall hurt her more than she let on? She stays seated while Trudy bustles from the table to the stove. It isn't like her to let someone take over her work. I've got to find out if she's all right before I leave to go out to Quitman's.*

Last night after Mary Lee had gone to bed, Jake had told Eli he would be gone for a while and went over to the Benders' to see if Trudy could spend the day. He told Ruby and Trudy about someone grabbing Mary Lee's foot, causing her to fall on the stairs.

"Somebody doesn't want her to have the baby and tried to send her headfirst down the stairs. I think I know who, but he's too much of a coward to do it himself. If I have to kill him to keep him from hurting her, I will."

"Lon Delano." Ruby spit out the name. "He expects to inherit the Circle C. It would put a crimp in his plans if Ocie takes a liking to Mary Lee's baby."

"Ocie has an interest, all right. He was out to the motor court tonight because he heard that she had fallen on the doctor's stairs. She doesn't want anything to do with him, but he doesn't pay much attention." Jake grinned. "She called him a nasty-minded old buzzard. I think he likes it when she talks back to him. He even told me to look out for her. He wants nothing to happen to her until that baby is born."

"Well, glory! That's somethin', isn't it? That old skinflint didn't have any use for his own son. Now he wants Mary Lee's."

"I have to say in defense of Ocie that Bobby wasn't a son a man could be proud of."

"I agree. He shoulda put his foot down on him when he was a tadpole. After Bobby got to be a frog, it was too late." The silence that followed was broken only by the squeaking floorboards beneath Ruby's rocking chair.

"Trudy can spend the day out at the court, that is . . . if she wants to. I can get along without her until the evening meal."

"I want to, Mama. It tears me up that someone wants to hurt Mary Lee."

"I'll pay you something, Trudy," Jake said. "But I don't want her to know about it. She'd have a cat-fit."

Trudy laughed. "She'd go up in blue smoke is what she'd do. You'll not pay me anything, Jake Ramero. Mary Lee was my staunch defender all the while we were in school. It's time I paid her back."

"You got feelin's for her, don't you, Jake?" Ruby asked bluntly.

"We're friends."

"Hockey!" Ruby snorted, then laughed when she saw the red come up under the tan on Jake's face. "You don't have anyone, Jake. Mary Lee has only that good-for-nothing mother. You need each other."

"I owe Scott Finley a favor for what he did for me a long time ago. That's all there is to it."

"All right, if you say so. But I'll bake a cake for the wedding."

Thinking about what Ruby had said caused a warmth to flood Jake's heart. He was jarred away from the pleasant thought when Trudy placed a dish of plum preserves beside his plate.

"Clean up that plate of biscuits, Jake. I've saved some back for Mrs. Finley."

Jake watched Mary Lee from the corner of his eye. When she turned to look back at the doorway, he slipped a half-dollar under the edge of his plate.

"More coffee, Jake?"

"Thanks, Trudy, but I've got to be going. Mary Lee, can I have a word with you on the porch?"

"Go on, boss lady," said Trudy. "I'll take care of things in here."

"I've no secrets from Trudy."

"Sure ya have," Trudy said briskly. "Better move around, or ya'll get stiffer than ya are."

Jake watched as Mary Lee put her hands on the table and eased herself out of the chair. He moved to the door and waited, then opened it so she could go out onto the porch.

"What did you want to talk about that you didn't want to say in front of Trudy?"

"Nothing. I wanted to see you move out of that chair. Where are you hurtin'?"

"My knees are sore and I'm stiff is all," she said crossly. "It's no more than I expected." She took a step back and leaned against the house. "I'll be all right by the end of the day."

Jake's eyes traveled from her face down

to her toes. His eyes lingered on her protruding abdomen.

"Gaston all right?" He grinned suddenly,
and it was so endearing she couldn't look
away.

"I've heard no complaints." It was a good
thing he hadn't asked about her back. It felt
as it were being jabbed with a hot poker.
Her belly felt so heavy this morning that she
could hardly resist the temptation to support it with her two hands.

"Good. I've got to go out to Quitman's. Eli
will keep an eye out and Trudy will be here."

"Trudy can't stay all day. I can't afford to
pay her."

"She'll stay as long as she can. I'll be
back before suppertime."

"Jake? I saw the money you put under
your plate." Her hands moved up his chest
and slipped the coin in his shirt pocket.

He tried to look shocked. "You don't miss
much, do you? I guess I'm not as slick as I
thought I was."

"I can't take the money."

"Then I can't eat here again—and I would
sure like to."

"You do so much for me."

"Nothing I don't want to do." Deciding

not to argue with her for now, he stepped close to her and put his fingers under her chin. "Don't deprive me of the pleasure."

"I feel I'm taking from you and giving nothing back."

"I've got a cheap place to live."

"For three dollars a week you can get a room in town."

"But the landlady wouldn't be as pretty as you." He took a step back. "Hey, now. I see you're getting your dander up. We're friends, remember?"

"Someone was trying to hurt me yesterday. Do you think they'll come out here?"

"I don't know, but I don't want to take any chances."

"Do Frank and his friends want Mama and the court that bad?"

"It may be someone who doesn't want your baby to be Ocie Clawson's heir."

"No! Why would he make my baby his heir when he disinherited his own son?" Her hands came up to grasp Jake's arms. "I'll not have my baby grow up under his thumb if Clawson promised to leave him the entire state of New Mexico!"

"I know that, but it wouldn't be a bad idea to accept his protection for now."

"I don't want to be obligated to him. He scares me, Jake."

"Don't worry about him. If the truth were known, he's just as scared of you as you are of him." Jake looked down the lane and saw Eli coming out of number five with an armload of towels. He watched him trot up to the porch.

"Mary Lee, they didn't even get under the sheets," he said with an expression of disgust on his young face. "Just on top. Do we have to change them?"

"I'm afraid so." Embarrassed to be holding this conversation in front of Jake, Mary Lee moved over to the porch post.

Jake remembered that when he was Eli's age, he was fascinated with anything to do with that mysterious thing called sex. Then one day he and Temple Clawson had a long talk while riding up the big hill to look for strays. Temple's explanation had been sketchy and on the rough side, but he'd gotten the message that man was pretty much the same as a bull or a stallion. That cravin' for a female, Temple had said, was God's way of keeping humans and animals on earth. He hadn't mentioned that it was the love a man had for a woman that made him different from a rutting stag, a bull or a stallion. His mother had explained that.

As Eli walked away, Jake called to him. "I'll be gone most of the day. Do you have . . . what I gave you?"

"Right here in the bib of my overalls."

"I've been meaning to talk to you about that, Jake." Mary Lee's face was creased with concern. "He showed me what you had given him and how he was to use them. He's just a boy. Don't encourage him to fight someone twice his size."

"He won't use them unless he's protecting himself or you. He's smart enough for that. I wanted him to have some kind of an equalizer in case someone jumped him."

"If you didn't think he'd need them you wouldn't have given them to him. I can tell that he's taken with you and will do whatever you say."

"How about you, *mi paloma*. Are you taken with me?"

"Darn it, Jake. I never learned to speak Spanish. I know that *'mi'* means 'my.' What are you calling me?"

His laughing eyes drank in her every expression. "It wasn't bad, *madrecita*."

" *'Madre'* means mother. I'm not your

mother, Jake." When she shot him an accusing glare, he flashed her a broad, guileless grin.

"Thank God for that."

"What was the other word?"

" *'Madrecita'* means 'little mother,' which you are or will be." He nudged her under the chin with his fist and walked away, still smiling.

Mary Lee hung on to the porch post and watched him. During the past few weeks he had become an important part of her life. She had come to depend on him. Now it occurred to her that she might be falling in love with him. And that simply wouldn't do. She couldn't afford a broken heart. It would distract her from her goal of getting this motor court free of debt so that she'd have a way of making a living for herself and her child.

When he reached his truck, he turned and waved. *How did he know that she was watching him?*

Her heart thumped painfully.

Chapter 15

It was a miserable day. Mary Lee was sure that she would not have been able to endure it if not for Trudy and Eli. They insisted on doing the washing and the cleaning of the cabins. They were like two thirteen-year-olds, fussing and teasing each other, making play of the work. Just watching and listening to them made Mary Lee feel old and tired.

Allowing herself to sit down often, she cooked beans and ham hocks and corn bread for the noon meal. In the middle of the morning she heard her mother in the bathroom throwing up. Later she tried to open the door, but it was locked.

After the noon meal and while the sheets and towels were drying on the line, she sent

Eli down to Mr. Santez's filling station to pay him the ten dollars she had borrowed for the mattress.

"You and Eli make a team," Mary Lee commented as she and Trudy cleaned up the noon dishes.

"I like him. He'll amount to somethin' someday."

"I'm going to do all I can to see to it that it happens." Mary Lee hung up a wet dish towel. "Thank you for helping Eli today. I didn't expect you to stay and clean cabins. I'll pay you extra for today."

"If you don't beat all," Trudy said. "You're so afraid that someone is goin' to do somethin' for you. You're not payin' me for this afternoon and that's that."

"I appreciate it . . . you know that. I'll not be so sore tomorrow."

"I think I'll stay tomorrow too. Stay and flirt with Jake," she added, and pinched Mary Lee on the rear. "Not that I stand a chance of getting him away from you."

"He isn't mine!"

"Oh, no? Have you told him that?"

The click of the bathroom door drew Mary Lee's attention.

"Mama's sick. She's been back to the bathroom."

"Do you think she's *sick* sick, or sick from a hangover?"

"She hasn't eaten anything today and very little yesterday."

"Why don't we fix a plate and I'll take it in through the bathroom door if she hasn't locked it."

"She'll say something mean to you. I'd better take it."

"She'll not get my goat. I know she's got a mean mouth. I'll put a few beans in a bowl. Butter a piece of corn bread, kiddo." Trudy placed a dish towel over a big platter and used it for a tray. "Do we dare take her a glass of milk?"

"Goodness, no! She'd throw it at you. Give her tea."

Carrying the food, Trudy followed Mary Lee to the bathroom, where she eased open the connecting door. Trudy breezed in. Dolly was lying on the bed.

"Hello, Mrs. Finley. I brought you something to eat."

Dark smudges circled Dolly's eyes, making them look like two burned holes in a blanket. Her cheeks were sunken, and her thin, dry hair looked as if she'd been in a whirlwind. She lifted herself up in bed and leaned on a bony elbow.

"Get out of my room, you ugly little bitch. Don't come back unless you bring me a drink of booze."

Out of sight in the bathroom, Mary Lee cringed, but Trudy didn't seem to take offense.

"Ah, shoot, Mrs. Finley. Ya don't mean that. My brother was a drunk like you are, and he'd throw up a drink if he took one on an empty stomach. It's just a waste of good whiskey. So you'd better eat before ya take another one. Eat the beans and corn bread, and by night you may be able to hold one down."

"I'm not a drunk!"

"You could have fooled me, Mrs. Finley. Seems to me like ya got the granddaddy of all hangovers or ya wouldn't be throwin' up your socks. I'll get a wet cloth so ya can wash your face and hands before you eat."

Trudy winked at Mary Lee when she went to the bathroom for the cloth, then hurried back to Dolly.

"If ya decide ya want more beans and

corn bread, Mrs. Finley, call out. Ya may want a glass of cold buttermilk."

The look Dolly gave Trudy made it plain that she wanted to kill her. "Where's Saint Mary Lee?"

"She's around here somewhere," Trudy answered matter-of-factly. "She may be in the washhouse. Want me to send her in?"

"Not less ya want me to throw this mess of beans at her."

Mary Lee was in the kitchen when Trudy left Dolly's room.

"I'm sorry, Trudy. She's mean when she's got a hangover."

"It's all right. She calmed down. She'd still be yellin' at you. I'll get us some tea. Then let's go sit on the porch for a while and watch the cars go by."

Mary Lee went to her bedroom and returned with her sewing basket and a handful of cloth.

"While we're sitting I'll hem a diaper or two."

"Why not use the sewing machine?"

"It's not here. I imagine Mama sold it for a couple of dollars. Several things are gone: Daddy's car for one, the mantel clock, the ice-cream freezer."

"Weeell . . . ," Trudy drew out the word, "for goodness' sakes. I'll take the material home and hem the diapers on our machine. Won't take but a jiffy."

Trudy led the way to the front porch, where it was shady this time of day. On the way through the living room Mary Lee picked up a cushion and dropped it into the old wooden rocking chair that had been on the porch for as long as she could remember. She dropped gratefully into the chair, fitted the cushion to the middle of her back and stretched her sore legs out in front of her. Trudy sat down on the top step and lifted her short arms up to hold her thick, curly, soft brown hair off her neck.

"Have you ever wondered where all the people are going when they pass by here?" Trudy leaned back against the porch post.

"Most of them are going on to Albuquerque or Gallup, but some of them have bigger dreams and are headed for the promised land of California."

"Have you ever wanted to go there?"

"Sure. I'd like to see it."

"It takes guts to pull out from all you know and resettle someplace else. I guess you know. You did it once."

"Yeah. I know now that I jumped out of the frying pan and into the fire."

"That bad, huh?"

"For a week or two it was all right. When the money started to run out, all Bobby did was whine. I realized then that I had taken a grown man to raise."

Trudy glanced at her friend, then back at the highway. "Look at that car? They've got everything they own in it and on top of it. Do you think they'll make it all the way to California?"

"They'll make it. They've come this far. Bet they're Okies."

"The April dust storm destroyed millions of dollars' worth of wheat crops, forcing people to leave their farms. I heard on the radio that dust piled up inside houses. Businesses and schools closed, traffic stopped and even the birds refused to fly. We're lucky that we just got a tiny bit of it here."

"I was in Tulsa. The sky was dark with dust. Everyone who was outside wore a handkerchief over their mouth and nose."

"Did you love Bobby?" Trudy asked bluntly, and turned her large brown eyes toward her friend.

"No. But I was fond of him at . . . first. I

felt sorry for him. He told me how awful it was growing up with a father who hated him. He told me stories about how cruelly he was treated when he was young. He was whipped every day until he got old enough to defend himself. He wanted so desperately to leave Cross Roads and get away from his father. I was tired of living in the same town with a mother who embarrassed me. Instead of staying and facing our problems, we ran."

"When did you stop . . . being fond of him?"

"When I caught him in lie after lie. When he didn't want to do anything but play cards and gamble at the pool halls while I worked nine hours a day six days a week, when he stole the money I was saving for the rent."

"Ah . . . Mary Lee . . ."

"But I don't regret a minute of it. I got the baby out of it. It's my baby. Bobby wouldn't have wanted it if he had lived. It would have taken my attention away from him."

"Will you tell the baby about its father?"

"I don't know. I'll have to decide that when the time comes."

Eli came back and sat down on the steps

beside Trudy and dug a paper out of his pocket and gave it to Mary Lee.

"Mr. Santez sent you a receipt and said you didn't have to be in a hurry to pay him back." Eli spoke to Trudy. "Are the sheets dry, short stuff?"

"You think you're so smart because you're taller than me. Didn't you ever hear that good things come in small packages?"

"Seems like I heard that somers, but I thought it was just hot air."

"You're nothin' but a brat." Trudy yanked the old straw hat off his head and slammed it down on hers.

"Gimme my hat!"

"Just hold your horses. Here comes someone."

They both watched the motorcycle with a sidecar attached come up the drive from the highway. The rider let the machine slowly roll to within a short distance of the porch, then cut off the engine. He sat for a moment fiddling with the controls, then swung his leg over and stood.

"Howdy."

"Howdy," Eli said.

"This the Cross Roads Motor Court?"

"It's what the sign says."

"Thank Jesus, Joseph and Mary. My rear is numb from sittin' on that seat."

The man pulled his goggles up over the top of his helmet, unbuckled the strap and yanked it off. The three on the porch gaped at him. His hair resembled a haystack. He was so homely, he was almost pitiful—pug nose, wide mouth and practically no chin. Dirt and whiskers covered his face. He stepped around the machine on short, bowed legs. His pant legs were tucked into scrubby cowboy boots.

"Deke Bales." He said his name as if he expected them to know who he was.

"Yeah." Eli stood. "You're Jake's friend. He said you'd be comin'."

"Got here a day or two sooner than I expected. Traveled some at night when it was cooler."

"Eli Stacy." Eli held out his hand. "This little squirt here is Trudy Bender and on the porch, Mrs. Clawson."

Deke shook Eli's hand, then offered his hand to Trudy. "Howdy, little squirt."

Trudy, for once, was speechless. She sat with her mouth clamped tightly shut while Deke stepped to the porch to greet Mary Lee. When Mary Lee looked into his large, friendly brown eyes with long, thick lashes, the rest of his face faded into the background.

"Jake said in his letter that a young lady ran the court. Guess you're it, huh?"

"I guess so. Welcome, Mr. Bales."

"Call me Deke, darlin'."

He was like a friendly puppy. She liked him immediately.

Mary Lee couldn't help thinking that Deke was the opposite of Jake in size and personality. Jake was big, rugged and quiet. She suspected that this little man never met a stranger. She remembered Jake saying they had met while working on a ranch in Oklahoma and that Deke was a first-class mechanic.

"Jake went out to a ranch to work with some horses," Eli explained. "He'll be back by suppertime. Would you like a drink of water, Mr. Bales?"

"Deke, son. Just plain, old, mud-ugly Deke."

"You can say that again," Trudy murmured.

"Did you say somethin', darlin'? Ya got to speak up. I been on that dang-blasted machine three days, and it'll be a while before my ears stop ringin'."

Trudy jumped to her feet and shoved Eli's hat into his hands. "I'll see if the sheets are dry." She hurried around the house.

"Sure is pretty here in New Mexico. We've 'bout forgot what green is, back in Oklahoma." Deke stretched and ran short stubby fingers through his damp hair.

"What part of Oklahoma are you from?" Eli asked.

"Around Sayre and Elk City. The dust was bad there, but not as bad as in the panhandle."

"Come on 'round to the pump, wash off and get a drink of the best water 'round here."

"Believe I will. I've got an acre of dust in my throat."

Mary Lee heard Eli proudly explaining to the little man who followed him around the house that he worked here. She was pleased at the way Eli had met Jake's friend, although she was afraid that the boy had hurt Trudy by calling her a little squirt. She got out of the chair, eased down the three steps of the porch and went around to where Trudy was taking the wash off the line.

"It doesn't take long for them to dry on a day like this." She reached for the clothespins. "Here, let me take them down and you hold the basket."

"I'm tall enough to reach the line, Mary Lee." There was a bite in Trudy's tone of voice.

"Uh-oh. Eli hurt your feelings, didn't he? I'm sorry, Trudy. Don't forget that he's only thirteen. He was trying to be funny and impress Jake's friend."

"He was funny, all right." She poked the sheets down into the bushel basket. "The towels will be dry by the time I get the beds made."

Mary Lee protested. "Eli and I can make the beds."

"Me and the little squirt will make the beds." Eli and Deke came up behind them. Eli bent and picked up the basket.

Trudy turned on the boy. "If you call me that again, Eli Stacy, I'll . . . I'll knock your block off!"

"Whoa! Why're ya mad? I . . . was just teasin'."

"I am sick and tired of that kind of . . .

teasing! I'm short. I know that I'm short, and there's nothing I can do about it except hit you in the mouth if you mention it again!"

"Yeah, why're ya mad at the boy, darlin'?" Deke said. "I'm short, case ya haven't noticed. Five foot two. All my life folks have called me 'little shrimp,' 'half-pint,' 'little weasel' 'n' other things. 'Squirt' sounds pretty good next to 'little horse apple' or 'little sh—' ah . . . 'hockey.'" He glanced quickly at Mary Lee, but her anxious eyes were on the girl.

"You . . . stay out of this, Mr. Whatever-your-name-is. And I'm not your *darlin'*."

"Name's Deke, *sugarfoot*."

"Yeah, I know, just plain, old, mud-ugly Deke. Come on, junior," Trudy said to Eli. "Let's make the beds. I've got to be gettin' home."

Mary Lee was dumbfounded. She'd never seen her friend so angry, so sarcastic. Eli looked stricken.

"Let me give ya a hand," Deke said. "I need to work the kinks outta my back. How many beds ya gotta make, darlin'?"

"Four!" Trudy shouted. "And I don't need help from a motorcycle cowboy!"

"Ya think I don't know how to make a bed? Darlin', my mama was a spit-and-polish housekeeper. You could eat off the floor at our house if the table was full. I started makin' my bed the day I crawled out of the cradle."

"When was that? The day you turned thirty?"

"I'm not thirty quite yet, darlin'. I lack a year or two. Bet yo're not much more'n sixteen."

"And you're full of bullshi—"

"Ach, ach, ach," he chided. "Yore mouth's too pretty to be spittin' out nasty words."

Trudy grabbed two sheets out of the basket and took off toward number five as fast as her legs would carry her.

"Wait up, sugar, and I'll help ya." Deke looked at Mary Lee and winked. "I don't think she likes me, but I'll change her mind." He hurried to catch up with Trudy and followed her into the cabin.

"Gee, I'm sorry I made her mad at me." Eli looked as if he had lost his last friend in the world. Mary Lee put her arm around him.

"She'll get over it."

"I've called her that lots of times 'n' she didn't get mad."

"I think it was because you said it in front of Jake's friend."

"She'll never like me again!"

"Of course she will. She was flustered. It was a shock to her to meet a grown man just inches taller than she is, one who didn't look at her like she was . . . different."

"I thought he was funny-lookin' at first. But after talkin' to him, I forgot about it, like I don't think of Trudy as being short anymore."

With Eli carrying the heavy basket, they went into one of the cabins. Mary Lee spread the sheet on the bed and tucked it in on one side. She and Eli worked together until the bed was made and the clean slips on the pillows. As they were finishing, Trudy came in and took more sheets from the basket. She looked at Mary Lee's worried face, winked, and dashed out the door.

Mary Lee's shoulders slumped in relief.

By the time the cabins were ready for occupancy, Trudy was in a better frame of mind. She put her arms around Eli and whispered in his ear.

"Why is she huggin' that kid for?" Deke complained. "I was the one who helped her make the beds."

"She's got a soft heart. I knew that she wouldn't stay mad for long." Mary Lee's ears, attuned to the rattle of Jake's truck, heard it turn into the lane. "Here's Jake. He'll be surprised to see you."

Jake drove past the motorcycle and stopped. The smile on his face was beautiful to see as he rounded the truck to meet his friend.

"You got here early. I wasn't expecting you for a couple of days."

"Howdy, big man." Deke sprang forward to shake Jake's hand, then took off his hat and slammed it into his arm. The two men clasped hands and shoved each other affectionately in their enjoyment.

Mary Lee was happy for Jake. Deke seemed to be genuinely fond of him. Eli and Trudy stood watching, both with grins on their faces.

Jake clamped a hand down on Deke's shoulder and grinned at Mary Lee.

"Has he been givin' you any trouble?"

"Not a bit."

"Yes, he has," Trudy said staunchly.

"What's he done? I'll clean his clock."

"He's mouthy."

"I should have warned you about that."

"Now that you're here, Jake, I'll go on home."

"Wait until I unload the truck and I'll give you a ride."

"You don't need to do that. I'll walk."

"How about me givin' ya a ride, sugarfoot? I'll throw this junk out of the sidecar." He tossed a couple of bundles in Jake's truck.

"All right, bigmouth. I've always wanted to ride in one of those thingamajigs." Trudy climbed into the sidecar and perched on a roll of blankets. "Fire this thing up, short stuff, and let's get goin'."

Deke threw his hat on the porch and, with a wide, pleased grin on his face, climbed on the cycle and stomped on the starter. The machine roared to life.

"Bye, Mary Lee. See you in the morning," Trudy yelled. She waved, then grabbed the sides of the car as the cycle sped down the lane and onto the highway.

"Well, now, don't that beat all?" Eli took off his hat and scratched his head. "Little bit ago she was about to bite his head off."

"There's no understanding women, Eli." Jake spoke to the boy, but his eyes were on

Mary Lee's smiling face. "Are you feelin' all right?"

"Oh, yes."

"Not sore?"

"A little. I can't believe that Trudy would go off with him on that thing."

"Don't worry. Deke is one of the most honorable men I've ever known. He'll see that she gets home or die trying. I'd stake my life on it."

"I like him, Jake. I really do. He sure livens up the place."

Chapter 16

Jake noted how slowly she moved as she bent to pick up her sewing basket from the floor of the porch. She lifted her eyelids, and the sadness in her eyes pulled him. He looked away from her and silently swore to make the man who tried to throw her down the steps sorry he even thought about laying a hand on her. Sooner or later, he would find out who the rat was.

"Is Deke going to stay?" Mary Lee asked, settling into the chair and pulling her skirt down over her skinned legs.

"For a while. We'll set up his cot in my room, if it's all right with you."

"Why wouldn't it be? You paid for your room."

"Trudy didn't like him at first." Eli grinned.

"Deke's got a way with him. He sweet-
talked her, and before I knew it, he was
helpin' her make beds. They were laughin'
and talkin' and havin' a high old time."

"He's got a soft spot for the ladies. I saw
him tie into a man twice his size for being
disrespectful to one. Don't let his size fool
you. He's a tough little son of a gun. When
he gets riled, he'll tackle anything."

"I hope Trudy isn't smitten with him."
Mary Lee was terribly aware that Jake was
so close that she could almost count his
long, thick eyelashes.

"Why?" He stood leaning toward her, one
foot on the porch, his forearm on his thigh.
His narrowed eyes were locked with hers.

"Not many men . . . have paid attention
to her. She might fall for him and be heartbroken when he leaves."

"Maybe he'll fall for her."

"He won't settle here. He'd take her
away."

Jake chuckled and said softly, "Little wor-
ryin' mother."

"Why do you say that?"

"'Cause it's what you are." He quirked a
dark brow, smiled, and dragged his eyes
away from her. "Come give me a hand, Eli."

He took a ten-pound pail of lard from the back of the truck and handed it to the boy, then shoved a paper sack into his arms. He hoisted a fifty-pound sack of flour to his shoulder and headed for the porch.

"You'd better come in and tell us where to put this."

"What in the world?" Mary Lee stood. "Where did all this come from?"

Jake grinned at her. "You won't believe this . . . but I found this alongside the road when I left Quitman's to come to town."

"You're right. I don't believe it."

"Open the door."

"Jake?"

Jake followed Eli into the kitchen. "Where do you want this?"

"I don't have the money to pay for that, and I don't have a tin big enough to put it in."

"There's a big tin with a good tight lid out in the washhouse." Eli set the bucket and the sack on the table. "I'll get it."

Mary Lee waited until the boy went out the door before she spoke.

"Didn't you hear me, Jake? I don't have money to pay for this. I was going to buy just a small amount at a time."

Jake eased the sack off his shoulder and onto the floor.

"I heard you, Mary Lee. I want to eat breakfast here and I want to pay more for my room. You've got this thing about paying me back for being around should you come up against something you can't handle. You won't take my money. I've got pride too. Don't be giving me any trouble over this." His hands gripped her shoulders and moved her back into a chair. "Sit down and stop worrying. You look worn out."

"All of this"—she waved her hand—"is too much."

"It's just flour, lard, baking powder and . . . a few things. I tried to remember what my mother used to make biscuits. She didn't make them often. She usually made tortillas."

"Why are you doin' this, Jake? You don't owe me anything." Mary Lee's eyes were swimming in tears.

Jake squatted down beside her. He took the red bandanna she had given him for his birthday from around his neck and gently wiped her tears.

"Ah . . . *querida*! Don't cry."

"I've never cried much . . . until lately,

that is. It just makes me so . . . mad to blubber like a baby when something upsets
me."

"It could be Gaston's fault," he said seriously with a teasing glint in his eyes.

"Poor little Gaston gets blamed for everything."

"Yeah, he's a little rascal, all right."

She smiled, and the tension in his face
was replaced by an engaging grin. They
gazed at each other, unmindful of where
they were. His hand sought hers, and without a trace of reluctance she grasped it and
laced her fingers with his.

"I don't want you to be upset about this."

"I don't understand why you're . . . why
you did it."

"Don't try to understand, *madrecita*.
You've had some pretty hard knocks lately."
He gently wiped the tears from her cheeks.

"Thank you," she whispered.

"You're very welcome. Better now?"

"I think so."

Dolly's sarcastic voice coming from the
doorway shattered the moment.

"Now, ain't this sweet? Ya proposin' to
her, jailbird?"

Jake stood. "No, ma'am."

"Shit fire! I thought maybe ya'd marry her and get her outta here."

Mary Lee got shakily to her feet. "Feeling better, Mama?"

"'Feelin' better, Mama?'" Dolly mimicked. "What the hell do you care? And what's a jailbird doin' in *my* house?"

Mary Lee straightened her shoulders, but before she could answer, Eli came in carrying the large tin.

"I found it and it's . . ." He struggled for words when he saw Dolly.

She looked at him as if he were a worm crawling out of her sandwich.

"Why's that little bastard here after I told ya to get rid of him? Why're ya wantin' him around for? Frank said ya was screwin' the kid. Ya screwin' the jailbird too?"

"Hush that filthy talk!" Anger made Mary Lee's voice shrill and drove her to take a step toward her mother. Jake's hand on her arm held her back. "You're . . . rotten and mean!" she yelled. "You'll do and say anything to hurt me. You don't care about anyone but yourself."

"Damn right! Scott cared till ya came along. Ya ruined everythin'. I didn't want ya. I told and told Scott I didn't want a kid. He said he'd kill me if I got rid of ya. I shoulda done it anyhow. That righteous shithead didn't have the guts to step on a cockroach."

"Don't you dare talk about Daddy like that!" Mary Lee shouted.

"Eli and I will go," Jake spoke softly, close to her ear. "Will you be all right?"

She nodded, her eyes on her mother's ravaged face.

"I'll be back and empty the flour in the tin."

Mary Lee nodded again and watched her mother take the ice pick from the holder beside the icebox and lift the lid to chip the ice. She spoke as soon as she heard the closing of the screen door.

"I don't know why you talk so nasty and say things that you know are mean just to hurt and humiliate me. You're not well, but that's no excuse. I've had about all of your meanness I can take. And if it doesn't stop you're going to have to find another place to live."

Dolly's cold, hate-filled eyes stared at her. "Ya . . . bitch. Ya think ya can run me outta my own house?"

"I don't want to. I've tried to get along

with you, but you just won't meet me halfway. You insulted Trudy, who came here to help. You treat Eli like dirt. He is just a boy without a home who is working for his keep. What has Jake done to you to make you take your spite out on him?"

"How about Frank and Pearl? Ya run 'em off."

"They were leeches, living off you."

"Ah . . . shit. Ain't no need to argue with ya 'cause ya know everything fit to be known. But I got news for ya, Miss Twitchy Twat, ya can't throw me out. Frank said that it's in Scott's will that I can stay here long as I live—and that's goin' to be a long time. 'Cause I'm goin' to stay alive as long as I can just to give ya as much hell as ya've given me."

"I can move you into the cabin with your friend, Frank."

"Just try it, and I'll burn the place down." Dolly tossed the threat over her shoulder as she left the room. The slamming of the bedroom door shook the house. Mary Lee sank down in the kitchen chair. She was too shaken to weep.

She sat at the table until she heard a car drive in. Wiping her face on the skirt of her dress, she picked up the registry book and went out onto the porch. Eli was talking to the couple in the car. After a few minutes, he stepped back and the car drove out onto the highway.

Eli came to the porch with a disgusted look on his face. "I don't know what's wrong with folks. They wanted to stay until midnight for a dollar. I told them two dollars and breakfast for the night."

"I'm glad you did. We don't want or need that kind."

"I didn't like their looks. They kind of reminded me of that couple that went around the country robbin' and killin'."

"Bonnie and Clyde Barrow? We don't have to worry about them anymore. Has Deke come back?"

"Little while ago. He came in the back way and parked down behind Jake's cabin." Eli sat down on the edge of the porch. "Jake and Deke are goin' uptown to eat. Jake said he'd take care of that flour when he gets back and that yo're not to lift that bucket of lard."

"He's getting pretty bossy," Mary Lee said irritably. "I've got to figure out a way to pay him for the things he bought. It would

take him a year to eat all the biscuits that
flour and lard would make. He'll not be here
that long." She glanced at Eli and saw the
set look on his young face. "You can understand, can't you, Eli?"

"No, ma'am."

"Why not?"

"It's between you and Jake."

"I'm embarrassed that he bought groceries. Please understand . . . ," she pleaded,
and fought to keep the tears from her eyes.

"Is it because he was in prison?"

"No! It's because . . . because . . ." Her
voice trailed.

*It's because I'm in love with him. I don't
want him feeling sorry for me . . . I want him
to love me—but after he heard what Mama
said, all he'll feel for me is pity! Oh, Lord! I'll
never be able to look him in the eye again.*

"You . . . like him, don't ya?"

"Of course I like him."

Before she could reply, two ladies in a
late-model car drove in. Eli showed them
the cabin. They came back, laughing and
joking with the boy, to sign the register. He
was grinning. Mary Lee couldn't help but
compare this Eli with the shy, tired young-

ster she had found in the washhouse a few weeks earlier.

It was an unusual evening.

The available rooms in the motor court were all rented within an hour. Before they could turn off the Vacancy sign, another car drove in off the highway. Eli directed the disappointed travelers to the hotel in town.

As soon as Jake's truck drove in, Mary Lee said good night to Eli and went through the dark house to her room, telling herself that she would lie down for a while, then go to the kitchen and set the table for the morning meal. After latching the doors, she eased down onto the bed. It felt so good to lie down that she almost groaned with the relief of it. She lay for a while listening for a sound to come from her mother's room, then decided that Dolly must have gone out the back door while she was on the porch.

Tears rolled from the corners of her eyes as her mother's words played over in her head. How could a mother hate her child? Since she was old enough to remember, her daddy had made excuses for her mother's cold treatment. He had known that she hadn't wanted the baby. *He* had loved his daughter and had tried to make up for the lack of her mother's love.

Daddy, why did you have to go and leave me?

Fatigue overcame her despair. She slept, then wakened suddenly. It was dark in the room. Someone was in the kitchen. She felt her way to the door, but Jake's voice stopped her before she opened it.

"Shhh . . . be quiet. Don't wake her. She needs all the rest she can get."

"When is her baby due?" She recognized Deke's voice.

"In a couple of months." Jake answered without a moment of hesitation. "It's already moving around in there pretty good."

Mary Lee put her hands to her cheeks. It was strange hearing her pregnancy discussed by these men. Strange but sweet.

"Where can we put this bucket of lard so it'll be easy for her to get to?"

"Leave it there," Eli whispered. "Trudy will know what to do with it."

"Hey, Jake. Does she want to keep this cloth on the table?"

"If it's clean. She wants things to be nice. Put three plates on each side and one on each end. Here's the forks and knives. Spoons are in the holder."

"Trudy said she'd be here by five-thirty." Deke had to be standing close to the door for Mary Lee to hear his loud whisper.

"You and Trudy must have got along like a house on fire," Jake teased.

"She can dish it out. She told me how the cow ate the cabbage right off."

"That's Trudy. Cute as a button too."

"Not bad. I've not had a gal look up at me since I was in the fourth grade. And she was in first."

"Mary Lee don't want Trudy to get to likin' you too much." Eli's voice was too loud to suit Jake, and he shushed him.

"Why not?" Deke was still by the door.

"'Cause she don't want her to get her heart broke." Eli spoke softly this time.

"Well, doggie. I never thought of myself as a heartbreaker." Deke sounded pleased.

Mary Lee groaned. *Does Eli tell everything he knows?*

"Are we through in here, Eli? If her mother comes back and finds us here, she'll raise a ruckus that will be heard a mile away."

"The old witch is out in number one."

"By herself?"

"Naw, she's got that man with her who was here with Frank the night Mary Lee 'bout tore his pecker off."

"Tore his pecker off? Hell's bells! What's this about?" Deke asked.

"Mary Lee had this plate in her hand and when he pulled it out to pee—"

"It's a long story," Jake interrupted. "We'll tell you later. Are we finished in here, Eli? If there's nothing else to do, turn off the light."

"Trudy will help her in the morning."

Mary Lee leaned her forehead against the door when she heard them leave the porch. She wished that her daddy could have known Jake and Eli. She swallowed the hard lump in her throat. They were very dear to her.

Would she be able to bear it when they left her?

Chapter 17

It was midmorning when Ocie Clawson drove into town and parked his car on a side street. He sat for a minute and watched a motorcycle with a sidecar go by and envied the man straddling the machine. If he didn't have the responsibility of the ranch, he'd be tempted to get on one of those things and ride down the highway to the faraway places he'd only heard about.

Heaving a sigh, he looked around, then got out of the car and turned into the alley behind the row of buildings on Main Street. He went up the back stairs to the second floor of the Bison Theater building, then paused before pushing open the door with gold lettering on the glass. WILLIAM MILLER AND SON, ATTORNEYS.

"Hello, Mr. Clawson." He was greeted by the woman behind the desk. She was his age or older and had two double chins. Her plump face was framed with soft brown hair, scalloped and held in place with long bobby pins. "It's been a while since we've seen you."

"Hello, Miss Dryden. Is Bill in?"

"Junior or Senior?"

"Senior."

"He was getting ready to go home for lunch—"

"Who's out there, Madge?"

The woman shook her head. "Nothing gets by that man. It's Mr. Clawson," she called.

"Did he come to see you or me?"

Madge rolled her eyes and jerked her head toward the back office.

"You, Bill," Ocie said, as he came through the door.

"Good. I'm not wanting to lose Madge to some clabberhead wanting a good cook and a warm bed. When I'm gone, Junior can get one of those flapper gals to sit out front. Sit down, Ocie. How've ya been?"

"Fair to middlin', Bill. You?"

"Not getting any younger. Hell, I'll be eighty my next birthday. It's a damn good thing the body goes downhill before the mind or I'd be a bloomin' idiot." His laugh was dry as corn shucks.

"Time waits for no man, Bill. That's why I'm here. I want to make out a will."

"A will, huh?"

"Yeah. You handled my father's will. He thought a great deal of you."

"Temple Clawson was one of the best friends I ever had. I would have trusted him with my life."

"He felt the same about you."

"In our younger days we even liked the same girls." A devilish glint came into the old man's eyes. "He was a good-lookin' son of a gun. I didn't have a chance after they got a look at him." He began to laugh, remembering. "There was this girl we both liked, but she had her eye on Temple. I had to think of something to get her attention, so I told her that Temple had fits about once a month. She dropped him like a hot rock. Hee, hee, hee. He was madder than a pissed-on snake when he found out. Later, he wished that I had got her. After she married, she turned to fat, and I mean fat . . . three hundred pounds."

Ocie thought about his sweet and gentle mother, so different from the sour, nagging woman he had married. His pa had been crushed when he lost her.

"About the will: I want to be sure the ranch is left to the grandchild Bobby's wife is carrying."

"Don't you think you should wait until the child is born?"

"No. I want to get things settled. If something happens to the kid, I want everything to go to Mary Lee. She's a Clawson by marriage. It's the best I can do to see that the ranch stays in the family."

"It's what Temple wanted."

"I know that. He drummed it in my head since I was old enough to stand to pee. I don't want anyone to know about the will or what's in it. Especially the girl."

"We don't blab what goes on in this office. You should know that."

"Not intentionally. Sometimes thin's slip out."

His father's old friend scowled, then said, "I heard that your daughter-in-law fell on the steps coming down from Doc Morris's."

"She claims someone grabbed her foot. Hell, I don't know if she was imaginin' it or not."

"Pregnant women get fanciful notions."

"She's working herself to death at that motor court."

"Dolly Finley is a sorry excuse for a woman if I ever saw one."

"She was even when Scott Finley married her. She was trash then."

"Her folks were hardworking. Whatever happened to them?"

"Killed in a flash flood over near Albuquerque. If she had other kin, I've never heard of them."

"Now, let me get this straight, Ocie. You want to leave Bobby's child everything. And should something happen to the child, to the mother. Is that how you want it?"

"Exactly."

"How about Lon?"

"How about him? He's a distant relative I signed on to work. He hasn't done all that good a job lately. Takin' a little too much on himself. If I could find a good man to take his place, I'd fire him."

"How about Jake Ramero? Gus Quitman

thinks he's top-notch. Swears he's the best with horses he's ever known."

"He's a jailbird, for God's sake." Ocie moved restlessly in his chair.

"Some say Lon railroaded him."

"The judge didn't think so."

"Fiddle-fart, Ocie. You and I both know how that goes. The judge had no choice with you up there siding with Lon. The boy's took what was handed out to him and did his time. He's back now and folks should give him a chance."

When Ocie refused to be drawn into a conversation about Jake Ramero, Bill changed the subject.

"I'll have Junior draw up the will. Come back in a day or two and sign it."

"Will he and Madge keep their mouths shut?"

"I'd stake my life on it."

Ocie got up to leave. "It's been good seein' ya, Bill."

"Hell, boy, it's been good seein' you. Your pa thought a heap of ya, know that?"

"I know that, Bill. We were both disappointed in Bobby, but that's all water under the bridge now. We play the cards dealt to us."

"Come in and chat—anytime."

Ocie had no more than closed the door to the outer office when William Junior opened the connecting door and came into his father's office.

"Did you hear that, Junior?"

"I heard. What're you going to do?"

"Make out the will just as he wants it."

"It won't be worth the paper it's written on."

"He won't know that, but it will ease his mind."

The old lawyer reached for his cane, got shakily out of his chair and stomped out the door.

Sheriff Pleggenkuhle came around the house to where Mary Lee and Trudy were hanging the morning wash on the line.

"Morning, ladies." He tipped his hat.

Mary Lee answered his greeting with a smile and a nod.

"And a howdy to you, Sheriff," Trudy said cheerfully. "Did you come out to arrest me for spitting my chewing gum on the sidewalk?"

"I've been looking for the culprit who did

that. So you're the one, huh?" A smile spread across his sunbaked face.

"Guilty. You gonna lock me up?"

"My jail is full right now. Jake around?"

"He and his friend went out to the Quitman ranch. Is something wrong?" Mary Lee asked anxiously.

"Not exactly. I wanted to talk to him for a little bit."

"About the other night?"

"Partly, I guess. I'm going to let Frank out in a few days. He's doin' some mouthin' off. I want to warn Jake to keep his nose clean."

"Frank won't come back here, will he?"

"Says he will unless you're willing to give him back the hundred dollars he paid for a month's rent. He claims his rent is paid up and he doesn't have anyplace else to go."

"A hundred dollars? I can't, and wouldn't if I could, give him a hundred dollars! He didn't pay rent. Mama is just saying that he did so she'll have someone to bring her whiskey," Mary Lee said heatedly.

"He said he paid Mrs. Finley. She swears that he did. She and Yancy Hummer were down at the jail talking to him last night."

"She wants him to come back here?" Mary Lee's shoulders slumped.

"Didn't she tell you that they're going to get married?"

"Married? Oh . . . Lord! Oh, good grief!" As soon as she could breathe easier, she said, "Why? When?"

"The when, I don't know. The why is so that he can live here with her. They tell me that it's in Scott's will, that she can live here as long as she wants, and as her husband, Frank figures that he can live here too. It might be a good idea to talk to Sidney Morales. He's your lawyer, isn't he?"

It took all the strength that Mary Lee could muster to hold herself together and not break down and cry in front of the sheriff. She turned away from him and looked off down the highway. Two cars went by while she batted her eyes furiously. When she turned back, her eyes were dry and her shoulders straight.

"Thank you for telling me, Sheriff. When will Frank be out of jail?"

"The judge said I must let him out in two days. He thinks that he has suffered enough for what he did, and sees no need to punish him further."

"I'm not a bit sorry I hit him!"

The sheriff chuckled. "I didn't think so."

"He'll do everything he can to ruin things here." Mary's disappointment and anguish were turning to anger. "I'm just barely hanging on as it is. If I don't pay what's owed the bank by October first, the bank will take over."

"That might be the best thing. The bank would put them both out."

"And me. Do you think I want to be out on the street with a new baby?" she snarled. "Maybe you think I could go to the hobo camp and eat at the soup kitchen. My daddy left this place to me, and I'm stayin' right here and payin' off the loan money that Mama squandered." After the outburst, Mary Lee's heart pounded with indignation.

"If Frank gives you any trouble, call me."

"What good will that do?" Trudy picked up the empty clothes basket. "The damage will be done."

"It's the best I can do. Believe me, if I had my way, I'd run him and a few others out of town on a rail. My job is to arrest them. The judge does the sentencing."

"I appreciate you coming by, Sheriff. I'll tell Jake what you said."

"You've got someone else on your side who's pretty powerful around here."

"Who is that? Mr. Santez? He was a good friend to my father."

"Ocie Clawson. He told Frank that if he touched you, he'd tear his head off. And knowin' Ocie, he'd do it."

"Ocie Clawson has absolutely no claim on me because I was once married to his son. I want to make that perfectly clear."

"That's between you and Ocie. I'm just telling you what he said. Jake was in town last night with that little fellow who rode in on a motorcycle. Is he staying here?"

Trudy rolled her eyes. "I suppose you know that he gave me a ride home on that cycle."

The sheriff grinned. "I didn't know that, Trudy. Thanks for tellin' me. I'll go right down and tell Lloyd. He'll want to put it in the paper."

"If you do, I'll never speak to you again!"

"Sure you would." The sheriff teased the girl whose head hardly reached his armpit. "You'd even vote for me."

"His name is Deke Bales and he's staying here for a while with Jake." Mary Lee, becoming more impatient, moved the bag of clothespins down the line.

"Where's he from?"

"Oklahoma."

"Did Jake say where he knew him?"

"Why the questions?" Trudy asked. "Isn't Jake allowed to have friends?"

"If he served time in prison, I want to know if there is a convicted robber, killer, or bootlegger in our town. Did he meet him there?"

"He met him while he was working in Oklahoma about five years ago. They've kept in touch. If you want to know more about him come back around suppertime." Mary Lee tried to conceal her irritation.

"I may do that. Good day, ladies." Sheriff Pleggenkuhle tipped his hat and went back to his car.

"Now, don't that beat all? I just never imagined that Mrs. Finley would do somethin' so foolish." Trudy clicked her tongue.

"She'll do anything to hurt me. We had an awful row last night in front of Eli and Jake. I thought I'd die of embarrassment."

"Was it over the supplies Jake bought?"

"It was over Eli and Jake being there. She didn't even notice the supplies. Trudy, I heard that sometimes people who drink a lot . . . lose their minds. Have you ever heard that?" she asked as they were walking back to the washhouse.

"Mama says that their brains get pickled when they drink a lot of that rotgut whiskey."

"That's what's happened to Mama. She's drunk so much since Daddy died that she can't think straight."

It had been hard to face Jake at breakfast after what her mother had said. When he and Deke came in, there was another couple at the table. Deke's chatter made it easier than she had expected.

"Mornin', darlin'. You look fresh as a buttercup this mornin'."

"Thank you, Deke, and good morning to you too."

"Thanks, sugarfoot," he said when Trudy poured his coffee. "You musta had a hard night. Ya got black all 'round them pretty eyes of yours."

"'Course I have, dumbbell," she retorted. "It's my eyelashes."

"Is that what it is? Golly damn!"

Trudy shoved a plate of biscuits across the table. "Eat and hush," she hissed.

Mary Lee had looked at Jake. He was smiling. He caught her eyes and winked.

"What did the sheriff want?" Eli's words brought Mary Lee back to the present.

"He had a warrant for your arrest," Trudy said. "We told him you had flown the coop."

"Why'd ya tell him that for . . . *darlin'*?" Eli skipped out of the way when Trudy ran at him. "Isn't 'darlin' ' your new name?" he teased.

Trudy dropped the clothes basket and chased him around the house. When they came back around the porch where Mary Lee was waiting, they were laughing like two ten-year-olds.

"When I catch you, you little dirt ball, I'm goin' to put a knot on your head." Trudy shook her fist.

"Who're ya callin' 'little,' *darlin'*?" he yelled back.

"I'll get ya. Just wait. We Benders never forget our enemies."

A cloud of steam drew their attention to a truck loaded with furniture that had pulled off onto the shoulder between the motor court and the highway. A man in overalls and a straw hat got out. He carefully unscrewed the radiator cap and jumped back. Steam and water gushed out. He spoke to the woman in the truck, then took a bucket from the back and walked up to where Mary Lee, Trudy and Eli stood beside the porch.

"Howdy, ma'am." He spoke to Mary Lee. "Would ya mind if I got a bucket of water?"

"Help yourself. Would your family like to get out, stretch their legs and have a cool drink of water?" Mary Lee asked, seeing the woman and two boys in the cramped cab of the truck.

"They'd be plumb pleased to, ma'am. Thank ye." He walked back toward the truck. "Marthy . . . ," he called, and motioned and waited. As the woman lifted one little boy down, another scrambled out. Both ran to their father. The woman followed. She was slender and obviously pregnant.

"Hello," Mary Lee said. "Come back to the pump and have a cool drink. It's good to move around, isn't it?"

"It sure is. The boys are good, but they get tired sittin' so long."

"Let's see if we can run a little steam off them." Trudy touched the older one on the shoulder. "Bet you can't catch me."

"Bet . . . I can." He looked at his father for permission, and when he nodded, he took off after Trudy. She ran around the washhouse and down to cabin number one before she let him catch her.

"You won." She pretended to gasp for breath. "Guess you get the prize." She took his hand, and they walked back to the house. "We'd better let little brother in on it, don't ya think?"

"What is it?"

"Come on in and you'll see. You, too, snookums."

The younger brother looked at his mother, then ran to take his brother's hand. The three disappeared into the house.

"She loves little kids," Mary Lee said with a smile.

"I can tell." The woman watched her husband carry the bucket of water to the truck and drank her second dipper of water. "The water in our well back home was hard as a rock before it dried up."

"Where are you from?"

"Kansas. Just above the Oklahoma panhandle. We got tired of fighting the dust." She looked wistfully around. "It's pretty here. Pretty and green."

"We're a little higher up here. It cools down at night."

Trudy came out of the house with the two

boys. They were eating biscuits that had been hollowed out and filled with strawberry jam. It was already smeared on their little faces.

Trudy smiled guiltily at the mother. "They're goin' to be a mess. I brought a wet rag so you can wipe them off."

"Did you thank the lady?"

"Yes, ma'am."

"They did. Both of them," Trudy said, and ruffled the hair on the young one. "He told me his name is Jeffy."

"Is this Calafornie, Mama?"

"No, honey. We've got a long way to go to get to California."

"We'd better be goin', honey. We need to get to that campground 'fore dark." The man stood beside his wife, his hand rubbing up and down her back. "Thanky kindly for the water, ma'am, and the treat for the boys."

"You're welcome. Good luck. I hope you reach your destination safely."

The family went back to the highway. The man hugged his wife for a minute and kissed her on the forehead before he helped her into the truck and lifted the young one in.

Mary Lee suddenly felt alone and teary. The couple didn't have as much as she had materially, but they were far richer. They had each other.

Chapter 18

Eli came out of the washhouse wearing clean clothes, his cowboy boots and a big smile. Mary Lee went to him before he reached the group waiting beside the back porch.

"One of these days soon you're going to have to have a haircut," she said softly, and pressed something in the hand between them.

"Ya don't need to do that . . . ," he whispered.

"Yes, I do. You've earned that and more. I want you to be able to pay your own way."

"Well . . . thanks—"

Mary Lee kissed him on the cheek. "I'm proud of you."

He clung to her hand tightly. "Ya'll let Jake stay with ya?"

"If he wants to."

"Oh, he'll want to."

"What do you mean . . . ?"

"Come on, kid," Deke called. "The little squirt's gettin' antsy. She'll be gettin' on her broomstick and flyin' off if we don't get goin' soon."

Eli and Trudy were going to the picture show with Deke. There had been a lot of teasing about it. Deke had said that he was afraid to be alone with the "little squirt" in a dark picture show and needed Eli to protect him. Trudy's face had reddened; and in order to hide the excitement of going to the show, she had snatched off his hat and hit him with it.

Since Deke's arrival three days ago, Trudy no longer came to the motor court wearing a faded old gingham dress but one that had been freshly washed, starched and ironed. Her mop of curls was tied with a ribbon, and her cheeks were flushed. It was plain to Mary Lee that her friend could see beneath the homely face of the little man who teased her. He was as sweet and caring and as vulnerable to hurt because of his size as she was.

Mary Lee watched the trio walk across the field behind the motor court and then turned to Jake.

"He's awfully nice. I've never seen Trudy so happy."

"They seem to like teasing each other."

"I wish he wouldn't leave, but when he does, she'll be heartbroken," Mary Lee said with a sigh.

"You like him?"

"Sure. I can't help but to like him."

"Are you tired, *madrecita*?"

"Why do you call me things in Spanish?"

"Why? So you won't slap me." They walked around to the front of the house.

"I wouldn't slap you for calling me little mother."

"How about *'querida'*?"

"What does it mean?"

"'Stubborn little mule.'"

She cast an accusing glance up at Jake, whose green eyes were dancing with unconcealed mischief.

"It does not! I'll ask Mr. Santez."

"Better not. You might hear something you don't want to know." He shook his head. When he extended his hand, she put hers in it. "Shall we sit here on the edge of the porch, or do you want to walk down to my place, sit on the step and listen to the radio?"

"I've missed the radio," she said wistfully. "But I'd better stay here where I can keep an eye on things. Mama is out there with Yancy. Frank will be released tomorrow."

Jake reached for the straight-backed chair on the porch. He placed it on the ground. After she was seated, he sat down on the edge of the porch.

"You don't have to stay with me."

"I want to. Besides, I promised Eli that I'd not let you out of my sight until he got back."

"Bless his heart. I'm getting awfully fond of him."

"He obviously feels the same about you."

"School starts in another month. He won't want to go and leave me here alone, but he must."

"Trudy will be here, won't she?"

"I'm . . . not sure. But regardless, Eli has to go to school."

"I agree. Maybe things will have settled down by then."

"I don't know. Mama is drinking more. It's

affecting her mind or she wouldn't have said the things she said the other day."

"Are Yancy and Frank furnishing the whiskey?"

"They must be. She's already sold everything she could carry out of the house."

"Someone is giving them money," he said thoughtfully. "Yancy's a cowhand. They get thirty a month and board. Frank couldn't be making much digging ditches."

"Could it be Mr. Clawson?"

"No. Ocie isn't sneaky. He wouldn't use deadbeats like Yancy and Frank to do his dirty work."

"Who, then? And for goodness' sake, why?"

"Maybe someone who thinks the motor court belongs to your mother."

"They should know better than that by now. Mama wanted Trudy and Eli to clean the cabin Frank claims to have rented. I told them they didn't have to do it, so they made themselves scarce. Mama threw bottles, boxes and all kinds of trash out the door along with the sheets and towels. Eli picked it all up, and I didn't even ask him to do it.

"Then she took clean sheets and towels off the clothesline. She's getting the cabin

ready for Frank." Mary Lee suddenly cried
and stretched out her leg."Oh, oh . . ."

"What's the matter?"

"I've got a . . . cramp!"

Jake grasped her leg, laid it across his
lap, and with strong fingers massaged the
hard muscles of her calf while holding her
foot with the other hand. When the muscles
refused to loosen, he got to his feet,
grasped her beneath her arms and lifted
her.

"Put all your weight on it."

Clinging to him weakly, she did as she
was told. When he walked backward, she
was forced to take a few steps. Then, with
his forearm beneath her armpit, he urged
her to walk. They made their way slowly
around to the back of the house.

"Does this happen often?"

"Every once in a while. It usually happens
at night. I get up and hold on to the end of
the bed until it goes away."

"How much longer?"

"Until the baby comes? September twenty-
eighth is the due date. It could be a week
sooner or a week later."

"Are you anxious to get it over?"

"Not really. I have a lot to do between now and then."

"Like what?"

"Well . . . I've got to make enough here to pay off the loan. I need to make baby clothes, although Mrs. Santez lent me some things. I need to get a basket for the baby to sleep in and—I'm worried about Mama. I don't think she would hurt the baby, but she wouldn't look after it either."

"Do you have names picked out?"

"Yeah. Gaston." She grinned up at him.

"If it's a girl will you call her Gastonia?"

Mary Lee's chuckle turned into a nervous giggle that kept on and on. Her head fell forward, her forehead resting on his chest.

Jake felt an urge to hold her. He couldn't resist. He put his arms around her, pulled her up to him and held her firmly but gently. His cheek was against the side of her head, his nose in the hair above her ear, breathing in the sweet scent of her.

Oh, God. I've got the whole world right here in my arms . . . this precious girl and her baby. Dear Lord, I'd give ten years of my life if the baby growing inside her was mine.

When he felt the miracle of movement against his lower abdomen, he whispered,

"I feel the baby moving." She started to lean away from him. "No, please . . . stay still," he said quickly. His hand moved soothingly up and down her back. "Gaston likes me. That's the second time he's kicked me."

She tilted her head to look at him. "When?"

"The night you took the starch outta Frank. I was holding you like this."

"Sometimes he really gets rambunctious."

"He's going to give his mama fits." Jake chuckled, then stilled when she took his hand and placed it on her stomach, keeping her hand over his.

"Feel that?"

"Yeah." There was a trace of awe in his voice.

Instead of being embarrassed at sharing this intimacy with him, Mary Lee felt a surge of elation.

Jake Ramero, this sometimes aloof man with eyes that can turn as cold as a frosty morning, a convicted rustler, hardened by years in the pen, truly cares about my baby.

He eased her down on the porch step and sat down close to her. With his arm around her he pulled her close while he stroked her rounded belly.

"Did you love him?" he whispered, his lips in her hair.

She didn't ask who he meant. She knew he wanted to know about Bobby, her husband.

"I cared about him, felt sorry for him. I didn't love him like I've seen in the movies or read about in books."

"Was he good to you? Did he hurt you?"

"He . . . hurt me only one time."

"The son of a bitch!" The curse came in the form of a hissed whisper.

"He died shortly after that."

"Did you like what he did . . . to make you pregnant?" His hand stroked her hair; his lips moved around to her forehead.

"Oh, Jake . . ."

"Did you?" he insisted.

"I knew nothing about . . . what happens between a man and a woman."

"I wish this baby was mine." His voice rose to a fervent whisper.

"I don't feel like the baby is Bobby's. He wouldn't have wanted it. Poor little thing. It'll only have me and I'll love it. I know how it feels not to be wanted."

"You're wanted, *querida.*" He tilted her

chin and kissed her sweetly, tenderly on the lips. It never occurred to her to turn away.

"We shouldn't be doing this."

"Why not? You like me a little, don't you?"

"I like you a lot, Jake. But look at me."

"I'm looking." His big, rough hand cupped her cheek and held her head against his shoulder. He lowered his face and gently rubbed his nose with hers.

"You see a woman with a shape like a watermelon, rough hands, sunbaked skin and a load of trouble."

"I see a pretty, sweet, spunky little mother with more guts than sense. If I had the world, I'd offer it to her."

"A lot of girls would love to have you . . . come calling. Don't you want a home? A family?" She wondered if he could feel her heart pounding.

"More than anything in the world," he whispered huskily, and kissed her again. His lips were warm and soft and gentle against hers. She felt cherished, protected, and wished she could stay in his arms forever.

"You'll have them someday. I hope you'll be happy."

"I'm a jailbird, *querida.* I'll be labeled a jailbird for the rest of my life. If I had any sense, I'd stay away from you so the stink won't rub off on you."

Mary Lee lifted her palm to his cheek. "It wasn't right that they put you in prison. I don't like to think of you in that place."

"It seems a lifetime ago that I sat here on this porch while a pretty little girl cried over me and watched her pa treat my sore feet."

"It does seem a long time ago. Tell me about yourself, Jake. Tell me about your mother and your father if you remember him . . ."

It was a night that neither of them would forget. Although no declaration of love was made, they shared a closeness, one neither had ever experienced with another human being, and it was precious to both of them.

He sat with his back to the porch post, with Mary Lee nestled close against him. He spoke in low, even tones while he told her about living on the Clawson ranch and about visiting his mother's people in the mountain villages. After his mother died, he had stayed on at Clawson's for a while, then worked on nearby ranches and in Oklahoma and Texas. His love for horses made him a good trainer.

"Nothing gets my dander up quicker than to see a horse mistreated. It's one of the reasons I left Clawson's."

"I'm not surprised."

"I've never seen Ocie mistreat an animal, but some of his men do when he's not around."

Jake skipped over the years he'd spent in the penitentiary. He shared his fear of heights and how he had to steel himself to climb the girders at the bridge site.

"Why did you do it?"

"For the money. I'm going to get my land back and raise horses. A few steers too, to help pay the bills."

"Why doesn't Mr. Clawson like you?"

"It started a long time ago. There was always competition between me and Bobby. Ocie would have liked for Bobby to outdo me, but Bobby wasn't as tough as I was. He'd had it soft all his life, while I'd been working since I was eight years old. I was a better rider, roper and all-around hand than Bobby. It made Bobby hate me and Ocie too, I guess."

"It wasn't fair."

"Many things in life are not fair, *querida*. A man has to play the hand he's dealt."

"Jake? I don't want you to get the idea that because I'm sitting here with you like this that . . . I'm a fast woman." Her hand plucked at the buttons on his shirt.

"Why in hell would I think that?" he growled, and tilted her chin so he could look into her face.

"You must know that a woman in my condition . . . doesn't act like this."

"Like what?"

"Well . . . I shouldn't have let you kiss me."

"Why not?"

She moved away from him and said irritably, "You only ask questions. I can't answer them all."

"Didn't you want me to kiss you?"

"Yes, dammit, I did. Are you satisfied?"

"I'm not only satisfied, I'm happy as a drunk hoot-owl!"

He reached for her, pulled her to him and hugged her, then fitted his mouth to hers and kissed her as if he were dying of thirst.

When she could get her breath, she gasped. "Oh, Jake. This is crazy." Then she slipped her arm around his neck.

*   *   *

The next day Mary Lee lived in a glow of
happiness up until the time Frank Pierce
was let out on the highway and walked up
to the motor court. Dolly came out of the
cabin and for a moment clung weakly to the
door. She was not steady on her feet, and
reeled drunkenly when she went to meet
him. She was wearing her most revealing
dress. Her thin, wiry hair had been frizzed
with the curling iron, and round spots of
rouge were bright on her sunken cheeks.
Her lips were scarlet.

Mary Lee felt pity for her mother and embarrassment that she would display herself
in such a fashion. She was also glad that
Jake and Deke were not here to see her.
Having Eli and Trudy stare at her was bad
enough.

Frank walked carefully. His eyes were
mean and searching the house as he
passed it. Mary Lee stayed beside the window, where he couldn't see her.

"Frank!" Dolly screeched. "I'm so glad
you're home."

Frank grunted and followed her into the
cabin.

That was the last she saw of her mother

until near suppertime. She came to the house and took food from the cupboard and the icebox, then went back to the cabin. She never spoke, and appeared to be weak. She paused every so often to hold on to the back of a chair.

It was late when Jake and Deke drove in. Trudy had gone home, disappointed, Mary Lee was sure, that she'd had to leave before Deke came back. Eli had teased her about Deke's insisting that he sit beside her at the picture show and the fact that he had to sit on the other side of Deke.

"Then on the walk to her house, Mary Lee, they just talked to each other and acted like I wasn't even there," Eli reported.

"We did no such thing," Trudy was quick to say. "You kept pushing me against him."

"I was tryin' to help you out."

"I didn't need any help, thank you."

The bantering between them had gone on all day. Mary Lee had thoughts of her own to keep her mind occupied. She had not gone into the house until Eli and Deke returned. Sleep had not come at once. Her mind had been busy with what had occurred between her and Jake. This morning he and Deke had come for breakfast; and when he left, he had placed his hand on her shoulder in passing.

"Thanks," he had said. "See you all to-night."

The cabins were filled except for one when Jake's truck came by the house and stopped at his cabin. Later he and Deke passed by as they walked to town. They stopped and said a few words to Eli. Mary Lee kept out of sight.

After the last cabin was rented and the Vacancy light turned off, Eli went to Jake's cabin to listen to the radio. Mary Lee went to her room, latched the doors and lay down on the bed.

"He didn't say anything about being in love with me. I know he is concerned about us, baby," she said silently to her unborn child. "That isn't the same as love."

Perhaps he had just wanted to pass a few pleasant hours hugging and kissing her. Bobby had been content just to do that until she told him that she was leaving Cross Roads. Then he had confessed his "undying love" for her, and she had been foolish enough to believe it.

Mary Lee undressed and went to bed. She lay for a long time listening to the cars pass on the highway until their song lulled her to sleep.

Chapter 19

If the day she heard that her father had died was the worst day of her life, this day was to be the second.

She and Trudy served breakfast as usual. Jake and Deke waited until there was room at the table before they came in to eat. Jake was quiet, his green eyes missing nothing, as he listened to Deke tease Trudy and to her sassing him back.

"How about goin' for a ride on the cycle tonight, darlin'?" Deke said when he and Jake were ready to leave. "We'll ride out into the hills where it's good and dark, find us a grassy spot and neck."

Trudy's mouth dropped open, but no words came out. Finally she said, "Are you talkin' to me?"

"I sure ain't talkin' to Mary Lee. I ain't wantin' this big gallot to squash me like a bug for flirtin' with his girl. How about it, darlin'?"

"Well . . . I guess I'll go for the ride part. But I'm not neckin' with you, buster."

Mary Lee had never seen her friend so flustered. Her face was rosy; her hands tightly gripped the back of the chair in front of her.

"Better not be sayin' somethin' you'll have to take back, sugarfoot." Deke snatched his hat up off the floor where he'd dropped it when he came in.

"Come on, jellybean. You can flirt with Trudy tonight." Jake's eyes caught Mary Lee's with a wink of conspiracy. She returned his smile.

After they left, Trudy sank down in the chair. Mary Lee was glad Eli wasn't there to tease her.

"Does he think that I'm the kind of girl who will go out in the dark and . . . you know?"

"I think he was as nervous about asking you as you were about accepting. I don't think you have anything to worry about.

Jake would have put the kibosh on it if he thought Deke would mistreat you."

"What'll I wear?" Trudy wailed, and Mary Lee laughed.

"That's the age-old cry of a girl being asked out on a date. We'll think of something before the day is over."

Mary Lee worked in the kitchen. It was a warm day. She worried about her mother being shut up in a room with only a couple of open windows for ventilation. Then it occurred to her that she might not be in there but out in the cabin with Frank Pierce. No, she vaguely remembered hearing her come in sometime during the night.

When the wash was on the line, Trudy, carrying a bucket of cleaning supplies, started on the cabins. Later she came to the house carrying a pair of white lace panties.

"Looky here, Mary Lee. I found these under the pillow in number four." She giggled. "What'll I do with them?"

"Put them in the wash, then in your hope chest."

"Oh, you! I don't have a 'hope' chest."

"Then it's time you got one started."

"It's a good thing Eli didn't find them. All

boys his age think about is . . . girls' panties." Trudy giggled and flounced out the door.

Mary Lee was chopping cabbage to cook with potatoes and carrots for a boiled dinner when she heard running feet, and Eli and Trudy burst into the kitchen. Eli's eyes were as big as saucers; Trudy was as white as the sheets flapping on the clothesline.

"Come quick!"

"What's happened?" Mary Lee dropped the knife and got to her feet.

"Fr . . . ank! Come look—oh, it's awful . . ."

Mary Lee followed the pair out the door and around to the side window of the cabin. The shade was drawn to within four inches of the windowsill.

"I just . . . looked in." Eli was so shaken, he could hardly speak. "And . . . and . . . saw him."

"What in the world are you talking about?"

"Look."

Mary Lee had to squat down to peer into the cabin. With the shades drawn, the light in the room was dim. When her eyes focused on the object on the bed, she gasped, closed her eyes, then opened them again. It was still there.

Frank lay on the bed in his underwear, the broken end of a bottle lodged in his throat. It was the most horrible sight Mary Lee had ever seen. Above the neck of the protruding bottle his mouth gaped open. His arms were thrown wide; blood covered his chest. He lay in a pool of it.

"Is he dead?" Eli whispered as if Frank could hear.

"He's got to . . . be. Oh, dear God!" Mary Lee leaned weakly against the side of the cabin.

"Someone killed him! He didn't do that to himself," Trudy whispered as Eli had done.

"Go down to Mr. Santez's station, Eli. Call the sheriff and tell him to hurry."

After Eli took off on the run, the two women held on to each other. Both of them were weak. Mary Lee swallowed repeatedly to keep from throwing up.

"Mama!"

"She isn't in there," Trudy said quickly.

"I heard her come in last night. She'll take this hard. She and Frank were going to get married."

"No! She wouldn't have married that . . . old thing."

"I . . . wish Jake was here. He'd know what to do." Mary Lee began to shake.

"Now, ya just better calm down." Trudy grasped her friend's hands. "It's not good for the baby for ya to get so upset. There wasn't nothin' we could do but tell you 'bout it."

"Who would have done such a horrible thing? I hated him, but that—"

"The sheriff will figure it out."

It seemed an eternity before Eli came back, followed by Mr. Santez. Then another eternity before Sheriff Pleggenkuhle drove in and got out of his car. The sheriff peered into the window and then tried the door. It was unlocked. He shoved it open and went inside.

Mary Lee, Trudy and Eli went to the house and sat down on the edge of the porch. The sheriff and Mr. Santez came out and talked for several minutes. Mr. Santez got into his car, and the sheriff came toward the house.

"Is your mother here, Mrs. Clawson?"

"She isn't up yet. Sometimes she doesn't get up until noon."

"Was she with Frank last night?"

"She was out there . . . for a while. I heard her come in sometime after midnight."

"Was anyone else out there?"

"I don't know. The man that was here the night you came here has been staying out there while Frank was in jail."

"Yancy Hummer?"

"He walked in from the back," Eli said. "I didn't see him last night, but other nights."

"Could you give me a list of the people who stayed in the cabins last night? You don't have to do it right now. I want to talk to your mother first. Will you ask her to come out? Keep an eye out, son," he said to Eli. "If anyone drives in, let me know."

He followed Mary Lee into the house. After knocking on her mother's door, she tried to open it. It was locked. She went through her bedroom and the bathroom to try the other door. It was also locked. Back in the living room, she knocked on the door again.

"Mama," she called. "Open the door. The sheriff wants to talk to you."

After thumping on the door several times, she said, "I'm sorry. She gets stubborn sometimes and won't open the door."

"Let me try." The sheriff thumped on the

door with his fist. "Mrs. Finley, Sheriff Pleg-genkuhle. I want to talk to you."

Silence followed. The sheriff looked down at the lock on the door. "Do you have another key?"

"No."

"We should see if she's all right. Do you mind if I put my foot against the door?"

"Go ahead."

The sheriff's number eleven cowboy boot struck the door, and it popped open. Dolly Finley lay on the bed, a sheet pulled up to her waist. She hadn't bothered to take off her dress. Lipstick was smeared on her face and on the pillowcase.

"Mama, are you all right?"

Dolly looked up with fever-bright eyes. "Whiskey," she whispered.

"Are you sick, Mama?"

"Whiskey."

"The sheriff wants to talk to you."

"Mrs. Finley, were you with Frank last night?"

She squinted up at him. "Frank?"

"Yes, Frank. Were you with him?"

She rolled her head from side to side, then focused her eyes on Mary Lee.

"What're you doin' in here?"

"You're sick. I want to help you." Mary Lee tried to put her palm against Dolly's forehead, but she jerked her head out of the way.

"Mrs. Finley, Frank was killed last night. Were you there?"

"Huh?"

"Frank is dead. Were you there when he was killed?" The sheriff spoke with brutal frankness.

Dolly looked at him for a minute; her mouth opened and a wail of intense pain came out of it. It was so loud and so poignant that Mary Lee stumbled back against the sheriff. Sobs racked Dolly's thin body. She doubled up on the bed, covering her head with arms that looked like sticks.

Pity for this woman whose love for alcohol had ruined her life welled up in Mary Lee. She reached out to comfort her but withdrew her hand. Her mother had not touched her in years and would probably not welcome her touch now.

"She's sick, Sheriff. It's been coming on for days. She won't listen to a thing I say."

"Doc Morris will be here soon to see Frank. You can ask him to take a look at her."

"Who could have done such a terrible thing?"

"Was Jake here last night?"

"Jake? He wouldn't have— He and his friend went uptown."

"What time did they come back?"

"I don't know. I went to bed about nine o'clock."

"How about the boy?"

"I don't know when he went to bed. I fixed a place in the washhouse for him to sleep. You don't think he— Oh, no. Eli would never have done anything like that."

"I'm not accusing anyone. Just covering all the bases."

"I won't have to close the court, will I?"

"You might have to for a day or two."

"I can't, Sheriff. Oh, good heavens. I can't close for even one night. I've a loan to pay the bank, and I'm just barely going to make it."

"I'm sure Mr. Rosen would extend your loan under the circumstances."

"No, he wouldn't, Sheriff. He wants this place. If I don't pay the first day of October, he'll take over."

"Let me see your register."

Mary Lee got the book. "Mr. and Mrs.

Sidney Thomas, Amarillo, stayed in number two. They were an older couple going to visit their son in the hospital in Gallup.

"A Mr. Samuel Cummings was in number three. He's a salesman for Acme Stove Company out of Dallas, Texas.

"Number four was rented to a Mr. and Mrs. John Jones. He said he was a banker from Flagstaff, Arizona. But if his name was Jones and he was a banker, I'm a fan dancer. Eli said the couple left while *Amos 'n Andy* was on. That would have been before ten o'clock.

"A couple with a baby was in number five. Mr. and Mrs. Richard Johnson. He gave his address as Little Rock, Arkansas, lately of Victorville, California. He said they were going home because his wife was homesick.

"Jake and his friend, Deke Bales, are in number six."

"Humm . . . Thank you, Mrs. Clawson."

Mary Lee sank down in the chair beside the window. Her mind went blank for a time, then came alive with concern for young Eli, who had witnessed such a terrible scene, and for her mother, who was sick in mind as well as body. She went to stand in the bedroom doorway. Dolly lay on the bed, curled on her side with her arms wrapped around her head.

How much longer before Jake would come home? With all her heart she wished he were here. She hadn't realized how much she had depended on his quiet strength. *Oh, Lord, what if the sheriff thought he had killed Frank!*

"Mary Lee, the doctor and the funeral wagon are here." Trudy spoke in hushed tones. "The sheriff wants to know if you have a couple of brown paper sacks."

"I never throw away a sack. They're stuffed behind the icebox."

Mary Lee followed Trudy out of the house and waited on the porch with Eli while she took the sacks to the sheriff. The long hearse was parked in front of the house. The doctor's car was behind it. It seemed forever before the sheriff and the undertaker brought Frank's sheet-wrapped body out on a litter and put it in the back of the hearse.

Doctor Morris came to the house. "Nasty business," he said, shaking his head. "Can I trouble you for a place to wash my hands?"

Mary Lee led the doctor through her bedroom to the bathroom and thanked the good Lord for telling her to clean it that morning and put out clean towels. When the doctor came back to the kitchen where she waited, he was buttoning his shirt-sleeves.

"I was told your mother is sick. Would you like for me to take a look at her?"

"Yes, please. But, Doctor, first let me warn you. She is very . . . unpredictable. She may not appreciate our concern and be . . . mouthy and vulgar."

"We'll not worry about that. How long has she been sick?"

"She didn't look well when I came home. She's really gone downhill lately. She . . . drinks a lot."

"I know that."

"Would you mind seeing her alone? I seem to bring out the bad side of her. She may be more cooperative if I'm not in there."

"I was going to suggest that." He went to the door and spoke to Eli. "Son, would you bring me the bag in the front seat of my car?"

While waiting for Eli, he asked, "How are you doing?"

"All right. I have some back pain once in a while and my ankles swell if I'm on my feet a lot."

"That's not unusual. Any other near accidents?"

"No." She shook her head as she spoke.

"Is the boy a relative?"

"He just wandered in. But I want him to stay," she added quickly. "He's had no one to care about him until now. I want him to be part of my family."

"He's a big boy. Is he fourteen or fifteen?"

"Thirteen. I couldn't run this place without him. I'd trust him with my life and my baby's. He's very dear to me."

The doctor nodded gravely.

Eli came to the door with the doctor's bag. "Mary Lee, the sheriff wants to talk to you when you're through in here."

"All right. If you want anything, Doctor Morris, Eli and Trudy will be here on the porch." She hesitated, then said, "Please don't be offended by anything Mama says. She's not been in her right mind lately."

The doctor placed his hand on her shoulder, patted it and went into Dolly's room and closed the door.

Mary Lee felt as if she had the weight of

the world on her shoulders when she stepped off the porch and went to where the sheriff waited for her beside the cabin where Frank had died.

"As bad as I hate to do this, Mrs. Clawson, I'm going to have to tell you to close the motor court until I can find out if Frank was killed by someone who knew him, or if he was killed by a person who wandered in from the highway and found the cabin door unlocked. I can't take the chance that whoever did this might try it again and kill someone who was just passing through town."

"I was afraid you'd say that. It'll mean I'll not have the money to pay back the loan. It's just not fair. My father worked hard to build this place."

"Maybe if you'd have come home sooner—"

"I couldn't. I didn't have the money. I didn't even know that Daddy had left the motor court to me until I got here. Is there any way we can stay open?"

"You're out here without a phone, Mrs. Clawson. I've got the whole county to patrol. I can't leave a man here to watch all night."

"Jake is here nights. He'll watch. Have you checked out his friend, Deke Bales?"

"I wired Sheriff McChesney over in Beckman County, Oklahoma. He gave him a good reference. He said Bales had a short fuse at times, but was fair and honest as far as he knew. Mrs. Clawson, when word gets out what's happened out here, it'll be a three-ring circus. What we'd better do is block off the drive and put out a Closed sign."

Mary Lee nodded numbly. "Do you think it was someone roaming the highway?"

"Or someone here who wanted to get Frank out of your hair. I don't know what to think at this point. I want to talk to Jake and his friend. I've already talked to the boy. I've not ruled him out. As soon as the doc gives the word, I'll try Mrs. Finley again."

"How about Frank's so-called friends? The drunken bums he hangs out with?" Mary Lee said heatedly.

"See what I mean," the sheriff said when a car came down the highway and wheeled into the drive. It stopped suddenly, stirring up a cloud of dust. Two men got out.

"I heard someone murdered poor old Frank Pierce, Sheriff. She do it?" He jerked his head toward Mary Lee. "Godamighty. Feller don't dare turn his back on a woman these days."

"Now he's 'poor old Frank.' When he was alive they probably wouldn't have given him the time of day," the sheriff said to Mary Lee. Then, "You're out of line, Berkhardt. Move along." When the man lingered, the sheriff said harshly, "Get out of here, or I'll arrest you for interfering with my crime scene."

"Well, shit, Sheriff . . ." The man got back in his car. "If she did it, she oughta fry the same as a man."

"Goddammit, Berkhardt," the sheriff roared, "get the hell out of here!"

The car stirred up another cloud of dust when it left.

"Where's the boy?"

"His name is Eli," Mary Lee said in a small voice.

Eli came when the sheriff called him. "Are there sawhorses around here or anything we can use to block the drive?"

"No, sir. But there's a couple of barrels and some rope we can tie strings onto. Will that do?"

"That'll do fine. Let's get it up."

"Are we closed?" Eli asked Mary Lee.

"For a while."

"Trudy will paint a sign, Sheriff. I have a board we can nail to one of the barrels."

"That's good thinkin', boy. Let's set up the barrels first."

Eli basked in the sheriff's praise. In less than ten minutes, the barrels were up, the rope strung, and Trudy was tying strings of cloth on the rope. When a car full of gawkers attempted to come into the drive, the sheriff waved it off. Not to be turned away so easily, the driver parked alongside the highway, and several men got out.

"What happened, Pleggenkuhle? We heard Frank Pierce was murdered out here. Know who done it?"

"Frank was killed and I don't know who did it . . . yet."

"Jake Ramero lives out here, don't he? Well . . . what more do you want? How about the little bitch who tried to ruin Frank's cockadoodle? Don't seem to me it's goin' to be hard to find out who done it."

The sheriff turned his back and walked away.

"Sheriff, if ya need a posse, count me in. Hey, is that the doc's car? What's he doin' here? Don't tell me he come to court old Dolly. Haw, haw, haw!"

"Jehoshaphat!" Sheriff Pleggenkuhle snorted. "Some folks got about as much brains as cow dung when something like this happens."

A deputy pulled up to the rope blocking the drive, got out and went around the barrels.

"I was on the other side of the county when I got the word. Santez didn't say why I was needed, but I stopped at the office and found out. It's all over town that Frank Pierce was murdered out here."

"We're going to have some trouble with sightseers. There hasn't been a murder here in more than five years. Keep an eye out and don't let anyone in. I need to talk to the doc."

Chapter 20

Work ceased at Quitman's ranch early on Saturday, giving the men time to clean up before heading to town. Jake drove into town with Deke, who had been working on a motor for Mr. Quitman while Jake put the horses he was training through their routine, and they headed for the Red Pepper Corral.

There were a number of people on the street, but it was not unusual for Saturday. Jake flung open the door, and Deke preceded him into the cool interior of the building. Before they reached the stools in front of the bar, they were met by three men who had leaped from their chairs at a nearby table the instant the pair entered.

One of them was Yancy Hummer, who charged forth with all the agility and temperament of a bull whose tail had just been twisted. On his right was a thin man with ferret eyes and the sharp, pointed face of a fox. The other man stood six feet two inches and weighed well over two hundred fifty pounds.

"Ya . . . murderin' bastard!" Yancy shouted. He was practically foaming at the mouth. "You son of a whore! Shit-eatin' Mex bastard!"

"Whoa, now, son." Deke was a couple of steps ahead of Jake. "Watch yore mouth."

"Shut yores, ya pig-ugly little turd. Get the hell outta the way unless this son of a bitch is gonna let ya do his fightin' for him." With a stiffened arm, he shoved Deke aside and turned on Jake. "Guess ya think screwin' that little bitch'll get ya the motor court. Nobody but a dirty, low-down half-breed would go where another man's already plowed the field and planted a kid."

"You worthless piece of shit! You're not fit to speak her name." Jake muttered a string of obscenities beneath his breath, took two steps and swung.

His rock-hard fist caught Yancy full in the mouth, smashing his lips against teeth. Yancy staggered back, then regained his balance and plunged forward, throwing wild punches. One caught Deke and sent him rolling. Quick and agile as a cat, Deke was on his feet. He lowered his head and drove it into Yancy's gut.

The big man stepped in and sent a ham-like fist toward Jake's head, connecting solidly with his right eye. The blow spun Jake around, and for a second or two he saw stars. His head cleared just in time for him to suck in his midsection before the ferret-faced man took a swipe at it with a long, slim two-edged knife. Enraged now, he kicked the arm holding the knife, sending the blade sliding across the floor, then gave Ferret-face a quick chop in the Adam's apple with the edge of his hand. The knifer toppled into a table, then onto a chair, which crashed to the floor.

Jake came around to see that the big man, who outweighed Deke by a hundred pounds and was a foot taller, had backhanded him with no more regard than if he were a pesky fly, sending him crashing against the bar. Deke lay in a heap on the floor.

Fearing for his friend, Jake focused on the man who was crouched in an attack stance. He put up his fists to distract him, then swung his booted foot. He viciously caught the man in the crotch with the toe of his boot. The pain was so severe it stunned him. His mouth opened, closed. His eyes crossed. Then he clutched the injured area between his legs and dropped to his knees. His stomach heaved, and he went over face-first in a puddle of vomit.

Jake and Yancy, the only two left standing on their feet, squared off only to have Paco dive between them, swinging the sap.

"Get the hell out of my place, Yancy, and take these sorry curs with you. Don't ever come back."

"Ya takin' the side of a damn half-breed killer."

"Get out, Yancy! I mean now." A murmur of protest rose from the crowd gathered around. "That goes for the rest of you if you've no more brains than to listen to this brayin' jackass yammer 'bout somethin' he knows nothin' about." Paco's eyes swept over the group, which quieted instantly.

Jake went over to help Deke get to his feet. The little man's mouth and nose were bleeding.

"Don't you know any better than to tackle a man twice your size?"

"Shit. He wasn't that big."

Jake's eye was rapidly swelling shut. He dug money out of his pocket and held it out to Paco.

"Sorry about breaking the chair."

"Keep your money." Paco went to the big man, who was now on his hands and knees, rocking back and forth like a stunned ox. He leaned down and took several dollars from his pocket. "That's to pay for cleaning up this mess." He took a bill from the ferret-faced man, then held his hand out to Yancy. "Pay up or your ass will be in jail before you can say Jack Robinson."

"Wait till the men at the ranch hear whose side you took in this. Lon will fix you. You'll wish to hell ya'd done different when you've got to close this place down." Yancy took a silver dollar from his pocket and slapped it into Paco's hand.

"Get out! I'll not have brawlin' or the soilin' of a good woman's name in my place."

"What the hell got into him all of a sudden?" Jake asked when the door slammed behind Yancy and his two friends.

"You haven't heard the news?"

"We just came in from Quitman's."

"Frank Pierce was murdered in his bed last night out at the court. The whole town's in an uproar about it."

"Madre de Dios!" Jake's mind scrambled for comprehension. He stared at Paco as if transfixed. Then words burst from him. "Who did it? How?" He grabbed his hat up off the floor.

"All I know is that he was let out of jail in the morning and someone slit his throat and buried a broken bottle in it last night at the motor court."

"Mrs. Clawson? Is she all right?"

"As far as I know. The sheriff's out there. They closed the place down."

"Thanks, Paco. I've got to go. Deke, are you all right?"

"Hell. It'd take more'n that tub of lard to lay me low." Holding a handkerchief to his nose, Deke slammed his hat down on his head and hurried out the door, trying to keep up with Jake's long legs.

Eli and Trudy cleaned the four cabins, locked the doors and hung the keys on the Peg-Board in the kitchen. Mary Lee had been in and out of her mother's room all afternoon.

The doctor had given Dolly something to make her sleep, and Mary Lee had taken the opportunity to clean the room, which was cluttered with trash and dirty clothes. Dishes from the kitchen had been shoved under the bed after Dolly had eaten the food she brought to her room. Mary Lee swept the floor and wiped months of dust from the furniture with a damp cloth. Trudy, standing on a chair, washed the windows on the outside while Mary Lee washed them on the inside.

Keeping busy helped to keep panic at bay. She tried not to think that if she was forced to keep the motor court closed for more than a couple of days, she would be unable to pay the bank the full amount owed by October 1. She had no doubt that Mr. Rosen, the banker, would foreclose and do so gleefully.

There would be the added expense of her mother's illness. The doctor had explained that there were so many things wrong with Dolly that it was a miracle she had remained on her feet for the past few days. Her heartbeat was faint and irregular; her blood pressure was soaring; her kidneys were failing. He had found pockets of water in several places beneath her skin. All this combined with the run-down condition of her body made it almost certain that her illness was terminal.

"Her heart could fail at any time. The best we can do is to keep her as comfortable as we can," the doctor had said. "Try to get her to eat when she wakes up later this evening. I'll stop back in the morning."

"She'll ask me for whiskey. She did this morning."

"If she asks again, give it to her. She's so far gone that it won't make any difference now."

"I don't have any."

"I'll bring some when I come again."

The sheriff had left a deputy to turn away gawkers while he made a trip back to his office. He was anxious to talk to Dolly and was disappointed that the doctor had given her a shot that put her to sleep.

Mary Lee was in the kitchen when she heard the slamming of a car door. She went to the front door to see Jake's truck parked along the highway and him striding toward the house. He passed the deputy with only a nod of greeting. Deke was doing his best to keep up with him. Mary Lee met him at the door and drew him into the house, out of the watchful eye of the deputy.

"Heavens!" she exclaimed when she saw Deke's bloody nose and Jake's eye rapidly swelling shut.

Deke went through the house and out to the pump.

"What happened to you two?"

Jake put his hands on her shoulders and peered down into her face with his one good eye.

"Are you all right?"

"Um-huh. A lot has happened since you left this morning." In spite of her vow not to do so, tears filled her eyes.

Jake pulled her to him as if he had every right, wrapped his arms around her and held her protectively against him. His lips caressed her forehead; his hand moved soothingly up and down her back.

"It'll be all right now, *mi bella.* You're not to fret," he whispered; then to lighten the moment he added, "Gaston won't like it."

"I'm glad you're here, Jake."

"I came as soon as I heard. Either Deke

or I will be here from now on until this thing
is settled."

"The sheriff wants to talk to you and
Deke," she said, leaning back to look into
his face.

"It's his job. I'd be disappointed in him if
he didn't."

She placed her palm against his cheek.
"Oh, your poor eye. What happened to your
face?"

"It ran into a big fist. Deke and I met up
with Yancy Hummer and a couple of his
friends."

"Come let me put an ice pack on it."

From the kitchen they could see Deke sitting on the porch steps. Trudy, with a cloth
and a pan of water, was fussing over him.

"Deke was hurt too?"

"Yancy had his tail in a crack. He seemed
to think I had something to do with Frank's
murder. I didn't know what the heck he was
talking about until Paco told me."

*I might not have hit him if he hadn't said
something insulting about you,* querida.
Then I wanted to tear his damn head off.

Mary Lee chipped ice, wrapped it in a
cloth, and held it to his eye. He wanted to
pull her down on his lap but was afraid to

push his luck. It was worth a dozen pokes in the eye to have her near, fussing over him.

She told him about Eli and Trudy peeking in the window and finding Frank's body. She spoke in detail about what had happened next.

"Someone slit Frank's throat with a knife, then poked a broken bottle in the . . . hole. It's too horrible to talk about. Doctor Morris says Mama is terribly sick. He doesn't think that she'll last long. She was staggering around yesterday like it took every bit of her strength to stay on her feet."

"I'm sorry, *querida.*"

"Poor Mama. Trudy washed her today and put her in a clean gown. We even changed the sheets and she didn't wake up."

"If she can't get well, it'll be a blessing if she can sleep till the end." Water from the melting ice chips was running down his cheek.

"The sheriff wants to talk to her. He thinks that she may have seen something. The door to the cabin was unlocked. The key was on the floor.

"Sheriff Pleggenkuhle said that it's possible that a tramp walking along the highway thought he'd have a place to stay for the night. He tried the doors, found one un-locked and went in. When he discovered Frank, he killed him."

"Was anything taken?"

"I don't think Frank had anything to steal."

"I wish I had put heavier latches on your doors. You'll not be in here alone if I have to camp out on the porch."

"Jake, I'm glad you're here," she said for the second time. Her wide eyes scanned his face, and she cherished every feature. "I may lose the court, but somehow things will work out. Daddy used to say that the Lord never puts more burdens on a person than he is able to bear."

"You'll not lose the court, *miel.*"

"That's another Spanish word I don't know. Don't tell me it's 'stubborn little mule.' It's not long enough for that."

" *'Miel'* means 'honey.' Is it all right if I call you that?"

"Oh, Jake, I don't know what to say. I'm afraid I'm bringing my troubles down on you when you've got enough of your own. If you hadn't helped me with Frank, you'd not have had to fight today or be suspected of killing him."

Jake dropped the ice pack on the table and was reaching for her when they heard a pounding on the door. Mary Lee hurried through the living room, hoping the sound hadn't awakened her mother. She knew before she reached the door who was standing there, and was grateful for Jake's solid body behind her.

"I heard what happened here last night." Ocie Clawson moved to the side when Mary Lee pushed open the screen door and went out onto the porch. "Who killed him? Do you know? Not that it's a great loss," he added.

"I don't know who killed him, and any death, even Frank Pierce's, is a loss."

"Did you kill him?" Ocie looked over her head at Jake.

"What do you think?"

"Wouldn't put it past ya and wouldn't much blame ya if ya had. How about that little dude stayin' here with ya? He one of yore jailbird friends? Gus Quitman tells me that he's a crackerjack mechanic. Wants him to rebuild that old motorcycle of his."

"It's what he said." Jake's answers were short.

"Hear ya had a run-in with my men at the Red Pepper."

"You're just full of news. One of them tried to knife me." Jake showed where the tip of the knife had ripped his shirt and had left a beaded red streak across his stomach.

Mary Lee drew in a gasping breath when she saw it.

"Was he a thin little weasel with teeth like a squirrel?" Ocie asked.

"That's him."

"He's handy with a knife. If I remember right, you're no slouch with a knife yourself."

"I know how to use one. You know who taught me."

"I should've kicked the hell out of them sons a bitches and put 'em off the ranch the minute they set foot on it. They're not welcome at Paco's—and won't be anyplace else when I get through with 'em." Ocie snorted. "The big galoot named Pete has a brain the size of a pea. Paco said ya ruined him . . . about."

"Yeah, well he got in the first lick."

"But not the last, huh?" Ocie grinned.

"When the odds are against me, anything is fair."

"I'll lay down the law to my men that as long as you're here lookin' after my kin, they're to steer clear of ya."

"I'm not your kin!" Mary Lee almost shouted.

"Maybe not," Ocie said, unperturbed by her outburst, "but the kid is. It's got Clawson blood."

"Which is nothing to brag about," she retorted, and tilted her chin defiantly.

"You stayin' here nights?" Ocie looked directly at Jake.

"That's none of your business, but I'll tell you this much: To get to Mary Lee you'll have to go through me."

Ocie snorted. "Don't get your back up. Do my men look as bad as you do?"

"Why don't you go find out?"

"I'll look 'em over before I tie a can to their tail." He looked over his shoulder. "The sheriff is here. I want a word with him."

"Don't let us stop you." Jake, standing behind Mary Lee, placed his hand on her shoulder in a proprietary manner.

After Ocie left to join the sheriff, Mary Lee turned to Jake.

"Come in and let me put some iodine on that cut."

"It's just a scratch."

"Then let me put some iodine on that scratch. The sheriff will want to talk to you and Deke." On the way to the kitchen, she said, "Why do you think Mr. Clawson keeps coming out here?"

"With Bobby gone, your baby is all he has."

"He'd better think again if he thinks he'll have anything to do with it."

"Ocie's pa, Temple Clawson, was great on family. They were both disappointed in Bobby. Ocie might think he's got another shot at raising a decent Clawson."

"My baby isn't his! How many times do I have to tell him?"

"Right now, I'm glad that he's looking out for you, *miel*. Whoever grabbed your foot on the stairs meant to hurt you."

"I've tried to think of something I might have done to cause someone to hate me that much."

"We'll see what happens now. I thought Frank had put someone up to it."

"The sheriff told me that Frank and my mother were going to get married. She took it hard when he told her Frank had been killed."

The sheriff came to the door. "Mrs. Clawson, is Mrs. Finley still sleeping?"

Mary Lee looked in the bedroom before she answered. It seemed strange to have the door to her mother's room open.

"Yes, she is."

"I'll be here for a while. Let me know when she wakes up. Jake, I want to talk to you."

Before Jake could move, Mary Lee whispered, "You and Deke come for supper."

He squeezed her hand and followed the sheriff out into the yard.

Chapter 21

"Ya dumb bastard! Ya stupid shit! Why'd ya have to go and show your hand? Ya ain't no good to me now."

Late on Saturday night, Lon Delano had come into the bunkhouse looking for Yancy.

"The jailbird killed Frank!" Yancy was in a foul temper. His lips were twice their normal size, and he had a cut high on his cheek. "It was him or the kid, and I don't think the kid could've caught poor old Frank unawares."

"No, but you could've."

"What're ya meanin'? I thought a heap of Frank. 'Sides, I was with Pete and Bowie."

"Shit. They'd say their own ma did it to save their hides. Were ya pissed cause Frank was takin' Dolly and the motor court?"

"Are ya crazy? You're the one who wanted him to marry the old hag."

"I told him if something happened to the girl, Dolly would get the court; and if he married her, he'd not have to wait long till it was his."

"Maybe *you* killed him 'cause he wouldn't do the girl in," Yancy said slyly.

"I've got a hell of a lot better alibi than Pete and Bowie." Lon's eyes were hard and angry. "Ya had to go and jump Jake at Paco's place. Right out there where God an' ever'body could see ya. Now, that took brains! What'a ya think's goin' to happen when Ocie hears about it?"

"I'll explain to him—"

"Shit. Ain't ya learned that ya don't explain to Ocie? Ya better start packin' yore gear 'cause he's goin' to kick yore ass outta here."

"Why? He ain't got nothin' to say 'bout what I do in town."

"He told me and I told you—to lay off Ramero."

"What's he so all fired up about that jail-bird for?"

"He thinks as long as he's out at the motor court, assholes like you will stay clear of it. He's usin' 'im as a guard dog for the bitch that's carryin' Bobby's kid."

"That don't make a damn bit of sense."

"To him it does. Christalmighty! You could've waited and caught him in an alley or out away from town someplace. Paco carries weight in this town. I heard that what riled Jake the most was you bad-mouthin' the bitch. That's not goin' to set good with Ocie a'tall."

"Well that's what she is—a slutty bitch! You ain't carin' a'tall that the bitch 'bout ruined Frank with that plate," Yancy jeered.

"No, I ain't carin'. She ort'a ripped it off of him for pissin' in front of her."

"Ya told him to get the jailbird to fight. He didn't, but I did."

"Ya better make yourself scarce. If Ocie see's ya he'll run ya clear outta the county." Lon headed for the door, then turned back. "Where's Pete and Bowie?"

"In town. At the livery. Pete couldn't straddle a horse. What'a ya goin' to do now, Lon?"

"Lucky for me that I've got more irons in the fire, and I'm not dependin' on dumbasses like you and Frank. Bastard got what was comin' to him."

Yancy looked into the cold, hard face of the ranch foreman and felt the hair rise on the back of his neck. *Frank had said flat out that he was through taking orders from Lon and that he wasn't going to marry Dolly. Lon couldn't afford to let him run off at the mouth about his plans. Now he was dead. It wasn't hard to figure out who had done it.*

Yancy began packing his gear.

Dolly didn't awaken until after supper was over. Mary Lee had cooked the boiled dinner and corn bread that she had started earlier in the day. When they sat down at the supper table with Jake and Deke, none of them had much of an appetite, but they ate anyway.

Now Deke had taken Trudy home to get a few things and to tell her mother that she was going to spend the night at the motor court. When Mary Lee heard a noise from her mother's room, she hurried there to find Dolly thrashing about, rolling her head back and forth, her eyes staring at the ceiling.

"Mama, are you awake?"

The sunken eyes turned to her daughter bending over her. "Whiskey," she muttered.

"I'll get you some. The doctor said that

you could have it. I'll be right back." Mary Lee hurried to the kitchen. "Jake, do you have any whiskey?"

"About a half bottle. Down at the cabin."

"I never thought I'd ask someone for whiskey for my mother, but can she have some of it?"

"I'll get it."

"Thank you. Eli, go tell the sheriff that Mama's awake."

Back in her mother's room, Mary Lee pulled a chair up close to the bed.

"Whiskey." Dolly's eyes suddenly focused on Mary Lee's face.

"I've sent for some. It'll be here in a minute." She picked up her mother's hand and held it between hers.

"You . . . hate me."

"No, I don't. You're my mother. How could I hate you?"

"I've not always been . . . a good mother."

"We won't think about that now."

Dolly rolled her head back and forth on the pillow. The hand in Mary Lee's was limp and cool. When Mary Lee heard footsteps on the porch and then in the living room, she tried to get her mother's attention again.

"Mama, the sheriff is here. He wants to talk to you."

"Whiskey," Dolly said, and her face puckered as if she would cry.

"Is Jake back?" Mary Lee called anxiously.

"I'm here."

"Pour some in a glass, Jake." Mary Lee looked defiantly at the sheriff. "The doctor said that she could have it."

When Jake brought the glass with a couple of inches of whiskey in it, Mary Lee slipped her arm beneath her mother's shoulders and lifted her so that she could drink. After gulping the strong-smelling liquid, she sank back down on the pillow, and Mary Lee got to her feet. Carrying the glass, she left the bedroom and nodded for the sheriff to go in.

In the kitchen, Mary Lee went straight to Jake's arms when he opened them. She pressed her face to his shoulder. She was too miserable even to cry. In her wildest dreams she could not have imagined herself holding a glass while her mother drank the hated spirits that had ruined her life and made her own and her daddy's a torment.

"Doctor Morris said to give it to her if she

asked for it," she said as if she needed an excuse for what she had just done.

Jake didn't know what to say. He held her, rocked her in his arms and buried his face in her hair. He would have given anything to be able to ease her sorrow. He felt guilty because her grief was giving him the chance to hold her. For the first time since his mother's death many years ago, someone needed him. It was a powerful tonic to be needed, and especially by someone as sweet and adorable as the woman in his arms. He breathed deeply the scent of her, and his heart pounded with love for her.

Sheriff Pleggenkuhle's voice came from the other room, low and coaxing. Mary Lee listened for the sound of her mother's voice but heard nothing. After what seemed a long time, the sheriff came to the kitchen door.

"She just stares at me. She's not said a word." The sheriff looked at the two of them accusingly. "You shouldn't have given her the whiskey. We could have bargained for it."

"You mean not let her have it unless she told you something?"

Sheriff Pleggenkuhle looked sheepish. "I

know it would have been a rotten thing to do, but there's been a murder and it will benefit all of us to find out who did it."

"Maybe she doesn't know anything. She came into the house just about midnight. I heard her in the bathroom. From the mess on the floor it looks like she crawled to the bed."

"It's likely that she doesn't, but still I've got to hear her say that he was alive when she came to the house and that she didn't see or hear anyone go in the cabin after she left it."

The sheriff noticed how close the two were standing and that Jake's arm was around her, holding her to him.

"It's a good thing, Jake, that Sheriff McChesney over in Oklahoma said the little dude was a straight shooter, or you'd be in jail. He said that if Deke Bales said you were with him, you were with him. That doesn't mean that you didn't sneak out, kill Frank, and sneak back in while he was asleep. So you're not off the hook yet."

"Are you accusing Jake!" Mary Lee punctuated the statement by stepping in front of Jake.

"At this point I'm not ruling anyone out.

Not even you. Some are wondering why you're not in jail, Mrs. Clawson. After all, you had as much reason to kill Frank as anyone."

"I didn't want him dead. I just wanted him to move."

"Whoever killed Frank was crazy mad at him, mad enough to bury the bottle in his throat after they slit it with a knife. And he knew who it was or they'd not have gotten close enough to him to do it. You were mad enough at him, Mrs. Clawson, to attack him with the plate. Did a good job on him too."

"You know why I did that. He was trying to draw Jake into a fight so he'd get in trouble and be sent back to prison."

"Looks like Jake's been in a fight."

"Yeah, and I struck the first blow. I plowed into Yancy Hummer six ways from Sunday, and I'd do it again for the same reason."

"I've talked to Paco. I know what happened." At the door of the kitchen, the sheriff paused. "If nobody here killed Frank, there's a killer running around out there. The women shouldn't be alone in the house all night. I can't leave the deputy here; I've got a whole county to patrol."

"They won't be alone. Deke and I will bed down on the porch."

The sheriff leveled his gaze on Mary Lee. "Like the fox watching the henhouse, huh? When will the doctor be back?"

"Sometime in the morning, unless . . . I need him."

"Tell him not to put her to sleep until after I talk to her again."

"I'll tell him what you said."

After the sheriff left, Jake and Eli moved the barrels so that Jake could bring his truck in off the highway and park it by his cabin. Shortly after they came back to the house, Deke returned with Trudy riding in the sidecar of his motorcycle.

Mary Lee was sitting beside her mother. Trudy looked in, then went back to the kitchen.

"Stupid sheriff. I ain't tellin' him nothin'." Dolly's voice was stronger. Her words were a surprise.

"Do you know anything to tell him, Mama?"

"Plenty, but I ain't goin' to."

Mary Lee sat quietly, rubbing her mother's hand. She didn't know what to say. After a minute or two she felt the tightening of her mother's fingers.

"Can I . . . have another drink? I'll not ask . . . for a while."

Mary Lee looked into eyes that pleaded, eyes that were dull and faded. Her mother spoke again before she could get out of the chair.

"I . . . know you hate it . . ."

"I'd be lying if I said I didn't. But the doctor said you could have it."

"He . . . thinks I'm dyin'."

"He never said that. He said to keep you comfortable."

"Is he comin' back?"

"Do you want him to?"

"I want to sleep."

"Then he'll be back tomorrow."

Mary Lee left the room and returned with some whiskey in a glass. She lifted her mother as she had done before and held her while she gulped the fiery liquid.

"Will you eat something now? I have corn bread, boiled cabbage, carrots and potatoes. I'll mash some of the potatoes and put butter on them."

"I couldn't get down a bite, lovey." Dolly closed her eyes.

Mary Lee was so shocked to hear the endearment that she went stone still, her eyes glued to her mother's face. Then, without her being aware of it, tears squeezed from her lids and rolled down her cheeks. When she was younger, she would have given anything to hear her mother call her "lovey." Now that she had done so, it was too late for her to love her as she should.

As soon as Mary Lee composed herself, she went to the kitchen, where Trudy was wiping the stove, making work for herself.

"Where's Eli?"

"Out on the back stoop. Jake told him to stay here while he and Deke went down to his cabin."

Mary Lee went out and sat down beside the boy. "Can I hug you?"

"If . . . ya want to."

"We've been through a lot together since you came here." She put her arm around his thin shoulders and hugged him. "I don't know if I could have managed without you." She rested her cheek against his shoulder. "Mama's dying, Eli," she whispered.

"Ah . . . you sure?"

"The doctor as much as said so. I never thought about her dying. I'm sorry now that

I wasn't more understanding of what was wrong with her."

"She was . . . hard to understand."

"You'll be my family now. You and the baby. Promise me that you'll not leave."

"Ya'll have Jake and Trudy."

"Jake won't want to be burdened with another man's child."

"It don't seem to bother him none. If I was old enough I'd marry you . . . if you'd have me."

"Why, Eli"—she lifted her head to look at him—"is this a proposal?"

"Kinda."

"Can I wait to see if you're goin' to be a famous lawyer or doctor or politician before I give you my answer?"

"I'm not goin' to be any of those thin's. I want to live on a ranch and raise horses."

"Like Jake, huh?"

"I wanted to before I met Jake."

"I hope you get to do that."

In the near-dark, she watched Jake and Deke come up the lane from the number six cabin. Each carried a canvas cot and bedding. When they reached the porch, they placed the bundles on it and Jake went back for a second load.

"Why're ya sittin' so close to my girl?" Deke demanded.

"I thought Trudy was your girl," Eli retorted.

"I can have two girls. Ain't that right, darlin'?" Deke was busy putting up the canvas cot.

"Don't count me as one of them, *darlin'.*" Trudy came out of the house.

"I told your mama that I'd take care of ya and that makes ya one of my girls, sugarfoot."

"You're as windy as a cyclone. Don't your mouth ever stop?"

"Yeah, when I'm kissin' my girl. Want me to show ya?" Deke made to grab her. Trudy let out a little cry and dodged around to the other side of Mary Lee.

"Don't you dare, you . . . you masher!"

"Masher? That cuts me to the quick, darlin'."

"What's a masher?" Eli asked.

"It's a . . . a flirt, a wolf, a skirt chaser—"

"You two. If you're not the limit," Mary Lee said, smiling at her friend. "Have you ever had a serious conversation?"

"Yes, ma'am." Deke went back to setting up the cots. "When she explained to me that she's been lookin' for a man like me all her life and—"

"You liar. I never told you any such thing!"

"What's all the yelling about?" Jake had returned. He carried his radio in his arms.

"Trudy just confessed her undyin' love for me, is all." Deke spoke as if bored by the whole thing.

"Someday . . . I'm going to kill you," Trudy gasped.

"Can it wait until after we listen to Ed Wynn, the Texaco fire chief?"

"I'd better go see about Mama." Mary Lee had just stepped inside the kitchen door when she heard Deke speak. She paused to listen.

"This little squirt was huggin' up to yore woman, Jake."

"I noticed that. I was about to bash his head in."

"I saw her first," Eli muttered.

"No, you didn't," Jake said. "I saw her when she was about six or seven years old—long before you were a gleam in your daddy's eye."

"Does it bother you that she's goin' to have another man's baby?" Eli asked.

Inside the kitchen Mary Lee's hand flew to her mouth.

"What do you mean, bother me?"

"She said that you'd not want to be bothered with another man's kid. If I was old enough, I'd marry her."

"Thank God you're not old enough. She thinks you're the prize in the crackerjack box as it is."

"Why don't you marry her?"

In the dark kitchen Mary Lee groaned.

"Eli Stacy!" Trudy said with irritation. "Didn't anyone ever tell you not to ask personal questions?"

"No, and if they had, I'd still ask it."

"It's all right, Trudy. He's concerned for her, as we all are. I don't have anything to offer her, Eli. She'd not want to hook up with a jailbird that's poor as a church mouse."

"You could help her run the court."

"And take your job?"

Mary Lee swallowed the large lump that was blocking her breathing passage. She didn't want to hear any more. She hurried through the semidarkened house to slump against the door to her mother's room. *An eavesdropper never hears anything good about himself.* The old saying popped into her mind.

Humiliation washed over her.

Jake couldn't come right out and say that he didn't think of her as a . . . a sweetheart in spite of the Spanish endearments, but as a pregnant woman who needed a helping hand. He would do the same if she were twenty years older than he was, weighed two hundred pounds and was as ugly as a mud fence.

Mary Lee's imagination sprouted legs and began to run away with her. He may have loved a girl, gotten her pregnant and lost her when he went to prison. Or, with his love of animals, he may have seen the suffering endured when one of his mares gave birth and had a special feeling for pregnant females. It was even possible that his mother had died in childbirth.

After checking to see if her mother was asleep, she went back through the house to the porch, knowing the others would come to see what was keeping her. Ignoring the vacant place between Eli and Jake, she sat down on the end of the bench beside Trudy and leaned back against the wall. Jake had run an electric line from the washhouse so they could listen to the radio. After the *Fire Chief,* Jake turned the dial to Nashville, Tennessee, so they could hear the *Grand Ole Opry.*

Roy Acuff was singing about careless love. The next performer was someone singing "There's An Empty Cot in the Bunkhouse Tonight." The sweet harmony of the Carter Family came from the radio. They sang hymns for almost a half hour.

Trudy and Deke were having a low, intimate conversation, not teasing each other for a change. Jake had not said a word since Mary Lee came back out of the house.

After a soft male voice sang "My Tumbledown Shack," his next song was "A Convict's Dream." Mary Lee thought that she couldn't sit still another minute.

"I'll go see about Mama, then I think I'll lie down for a while."

Jake was at the door when she opened it. "Are you feeling all right?" His hand was warm on her arm.

"Of course," she said, more sharply than she intended.

"You're not to worry. Deke and Eli will be here in the back. I'll be on the front porch."

"Thank you. I appreciate it." She stepped

into the house; his hand fell from her arm, and she hurried into the bedroom to sit on the side of the bed, her face in her hands.

Mary Lee was sure that the only misery she could compare to this was how she felt when her father died and she was far from home without money to come say her final good-bye to him.

Her mother was dying.

She was going to lose the motor court.

And Jake . . . oh, Lord, she had fooled herself into thinking that he cared for her when he only . . . felt sorry for her. How could she have been so stupid as to think his interest in her was anything but compassion for a pregnant woman who was having a tough time?

Chapter 22

Trudy moved quietly about, placing the plates on the table. She had stirred up a batch of pancake batter and was waiting for the round iron griddle to heat on the stove. Coffee was made, and syrup and butter were on the table.

When she heard steps on the back porch, she quickly went to the door and pressed her forefinger to her lips.

"Shhh . . . She's still asleep." Eli and Deke came in, followed by Jake. "She was up most of the night with her mother and she's 'bout worn to a frazzle."

"How is Mrs. Finley?" Eli asked.

"I don't know. One minute she's callin' for whiskey and before Mary Lee can get it, she's cussin' a blue streak." Trudy shook her head and clicked her tongue. "She looks terrible this morning. Sometimes she makes sense and other times she's out of her head."

Trudy went back to the stove and poured batter onto the grill. Deke poured coffee. Jake still stood hesitantly beside the door.

"Sit down, Jake. Your eye's not so swollen this morning but still looks bad. Can you see out of it?"

"Little bit."

"It's black as the ace of spades clear down onto your cheekbone. Reminds me of that big old white dog on the Victrola label with the black circle around its eye."

"The man had a big fist."

"Why're ya fussin' over him for, darlin'? I got a big lump on my head the size of a teacup and it hurts somethin' awful." Deke set the coffeepot on the stove and came to stand close behind Trudy.

"I'd be worried if the lump was anywhere but on your hard head, buster."

"Now, now, darlin'. I understand what yo're meanin', but ya ort to watch what yo're sayin' in front of the boy."

"You know what I mean, you . . . you

slimy toad," she hissed. "You've got a nasty mind."

"Is there any other kind?" he whispered back.

When Trudy heard a noise coming from Dolly's room, she quickly surrendered the job of turning the hotcakes to Deke and hurried from the room, her face hot and red.

"Do you want somethin', Mrs. Finley?" When she leaned over the bed, Trudy could feel the heat from the fevered body and smell the repulsive odor of urine.

"Where's Miss Goody-goody?"

"Mary Lee's sleepin'. She was here with ya most of the night. Would you like a drink of water?"

"Water?" she croaked. "I want whis . . . key, ya ugly little shit!"

"I'll get what there is left. You be quiet now until I get back." Trudy went quickly to the kitchen and grabbed up the nearly empty whiskey bottle, emptied what was left into a glass and added a little water. "I hope she doesn't notice the difference. This is the only thing that keeps her quiet," she said to the men seated at the table.

"I'll get more today." Jake was eating out of habit, not because he was hungry.

Trudy held Dolly's head and shoulders while she drank from the glass, then eased her back down onto the pillow.

"Is there anything else I can do for you? I'll rub your back, if you want me to."

Dolly looked at her for a long moment. Her eyes seemed to glaze over before she closed them wearily. Trudy had turned away when she heard her mutter.

"Ya . . . ain't so ugly. Guess I ain't . . . looked at ya real good."

She waited for several minutes before she went back to the kitchen. Three pairs of eyes were on her when she came through the doorway.

"She didn't notice that it was watered down. Maybe she'll sleep awhile. Mama says someone can drink so much of that rotgut whiskey that it'll fry their brains. I'm surprised she's not got jake leg. It's why she talks nasty. Poor thing. She's just skin and bones."

Jake got up and refilled the coffee cups. "I'm going to be gone for a little while this morning," he said to Trudy. "Eli and Deke will be here."

"Now, don't ya go off and get yourself in trouble. That would go hard on Mary Lee.

She's facin' enough as it is without havin' to worry about you. Maybe you ought to go along and keep an eye on him," she said to Deke.

"No." Jake spoke before Deke could answer. "He and Eli will keep an eye out here. Eli is good, but he can't be two places at one time. I'll not be gone but an hour or so."

"You're not workin' today?"

"When I get back, Deke will go out and tell Mr. Quitman that we'll not be out at the ranch until this thing is cleared up here."

"Will he fire you?"

"No. He wants me to train his horses and he wants Deke to build him a motorcycle. Besides, he's a decent sort and will understand."

As badly as he wanted to see Mary Lee and know that she was all right, he gulped his coffee and picked up his hat.

"Are ya takin' the truck?" Deke asked.

"No, I'll walk. No use advertising that I'm in town. Do you need anything from the store, Trudy?"

"Eli will take the wagon and go up this afternoon. Mary Lee will make out a list."

Jake dug into his pocket and placed two

silver dollars on the table. "Put this in the grocery pot."

"And not say a word about it, huh?"

"You got it right."

Jake walked across the field toward town. He'd had a sleepless night. Not only was the pallet on the front porch hard and uncomfortable, but his mind was awash with thoughts of the sudden change in Mary Lee's attitude toward him. During supper she had smiled at him and once squeezed his hand. Something had happened while he and Deke were at his cabin getting the bedrolls and the radio.

He had first noticed it when she came out onto the porch and sat on the end of the bench beside Trudy and Deke. She would have ordinarily sat farther away to give them some privacy. Although it was dark, she kept her head turned away from him. And when the songs about the convicts were sung, she had gone into the house.

Was she ashamed that she had let a convict hold her and kiss her? Was she ashamed that she was forced to accept his help because there was no one else she could depend on?

Jake's long legs ate up the distance to

town quickly. He took the stairs that separated the dry-goods store from the billiard parlor two at a time. At the top he hesitated, not sure whether he should knock or walk in. Deciding, he opened the door and walked into the office.

Sidney Morales was sitting behind his desk. He'd not had a secretary for several years. At this time in his life he didn't want to do enough work to require one.

"Howdy." The lawyer leaned back in his chair.

"Morning," Jake said. "Got a few minute? I'll pay for your time."

Sidney waved him to a chair beside the desk. "How ya doin', Jake? See you're sportin' a shiner."

"Yeah. I ran into a big fist over at Paco's."

"I heard Pete Hanna'll not be using his tallywacker for a while. He's been needing someone to give him a little of what he's been dishin' out ever since he came to town."

"When you go up against a bully as big and mean as he is, you got to use every trick you know."

"How are things at the motor court?"

"It's closed for now. Trudy Bender is staying with Mrs. Clawson. Mrs. Finley is bad-off. The doctor said her heart's giving out. She could go anytime. Mr. Morales, I've a favor to ask . . . sort of."

While he was talking, he lifted his shirt and took a money belt from around his waist. Jake counted out three stacks of one hundred dollars, then placed a single fifty-dollar bill beside them.

"Beside the fifty-dollar bill in my wallet, my truck and six horses out at Quitman's, this is the sum of everything I have. I want Mrs. Clawson to have it to pay off that bloodsucker at the bank, but I don't know how to give it to her. She's got pride she hasn't used yet."

"Why're ya doing this, Jake? Seems to me that if you have feelings for her, you could tell her and she would accept your help."

"She'll not have feelings for a jailbird. I'd not have my stink rubbing off on her if she did. Scott Finley did me a favor once. I'm paying his daughter back."

"Don't give me that line of bull about a favor to Scott. But why you're doing it is your business."

"She mustn't know where the money came from."

"Now, that'll be a problem. What the hell will I tell her? That I found it under a rock?"

"I have one idea. You can kick it around and see what you think. Her mother is dying. The doctor seems to think it could be anytime. He told Mary Lee to give her whiskey when she asks for it. What if Scott had taken out an insurance policy on her a long time ago and paid it up? When she passes, couldn't you claim the money is from the policy?"

Mr. Morales leaned back and eyed Jake. "That might work. I'll have to have a reason for giving her cash."

Jake got to his feet. "You're the lawyer. You figure it out. Another thing. Work around Rosen at the bank. He's not to know where she got the money. The greedy old fool is dying to get his hands on the motor court."

"Hold on; I'll give you a receipt for the money. Her bank loan is three hundred, but I suppose there will be an interest charge."

"It won't be over fifty dollars. It'll give her a little extra. As soon as I get a paycheck from Quitman, I'll be in and pay you for your trouble."

"You'll not owe me anything. I'll get my pay when I see the look on the girl's face when I give her the money, and again when she pays off Rosen at the bank. How's she doin'? Isn't her baby due in a little while?"

"She's holding up. Her baby is due the last of September." Jake grinned. "You should have seen her tie into Frank Pierce with that plate."

"The rumor is that someone came in off the highway and killed him."

"That's too pat for me. I think it was someone who knew him, maybe someone who was afraid that he'd spill the beans on him. But I'm hoping that it was someone who came in off the highway and has gone on down the road by now."

Mr. Morales handed Jake a receipt for the money. "Keep in touch and let me know what's goin' on."

"When Mrs. Finley passes, you'll probably know about it."

"Good-bye, Jake."

"Thanks."

Jake felt a little easier in his mind as he walked down the street toward the Red

Pepper Corral. Now, regardless of what happened to him, Mary Lee would be able to make a living for herself and her child at the motor court.

It worried him some that he'd not have the money he needed to buy a small herd, but that was a mild concern when compared to the ease it would give Mary Lee to know that she didn't have the mortgage hanging over her head. If he got too down-and-out, he'd sell a couple of his horses to Quitman.

The door of the Red Pepper Corral was closed. Jake looked through the glass door to see Paco mopping the floor. He rapped sharply on the window. At first Paco ignored the knock, but when Jake did it again, he turned with a scowl on his face. Seeing who it was, he put his mop aside and unlocked the door.

"Hey, *amigo.* Come in."

"Morning. I'm surprised to see the owner of this lofty establishment mopping the floor."

"I clean toilets too. How's the eye?"

"It hurts some, but probably not as much as Pete's nuts."

"Ohhh . . . ," Paco groaned. "It hurts to even think of it."

"If I learned anything in prison, it was how to fight dirty."

"I hear that Pete and that sneaky weasel he runs with spent the night in the livery. Pete couldn't fork a horse to get back to the Circle C."

"That's a shame. Has Lon been in?"

"Not for a day or two. Do you think he'd want to get rid of Frank?"

"Not unless he thought Frank had turned on him and was spilling his guts."

"What's Pleggenkuhle saying?"

"Not much. He would have liked for it to have been me or Deke. It would have made his job easier."

"He's counted you out?"

"Not yet. I came by to get a bottle of whiskey."

"Jesus Christ. When did you start drinking whiskey?"

"It's not for me. Mrs. Finley is bad-off. Doc doesn't think she'll last long and said to give it to her when she asks for it."

"Old Dolly is dyin'?"

"Yeah. She's been slidin' downhill for a month or more, and in the last few days she's taken to her bed. She doesn't eat. All she wants is whiskey. I had half a bottle I kept for snakebites. She drank that last night."

"Snakebites, my rear end."

"All right. I stole it off a man at the bridge site. I didn't want him drinking while I was attached to him on that high girder."

"I've got tequila." Paco went into the back room and came out with two bottles. He rolled them in newspaper and tied the bundle with twine. Jake placed two silver dollars on the counter.

"Is this enough?"

Paco drew one toward him. "This is enough."

"Thanks." Jake pocketed the other dollar. "What's the talk around town?"

"You know how it goes, *amigo.* There's not been this much excitement in town since two teamsters with bullwhips fought to the death out in the middle of Main Street."

"I've not heard about that. When was it?"

"Back in 1889."

"No wonder I've not heard about it." Jake gave his friend a disgusted look.

"*Yi, yi, yi . . .*" Paco's grin showed his gold

tooth prominently. "Yancy had some folks believing that you had killed Frank. Some thought Mrs. Clawson had done it, and others thought the little fellow from Oklahoma was the one. Now, I think they've settled on a tramp comin' off the highway or . . . you."

"Between you and me, I think it was someone who knew Frank or he'd have put up a fight. Sheriff said he was lying on the bed."

"Someone should be keepin' an eye on that girl. Sure as shootin', somebody tried to send her headfirst down that stairway coming down from Doc's."

"She won't be by herself. Trudy Bender will be staying with her, and Eli, the boy who has been helping out, will be there. He'd tackle a herd of wildcats for her."

"But he's still a boy. I've seen him pulling a wagon going to the store. Where'd he come from?"

"He wandered in. He was at the Circle C doing this and that for his grub until Lon ran him off. Mary Lee has taken him under her wing. He's a good boy and smart as a whip. You only have to tell him one time how to do something."

"How are you comin' along at Quit-man's?"

"He seems to think I'm doing a good job. He's getting a hell of a price for the quarter horses I've trained, and he's got a few more that look promising."

"But they're not your horses, huh, *amigo*?"

"No they're not my horses. It'll be a while before I have my own spread. This will do for now." Jake headed for the door. "See ya, Paco."

"I'll keep my eyes and ears open, *mi amigo*." Paco followed Jake to the door and locked it after he passed through.

Jake walked briskly down the street, nodding to those who acknowledged him, ignoring the others. He had been away from the motor court for a little less than two hours and was anxious to get back.

Coming across the field, Jake could see that Eli was hoeing in the little vegetable garden that he and Mary Lee had planted beside the washhouse. The sheriff's car was out front. Deke was sitting on one of the barrels that blocked the drive, so that he could watch the front of the house.

With hoe in hand, Eli went to meet Jake.

"What's going on?"

"Mrs. Finley's been in a awful state. She's cussin' the sheriff and ever'body else. I wish she'd just . . . go. She's killin' Mary Lee," he said angrily. "She's talkin' somethin' terrible to her."

Mary Lee was in the kitchen wetting a cloth in the wash pan when Jake opened the door. Her hair was in tangles, her face pale and pinched. She looked at him then quickly away, afraid that he might read in her face her newly discovered feelings about him and his about her.

He placed the bundle on the table and broke the twine. "I've brought tequila."

"Oh, thank goodness. The doctor is supposed to be here this morning. He said that he'd bring some."

Jake unwrapped the bottles and opened one. Mary Lee held a glass while he poured in a couple of inches.

"Is that enough?"

"Fine. Thank you. I'll pay for it, but first let me give this to her." She left the room hurriedly.

Jake could hear her talking to her mother and Trudy. When it was quiet, Trudy came out of the room.

"It's been just awful," she said as soon as she saw Jake. "She's out of her head most of the time, cussin' and swearin' somethin' crazy. She'd have nothin' to do with the sheriff. Called him the nastiest names I ever heard. She blames him for taking Frank to jail. Thank goodness you came with the whiskey."

"It's tequila. Alcohol is what she wants. She won't care what kind."

On hearing a knock at the back door, Trudy went to open it for a short, plump woman with dark, gray-streaked hair. She was carrying a pan wrapped in a cloth. Jake hastily removed his hat and held it to his side.

"Come in, Mrs. Santez."

"*Hola,* Trudy."

"Do you know Jake Ramero?"

"When he little boy. I see him." The large brown eyes twinkled up at him. "He big man now." She smiled and held out her hand. "My Ollie say you good man. He glad you here with Mary Lee."

"It's nice to see you, Mrs. Santez. And thank Ollie for the vote of confidence." Jake took the small, plump hand in his. A vision of his own mother, long gone, flashed be-

fore his eyes. She was much like Mrs. Santez, small and gentle.

"I bring enchiladas for supper."

"Thank you." Trudy took the pan and
placed it on the table. "They smell so
good!" She saw Mrs. Santez eyeing the
bottles of tequila. After glancing at Jake,
she said, "The doctor said to give Mrs. Finley what she wants. Jake was good enough
to get this for her."

"It's a shame. *Yi, yi, yi.* A wasted life."
Rosa Santez shook her head.

Jake edged toward the door and
slammed his hat down on his head. "Bye,
Trudy, Mrs. Santez." He was out the door
before they could reply.

Chapter 23

Ocie Clawson's booted feet were propped on the railing of his front porch. He liked to sit there in the evening and look at the hills that surrounded the ranch. Life was a bitch. He never thought that he would admit that he was lonely, but, dammit to hell, he was. He rattled around in this big old house with only María coming in and out to clean and cook a meal. He should have sons living on the ranch, running things, instead of a shirttail relation. And grandkids racing in and out of the house and driving him crazy with questions and rowdiness.

Hell, he should have married after Edith died. He wasn't too old then to have a houseful of kids.

Ocie saw one of the hands come out of the cook shack and called to him.

"Come sit awhile, Ben."

"Was goin' to," Ben said as he neared. "Was goin' to offer to beat ya in a game of checkers."

"Big of ya, Ben. How many times have I beat you over the years?"

"Harrupmt!" Ben came slowly up the steps to the porch and sank down in an old unpainted rocking chair. He tapped a forefinger on his head. "That's about the only thing workin' good anymore."

"You gettin' down in the back, old man?"

"Hell. Ain't it time?"

"Guess so. You've been here almost as long as those hills out there."

"Temple hired me. Musta been forty years ago. I was just a beanpole of a kid. Thought I knew it all. But when it come right down to it, I didn't know shit from Shinola."

"Time flies."

"I've been here so long, I expected to be buried here."

"Expected? You thinkin' of leavin'?" Ocie looked sharply at the old man. His hair was white, his legs bowed, his face so weathered it looked like saddle leather. The Circle C wouldn't be the same without him.

"Ain't wantin' to. Don't have no place much to go."

"Then why'n hell did ya say that for?"

"Thin's ain't the same here, Ocie. When's the last time ya saw the men gather 'round for a ropin' contest, or a-fiddlin' or just sittin' around a fire gabbin'? A lot of the old hands have been run off. Only me, Tom and Howdy is left of the old bunch."

"There's new ways of doin' things, Ben."

"Yeah, guess so."

During the long silence that followed, twittering birds began to settle in the trees for the night. A few stars came out. A truck with several cowhands in the back left for town.

"Didn't used to be no goin' to town 'cept on Saturday night," Ben remarked. "Used to be a man or a kid could come in here and get a bed and a meal for a day's work."

Ocie was quiet for a long moment before he asked, "What'a ya mean? Man or kid? There was a kid here a while back eatin' his head off and lazin' in the bunkhouse."

"That kid worked his tail off for the grub

he ate," Ben said bluntly, and clamped his mouth shut.

"Wasn't the grub good enough? Is that why he left?"

"He was run off and you damn well know it, Ocie."

"I know no such thing, dammit. Didn't know he was gone till I saw him at the motor court in town."

"Glad to hear he found some decent folks to take him in."

Things had changed here at the ranch in more ways than one, Ocie thought. He'd gradually let Lon take over the hiring, and what did he have? A bunch of men he didn't know, and most of them he didn't like. They had no loyalty to the spread or to him. They did the jobs assigned by Lon, took orders from Lon and ignored him for the most part.

One by one, the old cowhands, some of whom had been at the ranch for ten years or more, had left. He looked over at Ben and saw that he was gazing off toward the foothills. The old cowhand had lived most of his life here on the ranch and knew more of what was going on than he himself did. Hell, how had he let the running of this place slip out of his hands?

"Ben, you and Tom and Howdy have a home here at the Circle C as long as you want it, whether you can work or not."

Ben turned his grizzled head. "That's decent of ya, Ocie. Lon'd not stand for that. He expects a man to put in a full day's work."

"Lon doesn't own this ranch. I do."

"Does he know that?"

"What'a ya mean?"

Ben shrugged his thin shoulders. "I better be gettin' on back to the bunkhouse." He made an attempt to rise a couple of times before he got to his feet.

"Has Lon threatened to run you, Tom and Howdy off?"

Ben took a grip on the porch post before he answered. "Not in so many words, but he's workin' on it. He'd rather not have us around. Now, don't be goin' and sayin' so. I ain't wantin' a busted hip or a broke leg."

"Could that happen, Ben?"

"Wal . . . I ain't wantin' to chance it. Last few months three cowhands got busted up and had to leave."

"I never heard about it."

"Happened mostly while they was out

riding fence or roundin' up strays and you was holed up in here."

"And you think . . ."

"I ain't thinkin' nothin'. All I know is they wasn't no friends of Lon's. They'd bucked him some."

Ocie stared at the old man for a minute, then turned to see Lon coming toward them from the side of the porch.

"Howdy, Ben. Howdy, Ocie. Ben, I was lookin' for you. In the mornin' I want you to ride out to Rusty Ridge and take a look around. One of the hands said he found a couple of calves pulled down by wolves just south of there."

"I want Ben to work here in the house tomorrow. I think there's a leak in the water pipes. They got to be flushed out anyway."

"I'll take a look at it."

"Ben was here when the pipes were put in. Send one of the younger men to Rusty Ridge."

Lon's shuttered eyes went from the old man to Ocie. "If that's what you want."

"See you in the mornin', Ben."

"'Night, Ocie. 'Night, Lon."

After Ben left, Lon said, "What's he harpin' about?"

"Harpin'? Not a thin'. I called him over to talk about my water pipes."

"He's deadwood around here, ya know," Lon said between clenched teeth. "He's gettin' too old to carry his weight."

"You wantin' to put him out to pasture or shoot him like a broken-down old horse that ain't worth feedin'?"

"Ranchin' is a business, Ocie. Not an old folks' home."

"I'm the owner here, Lon. You just work for me. Don't send Ben out unless you check with me."

Lon shrugged as if the order was of no consequence, but his clenched jaws didn't go unnoticed by Ocie.

"Another thin'," Ocie said. "Get rid of Yancy, Pete and that squint-eyed knife thrower. Give them a half month's pay and tell 'em if they step foot on this ranch, I'll meet 'em with a shotgun."

"They're already gone. Ramero started the fight, but they could've backed off."

"Jake admitted it. Yancy was talkin' nasty about Mary Lee. Jake ain't standin' by and hearin' that kind of talk 'bout a decent woman."

"Decent? Horsecock! He's shackin' up

with her, hopin' to get his hands on the motor court."

"Ya know that for a fact?" Anger tightened the muscles in Ocie's face.

"No, but there's talk."

"And you're helpin' to spread it."

"Why're ya takin' up for that jailbird all of a sudden? He was a nasty know-it-all kid who turned into a goddamn thief."

"Maybe." Ocie was aware that Lon was making every effort to hold on to his temper. "I saw where your squint-eyed knifer tried to gut him."

"He wasn't *my* knifer," Lon said sharply.

"You hired him."

"And I fired him."

"Before you hire anyone else check with me."

"What's brought this on? Ben complainin'?"

"Goddammit, I got eyes! I know more about what goes on around here than you think I do. I don't have to depend on an old man like Ben to tell me."

Lon switched the matchstick in his mouth from one side to the other, letting his temper cool before he spoke.

"All right," he said smoothly. "You're the boss."

But not for long, you son of a bitch. I do the work around here and I'm sick of bein' talked down to by you.

After Lon stalked off toward the little cabin set alongside the bunkhouse, Ocie sat on the porch watching the bats flit here and there and remembered when Lon had come to the ranch some fifteen years ago. He had been a cocky kid who liked to be the center of attention. More than once Temple would have given Lon the boot if he hadn't been a relation.

Gradually over the years Lon had settled down, become a good hand. After Temple died and Bobby had turned out to be such a disappointment, Lon had stepped in and filled a void. Ocie had had no reason to doubt his loyalty until now.

Was he vindictive enough to pin a lie on a man that would send him to prison because of something that had happened when he was a kid?

Doctor Morris had gone out to a ranch to deliver a baby, and it was nearly noon when he arrived to see Dolly.

Mary Lee was sitting with her mother when Trudy brought the doctor to the bed-room. He placed his bag on the foot of the bed and nodded to Mary Lee when she stood to relinquish her chair beside the bed.

"Bad night?"

"Yes, sir. I got a little bread and milk down her, but all she'll drink is the tequila Jake brought."

"I thought that would be the case." Doctor Morris pulled down the sheet. His fingers swept lightly over Dolly's distended belly.

"We tried to change the bed, but it hurt her too much to be moved."

"Keep a dry towel under her. It's all you can do." He covered Dolly and put his hand on her forehead. "Are you awake, Mrs. Finley?"

The sunken eyes opened slowly. The lids were as thin as paper.

"Playing possum, are you?" Doctor Morris asked lightly.

"Am I dyin'?" Dolly spoke so low, he had to bend his head to hear.

"I won't lie to you, Mrs. Finley. You're on the road."

"Yeah? Well, it don't matter."

"The sheriff would like to talk to you. Do you feel up to it?"

"I ain't got nothin' to say to . . . that shit-head."

Mary Lee cringed, but the doctor didn't seem to mind the crude language.

"Will you talk to me?"

"Yeah. Whis . . . key first." She struggled for each breath.

Doctor Morris nodded at Mary Lee, and she left the room.

"Don't want her . . . to hear."

"All right."

Mary Lee returned and held her mother's head while she drank from the glass.

"When you leave, Mrs. Clawson," the doctor said kindly, "will you please close the door?"

Mary Lee returned to the kitchen, where Trudy was peeling potatoes from a bushel basket, and sank down in a chair. She had managed to avoid Jake since he brought the tequila. He was out now, talking to Sheriff Pleggenkuhle, who had been waiting for the doctor, hoping he could calm Dolly enough for her to give a statement.

"Where did the potatoes come from?" Mary Lee asked.

"Mama. Deke brought them when he went to tell her about Mrs. Finley and get a can of peaches for a cobbler. She's afraid they'll spoil before she can use them."

"Trudy, am I so stiff-necked that you have to lie to me?"

"Sometimes," Trudy said with a grin.

"Keep a list of who brings things so I can thank them later."

"I already started it. You want some tea or somethin'?"

"Not now. Did you turn the ice card?"

"We've got a chunk, so I turned it to twenty-five pounds."

After a silence, Mary Lee said, "The doctor told her that she's dying."

"She knew it already. Poor thing. She told me last night that she's known it for a while."

"I wish things could have been different between us."

"The whiskey got such a hold on her that she didn't care about anything else. Men will lie and steal to get it. I guess it happens to women too. Your mama wasn't strong enough to resist it."

"Daddy told me that. He loved her anyway."

"My mama has never got over losin' my daddy. I see her lookin' at his picture sometimes."

"Trudy, you're the best friend I ever had. I don't know how I would have managed without you."

"You'd a got by."

"At times I think that God has forgotten me; then I think of you and Eli."

"Just hush that or you'll make me bawl. Eli don't know what to do with himself. I thought of sending him up to the creamery to get us a pail of buttermilk."

"We won't be cooking for our stopover people for a while. I'll not be able to hold on to the court, Trudy. What money I've saved will go now."

"Maybe not. The doctor will let you pay later."

"I can't let the county bury Mama. The county buried Bobby and it was so . . . heartless and businesslike. It was like he was some unwanted garbage they needed to get rid of."

"Don't worry about it now. You've got six weeks before you have to pay the loan."

Mary Lee looked out the window to see Jake and the sheriff beside the water pump.

Jake was filling a bucket for Eli to carry to
the small garden.

"I wonder when the sheriff will let us
clean the cabin so we can rent it." Trudy
poured water over the peeled potatoes and
set them on the stove.

"We'll have to buy another new mattress," Mary Lee said worriedly.

"Two new mattresses," Trudy corrected.
"Hon, you can't use the one your mother's
on ever again."

"I know, but I wouldn't have to do it right
away." Mary Lee watched Trudy when Deke
rode in on his cycle and stopped beside the
washhouse. "You like him, don't you?"

"Yeah. He's like nothin' I've met before. I
don't think he minds that I'm . . . the way I
am."

"He sees what you are on the inside the
same as you see him. I like him, Trudy. He's
genuine."

"Yeah, he is."

"I hope he stays around here."

"He's not ready to settle down."

"Has he said that?"

"No. He hides his true self behind his glib
tongue." Trudy laughed. "You should have

seen Mama's face when he called her 'dar-lin'.'"

"Does she like him?"

"Loves him." Trudy laughed again nerv-ously. "She thinks he's cute. Says he re-minds her of a cocky little bantam rooster."

"Jake thinks a lot of him."

"Jake's in love with you." Trudy dropped the bomb into the quiet kitchen.

Mary Lee's head and shoulders swiveled around to where Trudy stood beside the window.

"You're . . . crazy! He feels sorry for me. He has a soft spot for pregnant women. Es-pecially those who find themselves in a bind like I am."

"Mary Lee Finley, the man is crazy about you."

"Hush saying that! There's no way a man like Jake would fall in love with a woman pregnant with another man's child, espe-cially Bobby Clawson's child."

"Then why does he watch you like a hawk watchin' a chicken? Why is he layin' off work to stay here in case you might need him? Why'd he sleep on that hard porch last night?"

"Well, for goodness' sake, I didn't ask him to."

"I know that. He did it 'cause he's crazy about you."

"He's a nice man. He'd have done it for anyone."

"Are you holdin' it against him 'cause he's been in prison?"

Mary Lee opened her mouth to make a firm denial, but the doctor came into the kitchen before the words could leave her mouth.

"Would you like a glass of tea, Doctor?" Trudy was already getting a glass out of the cupboard.

"That would go down real good. I doubt she'll last the night, Mary Lee. Will you have someone here with you?"

"Yes, sir. Trudy will be here."

"I'll come if you can get word to me."

"I will appreciate it. Is there something you can give her for the pain?"

"I gave her morphine. She may wake up again and she may not." He took the glass of tea and headed for the back door. "I'll be back in before I go," he said.

As he stepped off the porch, Doctor Morris motioned to the sheriff. They moved out into the yard. The doctor spoke for several minutes. Sheriff Pleggenkuhle listened intently, then took off his hat, scratched his head and put it back on. He went to where Jake, Eli and Deke were waiting beside the water pump and told the boy to bring him the garden rake.

The men went around the house to the front porch. Eli, followed by the doctor, came into the kitchen.

"The sheriff wants a couple of paper sacks."

"What for?" Trudy asked while tugging the neatly folded sacks from behind the icebox.

"He didn't say, but I reckon we'll find out."

After Eli left, the doctor said, "Mary Lee, there is no way to put this except to come right out and tell you. Your mother confessed to me that she killed Frank Pierce."

Chapter 24

Mary Lee was so shocked by the doctor's calm words that she was unable to utter a sound for a minute. Then she gasped, "That's impossible."

"She told me that she had cleaned the cabin for Frank when she could hardly stand on her feet. I believe that. I don't see how she could have done it in her condition. She said he was mean to her, refused to give her a drink from his bottle and said he'd not ever marry her. Called her vile names and told her to get out. When he lay down on the bed to go to sleep, she cut his throat with a knife, then buried the bottle she had broken earlier in his throat."

Mary Lee began to feel dizzy. She felt for the back of a chair and eased herself around and onto it. The reasons why it was impossible for her mother to do such a thing began to spew from her mouth.

"She wasn't . . . strong enough. She was too sick. She wanted to marry him. She couldn't . . . have done it unless she just went . . . crazy for a minute. She was a . . . drunk, but she wouldn't kill anybody."

"It didn't take much strength to do what she did," Doctor Morris said gently. "And it's very possible that she just went out of her mind and wasn't aware of what she had done until it was over."

"Maybe she's just saying she did it to protect . . . someone else."

"She threw the knife under the porch. Her dress, too, because it had blood on it. The sheriff is fishing them out with the rake."

"Will everyone have to know?" Trudy came to stand behind Mary Lee's chair.

"I'm afraid so."

"Could the sheriff wait until after . . . the funeral?"

"I can't speak for the sheriff."

"It would make things . . . easier," Trudy said.

"I've got to move along. Call me." The

doctor placed a comforting hand on Mary Lee's shoulder when he passed her.

"Thank you," she murmured.

Mary Lee went into her mother's room, sank down in the chair and looked at the pitiful creature that was her mother. How unreal it seemed that this woman had carried her in her body for nine long months, felt her move inside her as she felt the baby she was carrying.

Dolly nourished me. She had to have loved me a little.

Her mother was dying, and there was no one to mourn her except the daughter she had resented from birth. She picked up her mother's limp hand and held it.

"You'll not be alone, Mama. I'll be here."

The day seemed endless. Mary Lee sat beside her mother's bed all afternoon, aware that Trudy had prepared a meal and that the sheriff and the deputy were no longer there. Eli came in and squatted down beside her. He kept his worried eyes away from the woman on the bed, looking only at Mary Lee.

She stroked the hair back from his forehead, then hugged his head to her.

"I'm so glad I've got you, Eli. We'll be all right. We'll just have to figure out what to do after we lose the court."

"Ya think we will?"

"I don't see how we can scrape up the money now with this added expense and having to close the court for a while."

"Can't we open it tomorrow?"

"No, but we can open it in a few days though. We'll save every cent we take in and not be completely broke when we leave."

"I'll get a job and take care of you."

"We'll take care of each other."

"You still like Jake, don't you?"

"Of course. He's been a good friend."

"He says he'll move up into number one because when word gets out that someone was killed in that cabin folks might not want to stay there. Is that all right with you?"

"I don't suppose it makes much difference."

"We've been cleaning the cabin. Jake and Deke burned the mattress. We've scrubbed everythin' with lye soap. Jake fixed the door."

"I'm sorry he and Deke have lost work to stay here."

"Jake's worried about you."

"Did he say that?"

"No. But I can tell. He watches the house all the time, especially—"

Mrs. Santez came into the room, cutting off the conversation, and Eli left hurriedly. Trudy brought a chair for the gas station owner's wife. During the half hour she was there nothing was mentioned about Dolly being the one who killed Frank, for which Mary Lee was grateful.

When Mrs. Santez left, she assured Mary Lee that she and Mr. Santez were there for her if she needed them and that she would be back the next day.

Later, Ruby, Trudy's mother, came. By the time she left, it was dark and the bedroom was illuminated only by the light coming from the living room. Dolly's breaths were so shallow that at times Mary Lee leaned toward the bed to make sure that she was still breathing.

When the light coming from the living room dimmed suddenly, Mary Lee looked up to see Jake's big form filling the doorway.

"Are you all right? Do you need anything?" His voice was strained, husky.

"I'm all right, and no, I don't need any-thing."

He hesitated and turned as if to go. The light cast shadows on his cheeks and soft-ened the lines of his mouth. He looked younger and so vulnerable that a pain clutched Mary Lee's heart. She thought suddenly of the boy who had come hob-bling up to the water pump, exhausted and thirsty but too proud to take the water until he asked permission.

"I'll sit with you, if you want me to." His eyes were bleak, questioning.

"Yes," Mary Lee said in a strangled whis-per.

He came into the room, moved the chair Trudy had brought in closer, and sat down. He reached for her hand and held it tightly between his.

"You've been in here all day."

"I can't let her die alone."

"Did you eat?"

"A little. It's hard to."

"Yeah, I guess it is. How is she?"

"Just hanging on. The doctor said that she probably wouldn't wake up."

"That's the best way . . . if you have to go."

"Sometimes I'm not sure she's still breathing."

"Put your fingers here on the veins." He moved her fingers up to Dolly's wrist. "Do you feel the pulse?" he asked in hushed tones.

She looked at him with big, solemn eyes bright with tears and shook her head.

He took Dolly's hand and pressed his fingers to the veins in her wrists. "It's there, but it's faint."

When she took her mother's hand again, he put his arm around her and pulled her close. He heard her sniff and turned his head to put his lips to her forehead.

"Try to think that this is the best under the circumstances. She's been sick and unhappy for a long time. She'll not have to suffer a trial."

"Doctor Morris said that the reason she told him she'd killed Frank could be that she didn't want me to be blamed for it. Do you think that means that she loved me a little?"

"I'm sure of it. There would be no reason for her to tell otherwise. She drank rotgut whiskey all through Prohibition, and what you get now is not much better. The drink warping her mind is the reason she said mean things to you."

"I . . . can't imagine my not loving my baby."

"How is Gaston taking all of this?"

"He's been active. I've sat today more than I have since I came from Tulsa on the bus. I don't think he likes it."

It seemed natural for Jake's big hand to rest lightly on her rounded belly. It occurred to her that he was the only one who had touched her there except for the doctor.

"He's acting up a bit now. Maybe you should get up and walk around the room until he settles down."

"I can't leave her."

"Then lean on me, scoot down and stretch your legs. It'll give him more room."

His voice was the softest of sounds. He searched her face for assurance that he'd not been too bold. When she obeyed his instructions and nestled trustingly against him, his heart turned over.

Caught in sudden yearning, she held tightly to his hand as if he were a lifeline and she were being swept to sea. Her emotions were mixed. She was scarred from battling with her mother and from her struggle to keep the court going. It was comforting to pretend for a little while that Jake really and truly cared for her.

"That does feel better."

Time ticked away slowly. They didn't talk. There was no need for words. The house was quiet. A tightness crept into Jake's throat, and he thought how foolish he was to think that she'd even consider letting him hold her like this if not for the present circumstances. But he would take what he could get and store up precious memories for later.

It could have been minutes or an hour when Jake leaned toward the bed and took Dolly's hand from Mary Lee's. He held it for a minute, then stood and passed his palm back and forth across her open mouth.

"She's gone, *querida*."

He covered Dolly's face with the sheet, then reached down and lifted Mary Lee to her feet and into his arms.

"She's not breathing?"

"No. She just faded away."

"Oh, my," she whispered, and leaned her head against his shoulder and wrapped her arms around him. She was glad for his strength. Her back ached, her legs were weak and her heart sorrow-filled. She clung desperately to the security of his arms and strong, warm body. He held her firmly against him for a long while before he spoke.

"Deke will go for the doctor. He'll have to sign the death certificate."

"Then the funeral director will come?"

"Yes. You don't have to decide anything right now."

"I thought about it while I was sitting here. Folks will come to a service out of curiosity when they hear what she's done. I don't want that."

"We'll tell the undertaker not to announce when the burial will be."

"I want just a small service at the cemetery."

"Then that's what you'll have."

He led her out of the room and into the kitchen, where Trudy, Deke and Eli sat at the table.

"Deke, you and Trudy take the truck and fetch the doctor. Trudy can show you where he lives."

Mary Lee sat at the table while Jake made a pot of coffee. Eli moved around quietly and watched Mary Lee as if he expected her to fall apart. She looked at his anxious young face and took his hand.

"Don't worry. I'll be all right."

"I heard it marks a baby to be close when somebody . . . dies. Do you think it will have one of those red marks on its face?"

"If it does, it won't be because of this. If that was true, Eli, there would sure be a lot of people with red marks."

After the undertaker had come and gone, Ruby, whom they had brought back with them when they went to notify the doctor, helped Mary Lee look for something suitable for Dolly's burial. They found nothing in her room and went to look over Mary Lee's things.

Jake and Deke took the opportunity to remove the soiled mattress and the bedding from Dolly's bed. The foul-smelling mattress was left on the ashes of the previously burned mattress, to be set on fire in the morning. Eli started up the washing machine and laundered the bedding, not wanting to wait until morning.

When she was alone at last, Mary Lee went to the bathroom, washed herself from head to toe, put on her gown and went to bed. She lay there and cried quietly until sleep overwhelmed her.

Trudy cooked breakfast and, with Eli's help, cleaned the living room. Because Dolly had sold almost everything in the room, they added a few pieces of furniture from the other rooms so that it didn't appear to be so bare. Mary Lee greeted those who came to pay their condolences, and accepted the gifts of food. She thanked the callers and was grateful that none of them stayed very long. She was in constant fear that one of them would mention what her mother had done during the last days of her life.

In the late afternoon Ocie Clawson's car drove in. Mary Lee didn't think that she could cope with him today and was on her way to the bedroom when she saw Jake going to intercept him.

Jake had no qualms about facing him. He reached the steps as Ocie was about to go up onto the porch.

"Mary Lee's not feeling well. She's probably lying down."

"Not feeling well? What's the matter with her?"

"What do you think? The last few days have been hell for her. First Frank Pierce, now her mother."

"Yeah, well, Frank got what he had comin' and Dolly wasn't no saint."

"Maybe not, but she still was her mother."

"You ridin' shotgun here?"

"Doin' what I can to make it easy for her."

Ocie nodded and shifted the cigar from one side of his mouth to the other.

"Is she still pissed off at me about Bobby?"

"You'll have to ask her."

"He sold her a bill of goods. It's what he did best. Lying was the only thin' he was good at."

Jake didn't say anything for a minute. Then, "I don't think he fooled her as much as you think. She found out soon enough what he was like."

"A man's pretty low that'd steal from his own pa. Guess I shoulda helped her bury him, but I was so damn mad that he turned out the way he did."

"Yeah, you should have. It humiliated her to have to take charity from the county."

"Well, that's water under the bridge." Ocie went back to the car and reached inside for a package. "Here's a ham. Thought she could use it."

"She'll send her thanks."

"When's the buryin'?"

"Tomorrow. At the cemetery. She doesn't want a bunch of gawkers."

Ocie nodded and opened the car door. He hesitated before getting in, took the cigar out of his mouth and held it between his thumb and his forefinger.

"Jake, I've been meanin' to ask, what's between you and Lon?"

"Why do you want to know? It won't change anything."

"I'm thinkin' that maybe he lied to me about you stealin' my cattle."

"You're just now getting around to thinking that?"

"Well, hell, what would you have done? It was three against one."

"And I spent two years in the hoosegow for something I didn't do."

"They took your herd to pay your fine?"

"You know damn well they did. And the land I'd paid down on."

"I'll make it up—"

"Goddamn you!" Jake's green eyes flashed angrily. "Don't offer me charity to make up for the wrong you did me or I'll beat the living hell out of you. I don't want a damn thing from you."

"Pa thought a lot of you. I'd do it for his sake."

"I thought a lot of him. He was a decent man. It's too bad his son isn't more like him."

Ocie's face turned a dull red. "Guess I had that comin'." His eyes moved past Jake to where Eli sat on a stump, polishing his boots. "I never run the kid off. I didn't know he was gone until I saw him here. Lon run him off."

"Are you runnin' things out there or is Lon?" Jake's voice was laced with sarcasm.

"I want that girl and her baby at the Circle C." Ocie's voice turned hard. "The kid's a Clawson, by God. Clawsons take care of their own. When she loses this place she won't have anyplace else to go. You're in no shape to take care of her . . . if you wanted to."

"Don't you worry about it. Right now she'll go on the soup line before she takes a penny from you."

"You could help change her mind."

"Don't count on it."

Ocie got in the car and slammed the door. "Dammit, Jake, I'm not your enemy."

"Bullshit! If you're not my enemy, then who was it that helped put me in that hell-hole and took away two years of my life? I had a hell of a time surviving in there. I had to fight someone every damn day and sleep with one eye open every damn night."

"Shit." Ocie looked at Jake for a long time and saw no softening in his expression. "You ain't goin' to give an inch, are you?"

"No. Would you?"

"I guess not. Give her the damn ham and tell her I'll be at the cemetery."

"Why?"

"Out of respect for my grandkid, that's why."

Jake stood for a minute after the car had pulled out onto the highway and wondered what had come over Ocie. He'd been al-most decent for a change.

Chapter 25

The cemetery, on a knoll a half mile out of town, was dotted with aspens and pines. It was peaceful and quiet, except for the occasional birdsong, and blended perfectly with the background of the grass-covered, tree-dotted foothills of the mountain.

The small crowd that gathered for Dolly's burial was there out of respect for Mary Lee and her father. The casket was carried to the grave by Jake, Deke, Eli and Mr. Santez. The early morning service was short; and after a hymn was sung, the coffin was lowered into the ground where Dolly would rest forever beside the husband who had loved her.

Mary Lee, in a shapeless black dress, courtesy of Mrs. Santez, and a small black hat with a net veil that came down over her eyes, stood beside the open grave, holding tightly to Trudy's hand on one side and Eli's on the other. Her face was pale, and her eyes, dark-ringed from the sleepless nights, were clouded with fatigue. Her eyes were full of tears, and she drew her lips between her teeth to keep them from trembling.

Good-bye, Mother. Through the years I have been ashamed that you were my mother. I'm sorry for that now. I thought I hated you, but I don't. I love you. Not because of how you lived and how you made my life and Daddy's so miserable, but in spite of it. I realize now how sick you were. I love you, Mother, and I'm sorry that you'll never know the joy of holding your grandchild or the pleasure of loving and being loved.

She stared at the casket as it was lowered into the ground. After it was covered with soil, she placed the small bouquet of flowers Trudy had put in her hand on the mound and turned away from the grave.

She was surprised to see Mr. Morales, the lawyer, there. Mr. Santez, his wife and one of their daughters had come, as well as Ruby Bender and Trudy, Sheriff Pleggenkuhle, Paco García and his wife. Jake, Deke and Eli stood respectfully by while she spoke to each of them. Ocie Clawson was at the edge of the group, and good manners forced her to go to him and hold out her hand.

"Thank you for coming," she said, and pulled her hand from his.

Jake was watching, ready to go to her if Ocie tried to engage her in conversation. But for once he had the decency to keep his mouth shut. She was so pretty. Even with swollen eyes she was pretty. Spunky too. Maybe too spunky for her own good. Jake's eyes were drawn to her again and again.

Mary Lee rode back to the motor court with Mr. and Mrs. Santez. She was exhausted from the strain and the sleepless nights and went directly to her bedroom and closed the door. After removing the heavy black dress, she folded it carefully, then crawled into bed. Her problems were not going away. They would still be there a few hours from now, and she longed for oblivion. The minute she closed her eyes, she drifted into a deep, peaceful sleep.

*   *   *

"She's worn out." Trudy closed the door softly after she looked into the room. "Thank goodness word didn't get out about the buryin'. It went off as nice as she could make it."

"Word is out that Mrs. Finley killed Frank. The sheriff kept it under wraps as long as he could. Now the town is buzzin' about it." Jake had changed into his work clothes.

"You look nice, Eli," Trudy said. "Mr. Finley's white shirt was a little big on you, but no one noticed."

"How about me, darlin'? Did I look nice?" Deke playfully pinched Trudy's chin between his thumb and forefinger.

"Was that you in that blue shirt and your hair all slicked down? Glory! I thought I was seein' the back end of a mule."

"Now, darlin', you hadn't ought to talk to me like that when I'm fixin' to ask you to go to Sante Fe with me. I might even take ya out for a bite to eat at the five-and-dime."

"What's the catch, buster?"

"No catch. I'm goin' to get a couple of mattresses."

"On your cycle? How are you going to carry them—on your flat head?"

"I was plannin' on you holdin' 'em in the

sidecar, but Jake offered the truck. Now, come on, darlin'. Eli will be here in the house, and Jake isn't goin' to let that woman out of his sight once she comes out of that room."

Trudy glanced at Jake and saw his lips tighten before she went through the door Deke held open for her.

"I gave Deke money for just one mattress," Eli said worriedly after the truck had left the motor court.

"He can get a better deal in Santa Fe than he can here in Cross Roads. He may be able to get two for twenty dollars." Jake went to the stove to heat up the breakfast coffee and stepped in water in front of the icebox. "Hey, the water pan has run over."

"Shit, shit, shit! I forgot to empty it this morning." Eli pulled the pan out from under the icebox and emptied it in the sink. "I'll get the mop out of the washhouse and mop up this mess."

"You'd better not let Mary Lee hear you talking like that. She'll wash your mouth out with soap."

"I know." Eli grinned. "I'm careful."

Later they sat at the table eating a sandwich made from the ham Trudy had baked the night before.

"I wonder why Mr. Clawson came to the buryin'. He didn't talk very nice about Mrs. Finley the other time he was here."

"He came because he's trying to get on the good side of Mary Lee. He wants her to move out to the Circle C."

"She wouldn't like it out there. I hope she don't go. That Lon Delano is a son of a bitch. He's mean and sneaky. He didn't like me none a'tall. He was always accusing me of sittin' on my ass eatin' my head off."

"Did he run you off, or was it Ocie?"

"He did. Said the boss told him to get rid of me. Shit fire. I worked. You can ask old Ben or Tom. I ain't no sponger."

"So Ben's still there."

"Yeah, but I don't think Lon likes him. He has all the men in his pocket except for Ben and a couple others. I heard them talk sometimes. Ben was always telling the other two to be careful of crossin' Lon."

"Or what? Lon would run them off?"

"They'd end up with a busted leg or back. It'd happened a couple of times before."

"Did Ocie know about it?"

"Ben didn't think so. Lon has a shack out

east of the ranch that he goes to once in a while. He doesn't think Ben knows about it, but he does; and he and his friends stay clear of it."

"What does Lon do out there?"

"I don't know. Meets with fellers and such. One of the men—Howdy was his name—said he thought Lon was making cattle deals out there, but he couldn't prove it."

"Did they say where the cabin was?"

"It's on the range that runs along the Pecos River Canyon. Ben told me to keep my mouth shut about anything I heard or I might end up with a hole in my head. I've not said a word till now."

"Ben's right. Talk like that could get you killed."

Jake had a lot to think about. They finished their meal in silence. Eli put their soiled plates in the dishpan, and Jake moved the icebox out from the wall.

"I thought I might drill a hole in the floor so that the ice water will drain under the house. It would save her from having to lift that heavy pan."

"I try to remember to do it, but I forget sometimes. Do you have a drill?"

"No, but there's more ways than one way to skin a cat. I'll chisel a small hole in the floor. I saw a piece of old garden hose out on the trash pile we can use."

"Now that we know that someone didn't come off the highway and kill Mr. Pierce, there's no need to stick so close to Mary Lee. She won't like it."

"You don't have to breathe down her neck, but you should stay within shouting distance in case she needs you. Her baby could come early or she could fall."

"Trudy thinks you like Mary Lee a lot."

"I do. She's top-notch."

"Well, you could marry her and come help her run this place."

Jake noted the anxious expression on Eli's young face and thought a minute before he spoke.

"I'm a rancher, Eli. All I know is horses, steers and a little bit about welding. And don't forget, as long as I live, I'll be known as a jailbird. It doesn't matter if I was guilty or not."

"That wouldn't bother her."

"It would bother me. She's too sweet and proud to be known as the wife of a jailbird who can barely scratch out a living."

"She's goin' to lose the court and she doesn't know what she'll do or where she'll go. Can't somethin' be done to help her?"

"Let's keep our fingers crossed that something will happen and she won't lose it."

"Maybe something will happen and she won't lose the court," Trudy was saying to Deke. "That greedy old banker can hardly wait to get his hands on it."

They were sitting in the truck, eating the hot tamales Deke had bought from a vender on the walk in front of the Sante Fe telephone office.

"What do you do, sugar, when you're not at the motor court?"

"I help Mama at the café."

"Really? I'd a swore ya was a belly dancer, darlin'."

Trudy froze in shocked silence. Her mind shut down for seconds, then cleared with amazing speed.

"Where in the world would a belly dancer find work in Cross Roads?"

"Red Pepper Corral? Pedro's Place? Or I can think of another place where your talent would be appreciated." Deke lifted his brows.

Trudy let her arm fly out and thump him on the chest.

"Deke Bales, if I stripped off my clothes to belly dance it would scare you to death. You'd run for your life and I'd have to send Jake chasing after you."

"I'll tell you what . . . when we get back, let's rent a cabin for an hour or two. You can dance for me and we'll see who runs."

"You're an idiot. Did you know that?"

"Yeah, and bein' with you has been the most fun I've had in all my born days, darlin'. I've never met a sweeter or sassier girl."

"You're butterin' me up for somethin'. You wantin' to borrow money? I got twenty cents."

"There ya go," he moaned. "Can't ya see that I'm serious?"

"You don't have a serious bone in your body." Trudy spoke flippantly. She didn't dare look at him, afraid that he would see the longing in her eyes. Instead she focused them on an old dog going down the street with its tail hanging low. After a short silence, she asked, "What're you going to do after you build Mr. Quitman's motorcycle?"

"Well, darlin', I've thought of running for

governor. But then, I wouldn't want to live in Albuquerque."

"You wouldn't have to. You'd live here in Santa Fe." She looked at him now and grinned.

"Smart mouth! On the other hand maybe I'll hang around and keep an eye on you." He reached over and took her hand. "Is that all right with you?" He was serious and a little nervous. She could tell by his tone of voice and the tight grip he had on her hand.

"If . . . you behave yourself."

"Speakin' of behavin', darlin', I fully intend to kiss you before we get back to the court. I may pull off the highway and into the woods when I do, because it's going to curl your toes, and I don't want anyone to hear when you yell like a raidin' Apache."

Trudy's heart was chugging like a runaway train. "All right, Romeo, get this truck moving. We'll just see who yells the loudest."

It was late afternoon when they returned to the court. Trudy jumped out of the truck and ran toward the house, giggling.

"I'll get ya for that!" Deke yelled.

"What in the world?" Mary Lee hurried to the door. "What's going on?" she asked as

Trudy burst through the door. Her eyes were shining with happiness.

"That . . . that jackass!" Trudy looked over her shoulder to be sure Deke hadn't followed her to the house. "I pinched him."

"Pinched him? Why'd you do that?"

"Because he . . . because he deserved it."

"You two act like a couple of two-year-old kids. Trudy Bales, are those whisker marks on your face?"

Trudy's hands flew to her cheeks. A rosy redness rushed up her neck and covered her face.

"Does it show?"

"No, but I guessed that you and Deke would get around to kissin' before you got back."

"You . . . tricked me!"

Mary Lee put her arms around her friend and hugged her. "I'm happy for you."

"I'm scared, Mary Lee. I know it won't last."

"Maybe it will."

"I just can't believe that he likes me. He said I was . . . pretty."

"You are pretty. I've been telling you that for years."

"But . . . my legs are so . . . short. They're only half as long as yours. And . . . my butt is big." Trudy's brown eyes flooded with tears.

"I bet if you asked him, he'd say he didn't care. I bet he's glad he's met someone who has to look *up* to him for a change. Someone who likes him and is fun to be with. I don't imagine life has been easy for him either."

"But . . . he's always so cheerful."

"It could be a cover-up to hide the hurt he feels when someone calls him 'runt' or 'squirt.'"

"Every morning when I wake up, I wonder if this is going to be the day he leaves."

"Don't think about it. Get all the happiness you can out of each day."

"Hey, Jake! Get out here. It's goin' to rain." Deke's voice reached into the kitchen.

Mary Lee went to the door to see Jake come out of the washhouse and hurry around to where Deke and Eli were pulling a new mattress out of the truck bed. Jake grabbed one side, and they carried it up onto the porch. When Mary Lee opened the door, they brought it into the bedroom and hurried out.

Jake got in the truck and drove quickly down to number six. He had moved the mattress from that cabin up to replace the one they burned. They had just got the new one inside when the rain came pelting down.

In the house, Mary Lee looked at the mattress on her mother's bed with dismay. Her mind automatically counted the money left in the fruit jar.

"This is a nice one." Trudy began spreading a clean sheet over the blue and white striped ticking.

"Why did you get two mattresses when Eli gave Deke money for one?"

"That's a long story and a good one. You would have gotten a kick out of hearing the pitch Deke gave that store man." Trudy rolled her eyes toward the ceiling and tucked the sheet securely on one side. "Lordy, that man can dicker with the best of them. He dragged me to the door of the store twice, making out like we were leaving, before he got the man down to two mattresses for twenty dollars."

"He got both for twenty dollars? Mr. Collins at the furniture store here charged me fifteen dollars for one. I'll give Deke the extra five."

"You can try. He said that he owed you much more than that for meals and staying in the cabin with Jake."

"Jake paid the rent in good faith. It wasn't his fault that Mama let him have it so cheap. And he's entitled to share it with whomever he wants."

"You'll have to fight it out with Deke. But I'm warning you, he's as stubborn as a mule . . . *darlin'*." Trudy laughed, and it was such a happy sound that Mary Lee laughed with her.

The rain came down for an hour, keeping the men in the end cabin long enough for Mary Lee and Trudy to prepare supper from the leftover food. When all was ready, Mary Lee went to the front door and looked out onto the highway. Cars were going by slowly. She was sure that if the court were open she would fill the cabins.

It was strange to pass her mother's room and have the door open. Trudy would sleep in there tonight, and the canvas cot could go back to the washhouse. It was also strange not to feel the dread that Dolly would come storming out of the room and embarrass her.

She had locked her feelings for Jake in a little secret chamber of her heart. He had been kind, wonderful in fact. She could no longer deny to herself that she had fallen in love with him. He had held her at her mother's bedside as if she were a little child who needed comforting. She had felt his face in her hair, his lips on her forehead, but she couldn't let herself think that his feelings for her were anything near what a man felt for the woman he loved. He may have been alone when his mother was dying.

It would be over soon.

When she lost the court, Jake would go on his way. She and Eli would take what little money she could save between now and then and move to town. She had been thinking about what she could do and decided that she would look for work as a housekeeper where she could take the baby and Eli. Mr. Morales might know of a motherless home where she could work for their keep. She would talk to him soon.

Suddenly, it hit Mary Lee that both her close blood relatives were gone. She didn't remember ever having seen her grandpar-

ents. There were uncles and aunts some-
where, but Dolly had alienated them long
ago.

But she wasn't alone.

*Thank you, Bobby Clawson, for giving me
this baby, and thank you, God, for bringing
Eli to my door.*

Chapter 26

The first night after the court reopened, all five cabins were rented. Mary Lee and Trudy served breakfast to the occupants of four of them and to Jake and Deke, who had gone back to work. The second night they rented four cabins, but on the third night they rented all five of them again.

For three days, since the funeral, Mary Lee had managed not to be alone with Jake. It helped that he and Deke worked late every night and came back to the court hungry and tired. They never offered to pay for their meals, but Mary Lee knew that some arrangements had been made with Trudy because there was more money in the grocery jar than she had put there.

Trudy and Deke were in love. Trudy's face

glowed with a happiness she never dreamed would be hers. Deke's eyes found her the instant he stepped in the door; and although he still teased, there was a tenderness in his tone that had not been there before. Each evening as soon as the supper dishes were washed, they went to one porch or the other or walked across the field toward town.

Mary Lee was happy for her friend and prayed that she didn't end up with a broken heart.

Jake was aware that Mary Lee was avoiding him. She welcomed him to the supper table the day of the funeral and every night after that. She talked to him and smiled, but when the meal was over and the room set to order, she excused herself, went to her bedroom and closed the door.

Eli had tried to entice her to stay and listen to the radio Jake had left in the house. Her excuses were lame ones, such as, she had to wash her hair, do some sewing, write a letter. On the fourth night, Jake got up from the table and announced that he was going to town. He didn't invite Deke or Eli to go along, knowing that Deke wanted to be with Trudy and that Eli was too young to go into a beer joint.

The tension between himself and Mary Lee was wearing on Jake. His nerves were strung tight. He had fooled himself into thinking that she cared something for him. *Didn't she let me hold her the night her mother died?* Since that time she had made it painfully clear that she wanted only to be friends.

The undertaker had come, according to Trudy, and presented his bill. Mary Lee had paid it out of the money she had saved for the mortgage. Her eyes held a haunted, vacant look at times, and the smudges beneath them told him that she wasn't getting enough rest. She was worrying herself sick and wished that the lawyer would hurry and make his move in order to take the burden of waiting to lose the court from her shoulders.

Oh, Lord, Jake sighed. He never imagined that loving a woman could be so damn painful.

These thoughts were swirling around in Jake's mind when he opened the door to the Red Pepper Corral. It was early. Only one man sat at the bar, and another three or four at the tables.

"Hola, amigo." Paco stood behind the bar drying a glass. He placed it on the shelf and dropped the cloth to draw a beer for Jake, who straddled a stool at the end of the bar.

"How ya doin', Paco?"

"Fair. You?"

"Same."

"Well, that takes care of that. How's the little lady makin' out?"

"She's holdin' up real good."

"Glad to hear it. Stay away from Pedro's. Yancy and his bunch are hanging out there. Yancy is still talkin' big. He's sayin' Mrs. Finley had to have help killin' Frank."

"Yeah? Is he accusing me or Mary Lee?"

"He's not come right out and said. Guess he's afraid of Ocie. The man has a long arm."

Jake gave a snort of disgust.

"What're you down in the mouth about, *amigo*? Did someone tell ya there ain't no Santa Claus or did ya lose your job at Quitman's?"

"No. I've got two or three more months out there."

"A man was in here askin' about ya this afternoon."

"Yeah? What'd he want?"

"Don't know. Told him we were working out at Quitman's and you lived at the motor court."

"I'd have to be starving to climb those damn bridge girders again if that's what he wanted. They probably can't find another welder that'll go up there and they're looking for somebody dumb enough to do it."

"*Ai, yi, yi.* Speak of the devil. Here comes the dude who was askin' about ya."

Jake looked over his shoulder. When recognition dawned, he grinned at the pleasant surprise. The man's dark eyes swept the room and landed on Jake. In polished boots, tailor-made fringed jacket and a ten-dollar Stetson, the man would stand out in any crowd, not only because of his dress but because he was tall and broad, and well-dressed Indians were not a common sight in New Mexico.

Jake stood to greet him. He had worked on the Fleming Ranch in Oklahoma. It was there that he had met Deke.

"Howdy, Jake."

"It's good to see you, Mr. Fleming." The men shook hands like old friends.

"I just missed you and Deke at the Quitman Ranch. Had a good visit with Mr. Quitman, though. He showed me the horses you're working on."

"Mr. Quitman's a nice man to work for."

"I planned to get a bite of supper and then look for you and Deke at the motor court. I came in to have a beer first, that is, if the proprietor isn't afraid to serve a redskin."

"Name your poison, *amigo*." The grin on Paco's face was wide and welcoming.

"Same as Jake's." Barker Fleming straddled the bar stool with ease. "Nice little town you have here," he said to Paco.

"A village has been here a long time, *amigo*. But the highway has made it a town."

"It's the same with towns all along the way. They are calling this highway the Mother Road."

"Is most of it paved now?" Jake asked.

"All but a stretch over west of here." Barker emptied his glass. "Have you had supper?"

"Just finished," Jake said.

"Drink up, then come along with me while I have mine. I've got in the habit of eating; and when I miss a meal, it throws me completely out of kilter."

"Sure." Jake emptied his glass and placed two coins on the counter before Barker could dig into his pocket. "Thanks, Paco."

"I'll add my thanks too, for helping me find Jake," Mr. Fleming said. "I'll be back in before I leave town."

"Adios, amigos."

Outside the Red Corral Jake pointed toward Ruby's Diner, two blocks down the street.

"Not fancy, but the food is good."

"I'm not much for fancy. Let's go."

While the two tall men walked down the street, Mr. Fleming inquired about Deke, then told Jake that he'd had business in Albuquerque and was on his way back to Oklahoma.

At first, Ruby was a little awed by the well-dressed, exceedingly handsome stranger. But after he had eaten a large meal and complimented her on it, she visited with him as if he were a regular customer. He talked about Deke in glowing terms, telling her that he had known him all his life.

"His daddy was a crackerjack mechanic. By the time Deke started to high school, he could fix anything with a motor on it and had started building a motorcycle. He and I have talked about building a race car, but we both knew that it was just a pipe dream. You'll not find a more honest, hardworking man than Deke Bales."

When Ruby went back to the kitchen, Mr. Fleming lit a cigarette and offered one to Jake.

"I think you've set her mind at rest," Jake said. "Her daughter, Trudy, and Deke are kinda smitten with each other."

"I've always hoped that Deke would find a woman who would care for him. He deserves to have a home and family."

"They're well matched. You'll know what I mean when you meet her."

"Have you ever handled rodeo stock, Jake?"

"I understand that some of the quarter horses I've trained have been used for pickup and roping."

"Do you have any desire to get on a bucking bronco?"

"No. I like to keep all my bones inside my skin." Jake laughed. "I get my horses used to me with soft words and gentle handling. By the time I get on them they protest a little but do very little bucking."

"I'm thinking about going into the business of furnishing stock for the Dallas–Fort Worth Rodeo Association. I could use you and Deke—you with the stock and Deke to keep my equipment going."

"Before you say any more, Mr. Fleming, you'd better know where I've been for the last two years."

"I know where you've been. Deke told me. I think I'm a pretty good judge of men. Did you come back here to clear your name or to seek vengeance?"

"Someday my name will be cleared; and when it is, I'm going to be right here staring the folks in the eye who turned their backs on me."

"Then you're not interested in coming back to Oklahoma?"

"Not right now. I've promised Mr. Quitman I'd get his horses ready to sell. I figure that's going to take me two or three months. Maybe at a later date."

"If you ever want a job at my place, Jake, you've got one."

"Thank you. I appreciate your confidence in me."

"I'd like to say hello to Deke, then get back here to the hotel and get a little sleep. I engaged a room when I arrived this afternoon. The highway is paved now all the way to Sayre, and if I get an early start, I can make it home in one day."

As they approached the court, Jake saw that the Vacancy sign had been turned off. The cabins were filled again tonight. Then he felt a little spurt of anger when the big car stopped in front of the house and he saw Mary Lee sitting on the porch with Deke, Trudy and Eli.

She didn't go to her room early tonight because he wasn't there. Well, hell, that should tell him something!

Deke and Barker Fleming met each other like long-lost relatives. Trudy's eyes got as big as saucers when she saw the big, obviously well-to-do man put his arm across Deke's shoulders.

"It's good to see you, Deke. Lord, but I've missed you, and I've missed knowing you were handy when something went wrong with some of the machinery. I can't find anyone to fix that old tractor that pulls the hay baler."

"It's good to see you too, Barker. How's things at home?"

"Fine. Kids ask about you often. Especially Janna. She wants you to put a motor on her bicycle."

"She's a darlin'. She still sneaking out to ride the horses?"

"And I still give her a good chewing out when she does."

"How's Lucas?"

"He starts to school this year. My sympathy is with the teacher."

"He's a corker, all right. Come up onto the porch. There's some folks I want you to meet." He held his hand out to Trudy. "Come here, darlin'. I want you to meet the best man I know. This is Barker Fleming. His ranch is near my hometown of Sayre, Oklahoma. Barker, this is Trudy Bender." He proudly held on to Trudy's hand while she extended the other to the tall man.

Barker swept his hat off and grasped Trudy's hand. "Hello, Miss Bender. I can always depend on Deke to find the prettiest girls."

Trudy liked him at once and didn't seem to be a bit shy.

"I can believe that, Mr. Fleming. He's a flirty little cuss."

Deke said, "Now, darlin'—"

"I guess you're not ready to come home." Barker's smiling eyes went from Trudy to Deke.

"No, not yet."

Barker laughed. "I can see why."

"This is Mrs. Clawson." Deke made the introductions.

Mary Lee stood and extended her hand. "Welcome to Cross Roads."

"Thank you, ma'am."

Jake stood back where he could listen, look at Mary Lee and not be noticed. Where had he got the stupid idea that she might care for him? He was jealous of Deke's freedom to hold Trudy's hand even when he followed Mr. Fleming to the car. Not even in prison had he felt as lonely as he did now.

As soon as the car rolled away, he said a general good night to all and went to his cabin.

Lon Delano turned down the lamp when he heard the knock on the back door of his one-room cabin on the Clawson Ranch. When he opened the door, two men came in.

"Anybody see you?"

"If they did, they thought we worked here."

"Sit down. We're havin' a card game."

The young one snickered. "Oh, so that's what we're doin' here."

The men were unlikely companions. One was wiry and appeared to be in his early twenties. The legs of his britches were stuffed into high boots with white stars on the sides. Even though he had a sharp nose, flat cheeks, shaggy hair, and blond whiskers that looked like peach fuzz, he was good-looking. His pale blue eyes never seemed to settle on anything longer than a second or two. Some part of his restless body moved constantly.

The other man was older, calmer. His clothes were neat and of good quality, his face clean-shaven. He wore tan cord pants and highly polished boots. In town he would be taken for a lawyer or a banker.

"Did you find the shack?" Lon asked after they were seated at the table.

"Yeah."

"The motor court?"

"Yeah."

"See the pregnant cow?"

"Yeah."

"Well, dammit, can't ya say anything but 'yeah'?"

"Yeah." The young man grinned, showing overlapping front teeth.

"Goddammit!" Lon got to his feet.

"Calm down. Wyn's a smart-mouthed kid. You knew that."

"Why do ya put up with him?"

The older man's eyes turned cold. "State your terms."

"All right." Lon sat down. "Kill the woman—soon. The kid will be born anytime now. Take her to the shack out on the Pecos and kill her. I want it to look like someone came in off the highway and took her. Something like that happened over near Tucumcari last summer. Leave her in the shack. I'll go out in a week or two and burn it down."

"We can get rid of her without haulin' her way out there," Wyn grumbled.

"No," Lon said firmly. "I want to see her. I've got to be sure she's dead."

"He don't trust us, Lyle." Wyn snickered and fanned the cards.

"I'll pay you two hundred and fifty now," Lon said, ignoring the kid. "When I've proof she's dead, another two fifty."

"Five hundred dollars for a woman and a kid. Shit! We've been paid five hundred for a worn-out old cowpoke."

"Lyle . . ." Wyn was dealing cards. "I've never killed a woman. He'll have to pay more."

"Don't worry about it, kid." Lyle gently dismissed Wyn's protest and focused on Lon. "A thousand."

"I don't have a thousand . . . now. I will later."

"How much later?"

"Six months."

"No deal."

"I can give you seven fifty. Four hundred now and three fifty when the job is done."

Lyle looked at Wyn, then nodded. "A deal."

"I might have another job for you."

"We only take on one job at a time."

Wyn snickered. "Didn't I tell ya I'd get ya a man who knew what he was doin'? Didn't I tell ya that?"

"You sure as hell bungled the job when I sent you over to push her down the stairs."

"Hell, it was worth a try. How'd I know she wouldn't fall?" Wyn shuffled the deck.

Lon turned his attention back to Lyle. "Ten days after the word is out that she's missin', I'll meet you at noon at the post office in Santa Rosa with the rest of the money." He began to feel uneasy. He was with a couple of really dangerous men.

"If you're not there, we know where you are. Get the money."

"Wait for me by that dead tree behind the corral. I'm not fool enough to let anyone see where I keep my money."

Lyle nodded. "Can't blame ya for that."

Wyn threw his cards on the table and stood. "Hell, I had a good hand."

Chapter 27

Mary Lee, alone in the kitchen, took the calendar from the wall, placed it on the table and carefully counted the days. If she had figured right, the birth of her baby was less than three weeks away. The doctor had told her that she might have the baby a few days before or a few days after the due date.

She needed to find out how much time she would have before she had to vacate after the banker demanded his money on the first day of October. If she couldn't pay in full, would she be granted a few days' grace, or could he demand that she leave immediately? If that was the case, her baby would be only two days old if he came on time. How could she leave? Where would she go?

Each evening while she sat in the living room waiting for travelers to come off the road, she crocheted booties and caps out of the yarn she had unraveled from a shawl. In her mother's room she had found several things that she could use besides the shawl. One of them was a soft blanket. It would serve to line the dresser drawer she would use as a crib for the baby.

It had been a week since her mother died. Jake now came to the house only for breakfast and supper. Several times she had turned to find his eyes on her. He always looked away quickly. In the evening he sat on the washhouse steps with Eli or went to town.

In the middle of the week Deke had carried several grocery sacks to the kitchen. She had been in the washhouse and just happened to look out the door. Trudy was careful to have whatever he brought put away by the time she came to the house.

Mary Lee was completely miserable, not only in body but in heart. She felt as big as an elephant and . . . ugly as dirt. Her back ached; her ankles were swollen; her breasts were sore. She was on the verge of tears all the time. It was no wonder that Jake avoided her. He had spent all day Sunday away from the motor court. Trudy and Deke had gone to Ruby's after the cabins were cleaned, and Eli was enthralled with listening to the radio. It had been a long, miserable day for Mary Lee.

Now, on Monday afternoon, her spirits were at their lowest. Eli and Trudy were doing the daily cleaning; the wash was flapping on the line. Mary Lee sat down at the table, put her head on her folded arms and gave in to a storm of weeping. She had held the tears in for so long that now they seemed unstoppable. After a few minutes she lifted her head and dried her eyes on the handkerchief she pulled from the pocket of her daddy's old, faded shirt.

Stupid girl! That didn't change a thing.

She was at the sink sluicing water on her face when she heard a car drive in. After blotting her face with a towel and smoothing down her hair, she went to the front door. Mr. Morales was coming up the steps to the porch.

"Afternoon, Mrs. Clawson. Warm day for September."

"Yes, it is. Come in, Mr. Morales. You'll have to excuse me. I've . . . been working."

"I should have called and told you that I was coming."

"Had you done so, it would have been quite remarkable as we don't have a phone." Mary Lee smiled. "I'm glad you've come. There's something I've been meaning to ask you. If you don't mind sitting in the kitchen, I'll fix you a glass of tea."

"A glass of tea would go down real good."

Mary Lee was glad that the kitchen was as clean and neat as they could make it. She chipped ice for two glasses, then poured from the pitcher of tea.

"How are you doing, Mrs. Clawson?"

"Call me Mary Lee, please. I'm doing fine. Just fine."

"That's good. My, this tea hits the spot." Mr. Morales took papers from the inside pocket of his coat. "Did you know that Scott had taken out an insurance policy on his wife?"

"No. He never mentioned it."

"He took one out on himself too. A burial policy that I turned over to Mrs. Finley a few days after his passing." He fumbled around in his pocket and pulled out a fountain pen. "As soon as I heard that Mrs. Finley had passed on, I notified the company. They sent me a check for three hundred and fifty dollars and these papers for you to sign. I cashed the check."

From another pocket the lawyer pulled out a stack of bills, and to Mary Lee's astonishment, he counted out three piles of one hundred dollars and laid a fifty-dollar bill beside them.

She was stunned and couldn't speak for a long moment.

"You mean . . . you mean that this is for . . . me?"

"It certainly is. You're the beneficiary."

"I . . . can't believe this. You can't know what—" Her throat clogged; tears rolled down her cheeks.

"I think I do, my dear."

"I can pay Mr. Rosen, can't I? I . . . won't have to give up the motor court! Please, tell me it's true. There's no mistake?"

"No mistake. Now, read the letter. I've made two copies so you can keep one. It says I have performed my duties and passed the money on to you. If you will sign, I'll be on my way." He uncapped the pen.

Her hands were shaking when she signed

her name. She stood when he did and took his hand in both of hers.

"Thank you. I hoped and prayed that there would be a way for me to pay Mr. Rosen; I just never dreamed that my prayers would be answered."

"Well, they were. Now, what was it you wanted to ask me?"

"I was going to ask you if you knew anyone who needed a housekeeper. But I won't need to find a job now."

"From the looks of the court, you're doing a mighty fine job right here."

"Thank you. I can hardly wait to march up to the bank and wave this money under Mr. Rosen's nose."

"There will be an interest charge. I don't know how much because I never saw the contract between Scott and the bank. But it shouldn't be over twenty-five or thirty dollars. If it's more than that, tell him you'll see your lawyer."

"I will. Oh, I will, Mr. Morales." She was reluctant to turn loose of his hand and held it while they walked to the door. "Thank you."

"You're very welcome, Mary Lee. Take care of yourself now."

As Morales was getting in his car, Eli came running up from the last cabin. Trudy was behind him.

"Who was that?" Eli demanded, even as Mary Lee was waving.

A breathless Trudy stopped at the porch step.

"Eli 'bout scared me to death when he yelled that a man was in the house. I didn't know it was Mr. Morales until I was almost here."

"The most wonderful thing—I can't believe it—it's a miracle." *Oh, Daddy, bless you, bless you!*

Mary Lee led the way to the kitchen and sank down in a chair in front of the stack of bills.

"Holy shit!" Eli exclaimed, and Mary Lee didn't even think to correct him. "Where'd all this come from?"

"Three hundred and fifty dollars. Daddy had insurance on Mama." Relief had washed the worry and unhappiness from Mary Lee's face. She couldn't keep from smiling.

"Well, dog my cats!" Trudy exclaimed.

"Does this mean you can pay off old Tight-ass?"

"Eli!" Mary Lee giggled. "He is one, isn't

he? We'll pay off the loan. We can stay here, Eli." Mary Lee got up and hugged him. "You can go to school. You'll live here in the house with me. Trudy, you can come and work days; I know you want to be home at night."

"She'll marry Deke and go to Oklahoma if he asks her."

"You ornery little warthog! What gave you that idea?" Trudy hit him on the shoulder.

"See there," Eli teased. "You just mention Deke and she gets all red 'n' flustered."

"Stop teasing her and get our money jar. Let's see how much we have. We've got to celebrate. Can you stir up a cake, Trudy? Eli can go to the store and get a chicken, one that's already dressed. We'll be extravagant for once. We'll make chicken pie with biscuits."

"Jake's favorite," Trudy said.

"Well, yes, I guess it is. Is the work done?"

"Yup," Eli said. "Except for taking the sheets off the line."

"Can I make a chocolate cake?" Trudy opened the upper cabinet doors. "Reach up and get that cocoa, Eli."

"Deke's favorite," he grumbled, and lifted down the can. "What about my favorite?"

"You're my favorite." Mary Lee kissed him on the cheek. "Scoot, now. Get back so you can take care of the travelers while Trudy and I work on the supper."

When it was nearly dark, Mary Lee and Trudy had the table ready; yellow tiger lilies in a fruit jar sat in the middle of it. The chicken pie bubbled in the oven; the two-layer chocolate cake sat on the cabinet.

They had just changed into fresh clothes and tied ribbons in their hair when Mary Lee heard the familiar sound of Jake's truck going past the house, in between the cabins and alongside the washhouse, where he had parked since moving into cabin number one.

Anxious to share her happy news with Jake, Mary Lee ran out the back door, down the steps and across the yard as Jake was getting out of the truck. Alarmed to see her running, he hurried toward her.

"Jake! Jake, guess what?"

"What?" He caught her in his arms and scolded. "You shouldn't run. You could fall."

"I've got the money! Know what that means?" Her face was radiant. "I can stay here." Her arms encircled his waist. "Mr. Morales came. Daddy had insurance on

Mama—three hundred and fifty dollars. I can pay the loan. I couldn't wait to tell you . . ."

"I'm glad, *mi tesoro*. So very glad." He closed his eyes and hugged her as close as he dared. With his lips against her ear, he whispered, "My treasure."

"I was going to try to get a housekeeping job so I could have the baby and Eli with me—"

"You can take care of your baby right here."

"Isn't it grand?" She leaned back and looked up into his face. "We're celebrating tonight. Chicken and biscuits. Your favorite."

"That sounds mighty good," he said huskily.

"And cake."

"Hey, now, this *is* a celebration." He smiled down at her, his eyes devouring her beaming face.

"I'm so relieved. I just didn't know what in the world I was going to do."

"How's Gaston handling all this?"

She laughed happily and moved his hand down to rest on her abdomen.

"Feel him. He's kicking up his heels. He

can be born here. Not someplace where . . . nobody cares for him." The sudden tears that filled her eyes were happy tears. "Oh, it just makes me so mad. I even cry when I'm so happy I'm about to burst at the seams."

He laughed. It had been so long since he laughed that the sound was strange even to him.

"Don't do that. At least not before supper. I can't wait to tie into that chicken pie. I've got to clean up a bit. I can't come to a celebration smelling like a barnyard."

"I hadn't even noticed. I was so anxious to tell you about the money."

"Can we talk tonight? You'll not run off to the bedroom?"

"Not if you don't go to town."

"It's a date?"

"I've never been on a date."

"Then it's time you were." He kissed her forehead.

Trudy waited on the porch with Deke. They watched Mary Lee run to Jake.

"I told you that she was in love with him."

"Yeah, ya did, darlin'. The way she's been actin' has almost tore him apart."

"She can't believe that he'd care for her . . . the way she is now. She couldn't stand it if she thought he only felt sorry for her."

"If a man loves a woman, that's when he thinks she is the most beautiful, darlin'."

"But it's another man's baby?"

"The other man only planted the seed, darlin'. The important part is when the seed breaks ground. It will need food and water and lots of love to grow straight and strong. Without those things it will die."

"Ah, Deke. At times you show perfectly good sense."

"I've been tellin' ya that I'm smart as a parcel of lawyers, darlin'. No one's lookin'. Give me a kiss before I go clean up. I've been lookin' forward to it all day."

All the cabins except one had been rented by the time they sat down for supper. Mary Lee's happiness was contagious. Jake could hardly eat for looking at her. Her smiling eyes went to him often. Trudy told how scared Eli had been when he looked out the door of number six and saw a car in front of the house and a man on the porch.

"He tore out of there like his pants were on fire."

"Jake told me to keep my eye out. I'd a

done it even if he'd not told me," Eli said defiantly.

Mary Lee's eyes met Jake's. "There's no need now, is there?"

"It's always wise to be alert. Men, good and bad, travel the highway."

"Are Yancy and the other men who jumped on you and Deke still around?"

"I've not seen them."

They are here, querida. *I would watch over you every minute of the day if I could.*

"That's good. I didn't like that Yancy. His eyes were too close together."

"And I'd say that's a mighty good reason not to like him," Trudy said.

Mary Lee felt guilty being so happy when her mother had been gone only a week. She couldn't help herself. She felt safe here in the midst of her precious friends. Regardless of what happened between her and Jake, she would have this to remember. She was almost too excited to eat, but she ate the large helping Trudy had put on her plate.

When the meal was over, all that was left was a small piece of cake.

"Eli will eat this before the night is over." Trudy draped a cloth over the cake.

"Not if I get to it first." Deke got up to help Trudy clear the table.

When Mary Lee went to get the dishpan from under the sink, Trudy took it from her hands.

"Me and the motorcycle cowboy will do the dishes. You're too juiced up tonight. You just might break every dish in this place, and we'll need some of them for breakfast."

"For the love of heaven!"

"Mind the little darlin', Mary Lee. She's showin' good sense for a change." Deke gently shoved her toward the back door.

"Well, I guess I know when I'm not wanted."

"You're wanted, *mi amante*. Eli can stay in here and see that these two don't kill each other, and he'll take care of a car if it comes in."

"I should help. Trudy cooked most of the supper." Mary Lee was protesting as Jake, with his hand in the small of her back, was urging her out the door.

Eli watched until they reached the truck, then turned with a puzzled look on his young face.

"What changed her mind? She hasn't given him the time of day all week. He was so down in the mouth he'd gotten down-right crotchety at times—not that I blamed him."

"She's been worried half out of her mind about that loan."

"Do you think she likes him?"

"She more than likes him, clabberhead."

"Fiddle! I don't know anythin' 'bout women."

"Not many men do." She looked know-ingly at Deke, who grinned and chucked her under the chin.

"I know ever'thin' about women, darlin'. Just ask me somethin'."

"Do ya think she'll marry him?" Eli was like a dog with a bone; he wasn't going to let go.

"She has to be asked first. You heard what he said the other night. He considers himself a jailbird and not good enough for her, and she thinks he just feels sorry for her."

"That's a bunch of bull. He likes her a lot. I know he does! Hell and damnation! If all you're going to do is look at each other with calf eyes, I'll go listen to the radio so you can smooch."

"Thanky, son. I'll do the same for you

someday." Deke threw his arm around Trudy.

"One of these day's Mary Lee'll catch you cussin' and you'll wish you were in . . . China."

"Hush, darlin'. He's gone. Give me a kiss."

Chapter 28

"We have a date. Remember?" Jake's soft voice was close to her ear.

"Where are we going?"

"Out to look at the stars."

"We can see the stars from here."

"We've seen these stars. I know where there are new ones, bigger and brighter."

"Aren't you smart?" Excitement quickened her heartbeat.

"I put a clean blanket over the seat." With his hand beneath her elbow, he helped her step up onto the running board and into the truck.

"Where are we going?" she asked again when they turned west on the highway.

"California."

"California?" In the light from an ap-

proaching car she could see a flash of white
teeth and knew that he was smiling. "Do
you have enough gas?"

"When we run out we'll have to thumb it
the rest of the way." The face he turned toward her was relaxed, smiling. He looked
younger, more like the boy she had met
years ago. When he reached for her hand,
she put it in his. She could feel every nerve
in her body responding to his touch.

"I suppose you'll expect me to stand
along the highway and hold my dress up
showing my knees like Claudette Colbert
did in the picture show *It Happened One
Night*?"

"Why did she do that?"

"Show her legs? To catch a ride."

"Did you see the picture?"

"No. Trudy told me about it."

"We'll go to a picture show sometime."

Mary Lee didn't know what to say. Their
two clasped hands rested on the seat between them. He released hers when he
slowed the truck and turned off onto a dirt
road. A short while later, he pulled over and
stopped.

"It's high up here and might be a little
cool, but I want you to get out and look at

the sky. Wait," he said when she opened the door. He hurried around to help her out. "The ground is rough. I don't want you to fall."

He held her close to him as they walked a short distance. When they stopped, they were on a rocky ledge overlooking the river.

"That's the Pecos down there."

"I can hear it."

"Look at the stars, *querida*. Aren't they bigger and brighter than the ones in town?" He had moved behind her and, with his hands on her upper arms, pulled her back to lean against him.

"It's because there's no light anywhere out here," she said in an awed whisper. "It's beautiful and so quiet. It's like we're the only people in the world."

"Yeah. I see a big star with your name on it."

"Where?"

He tilted her chin. "Up there next to that little one."

"I see it now." She turned her head and laughed up at him.

"Several years ago, when I had my land, there was a place like this. Sometimes I'd go out there at night, look at the stars and daydream."

"What did you dream about?"

"What most men dream about, I suppose. A home, family, horses grazing on my own land."

"Then they took it all away, didn't they?"

"Not all of it. I still have the dreams." His arms moved across her chest and enfolded her. "Cold?" His lips were close to her ear.

"No."

"You shivered."

"Because what they did to you was so unfair."

"Do you have even a little bit of suspicion that I might have been guilty?"

"Absolutely none."

"Lord!" he sighed. "I was afraid to ask."

"After I met you, I knew you hadn't done what you'd been accused of."

"How did you come to that conclusion?"

"Well, for one thing . . . if you'd been guilty you wouldn't have come back here."

"I wouldn't let my accusers think they'd run me off."

"They'll think that when you and Deke go to Oklahoma."

"Where did you get an idea like that?"

"Mr. Fleming offered you a job."

"If I wanted to leave here, I'd sure take him up on the job. But my life is here and I suspect Deke's is too . . . now."

She took a shallow breath, then said, "Uh-oh."

"What's wrong?" he asked anxiously, and loosed his arms.

"Gaston's playing football."

Jake chuckled softly. "Little stinker wants our attention." He moved his hand down to her waist. "May I reassure him that we know he's there?"

"Do you think that's what he wants?" She guided his hand beneath the loose shirt until it rested on her roiling abdomen.

"We'll find out if he calms down. Calm down, little man," he said softly as if he were gentling a flighty little mare. "There, now, it'll be all right. You'll be out of there soon."

Mary Lee was moved almost to tears on hearing his soft voice talking to her baby. This big, rough, sometimes violent man was everything she'd ever hoped to have as the father of her children but never dreamed she would find.

His large hand moved slowly and carefully over her swollen belly. She could feel his heart pounding against her back and his warm breath against the side of her face as he stroked the lump that was the baby inside her.

"I can never get over the wonder of it," he said softly. "I can feel him moving. He's in a hurry to get out and face the world."

"He . . . might be a she." Mary Lee was so moved emotionally, she could barely speak.

"A pretty little girl with blue eyes and dark auburn hair." His mouth was close to her ear.

"I'll take whatever I get." Leaning against his strength, she closed her eyes. She would remember this moment forever: his strong, warm hand stroking her belly and the child within, the star-studded sky overhead and darkness wrapping them in its warm blanket.

"He's quieted down," he whispered.

"He must know how happy I am right now."

"Are you happy being with me?"

"Can't you tell?"

"You've hardly looked at me lately."

"I've been about sick with worry over losing the court."

"That's all settled now. You don't worry. Hear me?" His nose was buried in her hair.

"I hear you. Jake? Eli has got to go to school. He'll not want to go and leave me. You'll have to help me persuade him."

"Will Trudy be there during the day?"

"If she doesn't leave with Deke. I want her to be happy, but I'm selfish. I don't want her to go."

"Deke's crazy about her. I was hoping they would take to each other."

"I'll be able to pay her now for helping me, and I can have the telephone connected. I was worried about how I'd let the doctor know when the baby comes."

"I'd better get you back to the truck before you get cold." He drew his hand reluctantly from beneath her shirt.

They walked back, his arm around her holding her securely to him. Inside the truck, he reached for her and she went willingly to nestle against him. Her head was on his shoulder, her warm breath on his neck. She was soft and warm and so damn sweet. He wished to God they could stay here forever. He was holding heaven in his arms.

"Jake?" Her soft voice came out of the darkness.

"Yes, *querida mía.*"

"You told me one time that those Spanish words meant 'stubborn little mule.' I don't believe you now. What do they mean?"

"Are you sure you want to know?"

"Yes, unless they mean something worse than 'stubborn little mule.'"

His laugh was low, intimate. His arms tightened. "If I tell you, you might not want me to call you that again. I think of you as *'querida mía.'*"

"If you won't tell me, I'll ask Rosa Santez."

"Then I'd better tell you. You might get the word wrong and Rosa would come after me with a skillet. *'Querida'* means . . . 'beloved.'"

She caught her breath, and then there was a long pause before she spoke.

"Is it true? You think of me as . . . that?"

"I hadn't intended to tell you this when we came out here tonight." With fingers beneath her chin, he turned her face up to his. "It's something I've known for a while, thought about a lot and worried about what you would say if you knew. I had about given up thinking that I'd ever tell you. Now I'm afraid that you'll think me a stupid man reaching for the stars."

"What is it, Jake. You're scaring me." Her hand came up to his cheek.

"I love you, Mary Lee Finley. I've never said those words out loud, but I'm saying them now. I . . . love . . . you." He spaced the words for emphasis. "I'm in love with you. Completely, unconditionally, forever."

"Oh, Jake! Are . . . you sure?"

"I'll not burden you with it."

Her arm moved up and around his neck. "Jake Ramero, I love you too. It's been eating me up. I just couldn't see how you could have feelings for me when I'm so clumsy and . . . ugly. I was just sure that you only felt sorry for me."

"You're beautiful, my beloved. Just as beautiful as that little girl who cried over my sore feet years ago. Just as beautiful as that proud girl who came to the door a few months back, looked me in the eye, and told me to move." He was smiling when he touched his lips to hers and kissed her gently, reverently. "Even then, I was as smitten with you as I was when I was just a kid."

"But the baby . . ."

"I think of him as mine, *amor,* because he's yours. When he comes, I would like for his name to be Ramero and not Clawson. Do you think that's possible?"

"That would mean—"

"That we marry. I never thought I would ask you to be the wife of a jailbird. But, *querida mía,* I don't think I can bear the long, lonely years ahead without you. Think carefully, sweetheart, before you answer. Folks won't forget I spent time in prison."

"I'm the daughter of the town drunk, remember? It was even worse because the drunk was my mother. Folks won't forget that either."

"I don't have but six horses, a truck, and a heart full of love for you. I'll work my fingers to the bone to take care of you . . . and Gaston."

"We'll have the court. We'll get by until you can get back to ranching again. I know that's your dream and I'll help you in any way I can."

"Mother of God, don't let me wake from this dream." He breathed the prayer against her lips, then kissed her, and kissed her again. His mouth on hers was incredibly sweet and warm. His tongue stroked her full lower lip, and her arms tightened about his neck.

He lifted his head; his eyes, soft with love, drank in her face. Then, with a deep sigh, he held her head to his shoulder while he gently stroked her hair. They sat quietly for a while, hugging each other. Then he lifted her chin.

"I love you, *querida.* I will never say the words but to you and ours." His voice was husky and quivered with emotion.

"Beloved. I do—" The words melted on her lips when she tried to speak, swept away by his kisses.

His hand moved down over her breast. "Will they be this full after . . . ?"

"They're swollen now."

"I'll see them someday."

"I'll be all yours. You'll be all mine."

"Ahhh . . . that's what I want to hear." He kissed her long and hard, his mouth taking savage possession, parting her lips and invading them in a wild, sweet, wonderful way. His hand stroked her, touching her hungrily from breasts to abdomen. "Oh, love, I'll be so careful of you . . ."

"Not too careful, I hope."

His laugh was low and intimate. His eyes danced lovingly over her face. His hand curled possessively around her breast.

"I'll remember three days in my life for as long as I live: the day I hobbled to your house for a drink of water, my first birthday cake and this day, by far the happiest day of my life."

His kiss was long and deep and full of promised passion that flared whenever they touched. His fingers moved up into her hair, their touch strong and possessive. She took his kiss thirstily. She wanted to stay in his arms forever. His lips pulled away, but he drew her closer.

"My life has been empty up to now. You fill it completely." He kissed her again. Her lips were clinging moistly to his. His hand slipped beneath the loose shirt and cupped her full breast. Her nipple hardened. "You'll soon have milk," he whispered huskily.

"Uh-huh . . ."

His lips fell hungrily to hers. They were demanding yet tender. "I'd better stop this and take you home."

She laughed and pulled away from him. "This has been quite a day."

"I don't want it to end, but if I don't take you back soon, Eli will be coming after me with a shotgun."

"You'll help me persuade him to go to school?"

"He needs clothes, honey. He would be embarrassed to go in the ones he has."

"I'll give him money to buy some. I'll call it back wages or he won't take it. Jake, I want him to be part of our family." She looked anxiously up into his face.

"Of course. He loves you. But . . . not as much as I do." He started the truck. "No, stay here," he said when she attempted to move away. "I can see that I'm going to have to teach you how to shift gears."

Eli was stunned when Mary Lee told him that she and Jake were going to be married and that they wanted him to be a part of their family. When he didn't say anything, she looked at him anxiously.

"You do want to be with us, don't you?"

"'Course I do. I'm just surprised . . . is all."

"Why? I've told you all along that I want

you to be with me always. We both want you to be our son, the same as . . . Gaston."

"Gaston? Is that what you're goin' to call him?"

"Not on your life! Jake's been calling him that. Eli, now that I don't have to worry about the loan, I can afford to pay your back wages. I'm going up to the bank this morning—I can't wait to see Mr. Rosen's face when I give him the money. Will you come with me?"

"If you want me to."

"Jake made me promise not to leave the court unless I had you or Trudy with me."

"Does he think someone will try to hurt you again?"

"No. He's afraid I'll fall down, or the baby will come and I'll not have anyone with me. We'll go by the telephone office and have the telephone connected. Oh, it's wonderful, Eli, not to have to worry about that loan."

When the wash was on the line, Eli and Mary Lee left for town. Trudy would stay near the house, and when they got back, they would all pitch in and clean the cabins.

Mary Lee wore one of Rosa's daughter's

dresses, her small straw hat and the last pair of stockings she owned. They had only a small run that she hoped wouldn't be noticed. She was neat but felt as big as a barrel. The baby was all out front. They had walked just a few blocks when her back began to ache and she feared that she would have to sit down. She managed to get to the bank and sat down on one of the benches in the lobby.

After resting until her breathing was even, she went to the window and asked to speak to Mr. Rosen.

"He was about to go home for dinner. I'll see if he will see you. Your name?"

"Curtis Wessels, you know my name. We went to the same school. Stop acting so stuck-up and go tell Mr. Rosen I want to see him."

Clenching his teeth to hold back a retort, he knocked on the office door, then opened it and disappeared inside. He returned a short time later.

"Mr. Rosen will see you, but only for a few minutes. He's very busy today."

"That's very kind of him. Come on, Eli."

"No!" The young man moved to block the

swinging door so Eli couldn't follow Mary
Lee.

"Yes!" Mary Lee said with extra force. "He
comes with me."

"Mr. Rosen said to let *you* come in."

"Curtis Wessels, you're just as big a dope
as you were when we were in school. Now
get out of the way. Come on, Eli. Let's see if
Mr. Rosen is as rude as his hired help."

Mary Lee knew that this new courage had
come to her because of Jake's love. She
would never knuckle under or cower again.

The banker didn't give Mary Lee the
courtesy of standing when she entered the
office. Nor did he greet her or ask her to sit
down.

"Make it snappy. I've an appointment."

"I want to know how much interest I will
owe if I pay off the three-hundred-dollar
loan."

He twirled a pencil around with blunt fingers. "Forty-five dollars," he snapped. His
eyes were on her face, his brows drawn together while he waited for her to say something.

She remained quiet, opened her purse,
took out a handful of bills and placed them
on the desk.

"Three hundred and twenty-five dollars. The twenty-five is the interest."

Jumping to his feet, the banker was speechless although his mouth moved and his jaws puffed out. Mary Lee wanted to laugh. He looked as if he had swallowed a frog.

"Where did you get this money?" he demanded.

"That is none of your business. Count it and give me a receipt."

"I can't take this money until I know that it isn't stolen. How come it's in cash? It looks mighty suspicious to me. Are you bootlegging or running a house of ill repute out there on the highway?"

"That, too, is none of your business. But if you want to make a formal complaint, go ahead. I'll have reason to sue your socks off. Now, are you going to give me a receipt and the loan contract marked paid or will I send Eli for my lawyer?"

Mary Lee remembered the other time she had come to this office and this man had made her feel as if she were trash. Never again was she going to be treated as she had been that day.

The banker sat back down in his chair

and reached for the stack of bills. With fingers that trembled, he counted them slowly, placing them in stacks of one hundred dollars.

"I told you the interest on three hundred dollars was forty-five dollars."

"You've jacked up the interest and I'm not paying it. Show me the contract my father signed."

He jerked a pad of receipts from the desk drawer and hastily wrote on one. His jaws quivered with anger as he shoved it toward her.

"Now get out."

"Not without the contract stamped 'paid in full.'"

He went to a file cabinet, pulled out a paper, stamped it with a rubber stamp and pushed it across the desk toward her. Mary Lee looked at it closely, then said sweetly:

"Initial it, please."

After he scribbled something on it, she folded the paper and put it in her purse.

"Thank you. It wasn't pleasant doing business with you and I'm sure it will not happen again. Come on, Eli, Mr. Rosen is busy counting his pennies." They opened the door, and Curtis Wessels almost fell into the room.

"Did you hear it all, Curtis? I paid off the loan. Now the old skinflint can't get his hands on the motor court. Isn't that grand?

"By the way, Curtis, remember when you were in the fourth grade and you messed your pants? It went down your leg and all over the floor. My whole class got an extra recess while the janitor cleaned up the mess. I never did thank you for that extra playtime. How rude of me! I'll do it now. Thank you, Curtis, and good-bye."

As they went out the door, Eli was laughing so hard, he wasn't looking where he was going and stepped on a wad of chewing gum that had softened in the sun. It stuck to the bottom of his boot and almost pulled it off. Even that was funny and caused more laughter.

Chapter 29

The black sedan passed slowly by the motor court. A mile down the highway, it turned on a little-used road and came back toward the court through the woods, on what had once been a wagon trail.

"Godalmighty," Wyn said, holding on to the door. "These ruts'll tear up the car—my ass along with it."

"We can't have anything happening to your ass, now, can we, kid?"

"We've been watchin' that damn court for almost a week. I'm ready to make our move."

Lyle stopped the car when they were directly opposite the court and reached for the binoculars. The house and cabins were visible through the trees. It was early afternoon. Sheets flapped on the clothesline. The boy and the short, dumpy girl were working in the last cabin in the line. There was no sign of the pregnant woman. He put the binoculars down on the seat between them.

"We know we can't take her until after the folks who stay overnight are gone. We can't get close to her after the cowboy and the runt come back at suppertime. The cowboy sticks to her like glue in the evening. Our best time is while the girl and the kid are cleaning the cabins, preferably the end cabin where they are now."

"Why can't we just go in there in the night and take care of her and get the hell out of here?"

"She's not alone in the house at night. The boy is with her and the cowboy is in the cabin next to the house. I don't think I want to tangle with him."

"I'm getting tired hanging around this backwater."

"Santa Rosa isn't so bad, is it? We've got a nice room."

"Yeah, but we don't go out much."

"The most important thing in our business, kid, is patience and blending in so folks won't remember us." Lyle laid his hand on Wyn's thigh. "Killing a woman is different from killing a man. Killing a pregnant woman is really going to get folks stirred up. We've got to make sure we leave no trail behind when we take her."

"Yo're smart, Lyle."

"I've been in this game a long time."

"We could've got more money outta Lon. He wants that ranch. He's next in line to get it after the kid the girl's carryin'. After we do our job, he'll get someone else to knock off Clawson."

"I never concern myself with why someone wants a job done. I'm only interested in the money and saving my hide . . . and yours."

"The longer we hang around, the greater chance someone will remember us."

"Maybe you, not me. You're a damn good-looking kid." Lyle glanced at Wyn and winked.

"Why . . . thanks." Wyn grinned and winked back.

"In some places in the city you could name your own price. You'd need to be polished up some: clothes, a decent haircut . . . maybe grow a mustache."

"Ya think so?" In his excitement Wyn began to crack his knuckles.

"I know so. We'll make our move tomorrow or the next day. Then we collect the rest of our money, hightail it out of here and start living the high life."

"They haven't connected the telephone yet," Mary Lee said that night as they lingered at the supper table. "The man at the telephone office said it would be several days. They have to come from Sante Fe."

"It'll be connected before Eli starts to school," Trudy said. "I've got a stick all ready for him to carry with him."

"What'll I need a stick for?" Eli got up to bring the pitcher of tea to the table.

"To beat off the girls swarmin' all over you, what else?" Trudy grinned at him impishly. "Deke carries one all the time."

"But Deke carries his for protection against angry husbands when he flirts with their wives." Jake looked at Mary Lee and winked.

He had come back from their "date" a different man. A wildly happy man. He was no longer quiet or serious-faced. His green eyes danced when he smiled and laughed and teased. Love for him filled every corner of Mary Lee's heart.

"Love does funny things to a man." Deke spoke seriously to Trudy. "It will turn him to jelly, make him rat on his best friend. Darlin', if I get to actin' like that, you can hit me in the head with a board."

"*Darlin'*, I think someone has already hit you in the head. And after Sunday, you'd better not let Jake catch you flirtin' with his wife or he'll hit you with more than a board."

"I hope you have more control over your woman than I have over mine, Jake. At times she's as sassy as a dog with two tails."

"She's right, though. I'd hate like hell to have to break both your legs."

"Ouch! They're hurtin' already."

After the laughter died, Mary Lee said, "Seriously. What's the preacher going to say when Jake and I ask him to marry us? I can't hide my . . . condition."

"He'll say I'm damned lucky."

"Preachers don't say 'damn,' my love."

"There isn't a man alive who doesn't think it."

"You can tell him that you swallowed a

watermelon." Trudy spoke as if she had an answer to the problem.

"He might believe her if she said she swallowed a seed and the watermelon grew," Eli said.

Eli was happy about the wedding. He and Jake had had a long talk. Jake wanted him to go to school, and in a few years they would find a piece of land and build a horse ranch. They already had a start, Jake explained, and told him about the six good mares he had out at Quitmans. Eli readily agreed to go to school. Jake clapped him on the shoulder and asked him to go with them to Sante Fe when he and Mary Lee went to get married.

Trudy insisted that Eli and Deke would help her clear the kitchen before Deke took her home.

"My job is to look after you." Jake stood and pulled Mary Lee to her feet.

"If you're complainin', I'll look after her and you can do the dishes," Eli said.

"Honey, we'd better get our son out from under the influence of Deke and Trudy, or he's goin' to turn out to be a regular smart aleck."

"You'll be the head of the house." Mary

Lee looked up at Jake with love and gratitude. "It'll be up to you to see that he walks
the straight and narrow."

"Do you think he's too big to take a strop
to?" Jake glanced at the boy, who had
clamped his trembling lower lip between his
teeth.

"Much too big, my love."

"We could take a tube out of the radio so
he couldn't hear *Jack Armstrong, the All-
American Boy.* That would keep him in line."

"How clever you are, *querido,*" Mary Lee
laughed. "Did I say it right?"

"Right as rain, *mi tesoro.*"

Later they sat on the porch. Jake leaned
on a porch post; Mary Lee leaned against
him.

"I'll have to make us a porch swing."

"We used to have one. Daddy kept it
painted and the chain greased so it wouldn't
squeak. Mama must have sold it."

"Four more days, *querida,* and you'll be
mine forever." Jake's warm lips caressed
the side of her face.

"I'm already yours forever."

"I wish I had more to offer you," he
groaned. "I'd give you the world if I could."

"You're giving me yourself. I want nothing more."

Jake's hand rested on the side of her belly. "Gaston's quiet tonight."

"We should decide on a name. A real name. We can't keep on calling him Gaston. I've been thinking about Scott Jacob. What do you think?"

"Are you sure you want to put Jacob in the name?"

"You're going to be his papa. He'll never know any other."

"I'll be proud, *querida.*"

"What was your mother's name?"

"Juanita Anderson Ramero. Her mother was a beautiful Spanish lady. Her father was a Texas cowboy. When she was eighteen, she married a Mexican who worked at the Clawson Ranch. He was killed two days after they were married. He was a boy from her village."

"You grew up on the Clawson ranch?"

"The ranch is big. We lived on the land, but not near the ranch buildings."

"If we are married before the baby comes, his name will legally be Ramero."

"Is that what you want, sweetheart?"

"It's what I want. Mr. Clawson won't have any claim on him."

"He'll be our son."

"Will you be disappointed if it's a girl?"

"Not a bit. I'd have two girls to watch over and guard against horny cowpunchers."

"I love you, Jake Ramero. Did you see Eli's face when you talked about him as being our son?"

"He needs to feel like he belongs to us, honey. He tries to act grown up, but he's just a scared boy. Believe me, I know the feeling."

"If I hadn't loved you before, I would love you now."

Trudy came out to say that Deke was taking her home and that she would be back in the morning.

"Eli's listening to Jack Benny," she said.

One by one the lights in the cabins were turned off as tired travelers went to bed.

Reluctant to leave the haven of Jake's arms, Mary Lee cuddled against him. Between whispered confidences and loving kisses, they made plans for their future.

*   *   *

"Go on and get started on number six. I'll set the dishes in the dishpan, then go lie down for a while."

"Are ya havin' pains or anythin'?" Trudy was almost as much of a worrier as Jake.

"No pains. I get a backache from carrying this kid around all day."

"I wish they'd hurry and get the telephone connected."

"Maybe today. Eli will start school on Monday. I'll ask one of Rosa's girls to come help you. I don't expect you to do all of this by yourself. Jake thinks I should take the breakfast signs down. He doesn't think the profit we make is worth the trouble right now."

"He may be right. Come on, squirt," she called to Eli, hovering over the radio. "Let's get the work done; then you can listen to that thing while I take the wash off the line."

Eli grabbed up the bucket of supplies, the broom and the mop. Trudy went to the washhouse to get the clean, folded sheets and towels. The pair walked down the lane and disappeared in the cabin.

Soon a black sedan came swiftly off the highway, braked and backed up beside the house. Wyn was out of the car and in the house within seconds.

Minutes later he was backing out the door, dragging Mary Lee. She hung limp in his arms, her heels bouncing on the floor of the porch. Lyle jumped out, opened the back door of the sedan and helped Wyn put her into the car.

"Shit, she's heavy." Wyn tried to shove her legs inside so he could close the door.

Lyle hurried to the other side and pulled her across the seat.

"Hey! Hey!"

"Shit fire, it's the boy."

Wyn hurriedly crammed Mary Lee's legs in the car, slammed the door and jumped into the front seat. Lyle speeded out and down the highway as if demons were after him. The powerful engine in the sedan ate up the miles until they were a good distance from town.

"It's all right; he didn't see anything. We've got a good head start. She give you any trouble?"

"She thought I'd come to hook up the telephone. Don't that beat all? Do I look like a telephone man? I just walked up to her and popped her on the head. I didn't realize she'd be so damn heavy. She damn near took me to the floor."

"We'll get her out to the shack, then treat ourselves to a nice dinner in Sante Fe and a nice long evening in a high-class hotel room."

They were silent for a while, each with his own thoughts. The only sound came from Wyn, nervously cracking his knuckles.

"This is new to you, kid. But you'll get used to it."

"What bothers me is she's goin' to have a kid."

"Think about it like this—we wouldn't have the job if she wasn't going to have the kid."

"Guess yo're right."

Wyn looked into the back to see the woman sprawled on the seat, a trickle of blood on the side of her forehead where he had hit her. She began to stir. Her hand went to her head.

"Shit fire! She's wakin' up."

"There's some strong cord under the seat. Climb over and tie her up."

While Wyn was tying Mary Lee's hands behind her back, his forearm had rested on her swollen abdomen. He had felt the strong movement of the baby within. It jolted him. He stilled for a long moment, glad his back was to Lyle. When he finished tying her hands and feet, Wyn returned to the front seat.

Five miles down the highway Lyle turned onto a lane. They passed through a woods, then headed out onto rangeland.

"Shit, Lyle, can't we do the job here and dump her?"

"Kid, we go by the plan. You don't want to be ridin' around in a bloody car, do you? We give the buyer what he wants. Lon wants her in the shack. We get the rest of our money when he finds her there."

The shack was built from the earth, like the houses Mexicans had been building for hundreds of years. Set back amid a stand of Douglas fir, the structure was held together by rough logs that protruded from the sun-browned adobe walls.

Lyle braked a dozen feet from the cabin. Both men got out. Wyn lifted the crossbar on the door and threw it open. The shack was cool inside and windowless. A cot, a two-burner wood stove, a table and benches were the only furnishings.

"All right, kid, let's get this over with."

Wyn took Mary Lee's shoulders, and Lyle her feet. They carried her into the cabin and dropped her on the hard-packed dirt floor. Her head hit hard, and she groaned. Her skirt was up around her thighs.

"Want to see her pussy, Wyn? It's hard to see how that brat will come out of such a small slit."

"Naw. 'Sides, her legs are tied."

"I'll untie them if you want to see it."

"Naw. I've seen 'em before."

Lyle pulled a snub-nosed gun out from the inside of his shirt, spun the cylinder to check the load, then handed it, butt first, to Wyn.

"Go ahead, kid. You're going to have to get your feet wet sooner or later. It might as well be now."

Wyn hesitated, then took the gun.

"The side of the head is the best place, quick and clean." He threw his arm over Wyn's shoulder in a gesture of affection, then walked to the door. "Once you do one, the rest will be easy. Soon you won't think any more about it than if you were shooting a squirrel."

Wyn squatted down, took a handful of Mary Lee's hair and turned her head. He pointed the gun and pulled the trigger. The sound of the shot filled the room. Lyle saw her legs jerk, and he smiled. The boy was all right.

The kid rushed for the opening, pushed Lyle out and slammed the door. After dropping the crossbar, he reeled a few feet away, bent over and vomited.

Chapter 30

Laughing and tossing a pillow at Trudy, Eli went to the door to get the mop he'd left leaning against the side of the cabin. He casually glanced up toward the house, then looked again. A car was parked beside the house, and a man was shoving Mary Lee into it.

"Hey! Hey!" he shouted, leaped out the door and began to run. "Stop that!" He was halfway there when the car shot out of the drive and onto the highway. "Stop, you . . . bastards!" he yelled.

When Trudy caught up with him, she grabbed his arm. In shock, they stared down the highway, but the car was out of sight.

"They took her! Jake was dependin' on

me." Eli was crying openly and unashamedly. "If they hurt her . . . I'll kill the sons a bitches!"

"Get a hold on yourself." Trudy shook his arm. "Run down to the station and tell Mr. Santez to call the sheriff."

"We got to get Jake. He'll know what to do."

"Hell!" Trudy swore. "I wish we had a telephone. Go, Eli. Go call the sheriff. Ask Mr. Santez to take you to Quitman's to get Jake and Deke."

"If anybody comes, go in the house and lock the doors," Eli said, then took off running down the highway, oblivious of the auto horns that honked at him because he was running on the pavement. The fear in his heart fueled his pumping legs.

Trudy hurried into the house and went through the rooms. The house was as quiet as death. Some of the noon dishes had been removed from the table; a broken dish lay on the floor. She returned to the porch, numb with fear and dread, to pace and to wait.

After what seemed an eternity but could only have been fifteen minutes or less, a car pulled into the drive and braked in front of the house. Eli sat beside Mr. Santez. Trudy ran to the driver's side.

"The sheriff's on the other side of the county," Mr. Santez told her. "The telephone operator is trying to locate him and the deputy. When she finds him, she'll tell him to come here. I'm takin' the boy to Quitman's to get Jake." Trudy backed up, and the car sped away.

Eli clasped his hands together and clenched his jaws to keep from crying. Coming to the court had been the luckiest day of his life. Mary Lee loved him; she had told him she did. No one had ever loved him but his mother, and she had been gone for so long he couldn't recall her face. He would never forget seeing the man throw Mary Lee in the car, as if she were an old castoff, and slam the door.

Son of a bitch, bastard, dirty rotten shit . . . In his mind, he called the men every nasty name he'd ever heard.

Eli leaned forward and held on to the door and the dashboard. He had never been to Quitman's and had no idea where it was or how long it would take to get there. Mr. Santez turned the car into a long lane leading to a nest of buildings and a maze of corrals. They didn't stop until after they rounded the house and came to a stout corral connected to a barn. As soon as it stopped, Eli was out and running.

"Jake!"

Jake was leading a handsome, prancing roan out of the barn. When he saw Eli, fear rose in his throat. Something terrible had happened! He dropped the reins, hurried to the pole fence and jumped over.

"Some men came and . . . and took her!"

"Mary Lee?" Jake grabbed Eli's shoulders. "What do you mean, 'took her'?"

"Trudy and I was in number six. I looked out the door—they was puttin' her in a car. I . . . was supposed to take care of her—"

"Never mind that now," Jake said sternly. "Who were they? Do you know them? What kind of car?"

"Black car. They was carryin' her— I'll kill 'em!"

"We called the sheriff," Mr. Santez said. "It'll be a while before he can get here."

"What happened?" Deke came running up, followed by several others.

"Someone took Mary Lee away in a car." Jake's mind was trying to reason logically while his heart was like a cold lump in his chest.

Deke was speechless for once. Then, "Trudy?"

"She's back at the court."

"Did you see the men?" Jake's voice reflected his anxiety.

"Just one of 'em. I didn't see his face . . . but I saw his boots." Eli grabbed Jake's arm. "A man wearin' boots like that was working at Clawson's when I was there."

"Slow down and tell me everything you saw." Jake's face was hard as stone.

"I just had a glimpse, but he was wearin' boots that came about to here"—Eli bent over and touched his leg a few inches below his knee—"and his britches were tucked in. I remember the boots 'cause they had a big white star on the side."

"You're sure?"

"I'm sure a man at Clawson's wore boots like that. He was cocky and mouthy. He was younger than Lon Delano but hung around with him a lot."

"Son of a bitch!" A batch of cusswords flowed from Jake. "I should've killed that bastard a long time ago."

Eli shook Jake's arm. "It wasn't Lon Delano. I'd a recognized him."

"He never does his own dirty work."

"I'll get the cycle." Deke had been keeping his motorcycle at the ranch while he was working on one for Mr. Quitman.

"I'm going to Clawson's . . ."

"Ocie wouldn't have anything to do with something like this," Mr. Santez said.

"His foreman would. Go back. Stay with Trudy, Eli!" Jake shouted.

His words were almost lost in the roar of the motorcycle. Deke paused just long enough for Jake to jump into the sidecar before they roared off down the lane.

Eli repeated his story to Mr. Quitman, who immediately left for town to spread the news to the merchants up and down the street that Mary Lee Clawson had been kidnapped and to be on the lookout for two men in a black car, one wearing high boots with a white star on the side.

If his mind had been working clearly, Jake would have admired the way Deke handled the motorcycle. They traveled the roads, crossed rough range, dipped into a dry creek bed, scared deer and scattered a herd of whiteface steers. Deke drove fast but not recklessly. The wind whipped his hair and bloused the sleeves on his shirt.

Querida, querida, be all right. Please, God, don't let my love be harmed. I'll do anything, anything . . .

Jake had believed for some time that Lon Delano considered Mary Lee's baby a threat to his inheriting the ranch—especially since Ocie had made such an issue of wanting her to come out there to live. Lon was probably behind her near-fall on the steps leading to the doctor's office. If the bastard had a hand in this, he was a dead man.

The motorcycle sped toward the ranch house, leaving behind a trail of dust. Ocie came out onto the porch when it roared into the yard. Jake was out the instant it stopped.

"Where's Lon?"

"Hell, I don't know. Around here some-where. What's up?"

"Two men came to the court and took Mary Lee. If he's behind it, I'm going to kill him."

"Took her? The hell you say!"

"Have you had a kid working here who

wore boots with a big white star on the side?"

"Hell, a lot of men come and go. I don't pay attention to their boots."

"He wore his britches stuffed in . . . hung around a lot with Lon?"

"I know who ya mean." Old Ben came out of the house wiping his hands on a rag. "A bratty kid named Wyn was here until a few weeks ago. He wore boots like that."

"A man wearing boots with a big white star shoved Mary Lee into the back of a black car and sped away. If Lon is behind it he'll know where they took her."

"Are ya daft?" Ocie said. "Why'd Lon do that?"

"So he'd inherit the ranch, ya dumb shit!" Jake shouted. "Who's in line after Bobby's baby?"

Ocie's mouth opened, closed, opened again. "The bastard! I'll kill him myself if he hurts that girl."

"Lon has a shack down on the Pecos," Ben said.

Ocie looked at him. "There's nothing there but four walls."

"There is now. A few months ago one of

the boys saw that it was fixed up. The hands have been warned to stay clear of it."

"I know that old place. Why would he take her there?"

"Why not?" Ben said. "She could rot in that shack and no one but Lon would know."

"I'm going out there, then I'm coming back for Lon whether she's there or not." Jake stepped back into the sidecar.

"What can I do?" Ocie asked, coming off the porch.

"Gather your men to look for her. Quitman's probably already got his men out."

"Which way?" Deke asked.

Ben stepped to the edge of the porch. "Go through the gate behind the corrals, put your eyes on three fir trees standing alone. When you reach them, go east. It's a good five miles to the Pecos. Turn south. When you come to a dry creek bed, you're close."

Deke nodded, stomped on the starter, and the motorcycle came to life. Ocie didn't speak until they were out of the yard.

"You reckon Jake's right about Lon?"

Ben shrugged. "He's been actin' like he's owner here. He's got all new crew."

"I've been leavin' too much up to him, haven't I?"

"'Fraid so, Ocie. Ya better take control or ya'll be workin' for Lon."

"You think he'd get rid of that girl thinkin' I'll leave the ranch to him cause Pa was so hell-bent on keepin' it in the family?" Ocie frowned.

"You'll have to ask him. He just rode in." Ben went back into the house.

"By God, I will." Ocie went along the side of the porch to the back, where Lon was watering his horse at the tank.

"Who was that on the motorcycle? The damn fool'll spook the cattle."

"Jake." Ocie came right to the point. "He's looking for Mary Lee and seems to think you have something to do with two men takin' her."

"What? He's a crazy goddamn Mexican bastard who's always had it in for me."

"He'll kill you if anything happens to that girl."

"He might try."

"Goddammit, Lon, I want some answers. The kid that worked here for a while, the one who wore high boots with a white star, was seen at the motor court shoving her into a car."

"What's that got to do with me?"

"His name was Wyn and he hung around with you."

"I don't know who yo're talkin' about."

"Are you thinkin' the ranch will go to you if Bobby's kid ain't born?"

"I suppose I'd be next in line of kin, but that don't mean I have anythin' to do with her bein' missin'."

"Damn ya to hell. I can leave the whole goddamn place to the town whore if I want to."

"But you won't. This land has been in the family for more than a hundred years. I'm family."

"Ya'll never get it!" Ocie shouted. "Get your gear and get out. I've been meanin' to send ya packin' for a while. I don't like the way yo're doin' thin's. I'm thinkin' now you trumped up those rustlin' charges against Jake Ramero and got your men to swear to it."

"You swore to it too."

"I swore that they were my cattle, you lying son of a bitch! They had my brand on them."

"Ya ain't firin' me!" Lon's face turned a fiery red. "I've been runnin' this ranch for more'n ten years. If anyone goes, it won't be me."

Ocie snorted. "I own this place and I'm tellin' ya to be off my land by sundown."

"Who's goin' to put me off? You?"

"If I have to."

"There's more than twenty men work here. How many of them take orders from you?"

"So it's come down to this." Ocie shook his head and turned to walk away.

"The law'll give me this ranch when you're gone. By God! I'm next of kin. There's no blood kin standin' between you and me." Lon went behind his horse and opened his saddlebag.

"And I'm damned ashamed that yo're kin." Ocie turned. "If you've hurt that girl, it won't do ya no good. I've made out a will."

Lon's head jerked up. "When did this happen?"

"None of your business. You won't get this ranch . . . ever! I want you gone from here today. I'll leave your pay at the bank."

"Ya ain't got no will. It wasn't but a couple

weeks ago ya was talkin' that ya ort to have one."

Ocie turned and headed for the house. Before he reached it, Lon grabbed his shoulder and spun him around.

"If ya got a will, where's it at?" he snarled, and shoved Ocie back. When Ocie saw the gun in Lon's hand and the crazed look on his face, he became alarmed. But pride refused to let him back down.

"I'm tellin' ya nothin'."

"Ya'll tell me or ya'll not walk again." Lon pointed the gun and fired.

It happened so quickly, Ocie had no time to react. He screamed and fell back, his kneecap shattered.

"Ya ain't so smart now," Lon jeered. "I've been runnin' this place while ya've been lordin' it over me. I been takin' shit from you since I was a pup, but I ain't doin' it no more. Did Junior Miller make ya out a will? Tell me or you'll get a bullet in the other knee."

Ocie was rolling on the ground, holding his thigh and screaming with pain. Lon's words hadn't even registered in his brain.

"Guess ya want another bullet." Lon's

face was a mask of hatred. He stepped up close and fired into Ocie's other knee.

The pain was excruciating. Ocie never even heard Lon's next words.

"Have ya got a will in old Miller's office? Goddammit! Have ya? If ya ain't tellin' me, the next bullet goes into that shit between yore ears." He waited. When Ocie didn't answer, he pointed the gun toward his head. "When ya get to hell, say hello to old Temple, who didn't want to admit that Lon Delano was kin to the almighty Clawsons."

Lon never pulled the trigger. A loud blast came from a shotgun in the hands of old Ben. He had come out the back door. The heavy pellets struck Lon in the chest and threw him back into the dirt. His horse shied, then broke away and ran to the far side of the corral.

When the first shots were fired, all hands within hearing distance stopped work. At the blast from the shotgun, they hurried to the back of the house. Ben was on his knees beside Ocie.

"The bastard's dead, Ocie. We'll get ya to the doctor." Then he shouted, "Somebody get a board to carry him on!"

Chapter 31

Because the motorcycle made so much noise, Jake directed Deke by hand signals. It seemed to Jake they crossed rangeland forever before they reached the river. After they turned south, the terrain grew rougher, and they had to slow down. When they came to the place that Jake thought would be a half mile from the shack, he touched Deke's arm and motioned for him to stop.

"It's not far now. We'd better walk. I wish I had a gun. I never thought to get one from Ocie."

"I've got one." Deke lifted the seat in the sidecar, pulled out a small revolver, checked to see that it was loaded, then tucked it into his belt. "Let's go."

Jake wanted to run, but his high-heeled

boots made running difficult and he wanted to conserve his strength for what might face him when they reached the shack. As they hurried along, Deke did his best to keep up with Jake.

"A car has been here recently." Deke pointed to two sets of tire tracks. The blades of grass were flattened going in one direction on one set, and in the opposite direction on the other.

"They've been here and gone." Jake managed to speak over the huge lump in his throat.

He had never been so afraid in his life, not even when three hardened convicts at the state prison had backed him into a corner of the fence in the exercise area and he had believed that he might not get out of that corner alive.

Madre de Dios, he prayed, *I'll never ask for another thing if you'll let her be all right. I love her so damn much. She and her baby mean everything to me. They are all I want in this world. I can't lose her. I can't!*

His heart was pumping with dread at what they would find as they approached the windowless shack. It was quiet, serene, almost hallowed there amid the fir trees.

Not even the scolding of blue jays or the caws of crows soaring overhead broke the silence. Jake wanted his love to be there but feared that if she was, she was already lost to him.

Deke pulled the gun from his belt. Jake lifted the bar, threw back the door and sprang into the room. At first he saw what he thought was a pile of rags on the dirt floor; a second later a cry tore from his throat.

"Querida!"

Mary Lee lay on her side on the dirt floor, her hands bound behind her back, her knees drawn up as if she were trying to protect her baby. Blood had soaked the front of her shirt. The part of her face not covered with dirt was deathly white.

"Querida. Mi bella querida." Jake fell on his knees beside her, lifted her face out of the dirt with his cupped palm and smoothed the hair back from her neck. He searched and found a pulse. He gave a glad cry. "She's alive! Thank you, God!"

"See the powder burns on her shirt," Deke said. "She was on her back when she was shot." He slashed the ropes that bound her hands and feet, then made a cut in the shirt and pulled it off her shoulder. "Looks like it went through. We've got to stop the blood or she'll bleed to—"

"Cut the sleeve out of her shirt, it's cleaner than mine. Turn it wrong side out and pack the wound. She's got a big lump on the side of her head. Goddamn bastards left her lying in the dirt."

Working fast, they packed the wound the best they could. Jake ran his hand over her belly several times, searching for movement, and found none.

Don't be dead, Gaston. It would break her heart and . . . mine.

He lifted her into his arms. Deke jerked a blanket off the bunk. They wrapped her in it and, holding her high against his chest, Jake walked out of the shack.

"I'll get the cycle." Deke took off on the run.

Carrying his precious burden, Jake followed. He stopped once, kissed her soft mouth and whispered his love for her.

Mary Lee opened eyes that refused to focus. Someone was holding her tenderly and lovingly, cradling her against his chest. She wasn't afraid. *I'm dreaming,* she thought tiredly. Then she heard a beloved voice crooning to her. Jake's voice. He had come when she called to him.

Jake heard the motorcycle when it started, and kept walking toward it. Deke circled the machine and headed it back in the other direction before he stopped, then got off and reached to hold Mary Lee while Jake got into the sidecar. When she was settled in his arms, Jake gave Deke directions to the highway.

Knowing the bumpy ride was hurting her shoulder, he held her close, his head bent over her, his lips close to her ear. He told her that he loved her and that he had almost died until he found her. He murmured to her that Gaston was all right and they would be at the doctor's soon. Once he thought he heard a sound come from her, but he couldn't be sure because of the roar of the motorcycle.

When they passed the Santez gas station, Deke slowed and honked the horn to let the man know that Mary Lee had been found. When they reached the motor court, Deke turned in. Trudy and Eli were on the porch, and a deputy sheriff's car was there.

"Lock the door and come to the doctor's office!" Jake yelled.

The deputy yelled back, "I'll bring 'em!"

They roared down the main street of town and stopped beside the stairs going up the side of the building. Deke jumped off and bounded up the stairs to see if the doctor was there. He was back a minute later.

"Doc's gone out to Clawson's. Lon Delano shot up Ocie, and old Ben killed Delano with a shotgun. The nurse said to bring Mary Lee in and she'll do what she can until the doctor gets back."

People had gathered on the sidewalk, all offering helping hands. Paco was there. He came to lift Mary Lee out of Jake's arms so he could get out of the sidecar. Then, as if he couldn't bear to be parted from her, Jake reached for her and carried her up the stairs. Deke stayed behind to answer questions from the curious crowd.

The nurse was waiting and led him to the back room and a high sheet-covered table. As soon as Mary Lee was on the table, she took her pulse and lifted her eyelid.

"You'll have to help me with this. Go over there and scrub your hands."

Jake obeyed without hesitation. For the next half hour they worked as a team, the nurse giving the orders. The man who had shot Mary Lee had pressed the gun barrel against her shoulder. The shot had gone in and out and probably into the dirt floor where Jake had found her. The wound itself was not so serious, the nurse explained, but the loss of blood was.

Several times Mary Lee rolled her head and groaned as if she was trying to awaken.

"A few more hours and she would have bled to death."

"Why doesn't she wake up?"

"Probably because of the blow to her head. The doctor will have a look at it."

After asking him to leave the room for a few minutes, the nurse bared Mary Lee's belly and with the stethoscope listened for the baby's heartbeat. Jake took the opportunity to speak to Deke, Eli and Trudy, who were in the waiting room.

"Jake," the nurse called to him, and he hurried back into the room. "She's trying to wake up."

Mary Lee was moving her legs and rolling her head.

"She told me once that it was hard for her to lie on her back," Jake said. "Can we roll her over on her side?"

"I don't see why not. Take a good hold on

the sheet she's lying on, pull her over, then up to roll her over. I'll hold her arm so that the wound doesn't start bleeding again."

When she was on her side with her knees drawn up, she seemed to settle down. Jake pulled up a stool and sat down so that he was close to her face.

"As far as I can tell, the baby is snug as a bug in a rug. He has a strong heartbeat. We've done about as much as we can do, Jake. Watch her to be sure she doesn't wake, thrash around, and fall off the table."

"I'll be right here."

The nurse put her hand on his shoulder as she passed behind him. "You love her?"

"With all my heart."

"Does she love you?"

"She says she does and I believe her."

"I'm glad for you, Jake."

"Thank you."

As soon as he was alone with Mary Lee, he took her hand and, leaning over, kissed her still lips tenderly. He whispered to her that he loved her, over and over. He spoke reassuringly of their future together.

"With Eli and Gaston, honey, we'll have a good start on our family. Later we may be blessed with a couple of little girls who will look like their pretty mama. We'll have big gatherings on Christmas and birthdays. I'll teach our boys to be cowboys and you can teach our girls to cook and sew."

Minutes passed into an hour. At times he heard voices coming from the waiting room, Deke's or Trudy's. Several times the nurse came in and took Mary Lee's pulse. Jake left her side only to dampen the cloth the nurse had placed on her forehead.

He sat with shoulders hunched, eyes bleak, not caring how much he might be exposing his human frailty. They had taken off the bloody shirt and put Mary Lee in a gown that opened all the way down the back. She was covered with a light blanket.

Jake felt an urge to know if Gaston was all right. He slipped his hand beneath the blanket and felt her tight belly. Gaston was moving, but not boisterously as he sometimes did. Jake withdrew his hand and tucked the blanket behind Mary Lee's back and around her neck.

Shortly after that, she began to flutter her hands restlessly. He changed the wet cloth on her head and noticed that her lips were moving and a frown puckered her brows.

She jerked her head suddenly and let out a little cry.

Jake became alarmed. "Nurse!"

The nurse came and listened to her heart. "She's trying to wake up. Hold this pillow to the side of her head so that she can't turn it."

Mary Lee tried to lift her hand but didn't have the strength to bring it out from under the blanket.

"Oh," she murmured. "Oh, my head."

The words filled Jake with hope. Her eyelids quivered; she opened her eyes, shut them, opened them again and blinked as if she were trying to wake up.

"Don't move your head, *querida*." Jake's voice trembled with tenderness. "Can you wake up, sweetheart?"

"Jake . . ." Her lips trembled, and she began to cry. Tears squeezed out from under her closed lids. "I want . . . Jake."

"I'm here, *querida*. Don't cry. I'll not leave you." He brought her hand to his lips. "Lie still, my love."

"Am I dreaming that you're here?"

"No. Open your eyes and you'll see me."

"You came for me."

"Didn't you know that I'd cross the earth

to get to you if you needed me?" He gently wiped her cheeks with a corner of the blanket.

"I called you."

"I heard you calling me."

Her eyes flew open. "Jake! You *are* here!"

"Yes, *mi vida,* and I'm not leaving you for the next fifty years."

"Can't you stay longer than that?" Her eyes drifted shut.

"I'll try, sweetheart. Stay awake and talk to me."

"Where are we?"

"In Doctor Morris's office."

"Is my baby all right?"

"He's fine. The nurse listened to his heartbeat."

"Why did they do that to me? I thought I was going to die there and . . . and I'd never see you again."

"If you had, my world would have ended."

"The man told the boy he had to shoot me. Later, he said, he'd think no more of it than shooting a squirrel. I looked up and saw the boy looking at me. He didn't want to do it."

"He shot you in the shoulder."

"I woke up after they'd gone, and called you."

"I came as soon as I could, sweetheart."

Her eyes drifted shut. He could tell by her breathing that she was sleeping. After a few minutes he removed the pillow and stroked her hair.

It was near dark when the doctor returned to his office. The nurse briefed him on Mary Lee's condition before he came into the room. She was sleeping soundly, her hand in Jake's. He released it and stepped back.

"Hello, Jake," the doctor said wearily. "This little girl has had it rough since she came back to Cross Roads. I still haven't got it straight in my mind why someone would kidnap her."

"The truth will come out sooner or later. I think Lon Delano was behind it. He was afraid Ocie would leave the ranch to Bob Clawson's child. He wanted to get rid of the baby before it was born."

"Well, Lon's dead. The shotgun blast almost tore him in two. Too bad Ben didn't let him have it sooner. Ocie will never walk again. That'll be hard for a man like him."

"No charges against Ben, I hope."

"I wouldn't think so. Sheriff Pleggenkuhle is a commonsense kind of a sheriff. Ben saved Ocie's life, although Ocie may not thank him for it. It looks like my nurse did a good job on the shoulder wound."

"Will I be able to take her home?"

"It'd be the best place for her if there's someone there to take care of her."

"There will be."

Doctor Morris put his hands under the blanket and felt Mary Lee's abdomen.

"The baby has dropped . . ."

"Dropped? What does that mean?"

"It means that it won't be long until she'll be delivering. Step in the other room, Jake, and send the nurse in. I'm going to check and see if she's dilating."

Only Deke was in the waiting room. Eli and Trudy had gone back to open the motor court.

"They said they could help Mary Lee more there than sitting here."

"Have you heard any more about what happened at Clawson's?"

"Only that when Ocie Clawson fired Lon and ordered him off the place, Lon started shooting. Big slugs from that forty-five tore up the man's knees. They've taken him to Santa Fe to the hospital. The old-timer, they said, was calm as buttermilk. He told the sheriff that when a rattlesnake strikes, you shoot it. And that's what he did."

"Ben was there when I was a kid."

"As soon as Mary Lee is all right, I'm going hunting for a man in a black sedan and a kid wearing boots with a star."

"If he's smart, the kid will ditch the boots."

"If he was smart he'd never have got mixed up with Lon Delano."

The doctor came in, leaned against the desk and crossed his arms over his chest.

"She may be starting to dilate a bit. You can take her home; but if her pains start or her water breaks, come get me. I'm going home to get a bite of supper, then on to the hospital in Santa Fe to see about Ocie. I'll take you by the motor court unless you want another ride in that motorcycle car."

"Now, Doc," Deke said. "Don't be knockin' my cycle. It got us where your car couldn't've. Ain't that right, darlin'," he said to the nurse when she came in.

"You promised to take me for a ride."

"I'm not forgettin' it, darlin'. You'll have to

tie down that perky little white cap on your head." Deke winked at the doctor, slammed his hat down on his head and headed for the door.

Chapter 32

"Wake up, *querida*."

Jake, kneeling beside the bed, put his hand under Mary Lee's head and lifted it a little. His other hand was on her arm.

"Wake up. The doctor said to wake you about every few hours."

"Jake?"

"I'm here, sweetheart. Look at my hand. How many fingers am I holding up?"

"Two, silly man. Did you wake me for that?"

"Go back to sleep, honey. I'll not wake you again until morning."

"You're tired. Lie down by me and get some sleep."

"I might bump your shoulder. I'll catch some sleep when Trudy gets up."

When Mary Lee wakened again, light was coming in through the windows, and Eli was sitting beside the bed, staring at her intently.

"Mornin', Eli."

"You're awake!"

"I think so."

"How do you feel? Does your shoulder hurt where that pile of horse hockey shot you? I'm sorry I didn't protect you like I promised."

Mary Lee reached for his hand. "It pains me a little. I'm so glad you and Trudy were not in the house. They would have hurt you."

"If I ever see that kid that shot you, I'll blow his head off!" The boy's voice trembled in anger.

"The man with him told him to kill me, Eli, but he didn't. He saved my life. It was wrong of him to help the man take me, but when it came right down to it, he couldn't kill me." She held his hand up to her cheek. "Sometime during the night, Jake told me the reason they found me so fast was because you remembered the boots the man was wearing. If not for you they'd not have found me, and . . . and my baby and I would have died."

Eli swallowed the large lump in his throat, and his eyes filled with tears. Unable to speak, he held tightly to her hand and looked out the window.

Trudy helped Mary Lee to the bathroom, where she could wash her face and brush her teeth. Unable to get into a nightgown because of her shoulder, she put on one of her daddy's shirts and went back to bed.

The doctor came shortly after breakfast and put a fresh dressing on her shoulder wound. Jake was waiting in the kitchen when he came out of Mary Lee's room.

"Shoulder's healing. I'll leave supplies so you can change the dressing. She had a mild concussion from the blow to her head. It was mild or she wouldn't have drifted in and out of consciousness. If she runs a fever or has labor pains, call me. I expect her to deliver in the next few days."

Jake followed the doctor to his car, where they spoke for a few minutes. When he came back in, he went to Mary Lee's room and hunkered down beside the bed, leaned over and kissed her lips.

"The doctor said Gaston will be here in a few days."

"He told me. I'm anxious to get it over."

"Will you marry me, *querida*?"

"I want to, more than anything." She laughed nervously. "I don't think I could make it to the door, much less to a church to be married."

"I'll get the license and bring the preacher or the justice of the peace here. Later we can be married in a church if you want to. I want so much to be this baby's papa."

"So Ocie Clawson won't have a claim to him?"

"That, but not as much as I want him to be mine, carry my name."

"Poor Mr. Clawson. Trudy said that he'd never walk again."

"He should have seen through Lon a long time ago. My regret is that now I may not be able to clear my name of the rustling charges. If you marry me, *mi tesoro*, you'll be a jailbird's wife."

"Are you trying to talk me out of it? If you are, you're not going to succeed."

"Will this evening be too soon for you?"

"Right now wouldn't be too soon, my love."

"I want to hold you, but I'm afraid I'll hurt you." He spoke in a kind of desperate whisper, then lowered his head and kissed every inch of her face.

Her palm caressed his cheek. "You shaved."

"Of course," he said happily. "This is my wedding day."

After Jake announced that he and Mary Lee would be married that evening, the house became a flurry of activity. Trudy issued orders to Eli and Deke, and they jumped to obey.

Deke was sent to Ruby's to spread the word that there was going to be a wedding, and to ask her to bake the wedding cake. When he returned, he stayed with Mary Lee while Trudy and Eli cleaned the cabins in record time.

Then it was Eli's turn to stay while Deke and Trudy made a hasty trip uptown. They returned with a box that Trudy took in to Mary Lee.

"It's beautiful, Trudy!" Mary Lee exclaimed when Trudy opened the box and took out a white satin housecoat trimmed with fluffy white lace and tiny covered buttons. The sleeves were wide and the body of the garment generous.

"Jake said to get something white. We saw him uptown," she added by way of explanation.

Mary Lee looked at the price tag hanging from one of the sleeves and winced.

"It didn't cost that much. It was on sale. Deke and I want it to be your wedding present."

"Oh, Trudy, no. I can't let you . . ."

"Are you goin' to chase me around the house?" Trudy snipped off the price tag and carefully folded the garment and put it back in the box. "A girl doesn't get married every day."

"Especially a girl so pregnant she can't bend over and could have the baby at any moment. And one with a lump on her head the size of an egg."

"Just think of the story you can tell your grandkids. We saw Mama while we were gone. She'll ice the cake after she gets here. She got one of the Johnson girls to come serve the evening meal at the café. 'Course, she'll cook it this afternoon."

"Where did you see Jake?"

"He'd just come out of the mercantile

store. He bought new shirts for him and Eli. He was smiling from ear to ear. I've never seen a man so happy, and I don't think anyone else has either. He looked as if he had the world by the tail and was grinning like a jackass. Speaking of jackasses, I've got to set up the ironing board. Deke is pestering me to iron his shirt." She giggled. "Mama is bringing my dress. Deke is supposed to go get her about five. Jake said the ceremony would be at six."

"How could I have ever felt sorry for myself? I have the most wonderful friends in the world." Mary Lee choked on the last few words.

"Well, darn. You don't have to bawl about it and get your eyes all red and puffy," Trudy sniffed, and hurried back to the kitchen.

Jake and Mary Lee were married in the living room. Mary Lee, beautiful in the white satin robe, sat in a chair. Jake squatted down beside her, holding her hand. At the proper time, he slipped a wide gold band on her finger. After the words that made them man and wife, he kissed her tenderly, then winked at a beaming Eli in a white shirt and blue tie, who bent and kissed her cheek.

Deke and Trudy had stood with the couple, and Deke had insisted on his first right to kiss the bride. Jake proudly accepted congratulations and was tolerant as each man present kissed his wife.

The small room was crowded. Sheriff Pleggenkuhle had brought the justice of the peace. Paco and his wife were there as well as Mr. and Mrs. Santez and Mr. Morales. Ruby had made a beautiful two-tiered wedding cake. She and Trudy served it to the guests along with iced tea.

When Jake saw the lines of tiredness in Mary Lee's face, he picked her up, expressed their thanks to the guests for having come, and took her to the bedroom. Trudy closed the door behind them.

"You won't leave?" Mary Lee asked as he placed her gently on the bed.

"No, sweetheart. I'm staying right here with you tonight and every night for the rest of our lives."

"Will you lie down by me? You can't sit in that chair another night."

"I might hurt you."

"You won't. Thank you for the ring. I didn't expect it."

"It was my mother's. I took it to the jewelry store and they shined it up." He didn't tell her the shock he had experienced when he read the inscription inside.

"It was a lovely wedding."

"We'll have a *padre* marry us later, if you want."

"We can think about it."

"You're so tired you can hardly keep your eyes open. Do you want to take off your pretty robe?"

"I think so. If my shoulder should bleed in the night, I'd get blood on it."

After he helped her off with the robe and into the shirt, she lay back exhausted and closed her eyes. She could hear voices and laughter in the other room and wished that she could be in there celebrating her wedding.

"We'll have a party on our first anniversary," Jake said as if knowing her thoughts.

He took off his shoes, his shirt and tie and lay down beside his sleeping bride. It wasn't the wedding night he had dreamed about, but she was his, and he could wait.

* * *

Scott Jacob Ramero was born three days after his parents were married. Mary Lee had awakened in the night with pains but didn't waken Jake until early morning. He was so nervous that she wished that she could have waited until Trudy arrived.

The first thing Jake did was go to the other room and shout for Eli to wake up; then he hurried to cabin number one and pounded on the door for Deke. Finally Mary Lee managed to get him to sit still long enough to time the labor pains.

"The doctor said when they were five minutes apart to call him."

"I've already called."

"You didn't!"

"I did. I told him they were almost five minutes apart. I want him here in plenty of time."

"Ruby left some padding to put under me. It's rolled up there on the floor of the closet."

"Should we boil water?" Jake asked.

"Why? Are you going to cook me? Where is Deke going? I hear the truck."

"He's going to get Trudy and Ruby."

Eli stood in the doorway wringing his hands.

"Don't look so worried, Eli. Women have been having babies for hundreds of years."

"What can I do?"

"Make coffee. Jake will need some and so will the doctor."

Jake's hands were visibly shaking when he knelt by the bed and clasped hers. The stubble of whiskers on his cheeks and his tousled hair made him look roguish, but the green eyes on her face were filled with love and concern.

"Don't look so worried, my love." She caressed his cheek with her fingertips. He turned his lips into her palm.

"I love you so damn much. I don't want you to hurt."

"You don't have to stay, love. Ruby and Trudy will be here."

"I'm staying with you. Don't ask me to go."

He was on his knees beside the bed for the next three hours, wiping her face, giving her his hand to pull on, whispering encouraging words.

"Don't bite your lips, *querida.* Yell. It's all right to yell."

Tears sparkled on the cheeks of both by the time the baby arrived. The doctor held him up for them to see. He was crying lustily.

"You've got a fine boy, Mary Lee. Big one. Must weigh all of nine pounds." He took him to the kitchen, where Ruby washed him and wrapped him in a blanket. She brought him to Jake, who held him up for his mother to see.

Jake walked out with Doctor Morris when he was leaving.

"Watch for excessive bleeding, Jake. I don't expect it, but it's best to be aware that it can happen."

"I will, and thanks."

"You're very welcome. You were good, steady help in there."

"I've seen quite a few foals come into the world. But it's different when it's your wife. I was scared to death!"

The doctor chuckled. "I could tell."

"I'll be in and make arrangements to pay."

"We'll make it as easy for you as we can."

"I appreciate it."

Mary Lee's recuperative powers were amazing. The doctor wanted her to stay in bed for a week. She was up after five days when Jake was out of the house. Her shoulder was still sore, but she carried the baby on the other side. Everyone wanted to hold him. Eli swore that he smiled at him. Trudy didn't have the heart to tell him that Scotty probably had a gas pain.

The cabins were full almost every night. Jake and Deke went back to work at Quitman's. The news about Mary Lee's kidnapping and what had occurred at Clawson's ranch swept the area like wildfire. There had been no sighting of the man in the black car and the kid in the high boots. The sheriff reasoned that Mary Lee's quick discovery in the shack and Lon Delano's death had sent the pair scurrying out of the area.

Mary Lee enjoyed being slim again. She looked forward to the end of each day when her little family was alone. The first thing Jake would do when he came in at night was gather his wife into his arms, kiss her and run his hands down her back to hold her tightly against him.

"I miss something here," he said, stroking her flat belly. "As soon as you're able I'm going to put something back in there."

Always he would go to the dresser drawer where Scotty lay and say hello to his son and talk nonsense to him, enormously pleased when the baby grabbed his finger and held on.

"Look, honey! Look how strong he is. He's going to be a cowboy like his daddy."

Eli was fascinated with the baby too. When he came home from school, he headed for the crib to see if Scotty had grown any during the day. Neither Eli or Jake could stand to hear him cry, and the baby soon learned that that was what he had to do to be picked up and rocked.

Deke's courtship of Trudy was getting serious. They spent almost all their free time together—some of it in the cabin Deke and Jake had occupied until Jake moved into the house.

Jake had been wonderfully patient while holding Mary Lee at night. At times he trembled with wanting, but refused to satisfy his craving for her until after the full four weeks the doctor had suggested.

On this night, it was Mary Lee who initiated the consummation of their marriage. She locked her arms around his neck and whispered, "I want you."

"Are you sure it's all right?" His arms slid beneath her shoulders, and he pulled her to him. "Did I hurt your shoulder?"

"I only hurt in one place." Her mouth touched his softly, gently, and moved against it. The muscles in his arms quivered as he gently held her. She could have backed away and he would have let her go.

"I'm not going to break, sweetheart. Hold me tight."

A sigh trembled through him, and his lips moved against hers, seeking comfort. He lifted his head and rained tender kisses on her eyes, cheeks and throat. His hand moved to brush the tangled hair from her brow. His cheeks were pleasantly rough against her face.

Something deep within her was stirring.

His body was hard and big and warm. He cradled her to him with a gentleness that brought tears to her eyes. His hand roamed up and down her back, over her hips, raising the thin cotton cloth of her gown.

"Can I take it off?"

"You can do anything you want. I'm yours."

Her nipples were buried in the fur on his chest, and her flat abdomen pressed tightly to his. Her ragged breathing was trapped inside her mouth by his kiss.

"Tell me if I hurt you," he whispered urgently.

She couldn't speak. Her palms slid over muscles and tight flesh as if she had to know every inch of him. His sex was large, rock-hard, and throbbing against the thigh pinned between his. She was awed that this big man trembled beneath her touch and yet demanded nothing she was not willing to give.

He turned her on her back. His bare leg swung over hers and held her softness pinned to the yielding mattress. His masculine scent filled her nostrils. His fingers wandered through tight curls to sink into warm wetness. The roughness of his tongue on the buds of her breasts sent thrills cascading through her.

"I want just a taste. I won't rob our son of his dinner." He nuzzled the soft mound with his lips.

She gave a small, strangled cry. Tremors shot through her in rocketing waves. She grabbed the thick wrist of the hand resting on her belly and pulled the exploring fingers from between her legs.

A low moan came from him. He supported himself on his forearms, cupped her head in his hands and tenderly kissed her face. She wrapped her arms around him, spread her legs so that his thighs could sink between them, and pulled his weight down on her.

He entered her. Cradled together they rocked from side to side. He took her mouth in hard, swift kisses.

"Jake . . ." She arched against him in sensual pleasure.

"Am I hurting you, *querida*?" His cheek was pressed to hers, his words coming in an agonized whisper.

"No! My love, no." Even now, he demanded nothing, gave everything. His concern brought tears to her eyes. He turned his head and caught them with the tip of his tongue, then found her mouth and kissed her with lips wet with her tears.

The spasms of pleasure that followed were like a gorgeous dance throughout her body. At times she felt as though an enormous wave were crashing over her. At other times the sensation was like a gentle wind caressing her. Her whole world centered in the man joined to her.

It was so wonderful! She was sure that the tip of him touched her very soul. She had never known such an exquisite feeling. It was an ecstasy too beautiful for words.

She wasn't really aware of when it ended.

"Are you all right, *amor*? Was I too rough with you? I tried to keep control, but it slipped away and I lost myself in you."

She smiled against his mouth. "You were wonderful!"

Afterward, lying side by side, they held each other while their bodies adjusted to the aftermath of passion. Her head rested on his arm; her arm was curled about his chest.

"I feel so good. I'm more contented and happy than I ever dreamed possible."

"I'm glad, *mi bella querida*."

She smiled against his chin and nipped it.

Mary Lee had never been happier. She couldn't conceive of anything happening that would upset her world, but something beyond the realm of her imagination or Jake's did happen the very next day.

Chapter 33

All the cabins were rented for the night except one when Mary Lee set the last dish on the supper table. Jake had been holding Scotty and watching her. It was still hard for him to believe that she was his and that this baby they had called Gaston was his. He loved her so damn much. It scared him that one small slip of a girl was the sum and substance of his life.

He got up to put Scotty in the makeshift crib that rested on two kitchen chairs beside the table.

"You don't want to be off in that room by yourself, do you, cowboy?" Jake wiped the drool from the baby's chin. "You want to be in here where you can see what's going on."

Mary Lee, watching her husband and

child, looked at Eli, rolled her eyes and winked.

When their plates were filled, Eli began telling them about an event that happened at school.

"This kid got all smarty, and I said either shut up or I'll shut you up. That's no way to talk to a girl. I didn't want to have to—" He paused to listen when he heard a car drive in and stop beside the porch. "I'll go. Maybe we'll be filled up again tonight."

A few minutes later, he was back at the kitchen door.

"Someone to see you, Jake."

Jake left the table, stopped behind Mary Lee's chair and dropped a kiss on her forehead, then went through the house to the front door and out onto the porch.

"Hello, Jake. Remember me, Junior Miller?" The short, stocky man in the white shirt and tie held out his hand. Jake ignored it.

"How could I forget? You handled the case that sent me to prison."

"It was my job. The men who testified against you sent you to prison. I'm not here about that. My father is in the car. He'd like to speak to you. He doesn't get around very well anymore or he'd have come to the door."

"Is he willing to take my case and clear my name?"

"You'll have to talk to him about that."

Junior Miller led the way to the car and opened the door. Mr. Miller turned sideways on the seat and held out his hand.

"Hello, Jake. I've not seen you since you were a scrawny kid. You've grown to be quite a man."

"Time makes a difference, Mr. Miller." Jake shook the offered hand.

The old man laughed. "Truer words were never spoken. Seems like yesterday that I was a young buck like you. I hear you married Scott Finley's daughter. I never knew her, but her daddy was a fine man."

"He raised a fine daughter."

"I guess you heard that Ocie Clawson is home and in a rolling chair. Damn shame what Delano did to him, but at least he's alive."

"Did he send you here to tell us that he's going to try and claim my wife's son?"

"No. But I've been out to see him. His spirits are pretty low right now."

"I can believe that."

"Jake, I have something of interest to you and to Ocie. I'd ask you to come to my office, but the damn stairs are hard for me to climb and impossible for Ocie. So I'd like you to meet me at the Clawson ranch about ten in the morning."

Jake was shaking his head before Mr. Miller finished speaking. "I won't go there. The only reason I went before was that I was desperate to find Mary Lee after his foreman had her kidnapped. In case you've forgotten, it was Ocie and his men who are responsible for the jailbird tag attached to my name."

"I understand your bitterness, but it would be to your advantage to meet with me and Ocie tomorrow. He has paid for trusting Lon Delano."

"What's he cooking up now?"

"He has no idea why we are coming. Bring your wife. It's important to her too."

"I won't have him upsetting my wife by insisting our son is a Clawson. We married before that baby was born, and by law he's my son."

"I promise you that Ocie will not berate your wife."

Jake looked into the old man's eyes and

remembered his kindness when, as a kid, he had visited his office with Temple.

"All right, but I'll miss a half day's work."

Mr. Miller seemed to sigh with relief. "See you in the morning." He closed the car door, and Junior drove out onto the highway.

Jake watched them leave. He was puzzled and a little bit worried. He couldn't imagine what business would concern both himself and Ocie. He went back into the house to discuss it with Mary Lee.

The next morning, Mary Lee worried all the way out to the Clawson ranch that Ocie was going to raise a to-do about her son's name. On the birth certificate it was Ramero and not Clawson. Well, it did not matter. Her baby's name was Scott Jacob Ramero, and Ramero it would stay.

Jake worried that Ocie would want Mary Lee and Scotty to come live with him, and even offer him a job to entice them to come. No way in hell was he ever going to work for Ocie Clawson.

Mary Lee placed her hand on his thigh. "I love you. Nothing will ever change that. Whatever it is, we'll see it through together."

He took his hand off the wheel and clasped hers tightly.

She had never been to the Circle C and was impressed with the sprawling house with its long verandah and the buildings that surrounded it. She was still gazing at it when Jake stopped the truck beside Mr. Miller's car and came around to take the baby so that she could get out.

"It's pretty here."

"Yeah. When I was a kid it was like a castle that was off limits to me. I hated it then."

Jake cradled Scotty in one arm and with his other hand held Mary Lee possessively close as they walked to the house. Junior Miller was at the door to let them in. The house was cool and quiet. Mary Lee looked around at the heavy, dark furniture, the colorful rugs on the floor and the enormous cobblestone fireplace. It was spotlessly clean, but to Mary Lee it seemed more like the lobby of a fancy hotel than a home.

"Hang your hat there on the hall tree, Jake."

"*Hola.*" A smiling Mexican woman came from the back of the house to greet them. "I am María. I keep house for *Señor* Clawson."

"Hello." Mary Lee couldn't help but smile back at the pleasant-faced woman.

"Ah, such a *bello niño!*" She peeked at Scotty, nestled in the crook of Jake's arm. Scotty obliged her with a wide yawn.

"We think so," Jake said.

"You want I take?"

"No, thank you," Mary Lee said hastily. "I'll keep him with me. He ... might get hungry."

The woman smiled, nodded and backed away.

Junior motioned for them to follow. They walked through an archway and into an alcove. The first thing they saw was Ocie, sitting in a high-backed chair with large wheels and a footrest. His face was drawn, his eyes sunken. He had lost considerable weight.

"Come on in. I'm not going to bite," he barked when they hesitated beneath the archway.

William Miller got painfully to his feet. He greeted first Mary Lee and then Jake with a handshake.

"And what do we have here?" he said, pulling the light blanket back from Scotty's face.

"This is our son, Scott Jacob," Jake said

firmly. When Ocie snorted, he added, "Ramero."

"Well, now," Mr. Miller said, "he's a handsome boy."

"We think so." Mary Lee echoed the words Jake had said earlier. She reached for the baby. "I'll wait in the other room."

"No need for that, my dear. Stay with your husband."

Mary Lee had seen the anxious way Ocie's eyes had clung to the baby, and something inside her washed away her resentment of him.

"Would you like to see him, Mr. Clawson?" Without waiting for an answer or looking at Jake, she removed the blanket from around the baby and crossed the room to where he sat in the chair. "He's a big boy. He weighed nine pounds when he was born. He doesn't have much hair yet, but what he has is dark. His eyes are going to be blue, I think. You can't tell until he's a little older."

Ocie's eyes were on the child in her arms. She lifted the gown and showed him Scotty's chubby feet and legs.

"He's a good baby. He seldom cries, but when he does, his daddy is right there picking him up. I have to watch Jake and Eli or they'll have him spoiled rotten."

Mary Lee looked over her shoulder at Jake. From his expression she couldn't tell if he approved of what she was doing. She looked back at the man in the chair. His lids were lowered, but she saw moisture in the corners of his eyes.

"Would you like to hold him, Mr. Clawson?"

Ocie shook his head. "Naw." His voice was husky. "I might drop him."

Mr. Miller had sat down behind a long library table. Junior Miller got behind Ocie's chair and moved him to the end and indicated a chair in between for Jake. Before he sat down, Jake looked to see where Mary Lee would be. Her chair was away from the table but where he could see her.

Mr. Miller took a heavy brown envelope from his briefcase and placed it on the table.

"Ocie, I'm sure that you know that your papa and I were friends long before you were born. I grieved with him when your mama died and through the lonely years that followed. He gave a lot of thought to making out his wills. Yes, he made out two wills. After Temple died you saw the first one. He left the ranch and all his worldly possessions to you."

The old man's brown-spotted hands opened the envelope on the table and spilled out the contents.

"There was a second will, however, that I was not to make known or probate until after your death, or if you became so incapacitated that you were unable to manage the affairs of the ranch."

"Goddammit! Just 'cause I can't walk don't mean my brains ain't workin'."

"I know that and so does everyone else. But, Ocie, you must admit that you are no longer able to be out and about to see to the workings of this ranch."

"I'll hire a manager."

No doubt like your last lying foreman. Jake's face was expressionless in spite of his thoughts.

Mr. Miller continued. "Temple left a letter for you, Ocie, and one for Jake. But first I want to read to you a portion of the second will, which I will probate according to Temple's wishes.

"*By leaving two wills with my friend, William Miller, I have attempted to be fair to both of my sons. In the first will I left all of my worldly goods to my elder son, Ocie Lamar Clawson. He has been a good son and has worked hard to build and maintain the Circle C. Ranch."*

"Pa never had another son."

Mr. Miller ignored Ocie's outburst and continued to read:

"However, when Ocie dies, or if the time comes that he becomes incapacitated, for any reason, and in a way that will hinder his day-to-day operation of the ranch, I leave my entire holdings and all they entail to my other son, Jacob Ramero Clawson—"

"What!" Jake jumped to his feet. "I don't believe this!"

"Godalmighty!" Ocie exclaimed. "I wondered at the time, but—"

Mr. Miller read on: *". . . with the provision that he come and live in the house where he was conceived and that his brother, Ocie, and any family that he may have, continue to live on at the ranch where he was born and spent his childhood."*

"My mother never married him!" Jake blurted.

"Yes, she did, Jake. The marriage certificate is with the letter Temple left you."

"Why didn't they tell me?"

"I don't know. It may be in the letter. I do know that Temple fell in love with a girl thirty years his junior and she with him. They feared ridicule and chose to keep their love for each other to themselves. Temple thought Ocie would resent his marrying a young girl and think he was bringing her in to take his mother's place. And besides, Juanita wouldn't come near the ranch house because of Edith, Ocie's wife. She wanted only to live in the small house Temple had provided for her and their son.

"There's one other thing. Ocie, I think both you and Jake know how important it was to Temple that the ownership of the Circle C stay in the Clawson family. The will states, however, that should the two of you be unable to live and work together here on the Circle C, the ranch is to be sold. Each of you will receive one dollar, and the rest of the money will go to the state of New Mexico."

Jake stood. "That settles that. Come on, honey. Let's go. I wasn't wanted here when I was a kid. I don't want to be here now."

"Don't be hasty, Jake. You owe it to your wife and your son to think this over carefully. You and Ocie are brothers. Each of you would benefit from the other's experiences. Temple loved both of you. Take his letter. Let me know within the next day or two what you want to do."

"Hell," Ocie said. "What choice do I have? I either work with the jailbird or get thrown out of my home."

"Goes against the grain, does it, to be related to a jailbird?" Jake taunted. "Well, it doesn't sit well with me to be related to a first-class asshole like you."

"I had three men swear on the Bible that you stole my cattle!" Ocie shouted.

"I don't care if a hundred men swore on a hundred Bibles. They lied." Jake's voice rang out loud and clear. "I want my name cleared for the sake of my wife and my son. That is more important to me than this whole damn ranch and everything in it."

"Lon is dead, but I know where the other two are," Ocie admitted grudgingly.

"I'll talk to Pleggenkuhle," Junior said. "If we can get the other two men to retract their testimony, we can ask the judge to wipe the conviction from Jake's record."

Mr. Miller got painfully to his feet. "Do a favor for an old man who loved your father like a brother. The two of you spend thirty minutes alone together before Jake leaves. Mary Lee and I will wait in the other room. I want to get acquainted with Temple's grandson."

"I hear the truck. Deke is coming in." Mary Lee sighed contentedly in the aftermath of their lovemaking. Wrapped in his arms, she felt the thump of his powerful heart against hers.

"He's as happy as a kid with a new slingshot and a pocketful of rocks." Jake reached for her leg and pulled her thigh up over his. "*Amante,* I'm torn up inside. I grew up thinking my father was the cowboy my mother was married to for only a few days before he was killed. Then I'm told that I'm Temple Clawson's son and that he and my mother married."

"You're still the Jake Ramero I fell in love with and married. Nothing will change that." Her fingertips turned his face to hers so she could kiss his lips.

"Did you read the inscription inside your ring?"

"I haven't taken it off."

"It says, *'Juanita, mi querida.* T. C. 1910.' That was the year I was born."

"I wish he had told you that he was your father."

"I've been thinking about the many times he came to our house bringing meat and groceries. He ate with us a lot of the time and played with me afterward. I don't remember if he spent the night. My mother was always happy when he was there."

Mary Lee patted his cheeks with her fingertips, encouraging him to talk.

"He always took up for me when Bobby tried to get me in trouble. And the time I was left out on the range without my boots and walked here to the court, he was very angry and wanted to know who left me there. I was afraid to tell him it was Lon, because Lon had said if I told, some night our house would burn with me and Mama in it."

"What did you tell him?"

"That I'd slid off my pony and he had run off." He pulled her over on top of him, spread her thighs on each side of his and pressed her breasts to his chest. His lips nuzzled the side of her face as he ran his hands up and down her back and over her buttocks. "You feel so good. Maybe Lon did me a favor. I met my angel that day."

"I don't understand why Temple didn't acknowledge you as his son, but I was not walking in his shoes at the time. I don't know why my daddy put up with my mother for all those years. We just have to accept things as they are, my love, and go on."

"I'm kind of ashamed of thinking only of myself, *querida*. I resent it that I grew up feeling an outcast when I had as much right to be on the Circle C as Ocie and Bobby. But now I know that I had a father who cared for me, I have a wife and baby and Eli who love me. Ocie has lost his legs, his son, his grandson and now his ranch. I can't walk away and leave the man, force him to move out of his home, even if I don't like him very much."

"Then you've decided?"

"I told him that I didn't know anything about running a big spread. And he said that if I wouldn't be so bullheaded he would tell me how. I told him I would raise quarter horses. He said he didn't care how many damn horses I had as long as there was the usual quota of beef cattle on the Circle C." Jake chuckled, his breath warm against her face. "I imagine we'll have some good battles."

"Who is taking care of things now?"

"He said Ben, the man who shot Lon, and a couple other old-timers, were doing the best they could to hold things together. Some of Lon's friends have left. I imagine they took a few head of cattle with them."

"What about Mr. Quitman's horses?"

"I'll take them to the Circle C. I'm not letting that man down. He's been my friend through thick and thin. But what's more important . . . are you willing to leave the motor court, take Scotty and Eli and live out at the ranch?"

"Scotty, Eli and I go where you go . . . and willingly. You're our mainstay, our harbor in a storm, my husband, the boys' father. We love you and will abide by your decision."

She moved up, then down, allowing him to enter her slowly, reverently. His great body trembled with the effort it took to hold back. He penetrated deeper and deeper, making no sharp or hard thrusts. Only slow, sensuous motion, deliberate and controlled. When he was embedded to the hilt, the long release of his breath warmed her mouth.

"Look at me, *querida*," he whispered hoarsely. "I'll love you until the day I die."

"You are my love. Mine forever." They spoke mouth to mouth, sharing breaths and quick, hard kisses.

Then the movement of her hips drove him over the edge into blazing rapture. The joyous fulfillment raced through them, alive, pulsating, taking their breath. When they reached earth again, he gazed at her with intense delight, glorying in the loveliness of her face. Again and again he pressed gentle, sweet kisses upon her soft mouth. She wiggled and released a soft, purring sigh as she spread her fingers through his chest hair and tugged.

"That was for not telling me you loved me when you were ten years old."

Their laughter was low and wonderfully happy.

Epilogue

Thanksgiving, 1940
Circle C Ranch

A light snow had fallen during the night, leaving the landscape pristine white. When Mary Lee opened the door of the ranch house, a gust of cold air hit her flushed face. She slipped outside and hurried across the yard to the barn. Pulling aside the heavy door, she entered and closed it behind her. The barn was warm and smelled of hay and animals.

A big buckskin mare neighed a greeting as she passed her stall. Mary Lee paused and rubbed the mare's nose, then moved on when her husband came out of a stall at the far end and waited for her to join him.

"How did you manage to escape that madhouse?" Jake reached for her and pulled her to him.

"I'll not even be missed. Trudy is helping María with the dinner. Ocie, in his chair, is chasing Scotty on his tricycle. Deke is watching to make sure Patricia doesn't crawl into the fireplace or get run over by Ocie or Scotty. Eli is rocking Temple, who is enjoying all the confusion."

"Well, then, come here to me. We've got all of ten minutes to ourselves. Kiss me, sweetheart. Have I told you today that I love you?"

"Uh-huh. This morning, after you woke me up complaining that because it was a holiday you needed extra loving."

"That's right, I did. And you gave it to me."

"It was a chore, but somebody had to do it." She wound her arms around his neck and stood on her toes to reach his mouth with hers.

After several deep kisses they strolled arm in arm down the center aisle of the barn.

"Did I tell you that Eli talked to me about

going to veterinarian school as soon as he graduates this spring?" Jake asked.

"I had a suspicion he would want to do something like that. He spends all his spare time here in the barn."

"I wasn't so sure. He spends a good amount of time down at Deke's garage."

"Trudy's pregnant again. She said Deke wants to sell the motor court. He thinks it's too much work for her."

"He may be right."

Mary Lee snuggled in her husband's arms. "Can you believe it's been five years since we came here? I wasn't sure how living with Ocie was going to work out."

"The old goat sure was stubborn at first," Jake chuckled.

"He isn't the same man he was when we came here. He loves being with the children, and they love their Uncle Ocie. I was half mad when he ordered the tricycle for Scotty. He should have waited for Christmas. I won't have that boy spoiled."

"Then you'd better do something, little mother. I caught the two of them going through the Sears catalog." Jake laughed and hugged her.

"Have you been out here all this time looking at that new foal?"

"No, ma'am. I was in the bunkhouse for a while. Cookie's got four turkeys in the oven and six pumpkin pies on the shelf. Two poker games were going, and there was lots of cussin' and spittin'. Ben and Tom were playing pool."

"It was good of you to get the pool table."

"I like to play too."

"Now the truth comes out."

"But I'd rather play with you," he whispered, and nipped her earlobe.

"Jake Ramero Clawson, if you think I'm going to stay out here in the barn and roll in the hay with you on this Thanksgiving Day, you'd better think again."

"You've done it before."

"I didn't have a houseful of company and a dinner to get on the table."

"How do you feel about rolling around in the bed with me on Thanksgiving night?" They walked to the door and stepped out into the crisp air.

"That's a different matter altogether. I'll meet you as soon as the kids are put to bed."

"It's a date. Don't bother to dress."

"Are you planning on showing me the stars again, *darlin'*?"

"Where you'll be, there won't be a star in sight, *darlin'*." He bent and scooped up a handful of snow.

"Don't you dare!" she shouted, and raced for the door.